FOR CHINA SEA:

"Poyer's characters are as good as ever, and the action scenes lively."

—*Library Journal*

"The battle scenes are scintillating and satisfying ... Poyer displays a fine sense of pace and plot."

—*Publishers Weekly*

"Action, realism, and exotic locales ... an absorbing, exciting, and thought-provoking experience."

—*Chesapeake Life*

"An exciting story ... The author's vivid descriptions of life on a ship show us not only the *Anchors Aweigh* honor and dedication, but also the boiler-room sweat and frustrations of naval life."

—*Virginia Times*

"Poyer springs plenty of action on us ... his narration and dialogue ring true."

—*Jacksonville Times-Union*

"Poyer brings the courage, honor, and commitment of sea duty to life in this vivid portrayal of life aboard a Knox-class frigate ... the details describing life at sea are captivating as the action is continually rolling along, and each page pulls a new twist into the architecture of the story. In the end, the reader is treated to a fantastic battle that pulls each of the story threads together as a tightly woven yarn ... the scales of intrigue, from murder, piracy, and battle to international diplomacy, capture the imagination with lifelike characters of heroes and villains most naval readers can link to real people met during their own world travels... *China Sea* belongs in the library of avid fiction readers."

—*Shipmate*

FOR TOMAHAWK:

"There can be no better writer of modern sea adventure around today."

—Clive Cussler

"An absorbing narrative that whips along the author's usual firecracker pace . . . *Tomahawk* is very much a book of today."

—Norfolk Virginian-Pilot

"Poyer's characters are well-developed and frequently complex. His description is vivid. And he certainly knows the navy."

—Jacksonville Times-Union

"Sharp-edged . . . [a] tense tale."

—Florida Times-Union

"*Tomahawk* is a book of many levels. On the surface, it is a book of suspense—spies, secret missile strikes, murder . . . Dig a little further, and there is an officer who is troubled deeply by the effects of the weapons that he is developing."

—Proceedings

"The intrigues of bureaucracy have a ring of authenticity . . . If you're into military thrillers, you'll like this book."

—Wisconsin State Journal

"A gritty thriller."

—Microsoft Network

BLACK STORM

David Poyer

St. Martin's Paperbacks

This is a work of fiction. Characters, companies, and organizations in this novel are either the product of the author's imagination or, if real, are used fictitiously, without intent to describe their actual conduct.

Grateful acknowledgment is made to quote from the following:

"My Seven Bizzos," by the 2 Live Crew written by Luther R. Campbell, David P. Hobbs, Mark D. Ross and Chris Wong Won, Publisher Lil' Joe Wein Music Inc. By permission.

BLACK STORM

Library of Congress Catalog Card Number: 2001058562

ISBN: 0-312-98385-9

Printed in the United States of America

St. Martin's Press hardcover edition / June 2002
St. Martin's Paperbacks edition / June 2003

St. Martin's Paperbacks are published by St. Martin's Press, 175 Fifth Avenue, New York, NY 10010.

10 9 8 7 6 5 4 3 2 1

For those who do not make war,
but who are the victims of war

ACKNOWLEDGMENTS

Ex nihilo nihil fit. For this book I owe thanks to Eric and Bobbie Berryman, Ina Birch, David R. Bockel, Michael Boffo, Steve Butler, Al Cantrell, Robert D. Collinsworth, Jim Cross, Randy Culpepper, Sandra Dangler, Chuck Dasey, Drew Davis, Clark Driscoll, William S. Dudley, Edward Eitzen, Marie Estrada, Art Friedlander, Carl E. Gantt, Joel Gaydos, Louis Guy, Katy Haddock, Sloan Harris, Edward Herbert, Ken Hoffman, David Howe, Bob Hudon, Marty Janczak, Bob Kelly, Josh Kendall, Neil and Beth Kinnear, Brian Knowles, Marty Martinez, Bill McClintock, Kelly McKee, David McNamee, Paula Mills, Ed Miralda, Pete Mitchell, James A. Mobley, Scott Mosier, Barry Nelson, Gail Nicula, Dana Osterhaut, Tony Osterman, Bill Pelletier, Tracey Poirier, Lenore Hart Poyer, Lin Poyer, Ian Pund, Clifton Pye, Tommy Rayfield, Dennis Reilly, Sally Richardson, Ray Ruhlmann III, Sandra Scoville, Michael Styskal, Stewart Upton, Caree Vander-Linden, W. A. Whitlow, George Witte, Neal Woollen, Pat Worsham, and others who preferred anonymity. Thanks also to HCS-4, the "Red Wolves," to the US Army Medical Research Institute of Infectious Diseases, the Navy/Marine Corps Expeditionary Warfare Center, the US Marine Corps Amphibious Reconnaissance School, the Eastern Shore Public Library, the Joint Forces Staff College, and Headquarters, US Marine Corps. As always, all errors and deficiencies are my own.

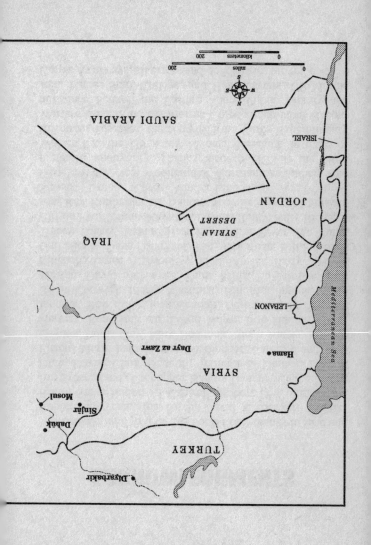

IRAQ AND ENVIRONS

Caspian Sea

Tabrīz

Al Mishraq
Irbīl
Al Qayyārah
A Sulaymānīyah
Karkūk

IRAN

Kermānshah

Sāmarrā'

Z A G R O S   M O U N T A I N S

Baghdad

Karbalā'
Al Hillah
Al Kūt
An Najaf
Ad Dīwānīyah

Al 'Amārah
Ahvāz

An Nāsirīyah

Al Basrah

Tigris River

Euphrates River

KUWAIT

Persian
Gulf

Kuwait

© 2002, Mark Stein Studios

And when We decide to destroy
A nation, We first send
Warning to those
Who are given Abundance in this life
And still transgress; so that
The sentence is proven
Against them; then,
We annihilate them utterly.

—The Holy Qur'an, bani Isra'il 17:16.5

PROLOGUE

0100 22 February 1991:
The Saudi Desert

No one spoke after the helicopter lifted off. The engine noise overwhelmed all other sound, walling off each mind within the compass of its own skull. The deck shuddered, tilting as the pilot pulled into a bank. Beyond the door gunner, hunched over the pintle mounts for the machine gun, impenetrable night hurtled by as they gathered speed.

The desert winter was cold and rainy, the worst weather in thirty years. For days now a black overcast had sealed off the stars. It opened only to loose soot-smelling, dust-gritty rain over the half million troops who waited, scattered across the desert or cooped in gray steel out on the Gulf, for the word to attack.

The helo dropped, steadied, hurling northward barely a hundred feet above the sand.

Seven dark figures lay tumbled in the crew compartment, where they'd thrown themselves during the thirty seconds the Navy combat search-and-rescue Seahawk had touched down at the pickup point. It held no seats, just bare aluminum-walled space lit by faint green lights to port and starboard. The team's camouflage battle dress had no rank insignia, no unit patches. They lay on top of gear and rucks and weapons and each other, like some composite organism only dimly coming to consciousness of itself.

The pilot tilted his head back, peering beneath night vision goggles as a line of blue-white lights lifted over the horizon. The Tapline Road ran parallel to the border. Under the glare both lanes were filled with tanker trucks and tank transporters, all heading west. The headlights passed beneath the speeding aircraft and fell quickly aft. As darkness retook the world he pulled the goggles down again.

A weird topography of lime and black floated up. A dry undulating sea of sand and sand and sand, of barren ridges and blasted wadis. And, fleeing close above it, the haloed green exhaust flare, pulled from the deep infrared by the lenses and amplifiers of the goggles, of another aircraft.

The black helicopter ahead was an Air Force Pave Hawk bird. It had better avionics and weapons, including a sophisticated terrain-avoidance radar, but the HH-60 had better navigation. The pilot tracked the Pave Hawk through the goggles, rising when it rose, dropping when it dropped. When he had the rhythm, he said softly into the intercom, "Gunny, you on the line yet? Slap a cranial on him, Minky."

"Six team leader on the line," said a voice. "That you, sir?"

"Welcome aboard the Baghdad Shuttle, Gunny. Intel hasn't changed, ingress is the same, but we may need to make some last-minute decisions re primary versus alternate LZ. How about reviewing that with my right seater."

A faint light clicked on, focused on an air chart. Across the lower quarter a dotted stripe zagged left to right, gradually angling down. North of it were a series of circles, carefully drawn in grease pencil. They grew denser and more closely spaced toward the top of the chart, where they overlapped.

The copilot's glove pressed a pencil point west of a blue-tinted scatter of lakes and marshland. It was covered by two of the circles, which marked the threat radii of antiair missile batteries. "We'll know a few mikes out if the primary's a go."

The team leader said, "It better be a go, sir. You were at the briefing. We've got too far to hump from there as it is."

"Well, we'll give it our best shot, Gunny. Just warning you there may be some turbulence en route. Tray tables in full upright position. You know the drill."

"Just get us there," said the team leader. "Sir."

"Roger that," said the pilot.

·

THE RECON team leader was thirty years old. He'd grown up as an Air Force brat, moving here and there around the country until he enlisted in the Marine Corps at eighteen. Now he looked closely at the map, reviewing the route for the thousandth time in his mind. Turn-around and jump-off, Point Charlie, Point Delta, objective. In an hour and a half they'd be on the ground a hundred and forty miles inside Iraq.

The air war had been underway since the UN deadline expired on 17 January. The bombers had been pounding the Iraqis for four weeks now, starting with command and communications in Baghdad, then shifting to the ground forces dug in around Kuwait. Some intelligence sources said they were decimated. Others said Saddam's Republican Guard was dug in so deep the bombing barely scratched them. The fog and rain hadn't helped.

He'd seen what happened when you underestimated your enemy. Night after night on the airport perimeter in Beirut, that hot fall of '83, listening to the crackle of gunfire as the Syrians, Israelis, Palestinians, Hezbollah, and every other faction in the Middle East fought it out. Someone with a direct line to God had set the Marine Corps down in the middle of it. He'd thought the locals understood they were protecting them. Till he'd been awakened one October night by an enormous explosion.

The truck bomb had killed two hundred and forty-one marines, sailors, and soldiers.

You didn't underestimate Arabs. They were courteous. They were patient. It was only when you thought they were finished that they became truly dangerous. Then they didn't care if they lived or died, as long as they could take you with them.

He stared into the darkness beyond the windshield. If he put on his NVGs, he'd see as well as the pilot. But it would be better to conserve batteries for the mission. For a second, fear pierced him, like a sharpened icicle jammed up his anus. He took a deep breath, reminding himself he had a good team and a solid plan. They'd briefed and trained, not as much as he'd have liked, but enough.

His own life didn't matter. Any justification for it had vanished in the blast of a shotgun a year ago. Bringing his men back was the only reason he still had to stay alive.

But no mission ever went as it was planned. And no one really knew what lay ahead in the dark, on the far side of the invisible line that separated the two armies built up over the last six months. Two massive forces, moving inexorably toward the final impact.

THE PILOT asked the copilot for the next vector. He'd already forgotten the men in the cargo compartment. He was too wrapped up in flying thirty feet off the ground.

The two helos had taken off from the Allied base at Al Jouf on a false course, then angled north and picked the team up off a deserted stretch of road. So far, neither helicopter had come up on the radio. The Pave Hawk blinked its infrared position lights each time they went over a checkpoint. They'd preplanned and timed the routes in and out, routing them through or beneath blind zones in the coverage of the SA-8 and Roland sites. If they did it right, they'd finish the insertion without a single transmission.

Which would be eminently desirable, considering the French- and Russian-trained technicians who manned the direction-finding sets, electronic intelligence posts, radar sites, and antiaircraft missile batteries ahead.

"Cougar, Red Wolf Two."

"Roll to Indigo, Red Wolf Two."

He snapped to the new frequency. "Red Wolf Two plus one, gate Tarzan, thence to xray kilo oscar papa, thence kilo uniform victor delta, charlie charlie mike papa, lima alfa uniform bravo. Read back, over."

The distant AWACS bird, orbiting in great slow circles thirty thousand feet above the Gulf, rogered his presence and read back his intended flight path. Now they were safe from the hunters above the clouds, Air Force and Saudi F-15s, Navy F/A-18s, French Mirages, Italian and British Tornados.

Unless someone made a mistake.

He was worrying about that, about the friendly fire this war called "blue on blue," when suddenly the Pave Hawk jinked violently. He hauled around too, just as a dune loomed out of the dark ahead and flashed past their rotor tips at a hundred and twenty miles an hour.

Instead of rising, the two aircraft dipped even lower, into a wadi, and increased speed, flashing along barely twenty feet off the lightless desert.

THE ASSISTANT team leader, twenty-eight years old, from Farmingdale, New York, was huddled close to the vanishingly dim green light in the crew compartment, a coverless, dog-eared, cola-spotted paperback held four inches in front of his eyes. His lips held a cool curve, lopsided, almost ironic, even though he wasn't thinking anything amusing. He was leaning against the med kit, which he carried along with the usual weapon and 782 gear. The turbines howled, the fuselage swayed, G forces pressed him against the bulkhead, but he didn't react. He was deep in *One Hundred Tips for Making Your Small Business Work*. The chapters had titles like: Focus on Service.

Automate Your Bookkeeping. Hire the Person, Not the Position. He was memorizing it, a page at a time. His lips moved silently, still tilted in that faint amused curve.

THIRTY SECONDS to the gate," said the copilot, who was simultaneously kneeboarding his map, working the GPS, and plotting each way point on the TACNAV display. The pilot risked a quick glance at the screen, then jerked his eyes back as the ground rose again, as if the land itself was reaching up to stop them. He blinked sweat out of his eyes, wishing he could see more clearly. Through the goggles the hurtling desert floor was blur and shadows, boiling with the random energy of amplified photons. He blinked again and squeezed his eyes shut, then popped them open and hauled hard on the collective as beside him his copilot sucked in his breath involuntarily.

If they hit one of those dunes, they'd never have time to realize they were dead.

BACK IN the crew compartment, the naval officer lay motionless for the first few minutes, trying to get control of his breathing. Feeling the others around him, pressed against him; feeling the angles of the Heckler and Koch nine-millimeter under his legs. Watching the door gunner, who craned down, looking into the blast of noise and darkness and icy wind.

What the hell was he doing here? He should be miles offshore, navigating a destroyer toward a naval gunfire support position. What was he doing with his face smeared with camo paint, carrying a submachine gun and an eighty-pound pack? Would he ever see his daughter again, or the woman who'd asked him once, one cool night in a darkened garden, if he thought they could make a life together?

Instead he'd put the Navy first. As he always had. Ahead of his ex-wife. Ahead of his daughter. But maybe he'd been making a mistake all along. Institutions knew no gratitude. But they needed people to blame when things went wrong; and all too often, he'd been the nearest bystander.

He touched the equipment lashed and clipped to his load-bearing gear. Night vision goggles. Gas mask. Grenades. Canteens. Knife, flashlight, magazine pouches, antitank weapon, compass, everything dummy-corded so a man couldn't lose it in the dark, no matter how clumsy or sleep-deprived he got.

If the team found what they were looking for, his mission would be to destroy it.

But now he struggled to sit up, feeling suddenly sick as he remembered what else he carried: not as gear or maps, but in his head. The Iraqis were set up to repel an amphibious invasion, a Marine Corps assault from the sea. But that threat was a sham. If Saddam ever realized that, he could wheel his forces south. Blunting, and maybe even stopping, the impending Coalition assault across the Kuwaiti border.

He hoped the men around him were good. Because as far as he could see, he was only going to be a burden until they reached the objective. Once they did that, he was pretty sure he could do what a very angry four-star general had ordered him to do.

If they got there alive.

PENETRATION CHECKLIST rechecked complete," the co-pilot said.

The pilot licked his lips but didn't answer. He squatted the helicopter even lower, shaving the last inches away between the terrain and the aircraft's belly. Now all light was gone. Neither sky nor desert yielded the faintest luminosity. Even through the goggles, the only illumination was the jittering, fanlike glow of the Pave Hawk's engine heat two hundred meters ahead.

"Wadi coming up. Tarzan gate, twenty seconds."

The "Tarzan gate" was a low-lying ravine, or wadi, that snaked across the border. Border crossers could use it as a tunnel under the Iraqi ground radars. But only if you flew low enough. He pushed the cyclic forward even more, fighting his way nearer to the earth. The earth was safety. But it was also mortal danger.

"There's the entrance," said the copilot, and at the same moment the Pave Hawk swerved. The pilot tilted the stick slightly, and the twenty-one tons of helicopter and crew and passengers swung onto the new heading and tracked down the looming-up escarpments, down through the blowing darkness, the clatter-slam of rotating blades carrying far out over the night-shrouded land.

AT THE very back of the compartment, the corporal held the butt of the Glock he'd stuffed into his cargo pocket after the preloading inspection. He was twenty-four, an E-4, the youngest man on the team. This was his first recon combat patrol, and he was trying with all his might to not crap his trou. He'd dropped them twice as they waited at the pickup site, but now he had to go again. It was the lousy raghead water. That and the shitty food, the Pak rice and the lettuce they trucked down from the Bekaa. He shouldn't've ate that lettuce. Everybody knew the fucking Ay-rabs shit on the fucking lettuce to make it grow, goddamn it, goddamn.

The other guys had worked together before. They had their own, like, code words. They acted like he was shit. But once they hit the ground he'd be out in front. The scout. The point. If he fucked up, they'd all get blown away. His lips drew back from his teeth and in the dark and noise he panted hard, trying to turn fear into hatred. Fucking ragheads. Smelly goat-fucking Ay-rack-ee motherfuckers. He hoped he got to score. God, come on, let me score.

His hand found the butt of the Glock again, and his finger lightly stroked the trigger.

•   •   •

MARK, THE border," said the copilot, over the intercom so their passengers could hear.

The pilot grunted. He was down to twenty feet now, and totally fixated on not flying into the ground. Voiding that ground-contact warranty. Gluing the shadow to the airplane. Jokes, his brain feeding back jokes so he didn't actually have to think about how close death was. It had happened to crews before. You didn't have any depth perception with the goggles, just light and shade and the blurry speckling seethe of amplified light. An HH-60 would make a hell of a big hole in the sand.

The Pave Hawk swung hard left and tracked up a side wadi, the bluff edges closing in, then rose, rose, as the land climbed. He pulled the collective and climbed too, following, then suddenly popped up over a rise.

They went over the Bedouin camp about ten feet up. He only realized what it was after they were past, retrieving from memory the conical tents a fraction of a second after they rocketed over them, the dark sparkling with gun flashes. The Bedoui gypsied back and forth over the border. Some were Iraqi, others Saudi, most pretty much independent of both sides, according to the briefers. Like the Arabs said, me and my brother against my cousin, me and my cousins against the infidel.

The pilot hoped he never went down out here. He was Jewish.

A brilliant flash jerked his head around. A climbing flame rose majestically out of the dark. He ignored it, knowing it probably didn't have a lock on. The border Arabs had Strelas, but they launched them blind, without waiting for a fire-acquisition tone. True to form, the glare wavered, then fell aft and at last plunged downward to lose itself in the chalk-dust and sand-cloud plume they were dragging across the desert floor behind them.

The lead chopper was getting too far ahead. He couldn't lose sight of it. They needed two birds in case one went down. Pushing the cyclic forward as he added power, he breathed very slowly in and out, and with tiny, nearly imperceptible movements of the stick threaded the hurtling needle of night.

THE COMMUNICATOR rolled himself awkwardly, humping the weight of ruck and radio and batteries and ammo slowly up the back of the aluminum column that enclosed the landing gear shock absorbers, till he could sit upright. Rifle and radio; defend yourself with one, save yourself with the other. Call in fire. Call in air support. Call in emergency extract if things went to shit.

He couldn't get over how cold it was. Seemed like the coldest place he'd ever been. He squeezed his eyes closed and tried to see the map. Made himself go over it again, how they were going to do the linkup, the passwords, the frequencies.

He'd left Guatemala when he was nine. He did not recall much of those days, of what his aunt still spoke of in mutters as *la violencia*. But he remembered listening to the distant flutter-beat of helicopters over the folded green jungle, the deep ravines and lofty mountains. The government troops could not catch the *guerrilleros*. So they wiped out the K'iche' villages they said supported the rebels. The troops came from the sky and killed everyone. Women. Children. Everything that lived. So that in the night he woke, hearing the distant pulse of rotor blades, and lay wondering if they were coming to kill his family.

And now he was a soldier. No, not a soldier, a marine . . . but he wore a uniform and carried a gun . . . and now he himself, little A Tun who was, rode the invisible helicopters through the night. Did children listen fearfully now below him, linking past to future in an invisible chain? When had that chain begun? When would it end? The fear in his belly, was it the fear of a child? When did a man stop being a child? When did a

Guatemalan become an American, cowboy-confident in himself and his gun?

He thought, but did not speak. He seldom spoke. Only when there was need.

Somewhere in there, thinking about it, he went to sleep.

THE COPILOT sat tensely, plotting fixes and trying to keep his hands from shaking. He wanted a cigarette, but knew he couldn't have one. The ground flashed by too close to look at. So he didn't, just kept his eyeballs pressed to the map and then the TACNAV, trying to keep his jitters under control.

An hour went by that way, and nothing changed except that now they were a hundred miles inside Iraq. The fuel-onboard gauge dropped gradually as they headed north-east, threading between two SA-8 sites and then swinging due east to pass the Roland battery at Mudaysis. The ground getting flatter, less cut by wadis. The relief going level, into what looked like meticulously graded gravel.

What terrified him was the emptiness. On and on and nothing living, no vegetation, no trees, not the smallest stunted bush. As if death itself had moved over this empty terrain. Some immense evil in the shadow of which nothing could live. Occasionally a tone in their earphones signaled the edge of a missile envelope, the invisible grope of a fire-control radar. But each time they heard it the Pave Hawk had already turned away, and they banked to follow and the deadly whine faded.

THE SNIPER was from Yauhannah, South Carolina. He was twenty-six. He'd rolled aboard folded over his rifle, tucking the scope into his gut, protecting his zero. He'd shot the Colt in every day during the lockdown. A heavy-barreled sniper-select M16 with a 203 forty-millimeter grenade launcher under the rifle barrel. The nine-mils were okay for close quarters, but you could reach out and touch someone with the 5.56. Day or night, he could put a bullet through a man's eye socket at four hundred meters. One shot. One kill.

Like at Khafji. When the Iraqi armor came through and surrounded them in that deserted town.

The colonel had climbed out of the tank in his natty greens and black beret like Saddam himself. From the rooftop overlooking the square the sniper had put the crosshairs down on him. Looked for a moment into his face; the heavy black mustache, the sunglasses, the self-satisfied smirk. He'd taken one more click for the wind, sucked a slow breath, and half let it out. Checked for shadow effect and quartered his target.

Then, one after the other, he shot the colonel and the three other officers who sat frozen in the staff car, still staring at the man whose skull had suddenly opened like a grisly tulip in front of them. By his third round the enlisted troops got wise, diving for cover, but the staffies just sat with their seat belts buckled as he killed them. When he had punched all their tickets, he'd gone back to the tank in time to see the colonel roll off his perch on the frontal armor and topple facedown into a sky-streaked puddle rut filled with the rain that had fallen all that day.

He hadn't felt bad about it. If they didn't want their asses shot off, they shouldn't have invaded somebody else's country. Shouldn't have taken on the US Marine Corps, and with it, package deal, the best damn sniper ever born.

He just wished he had something to chew. Aside from that, he was content. Rifle tucked protectively along his side, he stared out into the passing night.

AT 0150, the sky ahead suddenly turned to white fire. It outlined the lead helicopter black against white, so clearly the pilot could see its rotors going around.

He hauled into a hard bank, goggles flaring into a solid blinding brilliance as the light kept increasing. He pushed them up, close to panic, and saw the light pouring down across the desert as the fire climbed toward the sky. For a moment he couldn't tell what it was.

"It's a fucking Scud," breathed his copilot.

"Tag the way point, goddamn it, tag it now."

A wall of tracers rose suddenly and all at once out of the desert, blazing toward and then over them. They were huge, brilliant, but the pilot could barely see them. After-images chased across dazzled retinas, fear shuddered his hands. They were from ZSU-23s. A four-barreled, twenty-three-millimeter son of a bitch with a dish radar on a tank chassis, and for every one of those huge balls of tracer there were three high-explosive rounds in between. If they locked him up, he was dead. He popped chaff but knew it might not help.

Out of control, the helicopter lurched to starboard, rotor tips clawing toward the sand.

THE DOCTOR lay with her eyes squeezed tight, trying not to throw up. She'd felt sick to her stomach ever since they took off. She didn't think this was going to work. A squad of grunts, on foot, trying to find what a mad dictator had spent years and billions hiding? What the CIA couldn't locate, and Defense Intelligence said didn't exist? These people were insane. Totally unconnected to reality.

But they wouldn't listen to her. When four stars gave an order, that was the burning bush. But it wasn't just that. Even she had to admit it.

She'd studied with Fayzah Al-Syori. Fayzah worshipped Saddam. But could she do something like this? Could any physician? It was bullshit. It had to be.

But with that many lives at stake, you couldn't take a chance. You couldn't stand aside when people started perverting everything science had learned in the century since Pasteur first guessed what all those strange little wigglers you saw through the microscope were actually doing.

A terrifying roar came through the howl of the engine. Light played through the canted windows, throwing shadows across the grease-painted faces around her. She flung her arms out instinctively as the nose pitched up. Gay bright Independence Day sparklers she recognized after a horrified instant as tracers burned past the door gunner. Then the flame was *inside, with them*. A deafening bang cracked through the metal around her. And God help her, she hadn't meant to, but that was her screaming as they went down.

THE TEAM leader reached out, grabbing the people closest to him. If the helo went in, they'd ballistic through the cockpit windshield a fraction of a second after the pilots. Holding on to them wouldn't help. He knew that. But it was all there was to do.

The door gunner was firing. Not bursts, a steady clatter like he didn't care if he burned the barrel out. Another round punched through the fuselage, loud as a stun grenade in a closed room. Blinded, deafened, he braced for impact.

So they were right, the ones who'd said it was too risky. But Semper Fi wasn't just a motto. It meant accepting risk, when the mission called for it. Accepting the possibility that you, and the men you led, might not come back.

They were heading for the desert floor, bodies sliding toward him and then lifting off the deck as the aircraft nosed over. He wasn't afraid, though. Hadn't been afraid of anything since the night he'd shot his son.

Clamping his teeth together, holding tight to his men, he closed his eyes and waited for the end.

1

18 February: Ministry of Defence, Riyadh, Saudi Arabia

Those who knew him from West Point called the CINC "the Bear." Behind his back, those who had to endure his outbursts called him "Stormin' Norman"—and other things as well. Colonel E.H. Salter, his deputy intelligence chief, stood before his desk now, perspiring despite the air-conditioning, while the general read the message he'd just been handed.

The office the Saudis had assigned him was the size of a small ballroom. Winged-back chairs upholstered in cream brocade stood along the walls. At its far end hung life-size oil portraits of the king and the crown prince in gold frames. An easel tilted a huge map of Kuwait, Iraq, and northern Saudi Arabia. The desk was gigantic, blond Swedish modern, completely bare except for two black telephones, a tray of iced water and glasses, and a half-eaten instant Cup O' Noodles with a plastic spoon stuck in it. Behind it on a shelf was another phone, this one red, the scrambled direct line to Washington. This room was on the second floor of the Ministry of Defence building in downtown Riyadh, the capital of Saudi Arabia. It was 0300, and outside the windows the skies were dark.

The CINC—the commander in chief, US Central Command—was in chocolate-chip battle dress with the sleeves rolled. H. Norman Schwarzkopf's beefy bare forearms rested heavily on the desk. The four subdued stars of a full general weighed down his collar points. He was wearing a heavy chrome diver's watch, a wedding ring, and the reading glasses he didn't like to be photographed with. The intelligence officer noted that his face was slack with fatigue, and that he was gaining weight again. None of these were good signs. When Schwarzkopf raised his eyes from the paper, his expression had taken on a familiar chill, the one that all too often presaged the storm.

"Where the hell'd this come from?"

"It's a personal ultimatum from Saddam Hussein to you, sir."

"I can see that. I can read, damn it! How did it get here? How do we know it's actually from him?"

"Lieutenant General Ahmad handed it to the Swiss ambassador in Baghdad at ten hundred this morning with a request it go direct to you by hand. Not to State. Not to General Powell. Direct to you."

"Well, the son of a bitch has got that right. As soon as anything in writing gets to Washington, you can consider it compromised." Schwarzkopf scowled, fanning himself with the paper. Then he suddenly reared, throwing his weight back till the chair groaned. "Wait a minute. If it's supposed to come by hand, how did *you* get it?"

"We intercepted the Swiss embassy's report of the text," the intel officer said. He didn't look away from the general's eyes. The only way to deal with the Bear was to stand directly in front of him, know your shit, tell it straight, and give off no scent of fear. "You'll get the actual paper later today. The Swiss are sending a courier from Beirut by air."

"It's horseshit. It's a bluff." The general threw the paper down and looked at it with contempt. "What is this—if a single Allied tank crosses the border, he'll destroy Tel Aviv. Horseshit."

"Make it a crematorium, General," Salter said.

"What's that?"

"He says he'll make the city 'a crematorium,' sir. Not 'destroy' it."

"What's the difference?"

"He's making a historical reference," the intel officer said. He took a deep breath. "And I don't think it's 'horseshit,' General. He's threatened something like this before, back in July, then again in a broadcast in September. And he may be able to do something close to what he threatens."

"I don't think so. He's talking more Scud attacks. Even though he's not doing that much with them so far, not in terms of actual damage."

"Sir, with all due respect, the Israelis are taking this seriously. I have a back door to David Ivri. They want to know what we're going to do about it."

Ivri was the director general of the Israeli Defense Ministry. Salter watched the name take effect. Schwarzkopf sagged back, scowling, lips pursed. After a moment he said, "I won't even ask how *they* got hold of this."

"I agree, General. That's an interesting question in and of itself."

"Your point being I've got to hold their hands, or they'll send their own people in after whatever it is they think he's threatening them with."

"Yes, sir. They have to feel confident we're dealing with it."

Both men knew the Israelis had prepared a major air and commando raid to go into the western desert and root out the missiles that were killing families in Tel Aviv. And that if that happened, the fragile coalition of Arabs and Westerners would collapse, handing Saddam political victory no matter what happened on the battlefield.

The general sat thinking. Finally he said, "What exactly do you think he has? He can't actually pop a nuke, can he?"

A phone rang then. Not the red one, a plain black one.

Schwarzkopf picked it up, listened, then rasped, "You two work it out, Walt. You hear me? Settle it yourself. I'm trying to run a war. Don't call me again on piddly shit like this, General. Earn your goddamn paycheck." He slammed the handset down.

Salter went on, answering the question he'd been asked before the call. "No, sir, we don't think he can. Our belief is that if he had a working bomb, even a bread-boarded one, he'd announce it. He hasn't done that. Therefore, it's something else."

"Chemicals?"

"He's talked about that from day one. The tone of this message is different."

"You reading tea leaves on me, Salter?"

"Possibly, General. But the corporate-knowledge people think he's talking about something new."

"I still think it's a bluff."

"Sir, if I can interject a personal opinion."

Schwarzkopf nodded warily. Salter said, "The trouble is, Prince Bandar's right. Saddam doesn't make empty threats. The Al-Sabahs thought he was bluffing when he moved the Republican Guard to their border. He wasn't. We thought he was kidding when he said he'd use his Scuds. He launched them the day after we raided Baghdad. He's already proved he can reach Israel with conventionally armed missiles. Whatever he's got now, he thinks it'll do what he says. Or he wouldn't say so."

The general pursed his lips. He read the paper again. His heavy round face was set now. "Turn Tel Aviv into a crematorium," he said. "So what's he got?"

A gradually rising siren note outside came at the same moment the black phone purred again. Both the staff officer and the general reached automatically to check the gas masks slung at their belts. Schwarzkopf stood, holding the phone. When he put it down, he said tersely, "Three Scuds launched from vicinity of As-Salmān. Headed our way."

•   •   •

THE WAR room was seven stories down and eighty feet underground. Salter followed the general and his security man down a long passageway lit by fan-shaped sconces. Saudi and US sentries snapped to present arms. Past them, the three men went down another long stairwell, narrow, concrete-walled, echoing and empty, and through heavy steel doors that clanged shut behind them.

The room within was large but low-ceilinged and dim. A continuous murmur of voices and the hum of computer blowers floated from the desks and consoles. It smelled musty, like a tomb. Schwarzkopf stopped to pour black coffee into a plastic foam cup, exchanged terse words with an Air Force colonel, then looked around impatiently for Salter. They ended up in a small room deep in the JIC, the intelligence center where the photo analysts did bomb damage assessment.

"You asked me what he might have, other than chemicals," the intel officer said, going on as if they hadn't been interrupted. He took a lap briefing from his briefcase and laid it out in front of the general. "There are several possibilities. The Defense Intelligence Agency's appreciation of Iraqi military capabilities says Saddam might have, not a bomb, but a crude nuclear device that depends on radioactivity more than blast. It might take days, but it could still kill thousands of people. Also, sources inside the Soviet weapons program report that the Iraqis could have weaponized anthrax and possibly bubonic plague."

At each slide Schwarzkopf slumped farther in his chair. He took off his glasses. When Salter fell silent at last, he sat with pouchy eyes closed, rubbing his face.

A tap on the door. The security chief leaned in. "Sir, all three Scuds are down. One intercepted by Patriots. The other two impacted north of the city."

"Casualties?"

"No word yet, sir. I'll get that to you as soon as it comes in."

The CINC nodded and looked at Salter again. The intel officer said, "We might have an indicator. From the Iraqi underground, such as it is. We got a confused report about something called *hijurat ababeel.*"

"Meaning?"

"It seems to be a code name, a cover name," Salter said. "Literally, it means 'flying rocks,' or something like 'throwing stones.' Think of what David used on Goliath. It might also be a reference to the Qur'an, but I'm not clear on that yet. I have some of our people trying to mine anything else out of it."

"I'd better just have Buster Glosson bomb it," Schwarzkopf said. "Generate a B-52 strike."

"Sir, we could do that, if we could localize it."

"I thought you said you got a report from the underground."

"A rumor of its existence. Nothing like grid coordinates."

"You spooks must have *some* idea where it is."

"Only a general one." Salter laid out his last slide. It showed Iraq, pocked with a scattering of circles. On the scale of the map the circles were tiny, but each one was miles across.

Schwarzkopf stared at it, then looked up. "SAM batteries. The air defenses."

"Exactly, sir."

"So what are you showing me?"

"This weapon—whatever it is—is Saddam's last-ditch deterrent. His retaliatory capability, to put it in terms we'd use. Where do countries keep their deterrents? We keep ours in silos in North Dakota, or underwater in Trident submarines. The Soviets hide theirs in the Barents Sea, or deep in the interior." Salter's hand hovered over the map, then came down where dozens of circles interlocked. "You don't put them on the periphery; you put them in the heartland. Where is that for Saddam?"

Schwarzkopf looked at it. "In Baghdad?"

"The heart of his power," Salter said. "The best-defended site in the country. Also where the report about 'Flying Stones' came from. It's not much, but it's the best we have."

"Where in Baghdad?"

"That we don't know, sir. If it's there, it's too well hidden for overhead reconnaissance, or we'd have it by now."

Another tap at the door. It was a female captain with details on the missile attack. Two warheads had impacted in empty desert north of Riyadh. The Scud engaged by the Patriot had been damaged, not destroyed. It had fallen in a Koranic school and killed or injured thirty students and teachers, most of whom had been asleep.

Schwarzkopf pondered a moment more, then reached for a phone. "CINC here. For General Moore . . . Hello, Burton? I'm sending my deputy J-2 over with some bad news. Yeah. He'll tell you. He'll be right over." He hung up and said to Salter, "Don't leave this one to the system. As of now it's your number one personal tasking. Make it happen. Report to me every day. Call me personally if anyone gives you shit or stands in the way."

"Yes, sir," said the intel officer.

The general hesitated, then added, "Find it. But don't hit it until I personally approve it." He heaved himself up and stalked out. At the door he turned back. "Understand what I'm telling you?"

"Yes, sir, I do."

"If we've got to put the snake eaters in to find it, so be it. But find it. Before G day. *Verstehen sie*?"

"That doesn't leave us much time, sir."

"Five days. That's all any of us have, Colonel. I'm not going to postpone this thing again."

"Yes, sir. Oh—the message." Salter held it out. "Are you going to answer it?"

Schwarzkopf wadded the paper and threw it back. "The only answer he's getting to this is a bomb."

"Yes, sir."

"I still think he's bluffing. But if he isn't, this could be a show stopper, Colonel. Do not fail me. Do not fail the thousands of men who'll be putting their lives on the line one week from now. Do not fail the civilians who'll die if I'm wrong and he's actually got something held back."

He turned, lightly for so big a man, and a moment later was gone.

Deep beneath a terrified city, Salter stooped slowly for the paper. He smoothed it out, looking down at it.

2

19 February:
The Northern Gulf

Over the sea brooded a turbulent darkness deeper than any storm, blacker than any dusk. The smoke smelled like grease and acid, with a darker taste beneath: the stink of disaster and waste and war. The pall rolled a thousand feet deep over the uneasy waters between Kuwait and Iran where the Task Group was steaming. It left a slick on every surface and control in the helicopter, and it made visibility so bad that, banking away from USS *Tripoli,* the pilot didn't even bother to look up from his instruments.

Behind him, the lean, gray-eyed officer in sweaty khakis stared into the blackness with his mouth set. The burnt-oil stench made him feel like throwing up. He was remembering another time in these same waters, not that many years before, during the tanker-convoying effort known as Operation Earnest Will. Another time when war had loomed and men got ready to die.

And many had, when USS *Turner Van Zandt* had hit a mine. He rubbed his mouth, remembering how many had gone down with her. How many had slipped away afterward, of heatstroke and dehydration during days adrift. From the sharks and sea snakes, and the patrol boats that had attacked the helpless men in the water.

He seemed to have seen a lot of that in his career. Disaster. Loss. *Van Zandt. Reynolds Ryan.* Then deep in the China Sea, the frigate that had once been USS *Gaddis* but at the end had no name at all. When he closed his eyes, he saw men in the water, men burned, men torn apart by shells. Maybe he carried it with him, like a communicable disease.

Maybe that was why the board had decided to promote others while he stood still. Marking time as his career slipped away.

He remembered his way past the memories as they flew southward, till gradually his tension ebbed and he leaned back and closed his eyes.

They landed aboard *Blue Ridge* an hour later. He swung out of the aircraft, reached back for a flight bag, and jogged across black nonskid. The air was hotter here than in the northern Gulf. The sky had cleared too, turning the bright hazy tan he remembered from years before. He handed his cranial to a crewman. Beside a weatherdecks door a lieutenant with an aiguillette beckoned.

"Lieutenant Commander Lenson? Off USS *Tripoli?*"

"That's me," Dan said.

"Welcome aboard, sir. Follow me, please."

Belowdecks seemed very bright. Dan blinked, trying to keep track of where they were going in the white-painted passageways; then gave up. He was used to frigates, destroyers, not the labyrinth of this huge and nearly unarmed command ship. He barked his shin and started paying attention to the knee knockers. At last the aide pushed open a door. "The admiral's in here," he said.

"In here" was extremely dim, lit in hazy blue, and smelled of rubber and ozone. The deck was soft underfoot, padded by insulating matting. Petty officers and junior officers sat tranced before screens and keyboards. Radio nets spoke in muted whispers, and under all other sounds purred an unending drone of ventilation. He stopped, waiting for his eyes to adjust, then followed his guide to where three officers sat before large decision screens. Dan came to attention. "Lieutenant Commander Lenson, sir."

"Sit down, Commander." A tense-looking man in trop

whites sat gnawing a pencil in a padded leather command chair. To his left was a hefty marine in starched desert battle dress. To his right sat an air force officer in Class Bs. Dan hesitated, then sat where the admiral pointed, perching sideways before a console.

The decision screens showed Task Force 151.11's movement west. Minesweepers and gunfire support ships were probing in toward the coast of occupied Kuwait. The amphibious task force was forming behind them. To the south were four carrier battle groups. The air picture swept out hundreds of miles farther, over Kuwait, Iraq, southern Iran, and Saudi Arabia. It showed carrier air patrols orbiting and strike groups ranging far inland. Dan wiped his forehead. In the air-conditioned dim his sweat felt icy cold. A shiver wormed down his back.

"Just got in, Dan?"

"Just jumped off the helo, sir."

He'd met Wayne Kinnear during the planning effort that led to the impact of a hundred and twenty-two Tomahawk missiles on Iraq. Vice Admiral Kinnear was COMUSNAVCENT, commander of all US Navy and Marine forces in the Gulf. He wore the wings of a naval aviator and had shot down two enemy fighters in Vietnam.

Kinnear pointed his eraser at the air force officer, then at the marine. "Meet Colonel Ed Salter, from the CINC staff in Riyadh. And Lieutenant Colonel Anders Paulik, First SRI Group, I MEF. Gentlemen, you asked me for a Tomahawk targeter. Commander Lenson planned the TLAM strikes on Baghdad that opened the air war. He also planned the strike against the suspected chemical warfare aircraft at the Al Rashid base two weeks ago. Since then I've had him working for Pete Bulkeley in the Northern Gulf, getting ready for the invasion. I have to admit, I had my doubts about cruise missiles before I saw them live on CNN."

"You married, Commander?" said the Marine Corps colonel. Paulik was stocky, heavily built, with a crew cut and an accent Dan couldn't place. Not southern, like most marines, as if they'd all been born again at Parris Island and had become through that at least honorary South Carolinians. His skin was weathered as dark as old bronze.

He thought about Paulik's question, about Blair Titus and their long-distance, off-again, on-again relationship; decided to go for the short answer. "No, sir."

"Dependents?"

"A daughter. She lives with my ex."

The air force officer said, "You look like you're in good shape."

"I run, when I can," Dan said.

Paulik asked, "Any medical problems? Back? Knees?"

"None that I know of. What's this all about?" He glanced at Kinnear, but the admiral's attention was on the screens.

Paulik didn't answer, just asked another question. "And from what the admiral says, you're shit smart on Tomahawk?"

"Lenson was in Joint Cruise Missiles for the program development phase," Kinnear said. "He troubleshot the airframe when we had those crashes early in the program. Out here, he helped reprogram the Lacrosse radar satellites to give us the Iraqi terrain contours."

"Okay, that's good, but how about tactical employment? Targeting angles, warhead types?"

"Well, as Admiral Kinnear said, we've done quite a bit of targeting. I know what the system can do."

"And what it can't?"

"Well." He cleared his throat, not sure what they were getting at. "The missile has its limitations. The mission has to be planned in advance. To program in the terrain matching and the flight profile. Once your round's in flight, you can't reprogram or recall; you're locked in to that target. And you need contrast for the final homing phase; that's done with a separate visual matching system. And the warhead's not all that heavy. I've developed algorithms for optimal targeting against the various types of structures that make up the Iraqi military-industrial base—"

"Sounds like our boy," Paulik told the admiral.

"Here's the situation," said the bird colonel, Salter.

Lowering his voice, though the closest ear other than theirs was several meters distant, Salter explained they were trying to localize a rumored Iraqi threat. They had some intercept material. It confirmed their human intelligence, HUMINT as it was called in the trade, but they still had nothing precise enough to bomb with. They had to send in a ground team. CENTCOM's J-3, Major General Moore, had passed the mission to Lieutenant General Walter Boomer, commander of the First Marine Expeditionary Force—all the marine forces in the Gulf and Saudi. Boomer had passed it to the First SRI Group.

Paulik picked up there. "SRI stands for Surveillance and Reconnaissance Intelligence. We're the headquarters element between HQ I MEF and the divisional force recon units. This mission's short fuze, but it's the kind of thing we train for. We're sending a team in to find this threat, if it exists; localize it; and call in Tomahawks on it. We need a targeting guy. Thanks for volunteering, Commander."

"I didn't volunteer," Dan said, more or less by reflex.

Obviously following the conversation though he hadn't seemed to, Kinnear said, "Mr. Lenson here has gotten out of a few tight spots before. Not always smelling like a rose, but he came back."

Salter said, "Then he'll have to do. We're not using Tomahawks anymore in the northern theater. After that bunker strike that killed all those civilians, we've pretty much moved the air war over the Republican Guard and stood the TLAM shooters down—"

"That wasn't a Tomahawk—"

Salter backtracked smoothly. "No, it wasn't, Admiral, and I didn't mean to imply it was. The two events are unrelated."

"You bring your personal gear?" Paulik asked Dan.

"No. They just told me to get on the helicopter and bring my targeting kit—the templates and so forth."

Kinnear raised his eyebrows. "Now, wait just a minute. I understood this to be a consultation. Not a raid on my staff. It's true we're not firing Tomahawks just now, but we're going to need Lenson here for the amphibious invasion."

Colonel Salter cleared his throat. "You know there's not going to be an invasion, Admiral."

"Not the mainland—I know that's off. But Faylakah Island, we're going ahead with that."

Salter said apologetically, "Sorry, sir, that's not in the CINC's plan either. You'll get official word tomorrow. What you're executing is purely a deception plan. A diversion, to keep their eyes on the sea while the army goes in farther west. And I'm taking your man here with me. If there's a difficulty with that, sir, I suggest you call General Schwarzkopf direct." To Dan he said, "You won't need gear. We'll provide everything. We're leaving in ten minutes. You might want to drink some water before we go."

Dan had been sitting with one arm on the console, watching the volleys going back and forth. At the news that the landing was off, he tensed. It explained a lot of things he'd been wondering about. Such as why there hadn't been any preparatory shelling of the Kuwaiti beachfront, the liquid petroleum factory, the other facilities that could shelter Iraqi forces for a counterattack. But no one had told the eighteen thousand marines and thousands of supporting sailors out there getting ready. And the destroyers, cruisers, battleships, and minesweepers of Task Force 151, which—he glanced at his watch—should be just now entering the Iraqi minefield.

Kinnear had flushed, obviously angry. "If the CINC wants him, he can have him. The planning's done now anyway. But this about the landing not coming off—"

"It's not going to happen, Admiral," said Salter again.

"Both Secretary Cheney and General Powell are against it. But I'd keep that very close hold. If Saddam even gets a hint we're not coming in from seaward, he can swing those eleven divisions south and knock the hell out of I MEF coming up through the Saddam Line."

They were all silent, contemplating that. Finally Kinnear nodded. "Very well, take him. I'll have the helo called away for you."

AS THEY waited to board, Paulik stared off over the slowly passing sea. A small combatant, perhaps a missile boat, flying the green Saudi flag kept station a thousand yards off, and Dan recognized a British Sheffield-class destroyer on the horizon to the north; he guessed it was *York*. The smoke was thinner down here, and again he noticed the sky, faded like a master chief's khakis. And looking down into the sea he saw that it was the same transparent blue he recalled from years before. The cruise that had ended so badly for USS *Turner Van Zandt* and her strangely divided yet always courageous captain.

"Been in combat before?" Paulik said, interrupting but in a strange way paralleling Dan's thoughts.

"Yes, sir."

"Ground combat?"

"Oh—ashore, only once. I was on an amphibious staff in the Med. During the Syrian incursion. Colonel Steve Haynes was the MAU commander. I got ashore with the landing force, but I wouldn't say I know much about ground warfare."

"Well, what you need to know, we'll get you up to speed on. Let me explain a little more about this mission. You know what Force Recon is."

Dan tried to concentrate. "They're like Delta Force or the SEALs, as I understand it. Special operations."

"Well, yes and no. Our Force Reconnaissance community trains to the same standards, but we're not walled off from our parent service the way they are.

"Anyway, a couple years ago I was in Quantico working what we called the Urban Assault Team concept. The UAT trained with high-tech gear, new weapons, new tactics, new sensors in order to penetrate, operate in, and extract from high-density urban environments. We figured that's where warfare's going in the long run, urban environments like Beirut and Northern Ireland and so forth."

"Makes sense." Dan glanced back to see the chopper pilots climbing into the cockpit, the turbines start to whine.

"Yeah, I thought so, but we got defunded in eighty-nine and had to send everybody back to their units. Those who stayed in got deployed out here in the Desert Shield buildup. But as it happens, this mission's going into a built-up area. When I realized that, I thought of a couple of my sharp performers from UAT. I found them, MEF tasked the division to shit them out to me, and I'm using them as a nucleus to build the Signal Mirror team. You're gonna be what we call an attachment."

"You said 'Signal Mirror'."

"That's the code name. Right."

"Tell me again why you need a navy guy for a marine mission."

"I need a Tomahawk targeter in good physical shape, somebody who can think under pressure and come out with the right decision. The admiral seems to think that's you."

Dan wondered if it was also that ever since he'd tried to resign once, then taken it back, he'd had the feeling certain people considered him expendable. He dismissed that as paranoia, though. "Where exactly are we going?"

"Out west, to link up with the team."

"I mean, on this mission you're talking about."

"I can't tell you yet, but it'll be serious Apache man-tracking Indian Country." Paulik smiled broadly. "I got to do some of that in Cambodia. Livin' in the red. Does wonders for your nightmares."

"What are we looking for when we get there?"

"I can't tell you that either, because actually we aren't sure. We just got to get some eyes in there to look around, see what they can find." A crewman jogged toward them, and Paulik turned. "Okay, let's strap it on."

"Well, look, wait a minute. They need me where I am."

Paulik looked taken aback, as if the idea someone might question or object had never occurred to him. "Hey, I asked for their best guy and they shit you out. Don't worry, we'll have you back on your ship in a week. Two weeks, tops."

"Well, all right," Dan said, feeling like he'd just stepped overboard without a life jacket.

The aide, the one who'd taken him to the command center, came up to them. He said, "Admiral's got a last word for you, sir."

Kinnear was standing forward of the helo platform. The wash from the turning rotors ruffled his hair. Dan yelled, "Be there in a minute," to Paulik, ducked, and ran toward where the admiral stood.

"A couple Navy-only words," Kinnear shouted over the engines.

"Yes, sir."

"I don't know what this is about, but when it's over I want you back here."

"Aye, aye, sir."

"If there's anything I should know about, call me. This sounds like an army boondoggle to me."

"It sounds like a marine mission, sir. Colonel Paulik and all."

"It's assigned to them, but the tasking came from Schwarzkopf. Just keep your eyes open. Remember what's going to happen when this is over."

Dan stared at him. "When what's over, sir?"

"The war, Dan," said Kinnear.

"To Kuwait, you mean? And Iraq?"

"No, to the Navy Department. When this is over the army and air force are going to be at our throats again.

This time, they'll want our expeditionary mission. You know why we were ordered to stop firing Tomahawks?"

"They're an expensive round. We're using them up."

"Bull; we've got plenty of airframes. Schwarzkopf and Powell turned them off because we were getting too much network exposure."

Dan digested that as Kinnear went on. "I'm sorry to expose you to the ugly underbelly of interservice politics, Lenson. Just keep that in mind, when they start telling you you have to 'think joint.' I'll translate that for you. It means: we lie back and they do what they want to us."

Dan said he'd bear that in mind. Kinnear nodded curtly and turned away. Then he turned back. "One last question. What's your feeling on TLAM-N?"

"The nuclear round, sir?" He debated telling the admiral about his own history with the nuclear Tomahawk, how he'd been fired from the cruise missile office for objecting to its development. But it seemed too long to go into, so all he said was, "I'm not too keen on nukes in general, sir."

"Just keep that in mind," Kinnear said.

Dan stood looking after him as he walked away. Wondering, What did that mean? No logical answer suggested itself, and he turned and trotted for the aircraft as Paulik waved him on.

3

Ras al-Mish'ab Special Forces Base, Saudi Arabia

Gunnery Sergeant Sid Gault drove fast through the dark, wearing his night vision goggles. The Humvee had the troop seats in back and the canvas sunscreen and the AR/VRC-90 radio like a big green air conditioner between him and the shotgun seat. The antenna was copper wire strung between four swab handles bolted vertically at the corners of the vehicle. It looked terrible, but it cut setup and breakdown time to nothing.

The gate sentry bent to peer in, then waved him through. A hundred meters inside he parked at the watering point, leaning out to scan the sand where his boots would go. He'd started doing that after seeing a Qatari tanker get the meat blown off his leg by an undetonated cluster munition.

As the rest of his team rolled out he told them to bring him back a few liters; he'd stay with the vehicle. This far forward he doubted they had to worry about terrorists, but those were the orders. To the north, just visible through the NVGs, huge plumes of greasy smoke towered into the black sky. Tanks were still burning up there. Iraqi armor, destroyed in their retreat a few days before. The night rumbled with jets going overhead and the thud of bombs as they pounded at the dug-in Iraqis in Kuwait.

As his guys slogged away through the dark, moving with the slow, tired-looking gait you picked up after months on soft sand, Gault lowered his eyes to where his war had started, seven months before.

Ras al-Mish'ab had been a Saudi National Guard base before the war, a two-mile square of concertina wire and guard towers. Its flat, hard sand was spaced with hardstand, slit trench, tent areas, and one-story buildings of sand-colored concrete. Like the other bases the Saudis had segregated their infidel defenders to, it was miles from anywhere, far south of the abandoned city of Khafji and only connected to it by a dirt road that wound between the practically impassible sabkahs. To the east, not in sight tonight through the dusty air but not far distant, lay the Gulf. To the south, empty coast till Bahrain. To the west, desert forever, a thousand miles of it all the way to the Red Sea. Empty till a few months ago. Now, filled with the greatest concentration of troops and armor since the battle of Kursk.

He'd seen it first the August previous, two weeks after the Iraqis invaded Kuwait. Second Force Recon Company had been doing site training in Washington with the District of Columbia SWAT team when the CO called with orders. They'd closed up shop with the cops and bused back to Camp Lejeune for a predeployment briefing at Force headquarters. They spent one night with their families, those who had them, then mustered the next morning and trucked to Cherry Point Marine Corps Air Station. A day and a half in a C-130 and disembarkation at Dhahran, a sprawling airfield choked with fighters and transports, the whole noisy confused gaggle of forces pouring in on a bewildering mix of time-phased logistics and out-of-your-ass scrambling. He remembered that first breath of Saudi air, hot as flame on your skin, down your lungs, the gritty feel of powder sand.

Practically the first troops in-country, they lived in a hangar for two days, then got orders to Ras al-Mish'ab. Their initial tasking had been to establish OPs, observation posts, along the Kuwaiti-Saudi border. Which since the invasion had become the de facto border between Saudi and what Saddam was already calling the "nineteenth province" of Iraq. But the marines and SEALs and Special Forces, light forces hastily set out as a trip wire, didn't call it the border. They called it the fire support coordination line, the boundary between friendly and opposing forces.

Khafji, which lay between Ras al-Mish'ab and the FSCL, was a sizable city, with a port and a chemical factory, but no one lived in it now but mangy packs of pariah dogs. The population had pulled out when the Iraqis started shelling. It looked almost American, with modern buildings and four-lane highways. Vacant, abandoned, it felt like a postapocalyptic science fiction movie. Just the sly bony dogs, wary and skulking, and now and then a jeep full of Saudi troopers on what he figured was antilooter patrol.

The OPs were seven miles forward of Khafji, just south of the sand berms along the border. The teams moved into the customs posts, crenellated forts that looked like they'd been lifted from a Foreign Legion movie. They sandbagged the windows and dug fighting positions, did the basic grunt homework for a defensive position; fields of fire, avenues of approach, routes of egress, fire plan sketches. No artillery. No tanks. Just guys with rifles and radios, a warning bell that would go off if Saddam decided to wrap up all the oil in the Mideast in one neat package.

And there they'd sat for six months as the blinding heat waned into fall and then cool rainy winter. Living with the flies and the black bugs and the scorpions. Listening to REO Speedwagon and AC/DC and Guns N' Roses on the armed forces radio. Supply was fucked up, so they ate with the Saudis, rice and pita bread, lamb and chicken their hired Pakistanis cooked in fly-infested kitchens. Some of the men had gotten cramps, then got lethargic. Worms, the docs said.

It was usually quiet at the border. It was so flat they

could see fifteen miles into Kuwait from the tops of the police post. Occasionally a plume of dust sifted skyward in the distance. A few miles past that, the fortifications started. Wire, trenches, minefields, all the World War I stuff the Iraqis had used to stop the Iranians. Once Gault watched through binoculars as a camel wandered into a minefield and blew himself up. At night deserters would come in, hands raised, and the Saudis would take them away for interrogation. After a while the teams started rotating back to Al Mish'ab, for PT in the sun and what passed for liberty, taking Zodiacs out into the bay to spearfish or pick scallops off the reef. Or buy cream cheese in glass jars and canned beef, try to gain some weight back on Pringles and Twinkies and warm Pepsi at the gas station outside the gate. No beer. No magazines. Mail, but two weeks late. A couple of days off, then they'd rotate back to the border.

Which was where he'd been the evening the Iraqi Third Armored and Fifth Mechanized, moving between passes of the recon satellites, had come charging across with T-55s.

The guys came back, lugging plastic-skinned cases of bottled water. Their blouses were dark with sweat and spilled water. He looked around one last time, then climbed back into the vehicle.

"Let's go find us some Syrians," he said, and started it up.

INTEL HAD said the Iraqis couldn't attack. That was why there were no heavy forces there, just the OPs and then thirty miles back a jumble of Saudi Guard, Saudi Marines, Omanis, Bahrainis, and a not-real-well-soldered-together "army" of miscellaneous units from the other Arab allies. The Iraqis were hunkered down, they said. Half their combat effectiveness gone. Ready to run when the ground offensive started.

Like shit, Gault thought.

He and Vertierra and Abrahamson had been on the roof of the police post, watching Harriers and A-10s working over the Wafrah orchards all day long. OP-7 had called in movement, and the close air support had come out and circled and after a while the *crump* of bombs shuddered over the desert. Late that afternoon the jamming started, a scratchy buzz that wiped out their VHF.

Not long after dark they heard the tanks. They got their binoculars and NVGs and looked north over the berm. Gault couldn't see anything, but there was no mistaking the sound. They'd heard it before, far off on summer nights, but never this close, never this loud. The creak and squeal of bogies made the hair crawl on the back of his neck. He tried the radio again, but it was still jammed. He transmitted anyway, just in case Higher could hear him.

They stared out for a long time. He saw nothing through the sights. In fact, he couldn't even see the berm. He blinked, refocusing. But it was gone, replaced by a green night-cloud within which vague bright shapes swam like fluorescent ghosts.

Then Abrahamson yelled, "Tanks!" and the first three came out of what he suddenly realized was smoke, generated behind the attacking armor and pulled forward by the wind to cloak them. Because suddenly, like some evil conjuring trick, there they were, thin long barrels rising, then falling as the tanks' hulls slammed down, coming over the berm like boats coming off a wave, then charging, snorting out of the smoke and dust directly at them. T-55s, the round turret, but with—he stopped, gripping the barrels of the binoculars—with the barrels *reversed*, pointing back over their hulls.

In the corner Vertierra was still trying to raise Task Force Taro, speaking slowly and clearly to cut through the interference. And for a moment Gault's heart had surged as he thought, *They're surrendering.* Advancing with turrets reversed, wasn't that the sign for surrendering—

But then the turrets began rotating. And he'd realized

then what it all meant, the comm jamming, the reports from farther west of movement along the berm. The thud and roar of guns, the flashes of light that pierced the western sky. That flickered from the direction of the thin line between Saddam and the forward logistic dumps, ammo, fuel, water, food; everything he needed to disrupt and destroy the impending offensive.

One of the T-55s slowed. It rocked to a halt and the turret steadied. The barrel lifted. He realized it was pointed at them only as a flash obliterated the image. He ducked without thinking. The projectile whipcracked over their heads. A miss, but the next one might not be.

"I want a star cluster," he yelled over the rising clatter of tracks. Vertierra sprinted off for the pyrotechnic. "Then everybody in the vehicles. Right now!"

They had two Humvees, an M60, and their rifles. Nothing to face a brigade of tanks with. He told the men to get the logs, the crypto gear, and the night vision gear. When they had what they could carry, he took out two grenades, made sure the stairway was clear, then pulled the pins and laid them on top of the radios.

They were in the vehicles, speeding and bumping across the desert, when he saw that the tanks had already cut them off.

DAWN WAS limping in through the smoke and overcast when they caught up with the Syrians. He'd been assigned to them after Khafji, to get them used to Americans. They were well north of their assigned grid square location. That made no sense. The last he'd heard, they weren't going over the border on G day. They said they were there to defend Saudi Arabia, not to attack an Arab brother. Gault had pointed out Saddam had no problem attacking *his* Arab brothers, but they just laughed softly and smiled at each other like they knew something he didn't.

Major Amidallah was sitting on his tank as he drove

up. The Syrian Ninth Armored was equipped with Soviet-made T-62s. They were painted a dusty sand camouflage. He noticed they'd finally mounted the VS-17s, the big purple-and-orange reflective panels that marked Coalition armor against air strikes. He'd been trying to get Amidallah to do it for weeks. Maybe the Syrians were joining the team at last.

"Ah, Gunny Gault. Good morning. You are noticing our panels."

Gault stood up in the Hummer, trying to give as professional an impression as six feet of desert-gaunt marine, blue eyes and close-cropped blondish hair could convey. "Yes, sir. Good decision, sir."

"You see, we are on your side. I have been telling you that."

Amidallah hadn't told him anything of the kind, had in fact screwed, fucked, and misled the advisors as much he could. But Gault just said, "Yes, sir. And I know what famous fighters the Syrians are. Where you heading, sir? I had you two klicks south of here."

"We are taking our position as ordered."

"Are you joining the attack, sir?"

"We are in the reserve. Backing up our Arab brothers."

"That will hearten us all no end, to have such fierce warriors behind us," he said, troweling it on. Arabs loved compliments. Sometimes he thought they actually believed them. "Will you really stay back in reserve? Surely you won't let your brave brothers, the Qataris and Bahrainis, attack without you?"

Amidallah lost interest in the conversation. He shouted to his driver, who had stuck his head over the hatch, then climbed in. The engine roared, the tracks jerked and then rolled into motion. The other tanks and ZSUs started up and moved out after him, coughing black exhaust into the dark dawn light, throwing mud up behind the tracks.

Gault parked off the road, out of the mud, and watched them move out. President Assad had played both sides all through the buildup. He'd sent the Ninth to Saudi, but then offered it to Saddam to screen the Iraqi army from the Allies if the Iraqi dictator agreed to withdraw. They kept roaring by, swarthy, mustached faces regarding him from each tank. Some saluted. Most just stared, or let their eyes rove past as if he were a rock, or a pariah dog. Gault didn't care. He really didn't care.

The growing light turned a nearby shadow into an Iraqi armored personnel carrier, hit and wrecked during the retreat. The rear ramp lay on the sand twenty meters away. He went over, watching where he stepped, and peered into the cavern-dark interior. As his eyes adapted he tensed. Its crew was looking back at him.

They were still sitting where they'd been when the sabot round or TOW round had torn through the light armor and blown the rear ramp off its hinges. Only now they were leathery shadows of human beings. The explosion had crushed them back into the hull of the vehicle, molded them into seat backs and webbing and handholds. Portions of flesh and muscle had extruded through the firing ports and hung down outside, like beef jerky. They'd been flattened and scorched and then, over the days since, the burnt cooked meat had dried in the desert air till it was proof even against the flies.

One Iraqi corpse had a sign around its neck. It read DON'T FUCK WITH THE CORPS.

Once he'd have torn it down, then thrown up from the sick barbecue smell and the sight of human beings flattened like roadkill. Now he didn't feel anything. People died in war. They died every day. You didn't even need a war to kill them. Just a moment of inattention. Something as simple as not checking the bore of a shotgun.

He turned his head to find one of his men behind him, and had a momentary impulse to say something witty; something like "See what happens when you don't stay hydrated." But the words died as he looked again at what had once lived and walked and faced battle. Whatever he felt or didn't feel, they'd been soldiers. Other soldiers were dying right now, on the far side of those berms, and a whole lot more would end up like this or worse when the ground attack started.

He looked at the sign again. If one of the Saudis saw it, the manure would impact the propeller. But he found he didn't care about that either. So at last he just headed back to the Humvee. He climbed up behind the .50 cal and said to Vertierra, "Let's get back, Sergeant."

Half an hour later he was in his tent, and the hot shimmering rim of sun poking up over the desert signaled the end of another working day. He drank a bottle of water. Then pulled the flap closed and went to sleep.

MARCUS "SID" GAULT had grown up as an air force brat, trailing his dad all over the country. He did two years at Auburn, in forestry management. Then realized he didn't want to manage forests, and enlisted in the Marine Corps, for no good reason he'd been able to put his finger on other than that when he went into the office the recruiter hadn't seemed to want him. Had acted like he had to prove something, to be good enough to sign up.

At Parris Island he was in Third Battalion. In the winter series, which was good, the sand fleas weren't as bad and you didn't have to worry about heat stroke. Platoon Thirty-Eighteen, India Company, Third Battalion. When he played back boot camp he didn't get the rifle pits, or the run-down World War II barracks. What came back to him was the final parade, when your parents sat in the bleachers and you marched by in full dress, a Marine at last.

He went to infantry school at Camp Geiger. Squad tactics. Offense. Defense. The elements of battle. Did a float with Third Battalion, Second Marines, then screened for Force Recon out of Camp Pendleton. That was where he met Tina, working cashier at Lum's. They were married in '86, and Cory was born the same year. He picked up sergeant, then went to DI at Parris Island, picking up staff sergeant meritoriously on the drill field. He used his DI option to go back to Second Recon, where he'd picked up gunny just the year before.

He remembered that as the golden time. Loving his career, loving his wife, watching his boy grow day by day. Cory was a late talker, but the base pediatrician said that didn't mean anything, children varied in their developmental time lines. The boy wanted to be with him every minute he was home, would sit and watch him study or work.

Maybe that was why it had happened. The event, the accident, that changed everything about his life, his marriage—everything.

He'd been cleaning his shotgun in the basement den on Ivory Crescent, getting ready for duck season. Cory had been playing across the room. Four years old, talking happily to the plastic tyrannosaurs he'd named Newton and Stupid as his father worked with the spray can of Rem Action Cleaner and the screw-together aluminum cleaning rod. The sweet oil smell of Hoppe's Powder Solvent. The pristine white of the cleaning patches, turned black with sooty residue as they emerged from the action.

Then the recoil in his hands, the unbelieving moment as he'd stared down at the gun. Then lifted his head and looked where the magnum load of number-eight shot had gone.

The doctors said that with the brain damage there was no chance of recovery. He and Tina had let Cory go, the last thing they did together, and signed the papers to let what was left of him help other kids who needed it.

It was his fault. He'd loaned it to a guy to shoot skeet with, and hadn't checked the bore when the friend gave it back. A stupid thing. The kind of thing a boot would do. Tina left. Too many memories in the house, too many memories with him, she said. He kept going, but only because there wasn't anything else to do. All he had left was the Corps. The Corps in the day, and at night the half gallons of tax-free Jack Daniel's from the base package store.

So that when the Force went to war, he'd gone without

a backward glance. Not just because he was a marine. Because deep in the back of his mind was the hopeless hoping that someday he could find the only thing he wanted anymore: the secret of forgetting. Maybe someplace with sand instead of trees, clean and empty, might hold that secret. Like that river you were supposed to drink from when you died. The one that made you forget everything, and you could go across wiped clean, blank, reformatted, like an erased floppy disk.

When he looked back now, he could hardly remember the kid who'd signed up because the recruiter had acted uninterested. He couldn't imagine himself as anything other than a marine. He still had a soft spot for the air force, because of his dad. He respected the Rangers. Aside from that he didn't think much of the people the other services attracted. They seemed to see it as just a job. Which it wasn't. Maybe that was the pride.

But he didn't think a lot about it.

HE BLINKED awake inside the tent, holding his hand over his eyes. The gray daylight looked fierce, unnatural. The sand fleas were crawling over him, though they didn't bite. They slowed down when it got cold, but they never went away, the way you figured a bug ought to in the winter. His drying underwear hung on a bungee between him and the light. "What?" he muttered.

"Helo incomin', Gunny. Tower says it's for you."

He came awake. He swung his feet out, pulled his trou on, fumbled boots on over bare feet, and went out to the pad.

The helicopter dropped from a smoky sky. Gault didn't know the marine who jumped out, but the subdued railroad tracks of a captain and the jump wings registered. The guy was built like a refrigerator, solid chest and bull neck and buzz cut. The captain returned his salute, looking hard into his eyes. "Wake you up, Gunny?"

"Yes, sir."

"Usually sleep in till zero eight?"

"We're on reverse cycle, sir. We ORP at night and bunk up during the day."

The captain asked if he was the same Marcus Gault who'd led the team through the UAT concept development course at Quantico. Gault said he was, and the captain asked if he remembered a Major Paulik. Gault said no sir. The captain asked if he knew where the other UATers were. Gault said he still had three of them in the platoon.

"Get 'em," the captain said. "And load up your personal gear, Gunny. We're taking you TAD for a couple weeks."

And sure enough the captain was hand-carrying orders assigning one Gunnery Sergeant Marc S. Gault, USMC, for temporary additional duty with headquarters staff, First SRIG. Nor did he seem inclined to wait. So in the end Gault wrote out a radio message telling the rear what was going on and asking for a relief. Then he went back to his tent and started throwing his gear into his duffel. A few words of turnover with Abrahamson, and he grabbed his M16.

THE T-55s had crossed their front in a steady rumble, and Gault dismounted everyone, got them away from the Humvees. There was no cover, and they were safer on the ground. But the Iraqis ignored them. Not a shell came their way. He remounted and headed south again. Other vehicles appeared, angling in across the desert and from side tracks, all funneling at top speed toward the only way out: down the coast road, over the causeway into Khafji and out the other side. Looking back, he could see the tanks redeploying. There wasn't much time to escape.

But at the same time what a great target they made, a mass of armor on the move in daylight. He gave Vertierra the wheel and started working the radio. The jamming had faded as they moved south, and he raised Taro and asked for air strikes. But the air side was busy to the west, striking other armored spearheads. He got a promise of artillery, and several minutes later inverted pyramids of sand suddenly appeared out in the desert. By then, though, their targets had moved forward again. He called in adjustments, but realized he couldn't stay where he was. They'd roll over him.

The causeway was behind; the city rose ahead. Soon the heavy elements would counterattack. They'd need someone to spot fire for them, call air and artillery and naval gunfire from offshore. If they could find an observation point in Khafji . . . He told the guys what they were going to do. They'd have to abandon the vehicles, leave them some distance from wherever they holed up. Otherwise, if the Iraqis saw them, they'd do a house-to-house search.

By midnight they were barricaded in the cab of a container crane at the port, in sight of the Khafji Beach Hotel, looking down at the Iraqis as they edged into the deserted city and began looting. They stayed for two days, along with another team from First Recon, calling in fire on the Iraqis and dodging from building to building to evade them, until the Saudis retook the town.

THEY FLEW west. The sun gave him that much; and for a while he tracked the berm in the distance, the border between warring principalities and powers; then it angled off in the great northwest tangent that would end eventually at Jordan. He and the captain and Zeitner and Vertierra and Nichols sat wordlessly, butts cradled in nylon webbing, cranials and Mickey Mouse ears insulating them as effectively as if they sat in separate rooms. F.C. looked haggard. He had cammie paint in the creases behind his ears. Gault sign-asked if he was okay. He said he was. The sky went blue, then gray again, but they'd left the Destructo Zone of oil haze and overhead doom.

They landed only once, along a road that came straight as a taut wire over one horizon and disappeared over the other. A deuce and a half was waiting, and when the skids went down another marine swung out of it and trotted toward them. Gault didn't recognize him; a young guy. As soon as he was aboard they lifted off again and settled back into that western-heading groove. And gradually the droning vibration and the missing sleep got to him, and his head sank.

Arrowing westward over the empty desert, Gault slept.

THE ROOM was unpainted concrete block, with no windows and a buzzing fluorescent light. The floor was concrete painted brown, with a drain in the center. He didn't know what base this was. Coming in, he'd seen an airstrip, protective wire, guard towers. Cobras sitting in revetments. Tents. Conex boxes. More revetments around ugly warthog A-10s, like tadpoles with stubby wings, and off on the far side of the strip enormous mounds of green-painted bombs from which yellow forklifts shuttled back and forth. No chairs, so they settled on the concrete, looking up at a stand with a display. It was covered by opaque plastic marked SECRET. Vertierra broke open the shrink-wrapped case of water and passed bottles around.

The captain stood up front, looking even larger in the small room. Too large, Gault thought, looking at his bull neck, his tree-trunk thighs. The big guys didn't seem to make it in the recon community. The best physical type was neither tall nor short, neither skinny nor bulked. Team guys were buffed but not grotesquely so. Kohler passed out memo books and pencils, like a teacher before a test. Then went back to his modified parade rest.

"As of now, we're in lockdown for mission prep. No phone calls, no mail, no leaving the base. No discussion of the mission outside these rooms, even among yourselves. Everybody understand?

"For those who haven't met me yet, I'm Captain Kohler, with S-2 of First SRIG. Personel from I MEF and possibly from Riyadh will also be part of the briefing team. They're on their way here now. Lieutenant Colonel Anders Paulik is the S-3 of First SRIG. He'll be here shortly too. Till then, he's asked me to give you a quick mission brief so you can start planning.

"Why are you here? Two reasons. First, you're all recon marines. Second, we wanted street fighters. Most of you've been through the Urban Assault Team concept demonstrator, and if you were in Khafji or Beirut or Monrovia, you've done as much of it as anybody in the Corps."

Kohler turned the first sheet to a Magic Markered page. It bulleted HUMINT, Enemy Communication Intercepts, Visual Imagery, and Information Received Direct from Enemy. The bottom line was titled Flying Stones.

"Most intel work consists of looking for anomalies. Anomalies are abnormalities; items of data different from what you expect, or weird new shit you have no explanation for. One anomaly might be an error or a misunderstanding. When they pile up, you start looking for what's making that hump in the groundsheet.

"Putting the anomalies together, we think Saddam's got some kind of weapon of mass destruction held back. He's using conventionally armed Scud-Cs against Saudi and Israel. This is something else, something he thinks is so big 'n' bad it'll stop us kicking his ass out of Kuwait.

"We have a name. The Arabic translates as 'Flying Stones.' We have a suspected location: in central Iraq, under the coverage of the Kari integrated air defense network. Based on that, CENTCOM's handed us a 'black' mission: find, identify, and localize it."

He flipped the chart, and there was western Iraq.

"I'm going to read you the mission statement," said the captain. Gault took out his notebook. So did the others. Kohler read slowly, so they could get it down. "On order, UAT Reconstitute Twelve will insert into Iraq, link up with indigenous resistance, reconnoiter suspected nuclear/biological weapons site west of Baghdad, and squirt back targeting data before extraction. Mission has priority."

He read it again, and one by one they put their pencils up to show they had it. The bare cinder-block space was about as quiet as Gault had ever heard a compartment full of marines. Like everything else the captain had said so far, the words meant more than they said. "Mission has priority," for example. That meant that whatever happened in Kuwait, whatever happened elsewhere in the war, they'd stay till their mission was complete.

Kohler pointed in his direction, and he stood. "This is Gunnery Sergeant Gault. Gunny Gault will be the team leader." He pointed at another man. "Sergeant Jacob Zeitner, assistant team leader . . . Sergeant Tony Vertierra, RTO . . . Lance Corporal Fred Nichols, sniper and breach-course qualified . . . Corporal Denny Blaisell, scout."

Gault thought of telling him Nichols didn't go by Fred—he hated his first name—but didn't. He just sat down again. The others did too, with a shuffle of feet, some dry-sounding coughs.

Kohler rolled his head to one side, as if to loosen up. "We'll do patrol order, map study, and rehearsals over the next two days. The mission attachment's on his way. A navy Tomahawk targeter."

"Navy, sir? You mean SEAL?"

"I'm afraid not. We'll just have to do what we can to get him up to speed. We'll do basic quick reaction drills and a shooting package, but don't expect too much. He's essential at the objective, though, so your job's to get him there.

"This is about as short fuze as you can get. We have today, tonight, tomorrow, to train and plan. Then you're climbing on the helo and executing."

Gault finished writing *two days prep phase* in his book and closed it. He was evaluating what he'd heard, what he saw on the map. The zigzag line, presumably a helo insert track, leading into Iraq.

The mission itself sounded infantry-proof. Go in. Link up. Find this thing, observe, identify, report, and return. He'd been in Indian Country before. It could be dangerous, but only if they screwed up. Recon teams seldom did the Rambo-type, direct-action missions: snatching bodies, blowing up bridges. Going deep into hostile territory without support or heavy weapons, they avoided contact with enemy forces. Stealth and silence saved you violence. To be detected, to have to fight, meant they'd failed. They'd just have to plan as thoroughly as they could, practice as much as they had time for, then go out and do it. This was war. Some things didn't take a lot of thought.

But deep down he was worried. Usually you got a geographic objective, a specific place or at least an area to scout. The intel officer had given them no guidance on location. He didn't like the idea of only two days to prepare. He also didn't like going in with a mixed team. He knew Zeitner and Vertierra, Nichols less well, but he didn't know this Blaisell at all, except that he'd been with the LAVs during the battle around OP-4. A recon team trained together, deployed together, knew each other's strengths and weaknesses. You could accept risk, because you knew you could trust the guys around you. He wouldn't have that on this mission. Nor was he happy about having non-marine attachments. They could be a royal pain in the ass. Worse, they could be mission killers. Weak people who held the team back. Careless people who gave away their position. Untrained people who just plain fucked up.

He was thinking about all this. But he didn't say anything. Not yet.

The door banged open and a stocky lieutenant colonel came in. The captain shouted, "Attention on deck," and the men leaped to their feet. Gault recognized Paulik then. He'd seen him around the head shed in Quantico, as a major. Paulik told them to stand at ease. He asked Kohler, "Done the basic mission brief?"

"Yes, sir."

"Tell them about our source?"

"No, sir."

To the room he said, "Welcome to 'Ar'ar. My name's Paulik. I'm the ops chief for Special Reconnaissance Group.

"Our source says this thing's in Baghdad. But we shook the imagery shop and nothing fell out. So we suspect it might be *beneath* Baghdad. Baghdad's an old city. We're not sure exactly what's down there. They say you can go from one side of Rome to the other underground, in the sewers and tunnels. Maybe we can do that here. Maybe not. Anyway, that's why we're reconstituting the UAT. Specifically for the urban combat, underground navigation expertise.

"We have an agent in place. He's a member of the Shiite resistance run by the Syrian intelligence service. That is, an Iraqi who's a Syrian intelligence asset. The Syrians are Ba'athists, but they hate the Iraqis even though they're Ba'athists too. What can I say, this is the Middle East. He's agreed to meet up with the team, if you can make it in without detection, and guide you to the objective.

"All right, are we all tracking, before we get deeper into the brief?"

Gault stood up again. "Two questions, sir. First off—this asset, the guy who's supposed to take us in. Any chance he could be leading us into a setup? And does he really know where this thing is?"

"I'm not sure I can give you an answer that'll satisfy you, Gunny. He's not ours and we don't have a straight pipeline to him," Paulik said. "So basically it'll be up to you to evaluate him on the ground, decide what level of credibility you want to give him."

"I've had some experience with the Syrians, sir. They like to play both sides."

"I hear you, but we don't have a choice. What's your second question?"

"Baghdad's five hundred miles inside Iraq, sir. If they detect us—will there be an emergency extract package? Or will we have to E and E on our own?"

"You tell me. We'll back you up. You team oriented, Gunnery Sergeant?"

"Yes, sir, I am."

"They handed us the ball. Deep reconnaissance is our reason for being. Collecting and confirming the intel data. Being the commander's eyes and ears. This is a deep reconnaissance mission. End of discussion?"

"End of discussion, sir," he agreed. He sat down again, squatting on the hard concrete, and opened up his notebook.

4

'Ar'ar, Saudi Arabia

They reconvened in the same room after dusk; though since there were no windows and the lights stayed on round the clock, night meant nothing to Gault, who was used to sleeping through the hours of light. When he could sleep at all . . . this close to the runway, the concrete-block walls hardly muffled the howl and roar of aircraft taking off. So that now and then they had to stop and just look at one another while the ceiling vibrated and no word could be heard over the engines of American vengeance.

When he came in, he saw someone had liberated a folding table and a handful of chairs. As Gault came to attention Lieutenant Colonel Paulik pointed to one. He took it silently, squared his notebook in front of him, and looked toward where an overhead projector faced one of the unadorned walls.

The navy was there too, the tall officer who'd arrived that afternoon, and three people he'd never seen before, a women and two men. One of the men was in civvies. The other man and the woman were in battle dress cammies. The guy's service component tag said US Air Force, the woman's US Army.

Paulik cleared his throat. He introduced the female officer as Major Maureen Maddox, from Fort Detrick. The men were Major Anthony Bice and Mr. Charles

Provanzano. "Major Bice is a Middle East specialist from the Defense Intelligence Agency. Mr. Provanzano's a . . . civilian advisor to CINCCENT. They're here to help us plan the mission."

Gault said, "Do they know the team leader plans recon missions, sir?"

"We know that, Gunny. But they have background I think you'll want to hear." He waited and, since Gault didn't say anything else, looked at Bice. "Why don't you kick off, Major?"

Bice stood. Gault noted his knife-edged, starched desert battle dress, the brand-new leather boots that would destroy his feet in two days in the field.

"I'm Tony Bice, out of Riyadh. I've been asked to come out here and background you on what little we have on this thing. This'll be top secret." He slipped transparencies from an envelope and clicked the projector on. The first slide said simply, "985."

"For security reasons, the Iraqis give numbers to their weapons development projects. We believe "985" is their Manhattan Project. That is, a highly classified program aimed at production of nuclear weapons.

"Saddam started his effort to develop what he calls *'Aslihatel dammar ashammel'*—roughly, weapons of mass death—in the nineteen seventies. The Russians refused to help him, but he had more luck with the French. They built the Osirak reactors, later called Tammuz I and II. His plan was to breed plutonium in them. But the Israelis bombed them in 1981. That set the clock back to zero.

"When the war with Iran started, Iraqi atomic research stopped. But in 1987 Saddam gave it priority again.

"You may know there are two ways to get to the bomb: breeding plutonium in a reactor, or enriching uranium to a high concentration of fissionable isotope. This time they decided to produce their own weapons-grade uranium. They bought raw ore using various cover stories. This slide shows where it came from—Brazil, Portugal, and Niger—and how much was in each shipment. The total's at least six hundred tons. There's also some domestic mining going on up north, at Sarsenk, close to the Turkish border.

"Turning uranium ore to raw metal's not that big a deal. But enriching uranium by gas diffusion took us and the Russians and the Chinese enormous amounts of equipment and power and very distinctive chemicals. We watched Iraq, but we didn't see the filtration buildings, didn't see the chemical imports, so we didn't think they were that advanced.

"Then last July the Swiss raided a factory in Berne. They found out that seven gas centrifuges went to Baghdad in 1988. With centrifuges, they don't need huge buildings. They can churn out bomb-grade uranium in a bunker, in a gym, in the basement of a bottling plant.

"Now we have unconfirmed reports from inside Iraq that they assembled a uranium-based fission device last year. Originally they were going to test it in Mauritania. Saddam and the dictator there have a brotherly understanding. But now the test's off. Why? Our design guys from Sandia tell us the same components could be reassembled into a deliverable."

Bice took the last transparency off and shut down the projector. "So that's our call on 985, what I understand you're calling Flying Stones. It'll be low yield. Five, ten kilotons. But it'll be dirty. Lots of fission products. Over a city the size of Tel Aviv, it'll be enough."

"The Israelis would retaliate in kind," Paulik said.

"Right, they'll nuke Baghdad till you won't need streetlights," Bice told him. "But meanwhile, we can kiss off the Coalition. That's been Saddam's tune since August: the Arab allies are collaborating with America and Israel to wipe out the faithful."

"It resonates in the souk," Provanzano said.

"No shit. And even if they cap him, consider the payoff. Saddam Hussein, martyr, saint, and hero to the Arab world for the next thousand years. A bigger tombstone than you or I'll ever get."

Bice waited for more questions, then nodded. "That's DIA's call. An uprated Scud in an underground silo, with a quickie A-bomb or at least a heavy charge of very dirty isotopes on top. Probably located somewhere with transportation assets and heavy overhead crane access."

"Thank you, sir," said Gault. Paulik gave him a swift glance but did not object.

Provanzano stretched, then got up. He was in jeans and an open-collared shirt and cowboy boots. He walked back and forth a couple of times before he said, "It's not a nuke. Sorry, Tony."

"You guys are barking up the wrong tree again," Bice said. "Saddam caught you napping when he invaded. We had watch notices out a week before he went over the line."

"Watch notices aren't warning. I admit, there was an intelligence failure all down the line. But it wasn't just us."

"You gentlemen want to settle this somewhere else?" Paulik asked them. "Because we don't have a lot of time."

Provanzano grimaced. "All right. But I don't have any pretty slides."

He hooked his thumbs into his belt and walked the room again. "Tony's account leaves out a company that was originally called Arab Projects and Development. Saddam formed it in the seventies to recruit technical expertise in chemical and biological warfare. To be his hole card, if the nuclear program went sour.

"In 1979 the APD became the Ibn Al Haitham Institute, headquartered in Baghdad. The institute went shopping in the US, Britain, Belgium, Italy, and the Netherlands, mainly for chemical weapons production at first. Most companies reported the approaches and threw them out. They got a better reception when they went to Germany. Messerschmitt-Bolkow-Blohm, Karl Kolb,

Sigma Chemie, and Preussag provided the equipment. Other German companies built the plants.

"Iraqi gas production is the responsibility of a company called SEPP, the State Enterprise for Pesticide Production. They have plants at Sāmarrā,' Akashat, and Al Fallujah. They make mustard gas, cyanide, sarin, and tabun. Saddam used cyanide and sarin against Iran three years ago, the offensive on the Fao Peninsula. He dropped mustard on seventy Kurd villages in the north. We also have reports of something called 'blue acid.' It's supposed to penetrate masks and protective clothing. Our chemmies think it might be in the fluoroisobutene family.

"So that's one possibility for Project 985. A poison gas, either one of the classics or something new. You know what? I'd personally be glad if that's what it is. It'd be nasty. Nerve gas is not a nice way to die. But I don't really think that's it. And our second possibility's worse."

"Biologicals," said the army major, Maddox. She was sitting back with her arms folded, watching him.

Provanzano nodded, rubbing his chin as the thunder overhead swelled to a peak through which no one could speak. When it dwindled, he said, "Yeah. BW, biological warfare; what they used to call germ warfare. We're all behind the power curve on this one. They're a lot easier to cook up than nerve gas. You can produce them in the same lab you build a vaccine in. All you need's the bugs, the scientists, and something for them both to eat.

"When we pulled the lid off this can we found a whole lot of worms looking back up at us. Saddam's people got West Nile virus, dengue fever, and bubonic plague from the Centers for Disease Control in Atlanta. Legally. By mail. They ordered tetanus, anthrax, and botulism from a private company in Rockville, Maryland. They've also been buying a lot of monkeys. That's a bad sign, going through that many fucking monkeys. That means you have your bug production cooking; now you're working on your delivery systems. That's how you test spray and blast dispersal, stake down a bunch of chimps and set it off over their heads."

Provanzano looked down the table at Maddox. "I was going to tell them about anthrax, but now I remember where I heard your name, Doctor. Maybe you'll give them the bad news."

Maddox glanced at him, then got to her feet. She was a brunette, medium height. She looked stocky, but to Gault all women tended to in battle dress. Her voice was businesslike.

"I'm Dr. Maureen Maddox, from the US Army Medical Research Institute of Infectious Diseases. I'm in-theater with the Deployable Diagnostic Laboratory, which we've set up at the Ninety-third Evac Hospital in Rafhā' to give us early warning of any disease threat to the deployed force, natural or otherwise. I specialize in what are called zoonotic diseases—that is, those with animal vectors and reservoirs that also cause disease in humans.

"*Bacillus anthracis* is a large, gram-positive, non-motile bacterial rod that's the closest thing we know of to a perfect biological weapon. Most bacteria die in open air and sunlight. Anthrax goes inert instead, turns into a spore—until it enters a welcoming environment. It'll infect through the mouth, through open wounds, but its most effective infection route is the aerosol or airborne route—by breathing it in.

"The bug has three virulence factors: edema factor, a lethal toxin, and something we call 'protective antigen,' or PA. PA binds to lethal factor and edema factor to make two highly lethal toxins. The bacteria take about three days to incubate in the body. The first symptoms are like mild flu. Low-grade fever, malaise, chest pain, maybe a cough. Most people would not go to a doctor. After a day or so the symptoms fade. The patient feels better. Meanwhile the bacteria are taking over the lymphatic system and percolating into the bloodstream.

"Suddenly it starts releasing the toxins I told you about. They destroy the lungs and other organs. Every breath becomes more agonizing. Death comes by choking, convulsions, and asphyxiation as the lungs fill with fluid." She hesitated, then added, "I've seen one man die from it. He got it in Minnesota, eating contaminated goat meat. We tried to save him. But after the symptoms show, it's too late."

"What about mortality numbers?" said Provanzano.

"For inhalational infections? The death rate of the deadliest strains is over eighty percent."

Gault spoke, and their heads turned. "We got a lot of shots when we arrived in-theater. Would they protect us?"

"Yes," said Paulik; simultaneously Maddox said, "Maybe," and Provanzano said, "Probably not."

"Probably not?" said the naval officer, Lenson, speaking for the first time.

Maddox drew invisible figures with the eraser of her pencil. "That inoculation might protect you. It might not. You see, I happen to know the woman in charge of the Iraqi BW program. It would depend on the strain she's weaponized.

"The vaccine we're giving our troops is the same one veterinarians get back in the States. It protects against the most common natural strain found in North America, and we think it should protect against any strain where the PA antigen is what allows the toxins to enter the cells. But if a strain's been bred for increased virulence, or engineered in some way we haven't considered, it may not do the job."

Wanting to get this straight, Gault said, "It may not do the job—meaning what? We'd get sick, but not as sick? Or that we'd die?"

"You can't predict that on an individual basis," Maddox said quietly. "There are too many variables. Immune system response. Size of initial dose. Genetic similarity of the pathogen to the vaccine strain. It might protect you. You might get sick but recover. You might get sick and die." She paused as jets thundered, seemed about to add something, but at last didn't, and sat down.

Gault sat back, frowning. Paulik said, "Thanks, Doctor. Charlie, have you got anything else for us?"

"Actually I'm about done," Provanzano said. "I do have something on the delivery system, though. I agree with you, Tony, that whatever 985 is, it's strapped to an extended-range derivative of the Soviet Scud-B called Al Abbas. Our figures on that missile are a range of nine hundred kilometers, a payload capacity of about three hundred kilograms, and a Circular Error Probable at maximum range of somewhere between a thousand meters and a mile. With that CEP you go for an area target. Tel Aviv is just about nine hundred klicks from Baghdad. If it's anthrax, deployed in an air burst, our wind-drift and lethality models come up with various figures, depending on humidity, wind direction, and atmospheric conditions. If all those are ideal, we could be looking at as many as a hundred thousand casualties."

He let them think about that for a few seconds. "So that's our call for Flying Stones. Iraq can't produce a uranium bomb, even a simple gun design, that weighs less than the three hundred kilos I mentioned. Nerve gas? Isotopes? Could be, but I just don't think those'd be the mass killer Saddam wants. We've gone all through this with the psychological people, profiling him, analyzing language, and so forth. I met him in Baghdad, by the way. When he was on our side. He's a chiller, all right.

"So that's it. 985's anthrax. And if he's got it, Saddam's the guy to use it. This is a no-shit threat."

He nodded somberly around and pulled a folding chair under him. Its tinny scrape on the concrete was the only sound in the room.

"Anything else to say?" Paulik asked Bice. "You still think it's a nuke?"

"Yes."

"What about the payload-range problem?"

"That's not as big a bump as Charlie thinks it is," Bice said. "In the first place, *our* experts say you can build a primitive but effective enriched-uranium weapon with an all-up weight of three hundred kilos. And even if it comes in at four hundred or even six hundred kilos, it's not that hard to kick up a Scud's payload capacity. Strapping some solid-fuel boosters onto the first stage would do it. Or bolt three of them together and use them to boost a second stage."

Provanzano said, "It's not as simple as you make it sound."

Bice shrugged. "Maybe not. But his people have had years to think about it, brainpower from the Germans and Brazilians, and all the money they need. They know nothing deters like a nuke."

As they argued, Gault sat thinking. When the spooks disagreed, the point he got was that the team had to be prepared for anything. Chemical, nuclear, germs . . . or maybe something no one had guessed at yet, some subterranean horror from the basement of Saddam's hate and paranoia.

But did it really matter what it was? As long as they found it? All he, the team leader, had to do was get them there. The navy guy would write the targeting message and Vertierra would squirt it out in a comm shot. Then they'd hustle back to the extract site and Mission Complete. As long as they stayed covert.

But how would he know? Say they linked up with the asset and the guy took them to a site. Now Gunnery Sergeant Marcus Gault, USMC, has his binoculars on it from a couple of hundred meters off. The asset says that's it, that's Flying Stones. But the air force had just bombed a bunker full of civilians. This sounded like a golden opportunity for the same kind of truly resounding fuckup. Especially if it was germs, like the CIA was saying.

The ceiling shook; Maddox put her hands over her ears. When the sound receded, Paulik said, "You look doubtful, Gunny."

"Question, sir. We can take care of ourselves in Indian Country. But I'm not sure we're smart enough on the subject for ops against a biological target."

"Exactly what I told your colonel, Sergeant," Dr. Maddox said. "Your team needs to know what a bioweapon looks like; how to recognize a hazardous environment; what to do if you find yourselves in one. I'll help as much as I can, but I've already told him I don't think I can train you adequately in the time we have available."

Gault didn't like saying this. His whole training went against it. But whether he liked it or not, the mission demanded it. So he said, looking at the lieutenant colonel, "Sir, if this really could be some kind of biological weapon, I'd want somebody BW-qualified with the team."

"Along?" Provanzano stood suddenly, interrupting him. "Is that what this is about? You're sending people in after this thing?"

Paulik had been watching Gault and Maddox, who were staring at each other. He answered without taking his eyes from them. "That's our direction from General Boomer," he said.

But the CIA man cut him off, was in fact still speaking over him. "If that's your direction, it's bullshit. There's no need to send in a recon team. We can localize this thing close enough to bomb."

Gault looked up. So did the others. "You know where 985 is?" Paulik asked him.

"A surface-to-surface missile doesn't come bareboat. There's a troop unit that maintains and launches it. They eat, they shit, they communicate. When they communicate, we hear them."

"So where is it?"

"I didn't come prepared to brief that. I was told this was for background. Nobody said anything about inserting a team. How would you know where to go, anyway?"

"We have an asset," Bice said. "An insider, a mole

deep inside the project. An engineer, a guy who actually helped design the thing."

"An insider. . . . Give me a break. Not the Syrians. 'Pandemonium,' or whatever they call him—"

"I can't confirm or deny who it is."

"Get out of here. It's the Syrians, isn't it? Tony, you can't trust those assholes!"

"Syria's a Coalition ally."

"They're a Ba'athist state! They could flip any day. Or say whoever's running this agent decides he wants to be Hafiz al-Assad's left hand, earn some brownie points with Saddam for after the war. You're looking at compromise, capture, loss of your whole team. Call it off, Colonel. We'll localize your target for you. It's just a matter of going back and digging through the intercepts. Tony, if I convince you we've got the street address, will you go to Jack Leide with me and get this called off? These guys are laying their heads on the block."

"You convince me, and I'll go to General Leide," Bice said, but he didn't sound like he was going to be easy to satisfy.

Lieutenant Commander Lenson rapped the table then. They all looked over at him. "I'm going to have to say something about the targeting here. Specifically, the look-angle problem in the urban environment."

He explained how Tomahawk guided, and the warhead choices. "What that means is, if we're talking about an urban site, possibly hardened or buried, just having a geographic location or a signals intelligence fix isn't going to be enough. It's not like targeting in the open desert."

Paulik said, "So even if you know where it is, you can't destroy it?"

"That depends. See, cruises aren't ballistic missiles. They navigate by matching the terrain with a map in their head. Once they reach the target area, they home by matching a stored image with the scene they see through their onboard camera.

"We could design most of the mission ahead of time, knowing our final target's somewhere in western Baghdad. But are there buildings in the flight path? What's the best approach angle for penetration? The best fuzing? We need hard data. Pictures, if we can get them."

"So we *do* need a team on-site?" said Paulik, looking less and less happy with what he was hearing.

"No, you need another weapon," said Bice. "You want air strikes. F-117s, not navy missiles. This is an air force mission."

They were all talking at once now and, as the roar from overhead built again, shouting above each others' voices. Provanzano and Bice were face-to-face, shaking fingers at each other. Lenson and Maddox were both trying to talk. Paulik sat immobile. At last the colonel hammered his fist down on the table. Startled, they fell silent.

"All right, that's enough. Gunny, do you have anything more for these people?"

"No, sir, I don't. Far as I'm concerned, they've raised more questions than they answered."

"How do you feel about this mission?"

He didn't have any problem answering that. "Not good, sir. I thought I knew who I was meeting up with, what the objective was, and what fire I was calling in. Now I don't. And even if we did, with all due respect, sir, as the team leader I want somebody along smarter on this biological stuff than we are. Either the doc here or somebody real like her."

Paulik was shaking his head before Gault finished. "All right, that's it. Gunnery Sergeant Gault and his men are ready to take some risks. But what I'm hearing is bullshit. Guesses. Rumors. 'Unconfirmed sources.' I will not put a team in without a clearly defined objective and a clear plan to follow when they get there. I doubt Higher would. Period." He got up, face flushed, and was opening his mouth again when the engines began.

It was a major strike, plane after plane taking off, and they waited while above them, around them, the turbine roar built and built to a nearly unendurable crescendo, then slowly moved off into the distance. When Paulik could be heard again, he was shouting, "I'm bucking this up the chain of command. But if I don't get back something better than what I just heard, I don't care who orders me to do it. I'm not letting this mission proceed."

5

20 February: 'Ar'ar, Saudi Arabia

The next morning Maureen Maddox woke to a rap on her tent pole. "On deck, Doc. Breakfast in ten."

She scrubbed her face with a Wet Wipe and followed the murmur of male voices in the mist-streaming light that vibrated beyond the dunes. The sun wasn't up yet, but its gray preradiance illuminated sand, tents, and a wary-looking dog that stood watching in the distance, motionless as a forbidden image. Before one of the tents, men stood in line. As she came up they straightened, arms whipping up quivering-straight. She returned the salute, wondering if they knew they were asking for tendonitis when they were forty. When she fell in, they glanced at each other. The marine in front of her said, "You go ahead, ma'am."

"I'll wait."

"No, go ahead." He stood aside, and the others did too, not so much inviting as commanding her to go to the head of the line. So she did.

To stacks of green mess trays, containers of reconstituted eggs, toast and canned jam, a steel thermos of coffee. She saw Captain Kohler there eating. There was only one table; when she set her tray down the enlisted men, sergeants and corporals, stood immediately, though this time they did not salute. They wore DBU trou and green T-shirts with taped dog tags. The T-shirts were sweat-stained and she realized they'd been up for a while already, apparently doing PT. Without their blouses they weren't as muscular as she'd expected. They looked fit, their faces were lean and their arms ropy with muscle, but they didn't look like supermen.

Kohler stood too, at last. "Good morning, ma'am. You remember Gunny Sergeant Gault, from the briefing?"

"Yes. Hello, Gunny."

"Sergeant Zeitner. Lance Corporal Nichols. Corporal Blaisell. Sergeant Vertierra."

In one way she admired their military precision, their faultless bearing and straight-ahead gaze; but in another she suspected, though it was hard to say why, that it was less a show of military courtesy than posting a boundary between her and them. . . . She told them to stand at ease. They glanced at one another, then sat back down and resumed shoveling food.

"Anything new, Captain?" she asked Kohler. "Or are we still on hold?"

"No word, ma'am. Colonel Paulik flew out right after the briefing last night."

"So what's the plan?"

"I thought you and Commander Lenson might want to get in some shooting," Kohler said. He smiled, very faintly. "Just in case."

She looked at the others, but not one of them met her eye.

ONLY YESTERDAY she'd been seeing patients in Rafhā', at the Ninety-third Evacuation Hospital. Rows of ISO shelters—rigid-framed tents, complete with box-framed doors and plywood floors—pegged into the cold sand. Gray sky, dun sand, green tents.

"You can get dressed now, Warrant Officer," she said, snapping latex off her hands. As the patient slid off the examining table she turned away to give him privacy, dropping her gloves into the infectious-waste bin. As he dressed she went to the door to look out. The cold light of Arabian winter laid itself against the flat sandy waste beyond the compound entrance, over concertina wire spiraled through welded Xs of steel I-beam. Like the spiral of DNA, she thought, of some recurrent and malevolent virus or rickettsia.

The warrant asked her a question, and she answered patiently. He'd accomplished the nearly impossible task of catching a venereal disease in Saudi Arabia, or so someone thought, and had been driven over from the Sixty-second Medical Group at Log Base Charlie for evaluation.

That was her job, she and the four other MDs and lab techs in the Deployable Diagnostic Laboratory. Pulled together fast and ad hoc from Fort Detrick, they had a fairly sophisticated setup: polymerase chain reaction equipment, gel electrophoresis boxes, spectrophotometer, centrifuges, thermal cyclers. From the bags of urine and blood and the occasional live patient they coaxed leishmaniasis, sand fly fever, dysentery, and a dozen other bugs the Arabian Peninsula provided free of charge to visitors. Around their tent stretched a square kilometer of other, identical ISOs and the older-style GP Large tents. And the Ninety-third was just one of forty-four field hospitals scattered across Saudi Arabia and Bahrain.

The beds were ready. The instruments gleamed ready. Twenty-five thousand army medics in-country. No one knew when the offensive would start, but the computers estimated there would be thirty-three thousand dead and wounded, more casualties faster than the army had processed since Korea. Not only would they arrive en masse, they'd probably come contaminated with nerve gas, mustard, or biological agents. No wonder everyone walked around looking apprehensive, those who weren't in their bunks. Catching up on sleep before it started.

When the patient left at last—she suspected he had leishmaniasis, not syphilis, but the tests would tell the tale—she looked at her watch. She'd promised herself noon off. Down the center of the compound stretched a straight street screened from the desert by the acres of canvas. During the summer the women gathered there to sunbathe on towels and folding chairs. It was too cold now to think about tanning, but she could walk up and down the half mile of boot-scuffed sand. She could not leave the compound. The Saudis wanted American women kept out of sight. She pulled her scrubs off and went out into the little waiting area.

The techs and the warrant with leishmaniasis (or syphilis . . . or maybe, she thought for the first time, chancroid? The cultures would not lie) were sitting watching CNN. The picture was wavery, and there was no sound, but she recognized Wolf Blitzer. Then a video began, black and white, grainy, streaked with static. A squared-off building grew in a set of crosshairs. It rushed toward the camera, larger and larger. The last frame was of a pair of blast doors. Then the screen went blank. The watchers stirred uneasily, as if expecting something more, or something different.

"Doctor?"

Brockman was her sergeant first class; she took care of the details, Maddox only occasionally read what she was signing, to keep her honest. "Colonel Eitzler wants to see you stat. In the HQ tent."

She nodded and walked out. Not knowing that was her call to arms.

SIR, MA'AM, I'm not going to turn you into recon marines in a day. What I'm going to try to do is show you what you need to know to survive, and not to screw up so badly somebody gets hurt."

She and the naval officer, Lenson, sat down on the sand. Lenson looked uncomfortable in battle dress. They obviously weren't his; they were short in the legs. She said to the lance corporal, "Just a moment, Corporal. I'm not sure I understand why I'm getting this indoctrination, or whatever it is."

Nichols looked surprised. "Well, ma'am . . . the captain said, take you and the commander out and give you what you needed to know. Aren't you our attachments?"

She smiled. "He is. I'm not. I'm just here to give you the medical background on the threat."

Nichols still looked puzzled, so she just said, "Well, just go on and do what you have to do. I'll cooperate." It came in useful sometimes, knowing how the troops operated.

"All right, ma'am . . . as I was saying. We don't sit down in the field. When we stop, it's take a knee. When we're in a rest area, take a knee. Once you sit down you want to lay down, when you lay down you want to go to sleep," he told them. "So go to a knee instead. All right, now I'm going to show you how to cammy up."

"I know that," she said. She'd done it in field exercises, but he acted like he hadn't heard, just showed them how; a smear of green on their palms, a quick wipe down each other's face. He told them to forget the Rambo movies, different colors and fancy patterns. If their faces didn't reflect light, it was enough; hours of humping and sweating would make a mess of anything more elaborate anyway.

Nichols went from there to their gear. He explained how each item they carried had to be in the proper pocket. Each patrol member had to be able to find any item on his buddy's body without searching and without speech. Signal mirror, insect repellent, compass and maps, where to stow each one. Next he covered "deuce gear," a web-belt-and-suspenders combination that held canteens, ammo pouches, first aid kit, butt pack.

He showed them how to secure each piece of equipment with the green nylon line he called "ranger cord", how to insert the batteries upside-down in the flashlight, so a jostle wouldn't turn it on accidentally, revealing their location at night or exhausting the batteries in daylight; a dozen other tips she could see were designed for walking zombies, sleepless and exhausted. She nodded, and the marine moved on to the ruck, how to stow it and wear it. "You won't be carrying the mission gear. We'll be humping that. If an attachment can manage his own weapon and ammo, and what he'll need at the objective, that's enough."

That sounded good, but when she stood at last with full ruck and web gear, it was like being teleported to Jupiter. She hitched the belt up and regarded six full canteens with dismay. "I've heard of water retention, but this is ridiculous."

They stared at her, and she said, "Oh, never mind. What else?"

"Well, if you're ready, I was going to run you through some basic squad tactics." Nichols gave it a beat. "We patrol in what we call Ranger file. The point man first. Then the team leader."

They went to a knee and he selected some stones lying handy. He laid them out in a line, then began switching them around. He went through the drills for hostile contact, ambushes, sniper fire or air attack or artillery fire. When he was done, Lenson asked him to go over them again. Maureen nodded. Everyone in the team would have to know them cold; there would be no time for explanations in the rapid ballet of fire and movement. To hesitate or head in the wrong direction would be like jamming a finely tuned machine. The men sat hunched over, eyes locked on the pebbles as Nichols moved them about on the gritty damp sand under the gray sky. She looked at them, so intent it was cute, like little boys playing war, and asked herself wryly why she never met any guys like this back in Frederick.

HER FIRST husband had been a drummer, a musician, from Toledo, where she'd grown up. They'd dated in high school and for some reason she no longer remembered she'd married Mickey the year she entered med school. *No* married human being belonged in med school. But he said when she graduated she could support his career. And somehow she heard that as a bargain, thought *he* would help *her* out while she was in school.

Instead he started eating. He modeled clothes part-time, mostly suits, but as his waistline expanded, demand for his image decreased. Then one day he came home; they'd let him go at his day job, working stats at an ad agency. After that he spent his nights with the band and his days rolling blunts and eating pizza and chips in the apartment. When she told one of her instructors about her money troubles, he suggested the Army Reserve.

Their last day together she came home to find a new set of drums in the living room. Mickey had charged it on their Visa card. Her accession bonus, money she'd counted on to see them through the semester. That night she told him he had to take the drums back, lose weight, and get a job. She took his stash from under the waterbed and flushed it down the toilet. He'd left without a word, a pout on his puffy but still-handsome face. She'd wondered for years if it had been her fault, if somehow *she* had turned him into that overweight, apathetic slug.

COLONEL EITZLER was the CO of the Ninety-third. He returned her salute as she reported, told her to have a seat and help herself to coffee, all he had was instant but it had caffeine in it. He'd be back in a minute. She sat down, picking up a copy of the September *JAMA*. It wasn't a real office, just a medical headquarters tent, the kind she'd been in all over the world.

The funny thing was that she'd been in Saudi Arabia since October, but so far hadn't seen a single Arab. Landing at King Fahd had been like landing at a US base. Americans, American vehicles, what looked like light tanks, American aircraft and army MPs with guard dogs.

An enlisted man met her with a Toyota jeep. He told her they were going to Ascon Village. "What is that?" she said. He told her the Saudis had built Ascon for the Bedouin nomads, who'd stayed two days and decided town life wasn't for them. It looked like a suburb in Ohio, except for little raked-pebble front yards instead of lawns. From there she'd flown to Rafhā', and here, except for the occasional trip to a unit that had reported intestinal complaints, she had stayed.

Eitzler came back in. He introduced the stocky officer with him as Lieutenant Colonel Anders Paulik, US Marine Corps. The marine smiled grimly at her. "Major."

"Good morning, Doctor," she said, rather coolly. He raised his eyebrows and she noticed too late he wasn't wearing the caduceus. For some reason she didn't like this man. It was the kind of instant impression she tried to guard against.

Paulik was asking about her, if she was the one from Fort Detrick. She said there were several personnel here from USAMRIID.

"But you're the one who works biodefense?"

"No—at least, not the way I think you mean. I'm a preventive medicine officer. Right now we're having an outbreak of *Shigella* dysentery. We're trying to identify the source and put preventive measures in place."

"But that's not your specialty, is it?" Anders said. "Back home?"

"I specialize in zoonotic and other exotic infectious disease."

"Including anthrax?"

She didn't react for a moment. Then she said, "That's what I spend most of my time working on back at Fort Detrick."

Anders had been looking at her legs, her chest. She didn't like it, but she was used to it. From certain men. He said suddenly, "You play sports, Doctor?"

"I beg your pardon?"

"Sports. You into anything physical? Tennis, maybe soccer after work?"

She hesitated. Glanced at Eitzler, whose expression said, *I'm as puzzled as you are.* So she told the marine, "I don't have time for organized sports. I ride my bike around Frederick. Last year I got into rock climbing."

"Rock climbing?" That seemed to intrigue him.

"Yeah. I've been out to Seneca Rocks in West Virginia, and the New River Gorge. I'd like to do Mount Rainier someday."

Paulik asked Eitzler, "Can the major and I talk privately, sir?"

"Uh . . . sure. I was just going over to the physical therapy tent." She caught his curious backward glance, then the door closed.

She'd looked levelly at Paulik as he explained, and then, when she understood at last what he was asking her to do, had to sit down on the sofa. Her hand trembled as she stirred the coffee. Then she'd looked up, and said to the heavyset marine, "Did you know I went to school with Fayzah Al-Syori?"

SHE'D MET Fayzah, a rather mousy-looking brunette, at Ohio State. They'd worked under Dr. Richard Andrews isolating pyrogenic protein toxins derived from *Staphylococcus aureus*. The Iraqi spoke English with a British accent; said she'd done her undergraduate work at East Anglia. They'd gone to lunch together, to the library, done lab work together.

Maureen had gone to Fayzah's apartment once, which she shared with another Iraqi woman whose name she couldn't recall—Sela, something like that. Her brother, Fayzah said, had died in the Iran-Iraq war. "He was a hero. We are proud of him. He died for Saddam Hussein and the Arab people," she had remarked, hugging the girl. Something Maureen hadn't thought about twice at the time.

She hadn't thought much about it at all, really. Al-Syori seemed nice; gentle and self-effacing. She worked hard, but the projects she proposed were copies of previously done research. She seemed ordinary, a bit of a plodder, except when the results did not match the graphs. Then she'd cry and curse. Once she'd asked Maureen if she thought she was good enough to be in research. She'd replied reassuringly—thinking that not everyone could be a genius—till a shy smile had dawned through the tears, and Fayzah had kissed her. When they got a good mark on their project, Fayzah had given her a box gift-wrapped in gold foil.

She could still taste the sticky sweetness of those Iraqi dates.

HAVE YOU seen her since?"

"Two or three years ago . . . at the ICAAC; that's the Interscience Conference on Antimicrobial Agents and Chemotherapy meeting in Atlanta. That's a huge convention, college profs, CDC people. We said hi, that was all. She said she had a job in Iraq. I never thought it would be anything like . . . like what the magazines say."

"What do they say? We don't get to read many magazines where I work."

"Well, that she's the brains behind Saddam's biological warfare program. That she weaponized botulinum toxin and anthrax. Tested them on Iranian prisoners of war. Organized mass production . . . it's hard to believe."

"You don't think she could do something like that?"

"That's not what I meant. I think . . . what I mean is, it's hard to think someone you used to share pizzas with could . . . She's not a brilliant researcher, but none of this is original work. It's engineering, taking the lab processes and scaling them up. She admired Saddam Hussein. She and her roommate had a big poster of him in their apartment." Maureen sighed. "I have to say . . . maybe she could."

Paulik cleared his throat. "Let me say one thing up front, Doctor. I'm not a fan of women in the military. But they told me you were the best in the theater."

"I'll try not to take that personally. I know I'm not a combat-arms type. But if you think there's a possibility of . . . then of course I'll advise your men. Just tell me where to go and what you want me to do."

And Paulik had said, "We're taking you to 'Ar'ar."

SHE'D MET Curtis at an art show one of the microbiologists at Fort Detrick had dragged her to. He was an exhibitor, a glassworker. Not cute animals, but the most ethereal, exquisite collector glassware she'd ever seen. He used exotic metals to give his pieces a shimmering play of color, like cast rainbows. He was divorced, but not recently; he seemed to have the flower-to-flower syndrome out of his system. His day job was business development manager for the city of Frederick. They'd dated for a year, then rented a townhouse at Colonial Village in Walkersville. Then one day she'd run one of the tests that were just then appearing in the drugstores and found she was pregnant. But Curtis was nice and Curtis was funny; he was no Mickey with his grass and drums. So she'd told him, and he said that was terrific, he'd always wanted a family. They'd set a date for the wedding when she caught her experiment.

That was what they called it, catching your experiment. She'd been working with mice, looking at serum complement effects on O-polysaccharide side chains. Usually lysis didn't do too well against the smooth strains, but someone in the literature had mentioned that treatment with IFN-;γ in vitro inhibited intracellular replication, and she'd wondered if there was any reinforcing effect.

She worked in Building 1425. Green-painted cinder-block corridors, gray slick painted concrete floors, lit by greenish fluorescents that had been new when *The Brady Bunch* debuted. Heavy sealed steel doors with pressure readouts led to the biosafety level suites, close warrens of lab rooms, autoclaves, sample refrigerators, ultraviolet rooms.

She'd been working at BL-3, one level below maximum biocontainment. Biosafety Level Three was for deadly pathogens, but diseases you could treat with antibiotics if someone screwed up. A tiny room, fifteen by twelve, with white glossy walls and containment hoods and cages for the guinea pigs.

After the first thousand there was nothing even faintly cute about guinea pigs. They bit and they scratched. They didn't want to be part of the march of science. One of her nightmares was sticking the needle right through one of the wiggling little bastards into her hand. It happened. You got tired, you got scared, you got clumsy.

But what had actually gone wrong was that one of the centrifuges shorted out and caught fire. Not a big deal, unplug it, but two liters of toluene had been sitting beside it and when the solvent caught fire and exploded, everything else in the lab had too. During the confusion her brucella cultures—large thick flasks swarming with microbes—had overturned, smashing to the floor and throwing invisible particles packed with bacteria into the air. Brucellosis was easy to catch; a few panicked breaths were enough.

Brucellosis caused contagious abortion in cattle, sheep, goats, and other ruminants. In human beings too. Rifampin and doxycycline doused it, but it hadn't saved the fetus.

Curt had come to see her. He held her hand for a while, then said, "City's going to be announcing something big in the morning. Hoffman-LaRoche is coming to town."

"You landed them. Terrific."

"A major facility. Biotech. The latest stuff."

"Fantastic. I'm so glad, Wayne."

He'd smiled then, his Sales Face, and she'd seen even through her own pain and disappointment that he wanted something. "I talked to the human resources people, and the site negotiators, and they said they'll need developmental staff. New drugs. Gene sequencing. They were way over my head! But I told them about you, and they're interested. *Very* interested."

She'd frowned, not understanding. "In what? In me? Curt, I have a job."

"You have a job, sure. But now you see how dangerous it is. Okay? Are we on the same channel here?"

She'd struggled up on her elbows. "Honey, listen. There are some nasty things out there, being developed by some very nasty people. If one of them decides to use them, I want us to have another option than dying."

"You've done your time. Let somebody else take a risk once in a while. Go with Hoffman-LaRoche. Make some money, for a change." He'd argued with her, trying to make her see, and she realized he was really worried, he wanted the best for her. That was what had made it so damn tough to say that she was where she wanted to be and where she'd stay. Till finally he'd said that if she wouldn't, he didn't think they were really meant to be together.

Since then she'd stopped trying. Took up kayaking and then rock climbing, but though there were guys there, some of them seriously attractive, they seemed self-obsessed and afraid of her, somehow, when she told them what she did. So finally she bought a kitten and tried to resign herself to living alone.

THAT AFTERNOON Sergeant Zeitner and a wordless Saudi escort drove her and the naval officer, Lenson, north of camp. Two huge rocks rose out of the desert, like cloned Gibraltars. When the road ended, the assistant team leader pulled out a rifle case and a saggingly heavy canvas bag. They walked between the rocks—as she neared she saw how massive they were, the highest elevations for many miles—and came out on a gravel plain cut by worn paths. The ground twinkled as they neared, and she saw when they came up to the line that it was spent brass.

Zeitner held up a short-barreled black gun with a long magazine. "The MP5-N Heckler and Koch nine-millimeter submachine gun is our main weapon in the close-quarters battle environment. It weighs 7.44 pounds with a full thirty-round magazine. It fires nine-millimeter ammunition at an effective rate of eight hundred rounds per minute. The unit replacement cost is eight hundred ninety-four dollars."

She grinned. "Do we have to pay if we break it?"

"No ma'am, not if it's rendered inoperative in normal service use." Not a hint of a smile. "The MP5 fires from a closed and locked bolt in either automatic or semiautomatic modes. It is recoil operated and has a delayed roller locked bolt system, a retractable butt stock, a removable suppressor, and an integral flashlight in the forward handguard." Zeitner tossed it to her. "First we'll fieldstrip, then fire single shots; then bursts; then we'll strip again and clean."

Forcing the stubby cartridges into the magazine, she had a flashback to the one time she'd fired a gun before: the pistol familiarization in the abbreviated military course the army put its doctors through. This thing was heavier, steel and black plastic, short and ugly as a piece of pipe. Zeitner screwed another tube into the muzzle. "I thought silencers were illegal," she said.

"Common misconception. Law of war permits suppressors." He left them standing there and walked out a few yards and placed empty plastic water bottles at various distances. He showed her how to insert the magazine, how the safety and fire selector switches worked. Halfway through his explanation the gun went off, startling them both. "This trigger's too sensitive," she said.

"Just take it easy," Zeitner said. He backed off and gave her room.

She fired the full magazine of thirty rounds, one shot at a time. The suppressor didn't make it completely silent. It sounded like the noise a lawnmower made when you pulled the cord and it didn't start. She reloaded and thumbed the selector all the way down and fired the second magazine in short bursts. The muzzle tried to climb, but she could hold it more or less on target. The plastic bottles began jumping as she hit them. She was starting to have fun when Zeitner took the gun away from her. He took Lenson through the same drill, then showed them how to clear jams; how to do a quick magazine change; how to mount and dismount the suppressor and the flashlight, and last, how to tape the weapon in order to break up its outline. Then they fired some more. This time the target bounced almost every time she pulled the trigger.

"Feel comfortable with it?" Zeitner asked. She nodded. She didn't find the weapon that intimidating now, though she was still wary of it.

What she didn't like was what he took out of the canvas bag next: a grenade. "Oh no," she said. "I'm not touching one of those."

"Oh yes you are."

"Oh no I'm not."

An impasse. They glared at each other. Finally Lenson said, "Well, show me, Sergeant. The major can watch. She's not going, anyway, right?"

The marine didn't look happy about it, but finally nodded. She stood back, observing, hitting the gravel with her hands over her head after Lenson pitched. The explosion shuddered the ground. But she refused again when Zeitner gave her a last chance. She couldn't really say why. The gun was enough, that was all. Anyway, she needed to get back to Rafhā'. The bombing had been going on for four weeks now. Ramadan, the holy season, was coming up. She had the feeling the offensive was getting ready to roll.

At last Zeitner looked at the dimming sky. "That's all we can do here," he said. "Let's get back. Clean the weapons and see if there's any news." He looked at her and added grudgingly, "You shot all right. You got a good eye."

She followed them back to the Humvee, remembering the weight of the gun, the pushing kick of it against her shoulder. She flexed her fingers, noting a broken nail from loading the magazines. She worried the ragged sliver off with her teeth, not caring what it looked like at all.

6

21 February:
'Ar'ar, Saudi Arabia

The Scud landed about zero-four that morning. Corporal Denny Blaisell was standing in the air force mess tent waiting for early breakfast, or supper, or whatever you called it when you ate your last meal before you went to bed but it was before everybody else got up. Feeling relaxed, because the mission was off. Jake said they were headed back to their platoons to get ready for the ground attack. Tex-Mex, the Indian or whatever he was, hadn't said anything at all. He was a weird one. Blaze had tried stirring him up a little, just to see what happened, but he just looked at him and didn't say a word. So then he'd bitched to the gunny about the MREs, wasn't there anything else, and Gault had told them to take the Hummer and go eat on the air side, but to stay together and not to talk to anybody and to come right back as soon as they were done.

Blaze liked the air force mess. The airmen had cassette players. Tonight two were playing at once, Judas Priest and 2 Live Crew.

> On Sunday there's Connie,
> who fucks with slick Ronnie
> She's a tricky-dick bitch who's out for his money
> She's always schemin' and hot like a demon

I thought I came in her mouth, but I was only peein'.

There were even chicks there, "bomb dollies" they called them, like aircrewmen for the A-10s. One was in line in front of him. She was tough-looking, with short blond hair. He asked her where she was from. "Bumfuck, Florida," she said, and turned her back on him. "Fucking lezzbo," he muttered, loud enough for her to hear, but she didn't turn around again.

He was just about to the head of the line, smelling the bacon and listening to Desert Storm Radio talk about how somebody called Tariq Aziz was flying to Moscow, when the siren started going *wee-waw, wee-waw,* like when the Gestapo came for you in the old movies. Vertierra, in front of him, threw down his tray and grabbed for his mask. Blaze grabbed for his too. His hand found the carrier, but inside, his fingers encountered only emptiness.

He sucked air, remembering with a sick dropaway feeling how he'd hung it up to dry after scrubbing it out yesterday. It was in the *tent.* On the other side of the fucking *base.*

It wasn't a drill. They were announced ahead of time and after the first the team had just stayed in their tents and tried to sleep; the drills were always during daylight, in the middle of their sleep period. So this was for real; he didn't really need the guy who started yelling "Alert Red, missile raid, Scud launch, no shit, incoming." Everybody in the tent was like sucked out the entrance, the cooks clanging lids over the hot food before they scooted. He swallowed the fear and pushed and shoved his way out with the others, a mass of battle dress and flight suits, ground crew and navy and air force and marines all mixed up together.

Outside, the sky was dark as dark. The lights went out along the perimeter. The sirens screamed at the sky, whipsawing down through his brain. He didn't know where the shelter was. He didn't see Tex-Mex or F.C., so he followed the crowd, running with the other shadows, people stepping on the backs of his boots. Then suddenly the men in front of him disappeared.

He tried to stop, but somebody pushed him from behind and he half jumped, half fell down into a slit trench. He landed hard on mud-slick duckboards and his ankle twisted under him. He dog-crawled along the bottom of the trench, barely feeling the pain. He didn't feel safe till he was under the overhead cover, logs or something covered with dirt.

The last light went out. The sirens wailed on, *wee-waw, wee-waw*. Over at the airstrip, planes were taking off one after the other; it sounded like every engine on the airfield was turning up. He ripped open his pouch again, but the mask still wasn't there. Shit, shit, shit. "F.C.?" he yelled. "Tony?" and Nichols yelled back, "Here I am."

Shouts from farther back in the trench. They were yelling "Scud, Scud," and "MOPP gear." "Oh, shit," said a guy beside him. A nigger, by the sound of his voice. Blaze wondered what he should do. Finally he just lay still, tense as a coiled rattler.

A jolt came through the ground. No sound, no light, just the earth jerking under him. He clawed his fingers into sandbags hard as concrete. Seconds later came the sound, a supersonic *cra-a-a-ck* followed by a duller detonation like a sonic boom. They looked at each other in the dark. Then a cry of "gas, gas, don masks," from somewhere outside.

Oh fuck. Rubber snapped around him as the others started donning. He fumbled in his pouch again, knowing it was stupid but unable not to, as if it might somehow reappear. How fucking dumb could you be? Leave your fucking MCU-2 in the tent. He couldn't stop panting. His mouth was dry. His heart was speeding up, fighting like it was trying to get out of his chest. He could smell the gas. He could taste it. He was starting to choke.

"Anybody got a extra mask?" he yelled. And to his surprise and relief somebody reached up above his head and there must have been some there in the shelter because then he had one in his hand.

More guys hurtled over the lip of the trench and crowded in. He ripped the carrier open and pressed the facepiece tight, yanked the straps to snug it tight against his skull. Total dark. A choking smell of rubber and plastic. Sweating, wondering if it was true Saddam put nerve gas in the Scuds. Beside him the air force guys were talking about how there was nothing else out here, how in the hell the Iraqis knew exactly where the base was. Their voices buzzed through the mask diaphragms, like cockroaches talking. He lifted his head, trying to suck air through the filters and not getting enough, wanting to jerk the mask off, clutching his hands over it so he wouldn't.

A flare popped on in the distance, throwing a red glow into the shelter. A helicopter went over, lights out, tearing hell for leather out into the desert. He remembered, fuck, he'd left the Glock in the tent too. Hope nobody was up there now going through their shit. His breath panted loud and harsh in his ears, like Darth Vader, and his wide-open eyes stared through the twin lenses into the dark as beside him a voice from Kansas talked about the Last Days and the Battle of Armageddon and Romans 10:9.

They sat in their masks for half an hour before the all clear sounded. Vertierra climbed over him, stepping on his leg. They crawled out of the trench, dusted themselves off, the sand cold and gritty against their hands. The lights were popping back on over at the airfield. A PA system on the other side of the base was talking away, but he couldn't make out what they were saying.

"Are we gonna need new filters now?" he asked nobody in particular. Nobody answered. His legs were shaking so hard, dust was coming off his BDUs. He looked at the mask, considered putting it back in the shelter for the next guy. Then decided to keep it himself, for a spare.

●   ●   ●

THEY CALLED his dad "Blaze" too. His father was a small-town barber, a man with a recognized place in Ten Sleep, Wyoming. He owned his own shop and a little house behind it. He'd been a barber in Vietnam and had cut General William Westmoreland's hair before coming back to Wyoming. When he told the story, his father called the general "Westy," as if they were best friends.

Sitting on the vinyl seat after school, ripping through his homework or, better yet, reading a Spider-Man comic in the sun that came through the big plate glass window, he listened to his father talk. About the women who went into the big houses for money, and the divorcing and marrying for money, about the old ranchers who had land and money, and how much the big Lincoln that just pulled up must have cost. Sitting there listening to the buzz of the clippers and the roar of the stove in the winter, smelling woodsmoke and Marlboros and sweat and leather and hair lotion, he learned how the world really was and who was getting what, getting laid, getting the good job, screwing the neighbor's daughter, fixing the will. Not like they told him in school, but how the world really worked.

And at the end of the day it was his job to sweep all the hair up, pushing the old broom with its bristles curled like an old man's mustache, into a plastic garbage sack. His dad scattered it around the garden to keep the deer out. Deer didn't like the smell of human hair. Blond hair and gray, black and brown, everything but nigger hair. His father would let them come in and sit, but then he'd seat the men who came in after them. Never looking their way. Never saying a word. Till finally they'd understand and leave, sometimes curse him but more often just stand up and look at his father and at him and then push the door jangle and they were gone. But that had only happened a couple of times in all the years he was growing up, because there just weren't that many niggers west of the Bighorns and when they came they didn't stay long.

   He hadn't done too good in high school, so they put him in air-conditioning shop. It didn't matter what you did there; the grades were a joke and half the time the seniors skipped. So after a while he got a part-time job at the Texaco doing oil changes and hammering out fender benders when guys would run their pickups into the fences on Friday nights. He wore a Stetson and tight Levi's and then he got his own pickup, a red-orange Chevy with a 400 V-8 he bought from Frank Hunt for seven hundred dollars when Frank went to jail for statutory. He even left Frank's bumper sticker on it, the one that said THERE ARE TWO KINDS OF PEOPLE: THOSE WHO ARE COWBOYS AND THOSE WHO WANT TO BE. The first night he had it he took Donna out and they drank some Coors and made love real slow back in the camper cab. He remembered how she smiled down, pumping it out of him till he shouted.

   But then that November his dad died of emphysema and the lawyer said he didn't own the store or the house either—they were on leased land—and rented the shop to a woman from Sacramento who opened a bakery. Then Donna left for California; she was going to be in the movies. So he decided to get out of Wyoming too. And he didn't want to go in any fruity navy, ships full of fucking gays sticking it in each other's asses, or any fucking air force that sounded more like college than anything else. He liked the Marine Corps ads on TV, and he knew what the guys said at the barber shop. One old guy who'd been on Tarawa always said there was only one service for a real man.

WHEN THEY got back to the recon area, Gunny Gault was waiting for them. He didn't say anything about the Scud. Just told them to stand by. Blaze wasn't shaking now, but he was ravenously hungry. When they'd gone back to the mess tent it was secured, the food was there, but for some reason the fucking officers wouldn't let anyone eat it. "We still on hold, Gunny?" Zeitner asked him.

"So far, yeah," Gault told them. "Just hang loose, but don't go anyplace. Get your heads down and get as much sleep as you can, just in case."

BACK IN the tent they tore through some MREs, then he took out his Glock and fieldstripped it. A lot of guys in II MEF were Glockies. Something about the clunky little guns turned him on. Not like the Berettas, too big and with safeties all over it so dipshits couldn't shoot themselves. Or the modified .45s that were recon issue, good field sidearms but heavy. A Glock didn't have a safety, just a catch on the trigger so if your finger wasn't on it, it couldn't fire. They were mostly plastic too, so they were lighter in the field. He reassembled it, aimed it across the tent, and shot Miss February's tits off the centerfold. He followed up with a round up the snatch.

"Put it away, Corporal," Nichols drawled from the other side of the tent.

Blaisell looked at him. The sniper had his M16 disassembled, was stripping out the bolt assembly. "What you chewing?" he asked him.

"Copie."

"Can I have a rub?"

"If you beg for it," Nichols said. Blaze felt himself grinning foolishly, not knowing how to take that or what to say.

Instead he brandished the Glock, did a Wyatt Earp twirl around his finger. "Want me to order you one of these? I got an FFL. I ordered them for all the guys back in the LAV. Glock's a good weapon."

Nichols didn't answer, and Blaze aimed again and took out Miss February's eyes. "Ka bam, ka bam," he said. Vertierra glanced up, then went back to reading; he had a *Betty and Veronica* out of one of the packages people sent from the States. Whatever happened, they wouldn't run out of cookies or mouthwash. A guy in his platoon had gotten a no-bra shot of some fat girl. That

could ruin your appetite. He didn't care for the shit most
guys carried on patrol. PowerBars and granola shit like
faggots ate in San Francisco when they weren't eating
each other. So he'd gone into the tent where they kept the
things people sent from home to "Any Soldier" and "Any
Marine," the goodies and candy and homemade fudge—
it was fucking pogyville—and found a can of Planters
nuts and raisins and M&M's and some coconut cookies,
things like that, and made up his own gorp.

The five of them were bunked together in the same
tent. It smelled old, like it was from the Civil War. There
wasn't any heat except for a kerosene stove that stank so
bad they did without it. As long as it was dry you didn't
need a stove in this weather. It was when you got wet that
it felt cold. Zeitner and the gunny were over at the blockhouse. Blaze looked at the Glock again, spun it around
his finger.

"Put it away," said F.C. again, and this time there
wasn't any funning in his voice. Blaze quickly stuffed it
back to the bottom of his duffel, down where they
wouldn't find it if there was an inspection.

IT SEEMED like he'd just got to sleep when somebody
stuck his head into the tent. The armorer told them to get
dressed and get over to the blockhouse. That was all, but
something in his voice got them moving. He stuffed the
Glock, unloaded, down into his back pocket, just so it
didn't walk off while they were out.

Gunny Gault stood waiting in the blockhouse. The
lights were sort of half off, half on. Blaze looked around,
saw they were all there. The attachments, the light
colonel from First SRIG, the girl doc. Boxes of MREs
and ammo and Al-Ghadir bottled water were stacked
against the wall. He started to get a creepy feeling. The
gunny stood waiting till everybody was in and the door
was closed. Then he said, "We have a go order on Signal
Mirror."

"Same mission?" said Zeitner.

Paulik said, "Correct. I took it to Higher and it came back confirmed. For tonight."

Gault checked his watch. "I want to move out no later than twenty hundred. That means we got a lot to do before we emplane. First stop's medical. There's a Humvee outside. Major Maddox will take you over to the medical tent."

They rode over and got two shots, one in each arm. He asked what they were, and one of the corpsmen said for botulinum toxin. They each got a card of little white pills that were supposed to help protect you against nerve gas. They had to take them three times a day, eight hours apart, starting now. The first one was so bitter he could hardly swallow it.

AT 1400 the team filed back in. All the lights were on now. They sat down on the concrete and took out their notebooks. Zeitner was taping up a map of western Iraq, and another large square of taped-together 1:25,000's. A city, it looked like. Blaze went up to it: Baghdad. He figured this would be map drill again, where they went over their route until they could all draw it in their sleep. He was still sleepy, though now he was getting nervous too. The sand table was off in the corner. Zeitner and Vertierra had built it, showing the terrain from the LZ to the meet-up point. Usually in mission planning they had some kind of visual aid to plan what they'd do at the objective. This time, nobody seemed to know what or where the objective was.

Gault came in, carrying a clipboard, with Lenson and Maddox behind him and two aviators in flight suits. The pilots sat down in the back of the room. Gault roll-called the team. Everybody answered up and he went down the front handing out copies of the patrol order. Blaze looked it over, already knowing pretty much what it would say, because they'd been working on it since they got here.

The gunny started off, "This order and this briefing are secret. Don't discuss it with anyone outside the team. Okay, the Laws of Patrolling. Law One."

"Always look cool," they yelled, all together.

"Law number two."

"Never get lost."

"Law number three."

They shouted gleefully, "If you get lost, remember to look cool."

"All right. Patrol number UAT-12 is go. This'll be our prepatrol brief, and we'll follow it with patrol inspection at eighteen hundred."

First briefer up was an air force meteorologist. He described the weather over central Iraq as overcast, temperatures cold, possible sandstorms, winds from the north at between ten and twenty knots.

When the meteorologist was gone, Gault began on the patrol order. "We can expect enemy forces in this area, but specifics are missing. As we approach Baghdad we can expect heavier concentrations of enemy troops and population. Essentially Saddam has mobilized and armed every male of military age, at least those of ethnic groups he trusts.

"UAT-12 will patrol from this designated grid square on into contact with a reportedly friendly element. From there we will transition into a point reconnaissance mission. Special Forces and British SAS teams are operating west of LZ Lisa. After we leave the LZ heading east, any patrols encountered will be assumed to be enemy.

"Supporting fires: two A-10s on strip alert out of Al Jouf. Fire to be requested in emergencies only.

"Transportation: Det One of HCS-4 will provide initial lift into LZ Lisa. That will be Commander Jabo and Lieutenant Commander Lemoyne." The pilots raised their hands in lazy greeting. "They will also provide postmission extract. There will be no guaranteed extract available east of Majarrah. All requests for support or extract will be passed through HF.

"There will be two attachments to the team: Commander Lenson and Major Maddox."

Blaze looked around, startled. No one said anything, but he saw Nichols looking too. The doc stood in the back, arms folded. She didn't say anything, or return their stares.

Holy shit, he thought. This is too much. We got to drag *her* along?

"All right, mission," Gault went on. He read the next part slowly, because they all had to memorize it. "UAT-12 will establish and report geographic location of a possible nuclear or biological site in western Baghdad. Mission has priority . . . everyone got that? Blaze?"

He blinked, still thinking about the major, managed to get it back. "Uh . . . establish and report geographic location of a possible nuclear or biological site in western Baghdad. Mission has priority."

"Okay, Sergeant Zeitner will brief on execution."

Zeitner took over, sounding with his upstate accent like a cross of New Yorker and hillbilly, Blaze thought. He did the commander's intent and then they went to the terrain model.

"On order, Team Twelve will depart from friendly lines and load into aircraft along the pipeline road east of the base. We'll insert at primary insert point LZ Lisa and execute information turnover with SAS Team Charlie Two. Secondary insert point is at LZ Charlotte. After departure of aircraft, the team will move south seven hundred meters to clear the LZ, then turn east and move overland using cover as possible to rendezvous with friendly asset "Samir" at road junction at grid location Lima Bravo 710390. Identification will be a green cloth signal.

"The asset will escort us to the objective. Frag orders will cover movement to the final objective and action on the objective. Upon completion of observation, team will egress and move southwest in the direction of the Euphrates River, locate a secure area, and set up a comm site. After sending a SPOTREP to Higher we'll move west across the Euphrates in the direction of Lake Razzazah to extraction on D+2 at position Lima Bravo 300710, west of two pylons at the shoreline.

"Subunit tasks. We will be divided into two elements: recon and security. The recon element will be led by Gunnery Sergeant Gault and will consist of Gunny Gault, Commander Lenson, and Major Maddox. The recon element will be responsible for photographing, sketching, testing, sampling, and recording all information at the objective. The security element will be broken down into two security teams. Security Team One will consist of Sergeant Zeitner and Lance Corporal Nichols. Security Team Two will consist of Sergeant Vertierra and Corporal Blaisell. Team One and Two will be posted by means of frag orders at the objective, warning the recon element of any enemy movement in the area."

Gault said, "Commander, do you have a handle on the CCIRs?"

Lenson stood, looking ill at ease. He said, "Map coordinates; type of target; targeting data; any NBC indications. Covering forces; nearby civilian installations and centers of population."

Gault took over again, and they went through security during movement, what each individual had to do—for himself Blaze circled *Security at point, steady rate of movement, best route, danger area,* and *minefields.* The gunny emphasized that everyone was responsible for security, observation of enemy presence and movement, maintaining concealment, and sterilizing the area after halts or hides. Each team member had to know their location and route at all times, in case of unexpected contact. "We've walked through the SOPs for immediate action drills, halts, formations, and danger areas," the team leader said, but, as Blaze was afraid he would, he went over them all again, and then went into actions on enemy contact, at the objective, and at the extract point.

"Most of the time we'll move as a Ranger file. The

only way a column works is communication. Keep positive eye contact with the man in front and to your rear. Pass all signals quickly and accurately. The order of movement will be Blaisell, Nichols, Gault, Vertierra, Lenson, Maddox, and Zeitner. If we anticipate enemy contact I may go to a wedge by night or to traveling overwatch if we have to move during the day.

"I'll designate rally points every thousand meters, or when I notice a feature we can see some distance away. When that information comes down the line, repeat it to the man who gives it to you until he's certain you have it right. Then pass it to the man behind you and make him repeat it till it's letter-perfect.

"Danger areas: we'll do one-man bumps across roads, streams, and other danger areas. Mr. Lenson, remember the one-man bump?"

"Uh—hand signal for danger area; point man moves up; number two up beside him, right shoulder to danger area; number one sprints across to cover; number three moves up, then number two goes, till the last man's across."

Blaze sat hunched forward, thinking again about the woman, taking her with them. The navy dude was bad enough, but she was going to be dead weight. They'd end up carrying her. "This is fucked, man," he mouthed to Vertierra. The Mexican, or whatever the hell he was, just looked back at him, as usual not saying anything at all.

"Comment, Corporal Blaisell?"

"No, Gunnery Sergeant."

"Lieutenant Colonel Paulik."

Paulik told them that once they were in Baghdad there wouldn't be any extract. In case of compromise they should try to blend in with the population. Blaze caught F. C.'s eyeroll at this one and grinned back, *Yeah right!* He was laughing, but inside he was starting to get scared. It was sinking in. Another option, Paulik was saying now, was to escape and evade back toward Syria or Turkey via a series of predetermined rendezvous points. The Iranian border was closer to Baghdad, but he didn't recommend going to Iran.

Finally Paulik was done and the gunny said, "We got another briefer coming in, but before that, any questions for me?"

Nichols raised a hand.

"F.C.?"

"We dippin' on this one, Gunny?"

"No tobacco, F.C. Smokeless or otherwise."

"That sucks, Gunny."

"If it don't suck, it ain't discipline. Anything else?"

Surprising himself, Blaze stuck his hand up. When Gault nodded, he said, "I heard on the radio this morning the top ragheads were going to Moscow, the Russians got a peace proposal going. What if we go in and they all of a sudden call the fucking war off?"

"Good question, Corporal. Sir, you got an answer to that?"

Paulik looked grim. "I don't think that'll happen. Now that our heavy forces are deployed, this is our chance to destroy Saddam's ability to make war. But even if it does, it won't make any difference to this mission. Whichever way the big blue arrow points, Higher wants an answer on this one."

Gault said, "That answer you, Corporal? Okay, next up is Doctor Maddox."

He watched her tits jiggle under the cammies as she stood. A little old for him, but just knowing there were sweet little peaches under there was nice. So at first he was staring at her chest, not really tuned in. Then, just as he was getting hard, imagining what it'd be like, what she was saying started to penetrate. About the symbols for hazard-infectious areas, what they looked like. What not to touch, what not to do. Maybe she caught him staring at her jugs, because she pointed at him then, ordered him front and center for a gear demonstration.

The chemical protective overgarment was like heavy fatigues, only lined inside with charcoal. They didn't have desert pattern, only the woodlands pattern made for Europe. When he had them on, she told him, "Okay, now your mask." He showed her how fast he could don, a quickdraw from the pouch, heeling it to his face and snapping on the straps. Thank Christ, this time he had it.

But then she took out the tape. Regular silvery duct tape, like from a True Value. Using him like a dummy, she showed them how to tape the mask to the parka hood. The others squatted, watching as she gradually transformed him into a fucking moon man. Meanwhile he was getting freaked inside the mask. He started to feel dizzy again, like in the shelter trench. He tried to adjust it, wondering if the canister was actually working, but she pulled his hands down and started taping his gloves to his sleeves. The lady liked duct tape. Hey, maybe they could do a party. Bondage and discipline like in a *Hustler* layout. Nichols was grinning at him. "Stupid redneck," he muttered into the diaphragm, low, so all that came out was a buzz. "What was that?" she said, and he didn't answer, just grinned to himself. He was cool now. Deep breaths. Better.

When he finally got to untape, Gault gave them all a piss break, but got them right back in. The gunny kept looking at his watch.

An army engineer type unrolled another map, but this one wasn't military, or even a terrain map. It showed the Baghdad drain-and-sewer system.

Baghdad, he told them, had been one of the first cities in the world with underground drainage. There might be Ottoman- and British-era sewers and drains close to the river and even some from ancient times. A Finnish company had redesigned the system in 1980, entunneling the old wadi outlets and trunking neighborhood sewers together into large concrete-lined runs. Blaze stared in disbelief at red lines, blue lines, dotted lines, little elevation call-outs. The engineer cautioned that Egyptian and Pakistani contractors had actually carried out the plan, so what they found underground would probably differ from the map.

Zeitner raised a pencil. "You said 'sewers and drains,' sir. Is there a difference?"

Dork, Blaze thought. Just like high school, there was always somebody who had to make class longer by asking smart-ass questions.

"Good question. There is. Sewers in modern Western cities come in three categories. 'Sanitary' sewers, for sewage or wastewater, 'storm' sewers, for storm water runoff or drainage, and 'combined' sewers that serve both purposes. We used combined sewers till about the nineteen fifties, but the storm water tended to overwhelm the treatment plants, so now our preferred system is separate sanitary and storm sewers. Storm sewers go directly to a discharge point. Sanitary sewers lead to treatment before discharge."

He was starting on underflow and overflow when Gault said, "We're not going to be sewage engineers, sir. What do we need to know to navigate these things? If we have to."

The engineer said they needed to know about overflow and underflow because in a combined sewer system the underflow, or wastewater, went to a treatment point and the overflow, mostly storm water, went straight to discharge, in this case the Tigris. In other words, which system they were in would determine where they ended up. Gault asked if they got to keep the map, and the engineer said yes. He said again, though, that they might find anything under Baghdad, the city was so old. The thing to bear in mind was that although flow always went toward the river, the Tigris curved through the city in great lazy loops, so that 'downhill' could be east or west, north or south, depending on where you were.

And all of a sudden, Blaze didn't know why, but listening to all this it suddenly hit him: *They were going.* When they said the mission was off, he'd griped, but inside he was relieved. Now he felt like he had to shit. Felt fucking fear start to glow cold along the inside of his bones.

He touched the Glock, hard against the cheek of his butt, reassuring himself. Going to war. Just like his dad had in Nam. No, better than that; he wasn't a fucking barber. He was a marine.

If he had to go, he'd take some fucking ragheads with him.

DAN WENT outside after the briefing and looked at the sky. He understood for the first time what it might be like over there, on the far side of that line in the sand. The Iraqis too must know this disquiet, under a sky that no longer sheltered, but transported the instrumentalities of death.

He'd seen the missile come down. Had just happened to be looking at that quarter of the sky when it fell. A fireball, like a meteor at sea, but larger, closer, glowing a lambent red. At first he'd thought it was coming right at them, over the border and down their throats. Then as it drew its fiery line, he'd seen it would pass over, pass beyond. It disappeared over the horizon, still burning; succeeded by a flash of light. Then, seconds later, the rumble of detonation.

He couldn't shake the feeling the Iraqis had a bead on them. They weren't supposed to have any overhead reconnaissance. But what if the Russians were passing satellite photos? He glanced toward the ammo dump and shivered. No bunkers, no shielding, no revetments. If a warhead hit, there'd be nothing left of 'Ar'ar but a smoking crater.

Well, they wouldn't be here much longer. The knowledge moved like a reptile squirming through his belly. By tomorrow morning they'd be on the far side of that invisible line.

Standing there alone, he closed his eyes and sent his thoughts out wide, out past the horizon, past the night itself. Picturing his daughter, the way he'd seen her last: slim and tall and gray-eyed, a fresh new being molded somehow of himself and his ex. Wondering what she was doing tonight, whether she was happy . . . he figured he knew what Blair Titus was doing, though. Attending a fund-raiser, some party in Georgetown or McLean.

A puzzled frown creased his forehead, and he rubbed his mouth. He should call her. He should write. He'd do that, write her tonight. Maybe Nan and his mom too, though he'd already left in-case-of letters in his service jacket. But he didn't know what to say, which way to go. Maybe he should just hang it up. Chalk off another relationship to distance and separation and the Navy.

A presence to his right; he turned his head and opened his eyes to discover Gault beside him. The team leader was staring at the sky too. "Looking for Scuds, sir?" the gunny sergeant asked him. "You hear the one come down this morning?"

"I saw it," he said. "Pretty impressive. Looked like part of the sky was coming down."

Gault didn't respond to that. Instead he started going through his clipboard. "Sir, I wish we had more time for this, but I'd like to have you tell me and my ATL what you're going to need to do this targeting analysis. If we can get in there I want to be able to support you without a lot of discussion."

"Sure, when do you want it?"

"Well, the sked just slipped a couple of hours. Problems with the flight plan. Now we're launching at twenty-three. I want to do a final rehearsal before it gets dark. Junk on the bunk at twenty-hundred, final inspection at twenty-one. Then move out to the boarding site. So let's make it part of the final rehearsal, when we get to the part about what we do at the objective."

"All right."

"Can you sign this, sir?"

He looked it over. A list of their names, ranks, serial numbers, more numbers he didn't recognize, and what seemed to be serial numbers and weapons and gear. "What's this?"

"Kill sheet, sir. The flight manifest. Check your social and your gear, initial beside your name. I need your ID card too, and anything else you want to leave behind."

He didn't like the sound of that, but scribbled DVL and handed the clipboard back along with his wallet. "Final rehearsal, two hours," said Gault. "Be there."

Dan nodded, taken aback at being addressed in tones of command by an E-7; but he didn't have a problem with that. He'd take charge at the objective, when the decisions had to be made. He was turning away when Paulik came up. "Secure call for you in the comm tent," the colonel said.

"Which way's the comm tent?"

"I'll take you over."

Folding tables, scarred folding chairs, a bench press set in the corner, a coffee mess, banks of radio gear. A tech sergeant held up a red phone as he came in. Dan took it and keyed, staring at a photo of a smiling Saddam Hussein as he waited for the beep and the sync. Underneath it someone had printed in block letters YOUR FRIENDLY MIDEAST MUSTARD MERCHANT. "Lenson here," he said.

"Dan, this is Admiral Kinnear. Recognize my voice?"

Blue Ridge, a windswept deck, a warning to beware of the army and air force. "Yes, sir, I recognize it. How are you, sir?"

"Is Signal Mirror going in, Commander?"

"Yes, sir, mission is on. There was a last-minute hold but we're going in tonight."

"Remember I asked you about your attitude toward TLAM-N?"

Dan reached back for the conversation, got only a fuzzy recollection. He said cautiously, "I think I recall that, sir."

"Well, I wanted you to know, for your on-call fires: USS *Pittsburgh* is on station with a mixed loadout. The proword for special weapons will be 'Desert Moonlight.' Repeat back."

"USS *Pittsburgh,* mixed loadout, proword Desert Moonlight."

"That will be a recommendation, not a release. Release will be by the NCA on approval of the CINC."

"Aye, sir."

"Do not fuck up, Commander."

"Aye, aye, sir."

Kinnear signed off. Dan handed the handset to the sergeant, and noticed Paulik was still lingering. Had heard at least his side of the exchange. The colonel said, "Problem?"

"No problem," Dan told him. "Just last-minute updates on our Tomahawk assets."

Paulik nodded. "I don't have the whole picture on this mission, but they've got a hard-on about it in Riyadh. When I reported to General Boomer about what the CIA said, how they'd locate it for us?"

"Yeah?"

"He said, 'Goddamn it, do you work for me or the CIA? Stop second-guessing and get them the fuck out there.'"

Dan smiled faintly, more to show a response than that he felt like smiling. Because he didn't. Not looking at a covert insertion into hostile territory, a ground war about to start, a questionable mission without a clearly defined goal.

He was pouring himself a cup of coffee when he suddenly tensed, nearly dropped the steel container, and poured a scalding stream over his hand. He'd just realized what Kinnear had meant. *Special weapons,* he'd said. And given him the proword.

He looked at his shaking hands, felt the knowledge seep into him like a numbing draft of hemlock.

Kinnear had just cleared him to recommend a nuclear strike.

7

2100 21 February: 'Ar'ar

Gault glanced at his watch as the team fell in for patrol inspection. Past nautical twilight, now, and the dark was closing down. Engines howled from the strip, but there didn't seem to be as many strikes going out today. He wondered if it was the overcast. More rain, he'd believe. The armorer had rigged lights between the tents, so he could still see, but they were shielded from the rest of the base. The fewer people who knew they were here, the better. Which was also why they wouldn't take off from here, but meet the helo out in the boonies.

Everyone was in desert cammies, not the chocolate chip but the tricolor beige-tan-green pattern, and the desert bush covers. Their faces were cammied and they carried their weapons. When the attachments arrived Gault hitched his ruck and cleared his throat. He took inspection stance on Blaisell, square in front of him and a foot and a half away, and looked him up and down.

"Ready for this, Corporal?"

"Hot to trot, Gunny." The kid grinned wide.

The point had the standard load: eight quarts of water in plastic canteens, thirty-five pounds of ammo, grenades, light antitank weapon, and pyrotechnics, five days' rations in his ruck. They'd already done the junk on the bunk routine, so Gault didn't so much check gear as just run his eyes over the kid, making sure his day/night flare was pointing down, his knife and his weapon were dummy-corded to his war belt, and so forth. He jerked open Blaisell's mag pouch, got hold of the pull tab, and yanked one out. "Good mags?"

"Shot 'em all in last night, Gunny."

"What's the AWACS call sign?"

Blaisell told him. Gault started to move on, then came back. "Still carrying that Saturday night special?"

"My Glock, Gunny? Don't leave home without it."

Gault shook his head and went on to Nichols. The Southerner stood loose-hipped, thumbs tucked under his suspenders, cradling his M16 under his left arm. He was nearly the shortest man in the squad, but Gault knew he'd always be up. His jaw was working and Gault said, "I told you no smokeless on the mission, Lance Corporal."

"Roger that, Gunny. Goes overboard when we climb on the helo."

"The hell's this? What's these, SEAL Team Six gloves?"

Nichols didn't say anything. "Get rid of them," Gault told him.

He moved on to Vertierra, running his gaze over the communicator, his ruck, radio, down to his boots, where it stopped. Vertierra had on the nylon Vietnam-style hot-weather boots.

"I told you to get boots off the EPWs."

EPW meant enemy prisoners of war. Wearing Iraqi boots, instead of the distinctive US combat-boot tread, would make tracking them in-country that much harder. Vertierra said, "I was down there to the stockade, Gunny. Not one of them had my size feet. I got a spare pair of woolies I can pull on over these boots."

Gault considered that. The sergeant *did* have incredibly small feet. Finally he nodded.

He moved on to Lenson, and looked him carefully and minutely over from his bush cover on down. The attachments weren't loaded as heavily as the patrol members. He'd told Zeitner he wanted them light, the same water and chow, but only half the ammo and no grenades. Not only would that keep them up with the rest of the patrol, but giving a grenade to an untrained troop was asking for a casualty. Gray eyes looked steadily back at him. Gault gave him a half-reluctant nod of approval, muttered, "Commander." The navy man was a quick learner, and he seemed to be in shape. Not recon cross-country heavy-ruck-toting shape, but with the lighter load he'd probably be able to keep up.

He moved to the right, and looked down.

The war paint hardened her features, but it didn't do anything for her height. In cammies and ruck, with hair stuffed up under the bush hat, Maddox looked like a shrimpy, effeminate boy. She was scowling.

"Not a happy camper, Major?"

"Oh, hell yes, Gunny. Everything's fucking wonderful."

Swell, she had PMS. He grabbed her suspenders and pulled her ruck around, checking the adjustments on her pack frame, making sure it rode on her ass. Something about the way it hung looked odd, so he went around and lifted it. Her ruck was as heavy as his. "Jesus God," he said. "What you got in here, Doc?"

"Things we'll need."

He fingered a lump pressing out against the side. "What's this?"

"Dandruff shampoo."

He wasn't sure he'd heard that right. "Say again?"

"I got it from the medics. Poured it into a gallon jug and taped the cap on."

Gault looked at the sky, then at the others. They waited deadpan.

She said, "Dandruff shampoo contains selenium as the active ingredient. Selenium's the most effective sporicide I can come up with at short notice. If we need to decontaminate ourselves after an anthrax exposure, you'll be glad I brought it. The rest of the weight's medical and detector kits and five days' worth of MREs."

He looked at the others again, the snicker on Blaisell's

face, Nichols's lifted eyebrow, Vertierra's dubious glance. He ran through the possibilities. Let her take it all, ditch the excess later? No, what you packed in you packed out. Otherwise you were asking for compromise. He turned back to her and said, "I don't think you understand what it's gonna be like out there on the turf. It's gonna be a ruck hump. Maybe fifteen miles a night. More, if we get compromised and have to E and E cross-country. You've got to leave some of this snivel gear stuff here."

She said angrily, "This isn't 'snivel gear.' You don't go into a possible biohazard area without some way to figure out what you're dealing with, and protection against it. It's the minimum for the mission."

He studied her stubborn expression for another second, thinking, This is going to be fun. Then made his decision. "All right, you're the doc. You say we need it, it's got to go. But we got to lighten you up. Ever shoot a Beretta?"

"The nine-millimeter? Sure."

"Soon's the colonel's done with us, turn your MP5 in to the armorer. Draw a suppressed pistol and five mags. We'll break down your MREs so you don't have to carry that extra weight." He didn't wait for objections, just broke eye contact and went on to Zeitner. Ran his eye over the ATL, noting everything shipshape and tight, corded and strapped off. Jake was quiet, but in his upstate way he was always there. "Everything good to go?" he asked him. Zeitner just nodded.

He stepped back and looked at them all again. They looked all right. He just hoped *he* didn't screw up. He looked at his watch again as a formation of A-10s roared over, and caught a familiar stocky form threading down the tents toward them. The lieutenant colonel, with Captain Kohler trailing him.

Paulik moved down the rank, not saying much. He asked Lenson if he knew how to use a LAW. The commander said he thought so. He stopped again in front of Maddox, pointed wordlessly at how her ruck straps were cutting into her shoulders. Gault explained how he was going to cut down her load. The colonel nodded. "Pistol only? Okay. With any luck, you won't make contact."

"That's how I figure it, sir. Any way I can avoid a fire-fight, I will."

"All right, take a knee," Paulik told them all. The marines knelt in a smooth motion; after a moment Lenson and Maddox followed, wobbling as they balanced themselves.

"I know you've all memorized the mission data, but I'll say it once more: Establish and report geographic location of a possible nuclear or biological site in western Baghdad. Mission has priority. I have a lot of confidence in the gunny and in all of you. If you get compromised, we'll do all we can to get you out." Paulik glanced at his watch. "We'll move out to the departure zone in forty mikes. We don't have clearance from AWACS yet for the flight, but it should come through shortly. Maybe after we launch, but we can't wait too long or you'll run out of dark."

He cleared his throat and looked away. "You know SOP, there's always a major change of plan right before you leave. Gunny, you were briefed to meet up with an SAS team at the LZ. They were inserted a week ago to hunt Scuds and we frag tasked them to do a route survey for you. The original intent was for you to link up with them briefly near the LZ and get whatever they have on route info, enemy location and strength.

"The change is, Higher's decided that as long as they know the ground, one of them can help guide your team en route to the op area. The British concur. Their pass-word and response are 'Red' and 'Turkey'; your authenti-cator for the frag order detaching him is 'Ripper.'"

Gault held up a hand, and Paulik nodded. "Sir, what exactly are you saying? You're attaching this other team to me?"

"Not all of them, just the team leader. A sergeant Sarsten."

"Sir, I respect the SAS and all, but we don't need another attachment."

"I understand what you're saying, Gunny, but it makes sense to have somebody who knows the terrain. A route guide, to increase your chances of a safe movement to objective."

Gault looked at him, not wanting to argue but wanting even less another unknown added to his team. "Sir, I think that's a mistake."

"I'm sure you can deal with it," Paulik said. "I know what you're thinking. But if you have a source of information available, use it. He may turn out to be exactly what you need."

"Sir, I have to say again, I think it's a bad idea."

Paulik's face didn't change. "Let's step over there."

Twenty paces off, the colonel said, "I hear your objection, Gunnery Sergeant. Higher wants SAS along. That's the directive. But you're the team leader. As far as I'm concerned, you don't want him, he don't have to go. I know you're already concerned about taking Lenson and Maddox."

"Lenson I'm not worried about. The doc could be another story."

"Attitude-wise? Team cohesion? What?"

"Just hard humping over bad terrain. We could end up carrying her."

"She's mission essential. You came to that conclusion yourself." Gault was thinking, I said somebody *like* her, not *her*; but the lieutenant-colonel was still talking. "I don't think we have to class the Brits the same way. How about this: You talk to this Sarsten at the LZ. If you don't want him along, send him back and I'll deal with Higher."

"That's fair, sir."

"I'm glad you think so," Paulik said, a hint of sarcasm in his voice. Gault didn't really care. It was his responsibility, his fucking patrol, and he was getting eager to get to it, to get on the ground and carry out the tasking.

They went back to the team. Nichols turned his head

to the side and spat into the sand as they came up. The colonel looked at them, then at his watch again. He beckoned to Kohler. "Want a pre-mission photo?"

"Sure," said Gault. He went over to stand with the others and they looked toward the captain, who raised a camera.

A brilliant flash left them blinking at images. He stepped front again and told them, "Okay, if there's no more questions, Humvee in half an hour by the mess tent. Drink all the water you can hold, then drink some more. Crap or carry. Corporal Blaisell, stand fast with the gear." Gault shrugged his ruck off and propped it with the others'. Then he grabbed Maddox. He got her MP5 turned in and made sure she got a decent pistol, one the armorer had shot in, and well-used mags and a box of nine-millimeter. Then he went by the tent, saw that all the personal gear was secured, and made arrangements with Kohler to lock it in a conex till they got back.

He looked up at the night. Full dark now. Every minute lost was a minute they'd regret come first light. He went back to the gear and found Blaze spinning his Glock. He told him to put it away and break down the doc's MREs, leave the weight behind and take the food value. Then stood biting his fingernails, going over the checklist in his mind. He had maps, his Silva, his GPS. Had the thirty-five-millimeter Nikonos and extra film. What else would he need out there in the field? If they didn't take it with them, they'd just have to do without.

Ten till. The Hummer drove up and braked in a cloud of gritty dust that he could taste. He picked up his pack and Nichols and Vertierra did too. Lenson was just behind them. He shrugged it on, not fastening the waist belt, and carried it and his weapon to the waiting vehicle.

THE PIPELINE road blazed with blue-white light. Both lanes were filled with double columns of tanker trucks and tank transporters heading slowly west, so the chief kept the Humvee off the paved highway, paralleling it on the hard sand. Gault watched them pass, astonished at the sheer mass of it. It was sobering, watching the US Army go by.

An hour later they stood alone in the dark. The road lights glowed in the distance. The ground here was sandy and then hard, as if not far beneath was rock. He didn't put the team on security. They'd be doing enough of that in Iraq. He let them hunker, rucks off and weapons laid across them.

He lifted the night vision goggles around his neck and turned them on, checking them one last time. The landscape leapt up, wavering green. He could see every rock. He turned slightly, checking out the team. The marines looked calm enough. They'd all been through this kind of thing before. Lenson paced back and forth, ten feet each way, as if he was on the bridge of a ship. Maddox had her cover off. He could see her abstracted expression as she fiddled with her hair, twisting it up and pinning it before she jammed the shapeless bush hat down again.

Right on time, the flutter of blades in the sky. He didn't see the helicopters at first. Then he did, they both had their lights on, coming in from the southeast. The team got to its feet. Zeitner aimed his flashlight at the lead chopper. The sound of the rotors changed, like they were taking deeper bites of the air, and the lights wheeled and grew, brighter and brighter. Sand blew up into their faces, stinging their bare skin.

Gault looked past them at the black sky. No stars. No moon. A dark night, maybe rain. Just right for insertion. He didn't believe in omens. He believed in luck, though. He hoped they got some.

The sound of the engines grew deafening, and then came the *whomp* of the landing gear. The black square of the hatch slid open. Without a word, speech useless now, he waved his team in, then tumbled in last as hard metal cut off the night and the smell of burning JP-5 surrounded them. He blinked, registering bare aluminum-walled space lit by faint green to port and starboard. Before his eyes adjusted, someone's hands felt for his head and clamped a headset over his ears.

"Team leader, you set for lift?"

"Affirmative, let's go."

A click and hiss, a new voice on the line. "Gunny, you on the line yet? Slap a cranial on him, Minky."

"Six team leader on the line," he said, feeling how dry his mouth was all of a sudden. "That you, sir?"

"Welcome aboard the Baghdad Shuttle, Gunny."

Cocooned in the roar of engines, they grew heavy, lifting into the night.

8

21–22 February: The Saudi Desert

No one spoke after the helicopter lifted off. The engine noise overwhelmed all sound, walling off each mind within the compass of its own skull. The deck shuddered, tilting as the pilot pulled into a bank. Beyond the door gunner, hunched over the machine gun, impenetrable night hurtled by as they gathered speed. Then dropped, steadied, speeding northward barely a hundred feet above the sand.

Sergeant Antonio Vertierra lay blinking at the overhead in the crew compartment. He lay against something hard, an angular metal box that jutted up from the floor. His weapon was under him, and his ruck. His legs were spread, knees crooked around someone whose back was wedged against him. It was uncomfortable. But he didn't move. Pain didn't bother him. Not that he didn't feel it. But life began in pain and was lived in pain and could not exist apart from pain. So why let it rule; above all, why lose one's dignity by acknowledging it aloud?

So now they were on their way. Into Iraq. Past the door gunner, as they gained altitude, a straight line of blue-white light tapered off to the far horizon. He recognized the road they'd come down, so many tanks and transporters the eye found it impossible to grasp. The richness and power of America. Then the lights wheeled past and darkness replaced them, suddenly and at once darkness so intense that when he waved his hand in front of his eyes he couldn't see a difference. Only as seconds passed did he become aware of a radiance bleeding up from tiny lights at deck level, barely bright enough to sense.

When the roar of the blades and engine lessened, he made out someone talking. Sounded like the gunny, but his voice was muffled. There was no answering murmur, but he spoke on. Vertierra couldn't make out what he said, but a moment later the man who was wedged into him turned his head.

It was Zeitner. "Pilot says there's gonna be some turbulence," the staff sergeant yelled. "If ya can find a handhold, grab on."

OUT OF nowhere, not understanding why he thought of it just then, Tony Vertierra found himself remembering a hot day in Lott, Texas.

He'd been hunting crows for Mr. Henderson. The farmer paid him ten cents for each ragged, limp bundle of feathers he presented at the back door. He killed them with his slingshot. Back home the boys could all shoot iguanas out of the mango trees, and their mothers would make a mole sauce with the roasted lizard, with tortillas and black beans, and sometimes a delicious white salty cheese.

He had much time to remember all this because in the open land of Mr. Henderson's fields he could not hide himself from the black birds who circled endlessly above. Instead he lay for long hours motionless on the dusty ground. But this too brought the memories. On their way to this country he and his aunt had to cross the desert before the Rio Grande. When the planes went over, looking for them, they had to lie motionless as the dead. Hoping the *oficiales* would not see them.

So that was how he lay in Mr. Henderson's fields. Like the dead. Till the cunning and suspicious birds had given up at last, and fluttered down.

Saudi reminded him of Texas. Not the cold, but the bareness, the sand interspersed with patches of rocky gravel, the sparse brush that smelled of a delicate sweetness when you rubbed it between your fingers and held them to your nose. A smell that clung for a long time after.

Lott, Texas, was where the Quakers who helped the refugees had relocated his family. One bank, one grocery store, not even a jail; when someone had to be locked up, they had to take him to the next county. He'd grown up in Lott, but he wasn't a Texan. The other kids called him a Mexican, but he wasn't Mexican either, though his family had lived there in the camps after they left Guatemala. It was difficult for them in Mexico because even their Spanish was half Mayan, the gutteral harsh-sounding dialect of the K'iche'. The *oficiales* despised the Indios, and stole or tore up their *documentos* unless they had money to pay. His aunt cried when they were finally safe in America. But still they were not Americans. He would have to apply, to become a citizen. He would have to beg.

This he did not like. At the school, a teacher had taken him into an office once and offered him money to buy clothes. He had thanked her gravely and walked away. To earn the clothes, to buy his lunch at school instead of signing to be given it for nothing, he shot crows for the farmers, sold fruit from door to door, stood by the road in front of the Al-Lyn trailer park, silently holding a sign that said he would wash cars for a dollar.

Not many cars came through Lott, Texas. But one day a man stopped to have his truck washed. His camper cab had many stickers on it in red and gold. Overcoming his shyness, Antonio had asked what they were. What Semper Fidelis meant. And the man had told him, and told him something else: that if he joined the Corps he could become an American because he'd earned it, not gone begging for it.

In boot camp he became Tony, not Antonio, but he still wore the silver medal of Our Mother Guadalupe his aunt gave him when he left Texas. He was skinny and strong, but with much meat and much exercise he became even stronger, though he was always the shortest man in any squad. The Corps made him an 0451, a parachute rigger, for no reason he'd ever been able to figure out. He wanted to make sure he earned the money that came every month in a green check. For that, he volunteered, holding up his hand silently whenever the platoon sergeant asked for men for a special detail, a piece of work harder or more demanding than straight duty. He put in for recon twice, got turned down both times. His platoon commander said he was too good at the chutes, but he finally requested mast and then the lieutenant let him go. They didn't have many Hispanics in recon. Blacks either. They said it was the swim test, but he wasn't too sure about that.

Or maybe it was. He'd almost died in the pool the first time, and got sent back to his grunt-side platoon. But instead of giving up or quitting he'd gotten up at 04 and gone down to the base pool before dawn. Swimming every morning. Ignoring the panic that laced up his chest and made him feel like he couldn't get any air, the fear that made him want to go crazy and try to claw his way up out of the water. Plowing on until he could swim a half mile, then a mile. The second time, he passed.

He was still afraid of the water, especially when he had to put his head under. But he could do it. He was a Marine.

He checked his MP5, pulling it around in front of him, making sure the loop of ranger cord was taut.

HE WAS feeling sleepy when suddenly the helicopter jinked violently. The forms around him stirred, cursing or muttering. He said nothing. Just spread his arms and legs, trying to cling like a fly to a ceiling. He heard the engine wind up, felt the airframe around him tilt forward as their speed increased. He could see nothing past the gunner, nothing but blackness, but from the roughness of the air he guessed they were lower now. Much lower.

Maybe they were in Iraq already. Would the gunny tell them? He didn't know.

He rolled himself awkwardly, humping the weight of ruck and radio and batteries and ammo slowly up whatever it was he was sitting against, till he was upright. The radio meant you were not alone. You could call in artillery. Call in air support. Call in emergency extract if things went to shit.

The wind was a steady blast through the open door. He couldn't get over how cold it was. He could not remember ever being this cold. He squeezed his eyes closed and made himself go over it all again, how they were going to do the linkup, the passwords, the frequencies.

Suddenly, without warning, the aircraft tilted below him, bent into a wide shallow curve that pinned him against the bulkhead. He felt himself trembling.

"Mark, the border," someone shouted into his ear. "Indian Country now."

He couldn't help smiling inside at that. Indian Country. Did that mean he was home? He didn't think so.

He was about as far away from home as a man could get.

HE COULD just remember Guatemala. He'd been so little then. Even his name was different. A Tun Rash Ulew. A Tun meant the same as Antonio. Rash Ulew was his family, named after the green land itself. Sometimes it seemed as if he ought to remember more. As if there was a hole where that remembering ought to be. He did know that it was very bad there. He often heard his aunt and her friends in the kitchen talking of what they called *la violencia*. They kept their voices low, as if even in Texas, the government or the *guerrilleros* might hear them.

He remembered, as a child, lying awake and listening to the distant flutter-beat of helicopters moving over the folded green jungle, the deep ravines and lofty mountains of El Quiché Province.

He could close his eyes now and be that child again. Hearing at the same time, in a strange echo so much louder and more present, the roar of the engines around him now.

The government troops could not catch the *guerrilleros* of the ORPA. So they wiped out the K'iche' villages they said supported the rebels. It had happened in a village not that far from theirs. Someone, maybe the guerrillas, maybe a robber, had killed the Ladino landowner. A few days later planes dropped fire on the village. Then troops came from the sky and killed everything. Men. Women. Children. Pigs. Everything that lived. So that in the night he had awakened, hearing the distant pulse of rotor blades, and lain wondering if they would land in his village, and come and kill his family.

And now he was a soldier. No, not a soldier, not like the men in the green trucks with their *automaticas*. He was a marine . . . but he wore a uniform and carried a gun . . . and now he himself, little A Tun who was, rode the invisible helicopters through the night.

Did children listen in fear now below him, linking past to future in an invisible chain? When had that chain begun? Would it ever end? The fear in his belly, was it the fear of a child? When did a man stop being a child? When did a Guatemalan become an American, cowboy-confident in himself and his gun?

He thought about this for a time, wondering. All Americans came from somewhere else, didn't they? When did they stop remembering, stop being what they'd been?

Gradually his lids drifted downward again.

HE AWOKE again, how much later he didn't know; woke amid yells and the clatter of the door MG, woke to someone grabbing him at the same moment blast and flame tore through the fuselage.

They were turning over, he was sliding downward. Floating in the air. The gun kept clattering, the flame visible past the bent figure in the door. Not bursts, just a steady clatter like the gunner didn't care if he burned the barrel out. Another bang lit the inside of the fuselage, and he heard the sound of tearing metal as something punched past not far from him.

The flash showed faces around him. They thought they were in darkness, but they were revealed by light. In that light he saw revealed their fear in the face of death. His heart went out to them. They were his team. His people. The closest thing he had to a country, now.

They were heading for the desert floor, bodies sliding toward him, then lifting off the deck as the aircraft nosed over. He felt the gunny reaching for him, and reached out too. Gripping rough cloth, feeling the hard muscle beneath.

Twining their arms together, they waited for death.

9

0400 22 February:
Western Iraq

Gault had no idea how they did it, but at the last possible moment the guys up front got the aircraft back under control. More rounds punched through the fuselage, whanging like a rivet gun perforating the aluminum, but they lurched level again and seemed to pick up speed. At any rate, they hadn't crashed. Yet. He let go of the others and shoved up to look past the door gunner. Reached to turn the NVGs on, and was instantly sorry. The ground was too close to look at. He turned them off again and grabbed for a handhold as the deck bucked upward, then down, sending them floating in a jumble of straps and rucks, weapons and legs and arms all meshed and thrashing in the weightless dark.

But somehow they were still alive, despite the wind whistling through the holes and the acrid stink of incendiary compound.

The copilot came on the line. "I need help up here," he said, voice no longer as cool as before.

"What you got, sir?"

"Commander Jabo's hit. There a corpsman back there?"

"We're all trained in battlefield medicine, sir." Gault fought himself free, twisted to look forward. The narrow passage between the cockpit and the after compartment was a well of darkness. Nothing but dim phosphors of instruments.

"Well, can one of you get up here? Wait, I think I . . . seat restraint's off. Can you take care of him back there? I've kind of got my hands full."

WITH THE pilot's seat empty, the copilot tried to bear down and concentrate. He brought them up another fifty feet. Too high, radar visible; but the way his hands were shaking, if he stayed low they'd fireball into a dune or a rock outcrop. They were flying over villages, some sort of industrial facilities, pumping stations or what he didn't know. AAA twisted up, ribbons of lovely light like the fireworks at Disneyland if you didn't think about what they could do. What they'd damn near done.

He didn't know if it was a shell or bullet, but it had come through the right-side fuselage with a jolting bang, traversing upward from the right chin side across the cockpit and out the overhead. The cockpit had filled instantly with smoke, biting into his lungs. He'd clawed at his mask, then relaxed as the cabin ventilation cleared it almost instantly.

But then they'd twisted off and headed for the ground, and he'd glanced over and seen the pilot slumped back, and he'd grabbed desperately, knowing that it was too late, the ground was coming up.

He pulled his mind off that and ran his eyes over the instruments. Airspeed. Attitude. Gyro. He lined up on 040 again. Fuel needle steady, thank fuck they hadn't magic-BB'd the gas. But the TACNAV was dark. Now he had to fly and at the same time navigate from his knee pad. He squinted through the goggles at the chart. They should be crossing something called the Wadi Abu Gher.

When he looked up, the ground was in his face again. Shit! This wasn't gonna work. His hand cramped on the stick. He got the nose back up and peered through the windscreen, only then realizing the Pave Hawk was gone. Somewhere in the chaos of being hit he'd lost the lead helo.

They flew at 150 knots through the Iraqi night, and in his earphones pealed the peremptory *peep peep peep* of the radar warning signal. Someone down there had locked on.

ZEITNER GOT a body dumped in his lap without knowing what the hell was going on. Gault was yelling, but it was unintelligible above the storm of rotor blades and wind whistle. The airframe shook like a rattletrap pickup. Suddenly everything went slanted and he grabbed the guy in his lap to keep him from sliding toward the door.

The team leader put his mouth next to his ear. "It's the pilot. He got hit, check him out," Gault was yelling.

Zeitner felt for his combat flashlight. Couldn't help the guy if he couldn't see. The light gleamed off black blood. It covered the front of the flight suit. He checked the airway first, thrusting his fingers in rough and deep. Clear, but the guy didn't react the way he should when somebody stuck fingers down his throat. So he put the light in his own mouth and pulled his KA-BAR and ripped the suit apart up to the shoulder.

Classic sucking chest wound. He kicked savagely at somebody else who was pressing in on him, the helo still jinking and howling around the sky. He turned his head and vomited and groped for his kit and found a field dressing more by feel than by sight.

Gault again. "Copilot wants that light out, it fucks up his NVGs."

"I got to have light, Gunny. Move over here and shield me."

He was ripping the packaging off the dressing when two hands in surgical rubber gloves came into the lit area. He hadn't wanted to touch the wound, but they went right to it, spread it, and went in. He stared as they felt around, then as one dug deeper, into the chest cavity. A jagged piece of golden-colored metal came out, amid a pulsing welter of bright blood.

"Is there a needle in that kit? Sutures?"

Relief flooded him. Shit, he'd forgotten they had a doctor with them. "Uh, yes, ma'am," he said, and backed off to give her room.

He glanced up to see the other team members sitting with their backs against the forward edge of the compartment, sealing the light off from the copilot. The gunner began firing again. Cartridge cases clattered to the deck. The engine spooled upward, and he swallowed. Then the major said, calm in his ear: "Just hold the flashlight. I'll take over from here."

GAULT AND the copilot were arguing over the mission. The copilot said he was aborting. They'd been seen, they'd been hit, he couldn't navigate and fly at the same time, and they'd lost the lead aircraft.

"Lost as in shot down?"

"Lost as in, he's not in VFR."

"What?"

"I can't see him. So I can't follow him. So I'm aborting."

"This is a go mission," Gault shouted as evenly as he could. He was trying to stay cool but the motion was getting to him. There was something wrong with his NVGs too. When he turned them on, they flickered. Maybe from getting banged around during the evasives. If they aborted they'd just have to do it all over tomorrow night. He snapped the rubber band on his wrist, the one with the freqs on it for the rapid reaction force. They were supposed to come get you if you stepped in a shit sandwich, but he didn't think it'd happen this deep in Iraq. He said again, "This is a go mission. There's too many wheels turning. Your pilot's doing all right back there, the doc's operating and he's doing all right."

"He still alive?"

"I told you he's doing all right."

"I better abort. We lost the Pave Hawk."

"Stiffen the fuck up, sir. You just get this fucking bird there, okay?"

The copilot found himself getting a little calmer. No one had shot at them for the past few miles, for one thing, and the radar tone had peaked and then faded without their getting in range of whatever missile or gun battery had locked on. He took deep breaths, then reached for the mike.

The Pave Hawk answered and gave him a radar bearing. He came right to 055 and in about four minutes picked the other helo up, the two dim IR beacons snapping off as soon as he called them in sight. He saw he was eighty feet up and forced himself to bore in, bear down, snuggle down into the fuzzy fur of Mother Earth. The mama who'd keep you safe, or kill you. Depending on just how close you got.

Point Delta. He glanced at the chart and saw the radar must have been the Mudaysis airfield. They were threading south of a big SA-6 envelope, coming off the flat desert into hilly country broken by wadis. The Pave Hawk lifted and so did he. A warning tone ululated again but faded. The last turn. Thirty more miles.

"You guys can get ready," he yelled back. "Fifteen-minute warning."

THE GUNNY told them to load mags. Blaze pulled the MP5 around where he could get to it. It caught on his ruck and he cursed and fought it around till something tore free. He didn't care what; he wanted that weapon in his hands.

His mouth was dry. Seeing the red glistening inside of the pilot's lungs had taken him back to when he was a kid, nine, third grade, and his mother went away, left them and left town and they never had even a letter from her. His uncle came over to the barbershop and said to his

dad, "Blaze, let's celebrate, where do you want to go out
for dinner, just you and me and the boy." And he'd yelled
for Cake 'n' Steak and when they got there he ordered his
rare, because that was what they said on TV. But then
he'd cut it open and it had been bloody raw but he'd eaten
it anyway and halfway through threw up, right there in
the restaurant . . . the red glisten was just like that, like
raw meat. . . . He slammed in a mag, heard it click seated,
worked the bolt an instant before he remembered not to.

The hand fastened to his shoulder, painful even
through the battle-dress jacket. "Unchamber the round,
Corporal." He pulled the magazine and worked the bolt
again, heard the cartridge flick out and clatter heavy-
bulleted somewhere down onto the metal deck. Let the
bolt slam and reseated the mag. Zeitner's hand released
and went away. He sat feeling sweat ooze over him, all
over his face.

"Five mikes. Get your gear buckled," the gunny yelled
over the drone of the engines, the whine of the wind
through punctured metal like a chorus of cheap whistles.
"Get your shit on. Look like fuckin' recon marines."

And suddenly Denny Blaisell understood there wasn't
any way back, there wasn't any way out. Face-to-fucking-
face with it, man, he thought, both terrified and so excited
his dick went rock hard. Full auto rock and roll.

"One minute. Lock and load, weapons on safe. One
minute!"

Lips moving, so scared he panted, "Blaze" Blaisell
fumbled with his weapon, staring wide-eyed into the
roaring night.

I'M GONNA land straight ahead two hundred yards."

The gunner: "Okay, skipper, got it."

"Passing forty knots—landing configuration." He
fumbled for the landing checklist, found he couldn't read
and fly at the same time, staring through the goggles like
through two toilet-paper tubes with green cellophane

taped over them. So he did it from memory, snapping switches by feel. Contingency power. No lights. AFSC on, check harness.

"Crewman checklist complete."

"Roger that . . . give me a call."

"About thirty feet . . . twenty . . . LZ looks clear. Slight slope to the right."

The crew chief: "LZ good on the left."

"Ten feet."

The gear thumped, absorbing the shock as he slammed twenty-one tons of American metal onto the gritty soil of Iraq. "Clear to depart, Gunny," he told the marine. "Unass quick and get those other people in here. We don't have a lot of fuel or a lot of time."

But when he looked back they were already jumping out.

GO, GO, go," Gault yelled. "Move, move, move. Get in the fucking vege. Fire discipline, watch for friendlies." He waited as Vertierra, then Blaze and F.C. rolled out through the starboard door. As they left he swept the interior with his strobing flickering night vision, making sure nothing got left behind. He hoped the radio didn't lose its fill in all that banging around. If they couldn't phone home they'd be in the hurt locker come time to extract. The attachments hung back, looking toward him, and he hustled them out, yelling; it didn't matter about noise discipline with the engine blasting and the rotors whipping around. A last look at the pilot, who was lying against the landing gear housing, the crew chief bent over him. Then he scrambled to the door and jumped.

To hit and tumble and roll back up, weapon shouldered, aiming out into the flickering darkness. He sprinted over uneven ground, buttonhooking around the tail and heading out to port like they'd rehearsed. Faster to use the aircraft for orientation on the LZ, instead of the compass. He couldn't see the others; the goggles' field of vision was too narrow.

Twenty meters out he dropped to prone firing position. The strobing got worse, till he could barely see. They were in a wadi, gravelly sand studded with little bushes and, here and there, coarse grass. Cold rain brushed his face. He smelled wet earth and a scent between turpentine and jasmine that was probably the bush he was lying on. It was colder than he'd expected. They'd come four hundred klicks north, into a whole different weather system. This was the overcast and rain that had stopped the air strikes on Baghdad. But the worse the weather, the better for the insert. He shivered, staring over the suppressed submachine gun, the wet gravel cold against his balls. Nothing moved in the darkness.

He tucked the weapon into his elbows, rolled on his back, and pulled the goggles off. He opened the battery compartment and reseated the batteries and screwed it down again as tight as it would go. When he put them back on, they still flickered but not as much. He went up on a knee, did a three-sixty, checking the shadows.

The helo was a bright green double blob of infrared. The rotors, still engaged, a shimmering halo above it. It would stay for ten minutes, in case they had contact jumping off. Meanwhile he was supposed to link up with the Brits. But where were they?

He was wondering if they'd missed the meet when light pinpricked the darkness. He lifted his goggles to make sure it was red. Check. He blinked two from his own flash. One came back. He got to his feet and jogged toward it at port arms. As he passed, his team rose from scrub and rocks as if being born from the ground. Zeit was moving them out, covering him. Gault felt uneasy. He hated linkups.

Up a little rise, and men rose up suddenly around him, silent, the outlines of their weapons green against black.

They were pointing at him, and he stopped, looking at them. One wore what looked like a black sweater.

Another, some sort of camo uniform. A third had a stocking cap on. Another, what looked like an Iraqi helmet. Two were carrying a third, and others were limping and weaving as they walked.

Gault called in a low voice, "I used to have a red bird."

"What kind, a turkey?"

"Red" and "Turkey" were the challenge and passwords, used in a sentence to confuse anyone who overheard. The weapons swung away. Their leader, a large-chested man in a black watch cap, circled his arm in the air and pointed down. They fanned out into their security, and Gault went to a knee with him.

"Who're you wankers?" were the first words out of his mouth.

"US Marines. You Sarsten?"

"Sarsten, yeah. The head shed said to meet you at the RV but didn't say what for. We're in shit state, you can see that. What's the problem, mate?"

Up close Gault could see him pretty well now that his NVGs were working. The SAS patrol commander had black beard stubble and a heavy mustache and sideburns. Dark curls poked out from under the stocking cap. He looked big and rough and very wired. Gault decided not to start with the bad news. He said, "We're headed east. What have we got in that direction?"

"Hostiles. There's fooking ragheads all over starting at first light. There's an antiair battalion eight klicks east of here. They've got ZSU-23s or M53s and good security. Dogs. Lights. Wire."

This didn't sound good. Gault said, "I see you've got wounded."

"We had some drama. I'm the only one not hit."

Gault rose, started to aim his flash back at the helo. Sarsten's hand closed over it. "What the fuck you doing?"

"Letting the helo go."

"He's taking my wounded. Then we're getting out of here."

"Get your wounded into the chopper, Sergeant. The rest of your team too. But you personally are attached with us now."

Gault put his hand on Sarsten's shoulder, getting ready to explain. But the other man knocked it off instantly with the butt of his weapon and in the same motion pushed the muzzle into Gault's neck. Gault froze. Something about the man's eyes, imperfectly visible though they were, warned him not to move.

"What are you telling me, mate?"

"We're on a hot mission. We've got to know what's between us and our objective point. Especially if there're hostiles. Get your team out of here, but you're staying. We've got extra rations and water for you. Ammo too."

Sarsten stared at him. His camo paint had smeared in the rain. "The fuck you say. Where you getting this shit?"

"Those are the orders."

"Orders from who? . . . Those rear-echelon *fuckers*, don't tell me they . . . I said, orders from fucking *who?*"

"From whoever your chain of command is. The authenticator is 'Ripper.' "

The mustached man began cursing. The rain increased, coming down out of the black with stinging force. Engines revved behind them; the copilot, telling them he was about to lift.

Sarsten yelled at the shadows around them to get in the helo, and left him standing there. Gault's goggles started flickering again then, and he had to take them off to reinsert the batteries. As he fumbled in the rain, the world was an immense and impenetrable dark, broken only by the occasional flash from the east. Like lightning, but silent. He didn't know what they were.

When he got back to the helo, the British team was boarding. Two walking wounded stood by, one with a slinged arm and the other a bandage round his head. He leaned into them and yelled, "Sorry we have to keep your team leader."

"What? Keeping the Devil?"

"Good fucking luck on you," said the man with the head wound.

Gault hesitated. "Who?"

"The Devil Incarnate. But I didn't tell you, mate."

The other man muttered something, lost in the clatter of rotor blades and the rain. Gault said, "Say again?"

"Said, you don't want to all get slotted, better ship him back with us. He's right round the bend, that one."

Sarsten came up and the wounded men fell silent. He asked if they had any ammo or food or water left. They said no. Gault watched the body language. The sergeant's men turned away, edged apart from him. Put distance between them.

For a moment he wondered if he was making the right call. Paulik had left it up to him. But if there were enemy forces between him and the objective, he had to know where they were, how they were armed, how they patrolled . . . things Sarsten's team had obviously paid in blood to learn.

The last SAS merged with the blurry heat-shadow of the aircraft. The pitch of the blades increased. A blast of dust and grit whipped up to sting the backs of his legs and neck as he jogged away. He was unable to shake the feeling that he'd have been safer, for some reason he couldn't put his finger on, if he'd told Sarsten to leave too, join his wounded and go. But it was too late now. So he just stood silent in the rain, then got the team on their feet and started them moving out.

AN HOUR later Dan came up over a rise and saw a fiery rainbow in the distance.

They'd been moving steadily since the helo lifted, since it turned from a roar to a clatter in the sky to silence. Into that silence gradually filtered the sigh of the wind; the patter of rain; the rustle of the brush; the crunch of boots on wet gravel. No one spoke. Back at 'Ar'ar, Gault had made it plain that once inserted there'd be no

coughing, no grunting, no sneezing, no speech. Everything metal was taped to prevent clicks or jingles. In what
the marines called Indian Country, the Bush, the Vege,
the Zone, silence was life.

They'd humped fast off the LZ for an hour, moving in
column formation. Every fifteen or twenty minutes the
Gunny lifted his cover and they halted to listen. Dan went
to a knee with the rest, resting the MP5 across his thigh as
he looked, listened, and sniffed. To sense only a dog
barking far away, and once a droning that might have
been a vehicle on a distant road. Gault had angled away
from it. They had to avoid roads, villages, anybody who
might report their presence. The distant flickering he'd
noticed had died away too, leaving them in a void. Dark
and the rain.

Now sound came to him, a distant hollow popping,
and he suddenly understood it and the fiery rainbow were
one; antiaircraft fire arching upward. Directly ahead.

The gunny lifted his cover and Dan took a knee again.
His bladder ached. He laid his weapon carefully across
his boot the way you were supposed to, and fumbled his
dick out. Maddox must have had the same need; she
moved a few yards off into the dark.

He couldn't get over how cold it was. The rain came
and went, but the freezing wind went on. Any depression
in the ground cupped water at its heart. He wondered how
long they stayed filled and how deep the aquifer was. This
could be a fertile land, given wells and pumps. He buttoned after completing his contribution, shouldered his
weapon, and scanned the horizon again. The AAA fire
died away, and the night grew still again.

GAULT WAS huddled with the British patrol leader,
Sarsten, both men down on one knee and speaking lover-
soft into each other's ears.

He'd rehearsed the order of movement back at 'Ar'ar.
Blaze at point, then Nichols, then him. Vertierra behind

as RTO. Then came the two attachments, followed up by the assistant team leader. About five yards between each man. But now he had Sarsten too. Finally he'd put the SAS man ahead of him. Now he whispered, so low he barely heard himself, "That's your triple-A battalion?"

"Correct." Sarsten was breathing hard, but then, he'd already been out here for days, had been in a firefight; he had to be exhausted. Again Gault wondered whether bringing him along had been a good idea.

"Which way around them, Sergeant? Got a recommendation?"

"Might have. Let's see your map, mate."

Zeitner threw a poncho over them, hiding their light while they laid the chart out on the ground. Gault set the GPS out and took a first position with it. It was about the size of a brick with a little squared-off antenna pivoted from the side. They'd issued it to him back at 'Ar'ar and he was wary of it. Easy things let you down in the field. But the glowing green screen gave him a lat and long, and when he had that plotted, Sarsten pointed out the Iraqi position ahead and a wadi, on the map, that led south around it.

Gault didn't like going down into wadis, but he liked enemy antiair battalions even less. What worried him was that it'd take time to square his way around it. Maybe four hours. It'd be dawn before they could go to a hide site.

He decided to put that choice off, try the wadi and see what progress they made. He put the gear and map away and got the team on their feet again.

He caught the back-turned blur of Blaisell's face. A stab of doubt. Had *he* ever looked that young? The kid had been to UAT, but not on his watch. Still, he was a marine. He'd do all right. Maybe it'd be a good idea to swap him out with Nichols occasionally, give him a break on point. He'd think about that later too.

He caught the kid's eye and gave him the signal to move out.

•   •   •

MAUREEN HEARD the dogs, not that far away. She was getting tired. Seemed like they'd been marching for hours through the dark. She didn't have goggles, like the marines. There weren't enough to go around. So she couldn't see where she was putting her feet, and often stumbled on rocks or uneven footing. She couldn't believe how heavy her ruck was. She tugged at her deuce gear, bowing to give her back a moment's rest. She was sweating despite the cold, and her calves were cramping. So far she'd kept up. She hoped they stopped soon, though. Surely they had to rest once in a while.

Her mind moved ahead, to what they were going to find. If this wasn't just another bullshit exercise, another of Saddam's empty threats. The Mother of all Bullshitters. She hoped it was gas. Tabun or sarin in a Scud warhead. Nothing to laugh about, but the Israelis had masks and safe rooms; they might get through without too many dead.

But if he was talking about a biological, ten to one it'd be the big A. Onset in one to six days, dose-dependent. High mortality. A tough bug, one you could pack into a warhead and expect to do some damage. She wasn't afraid of it. The team should never get in range of infectious *B. anthracis*. Even if they were exposed, the inoculations should protect them, unless Fayzah had bred some sort of variant, and even then she was carrying enough oral ciprofloxacin to bring the team back. Max-dose them till they shit their guts out. Cipro would screw up the intestinal flora, but they wouldn't die.

No, she wasn't afraid of anthrax. What she feared was the dark around them, the distant popping and the floating light. She touched her pistol. Back at 'Ar'ar she'd wondered if she could actually shoot somebody. Out here she felt more confident of it. But the thought made her guts move inside her belly.

Someone trod on her heel, Zeitner, and she sucked air at the pain. She turned her face and whispered, "When are we going to take a goddamn break?"

For answer she felt his hand slide across her throat . . . the signal for silence. That pissed her off, but she said nothing more. Just set her unseeing gaze forward again, bent under the weight, and grimly pressed on.

BEHIND HER, Zeitner was worried. They had to preserve noise discipline. If she was going to talk . . . he adjusted his goggles, watching her ass move under the butt pack . . . he remembered the pilot and how she'd stitched him up. Reaching in, finding the artery somehow, and sewing it up so fast and deft he couldn't believe his eyes. While all he was going to do was put a pressure bandage on, so the poor shit would have probably just bled to death, that artery pumping away there inside his chest.

Jake Zeitner had actually resigned from the Marine Corps last June. But two weeks before he was due to get out, go to Cuba, New York, and start setting up the franchise with Joel, Daro's cousin who was going to be his partner—Joel handling the shop and him the office and the relationship with Firestone—the Marine Corps had issued what it called a stop loss. Everybody who was due to get out, retire, resign; they were on hold for the duration.

This had put him in a jam. They'd already paid Firestone the franchise fee and signed the lease on the land, the curve going out of town on 305 North between Moonwinks and the North Star Grill. Joel had put in all his savings. It was up to him to keep up the lease payments. Meaning Daro had to move back in with her folks in Salamanca. She'd disliked the Corps even before that, had pushed him to get out, make something of himself; the stop loss had made her wild.

Running a business wouldn't be easy. The package

Firestone sent made that clear. The lines, the margins, financing, you had to know what was going on in your shop and in your office, had to understand compound interest and labor relations and contract law.

He was going over the numbers again when he remembered where he was and pulled his mind back, astonished at himself. He was rear security, for Christ's sake! He half turned, checking their rear, first the left, then the right. Looking for anyone tracking or trailing them, someone cutting in behind. But the black hills, the faint green-sparkling sky, were empty and void.

You better get your head together, he told himself. Quit zoning out. Secure thinking about the major's ass and selling front-end alignments. If the fucking Iraqis see us we're in deep fucking shit.

Sweating now, he kept looking back, sharpening his sight into the darkness that followed them.

GAULT WAS thinking the overcast was good, the rain was good too. People would stay inside in this weather. The occasional distant flashes, which he figured for bombing, meant the troops they were passing would be looking up, not focused on their perimeters. He hoped.

They had a long way to go, and not much time to get there.

Gradually the ground dropped away. The wadi was peppered with gravel and the bushes grew thicker as they descended. Here and there the undergrowth was almost continuous, almost a brush line.

They had to hump thirty klicks to the linkup. Make it thirty-five, with this dogleg. One night and a day hide and part of another night, he'd figured. He hoped the Syrian asset showed up. If this Samir or Shamir or whatever his name was—Nichols called him "Shamu"—didn't show, they'd just have to strap it on for the extract site. That or try to capture somebody, see if they got lucky.

Flying Stones. He wondered again what it was, then dismissed it as his boots splashed into water. Shallow at first, an inch or two. Then it flooded his boots. Damn, he hated to march with wet feet. Have to watch out for hypothermia. He was shivering, but it was the attachments he was worried about. A navy missile geek and a female army bug doctor. He'd done his best, but there was a limit to how much bush sense you could hammer in in two days.

Pushing through the water, he flipped his compass open and sighted along the line of march. Trying to imagine what lay ahead, putting the map and what he could see of the terrain into a coherent picture.

The wadi led east, following the sloping land down toward the three lakes that shielded Baghdad from the west. He hugged the north side of the ravine as much as he could. The water deepened as they pushed on. He took each step warily, fearing sinkholes, quicksand, mines, but all his boots encountered were submerged bushes. Rocks too, making the bottom uneven, but there didn't seem to be any sudden drop-offs. The water rose over the course of the next hour till they were wading thigh-deep. Icy cold, numbing his feet inside the thin Iraqi boots. The up side was that you didn't leave tracks on water. The down side was that they were real fucking exposed. He hadn't been at Khafji, but Nichols said the Iraqis there had night vision goggles they'd bought from the Dutch and Belgians. He figured Saddam had gear like that at the front, not as far behind the lines as they were now. But it still made him feel like there was a target painted on his back.

He started skipping breaks. If they went to one knee they'd be under water. Besides, they were running behind schedule. So he just kept mushing. At one point he thought he heard the woman's voice, but when he turned, her head was down and she was slogging. She was shorter than the men and the water was up to her chest. Her deuce gear and ruck were dragging through it. He thought about relieving her of some of that weight, then remembered he'd already lightened her load. She'd just have to keep up.

He stopped and took another bearing, standing erect as around him the others bent to prop their hands on their thighs. He signaled the pace man. Three klicks since they hit the wadi. The map showed it intersecting with another ahead, two shallow flooded ravines meeting in a V. Right now they were just about abreast, due south, of the troop position Sarsten had told them about. Give it two more miles east, then he'd cut left, get up onto dry ground, and look for a hide site.

He checked his watch again, holding his wrist away so that he could focus on the face through the NVGs. An hour and a half till BMNT—beginning of morning nautical twilight. That didn't leave a lot of time to get dug in.

He folded the map and slipped it into his leg pocket. Waved Blaisell forward again, and the barely audible splash of their movement resumed.

F.C. NICHOLS slogged steadily along, not thinking of much in particular. Just keeping his head up and eyeballs roving, punching the goggles on every few minutes to track along the tops of the ridge lines between which they were moving. Couldn't see too good; they were two or three hundred meters off and the rain degraded vision. But that meant nobody could see them either. He shifted the rifle in his arms, keeping it clear of the water and the mud. If they had contact the last thing he needed was a stoppage under fire.

He hadn't been able to sleep last night. He was wet too, and cold, but none of that bothered him as much as missing the pinch of Copie he usually tucked into his cheek. Unfortunately you could smell smokeless tobacco way downwind and nobody but Americans used it. He just had to stop thinking about it. Maybe chow down on a PowerBar next time they stopped.

Eyes flicking around him, F.C. Nichols waded on.

. . .

WHEN GAULT saw the other wadi ahead, the light was coming, the night was waning, he was racing the sun. When he lifted his goggles again, he was shocked to be able to see. The gray-silver half-light did not fall from the sky, did not seem to come from anywhere, really. Just light, visibility, bleeding up through the rocks and sand around them. He turned the NVGs off to save the battery, dropping them to hang around his neck. He looked at his watch again, then at the flat dropping-away of land ahead. No concealment there.

He walked faster and came up with Blaze. The point man flinched around, half pointing his weapon. Gault jerked a thumb over his shoulder. Blaisell looked doubtful, but led them back in a sharp zag, nearly retracing their tracks toward the rise where the two wadis met.

He stood back and let them pass, inspecting each as he went by. Sergeant Vertierra, small and spare and incredibly strong, darting him an emotionless glance out of dark eyes as he moved past with a tireless lope despite thirty extra pounds of comm gear and batteries. Never any empty chatter from the Guatemalan. Then the SAS man, stocking cap pushed back, trousers black wet as he came dripping up out of the water. His face was gray with exhaustion. After that, the navy commander, bent into his load straps, mouth set in a grim line.

The major walked as if her feet were bleeding. Water ran off her gear. She stared at him with dull hatred. He nodded and she switched her eyes past him and went on. After her came Zeitner. Gault signed to the ATL that they'd hide-site on the knob. Zeitner nodded wordlessly, looking up at it.

The gray ground at the top was strewn with rocks. Some were arranged in circles, as if shepherds had camped here. Last night, or ten centuries ago, there was no way to tell. Gault looked carefully around over his front sight. Nothing but the gray mist of rain, the gray light of dawn, coming fast now. A good position, with good observation. Already he could see maybe a quarter mile. By full light they had to be under cover.

Zeitner signaled from ahead, pointing at a darker area of soil some distance off.

It was a dent in the ground ten meters across. Larger stones lined one side of it, fitted in what might once have been a wall or part of a foundation. He did a slow 360 and nodded. Zeitner pointed Blaze and Vertierra and Nichols out on security as he stripped his ruck off and snapped his entrenching tool open. He jumped down and probed the blade around the bottom of the depression. When he was satisfied there were no mines, he called Lenson and Maddox down with him.

Not too much later they had something like a skirmisher's trench hugging the stones, a foot and a half deep and about six by six. Zeitner was still digging as Gault started arranging the sheets.

"What kind of trex is this?" said Sarsten, looking down.

As soon as they'd stopped he'd gone to one knee and faced out, helped secure the perimeter. That was good, but his tone now wasn't. In the growing light, seeing him clearly for the first time, Gault saw that the SAS was wearing what looked very much like an Iraqi uniform. He kept his voice low. "This is our RON position."

"Our fucking what?"

"Remain overnight. We're hiding up here today."

"Okay, I got that, but there's no fucking cover up here. I told you, there's going to be all kinds of people around come sunup. That's how we got topped."

Gault wasn't sure what to make of this. So far he hadn't seen a village, a cairn, a trail, any sign of life. The CIA map showed this area as unpopulated. Finally he said, "It's dawn. We're staying here."

Sarsten kicked the sheets. "And what the fuck's this? This isn't a proper spider hole."

He explained about the sheets and the sand, that kicked-out dirt was a different color than the topsoil. The

Britisher listened skeptically, but at last shrugged and slid in. Zeitner motioned the rest of the team inside, then dragged the cover over their heads. He tossed handfuls of sand scratching and rattling over it, then crawled in too. Eight bodies and gear huddled close together. The edges of the sheet rattled, flapping like the sail of a derelict lifeboat, till Gault reached up and tucked the flap under. Then the only sound was the eternal whisper of the desert wind.

10

22 February: Western Iraq

The team lay at the bottom of the hole like tadpoles stranded in a footprint. Gault with Vertierra, back to back, taking the first watch. Nichols and Blaisell; Zeitner and the Brit, Sarsten, with Lenson closed up too. Only Maddox sat by herself, or as much so as a six-by-six hole would permit, with her knees drawn up and her back to the fitted stones that formed the north side.

Not long after dawn, rain began tapping on the sheet, then gradually became the hiss of wet sleet on gravel and rock. They huddled together, sharing warmth from ponchos and each others' bodies. The marines lay prone on their rucks, alert and motionless. Their breaths were white mist. The sheet that covered them was propped open along its edge with rocks so they could see down into the wadis. Claymore clackers dangled inside it.

F. C. Nichols was cold, wet, and tired, but he liked this position. He had a clear field of fire for three hundred yards, limited only by the gradual slope down to the wadi. At first light he'd dug elbow holes and marked out his sectors with rocks. His rifle lay across his boot, a National Match cartridge chambered and the safety on. Water dripped from the center of the sheet, pulled down by the sand and rain into a sagging teat. He'd already refilled his canteens and drunk as much as he could hold. Only trouble was, when you hydrated you had to piss. And in a hide site that meant letting go in your trou, or at best half-turning to urinate into the grenade sump they'd spaded. Water stood inches deep in it already.

Daylight, and all day ahead of them. Back home they thought the desert was hot. His wife had sent him a big bottle of sunscreen in the Christmas package. Now it was sleeting. Not a problem. As long as they stayed covert. He leaned against the side of the hole and drifted into a light sleep.

When he awoke, it was 0840 and something hard was digging into his back. He reached around very cautiously, so as not to dislodge any of the gravel that formed the side of the pit, and shoved. Blaisell shifted an inch or two, snorted in his sleep, and relaxed again.

Dan swam slowly up into consciousness. His stomach rumbled. He was shivering, leg muscles iron-taut with cold. He rolled to his ruck and got a Ziploc of gorp. Crammed nuts and grain into his mouth, washed it down with flat-tasting rainwater. Everything was soaked. He caught a glance from Sarsten, and held the food out. The other shook his head and returned to his silent contemplation of the desert. Dan noticed the Britisher's eyes were rimmed with red. He couldn't have gotten much sleep out chasing Scuds, but he didn't seem to be trying to catch up now.

A distant bell rattled, hollow and cracked-sounding. He ducked, peering beneath the cover sheet toward the flooded wadi below. Its gray surface shivered with cat's-paws of wind. It steamed faintly in the cold air. The hillside was brown and gray rocks, like the moon. The sleet seemed to be letting up, turning back to rain.

He lifted his head, frowning.

Something had moved, in the slowly rising wisps of vapor ghosting up off the water. He glanced around. The marines had picked it up too. Nichols was staring in that direction, and the gunny had a small pair of binoculars focused on it. Vertierra leaned toward him, and they held a conversation that four feet away he couldn't overhear.

Dan looked out again, but whatever it was had gone away, or stopped moving; at least was no longer visible. There, Gault was putting the binoculars away; it must be okay.

Rolling over, curling his boots up out of the icy water that was gradually filling the pit, he pillowed his head on his rucksack, hugged himself, and closed his eyes again.

A foot away, shivering, Maureen Maddox massaged her cramped legs. *Solens, gastrocnemius, Triceps surae; the tendo calcaneus is the thickest and strongest in the body* . . . Her feet had gone numb during the night march, and she still couldn't feel her toes. Her shoulders hurt where the ruck straps cut, and her throat and lungs were raw. She was very tired and very cold, so exhausted she could only sleep in snatches, drive-by glimpses of nightmare she jerked up from at the slightest movement from those around her, the slightest drip of rain on her face. She was even more frightened, a bone-deep apprehension that made her feel sick, each time she woke to remember where she was.

After an internship at George Washington University Hospital, the world capital for gunshot trauma and emergency medicine, missing sleep didn't bother her. But she'd barely made it through the hump last night. Those last few hours had been a corridor lined with red velvet hangings of pain. She groped for her butt pack, shook another six hundred milligrams of ibuprofen into her palm, and swallowed the fat white tablet dry. If they went like that again tonight, that fast, that far, she'd never keep up.

Then she set her mouth in a hard line. She'd keep up, all right.

She lifted her head slightly, sure she'd heard voices. Listened for a long time, but didn't hear them again. Just the hiss of sleet, the drip of the sheet. A fart from one of the men. Charming. She wished the guys back at Fort Detrick could see her now. Be All You Can Be . . . assdeep in a hog wallow in western Iraq.

A faint clear tinkling sound, delicate and wistful . . .

she was peeping out under the sheet when a pair of legs went by. Not twenty yards away, and the bell-clear jingle rang out again. She stared. The legs were in saffron cotton and the ankles were bare. The feet were wearing what looked like shower shoes, blue rubber flip-flops with the thong between the toes. Her first thought was that they must be freezing. Her second was to reach out and grab the nearest guy, who happened to be Lenson, and shake him awake and turn his head so he was looking where she was. She felt him stiffen. The others were looking her way now. She made walking motions with her fingers and pointed.

Gault nodded. He rolled quietly over and came up on a knee. He had his submachine gun to his shoulder, looking along the barrel. She remembered her pistol and fumbled for it. The muzzle was muddy and she wiped it on her trouser leg, hoping he hadn't seen.

The legs moved off and were followed by more; this time hairy and thin, ending in dainty black hooves that picked their way delicately among the rocks. A low *m'a'a'* came to them.

They lay rigid, not breathing, not speaking. The men had picked up their weapons. Only their eyes moved now. She felt her heart hammering, shaking her chest, and breathed slow and easy, in and out.

The goat baaed again. The bell tinkled. They seemed to be moving away.

Gault was following things from his peephole. His face crowded close, he could see the western side of the knob and beyond it the curve of gray-clouded sky. Beyond that, nothing. Then they moved into his sight, climbing up from the direction of the water, and he narrowed his eyes.

Three goats and one shepherd, goatherd, whatever you called them. A short woman in a worn padded cotton coat whose embroidery might have been colorful many years ago. Dingy yellow trousers stained with mud. He couldn't tell her age. Her face was concealed by a black cloth wraparound. She carried a carved stick and seemed to be following rather than leading the goats. The biggest one, a bearded male, was walking point. It picked its way among the rocks, peering about like a nearsighted old man. Occasionally it stopped to nuzzle a bush. Each time it lifted its head, the bell around its neck gave a cracked rattle.

He focused the binoculars on the woman, watching every motion of her head, every step she took. She kept her eyes on the goats, or looked occasionally back down the wadi. She hadn't glanced in their direction, called out to anyone, or evidenced any interest or surprise. Now as he watched she blew her nose casually in her fingers and wiped them on the coat. She didn't sing or speak, just trudged flat-footed and weary after the animals as they drifted on up the ridge.

He watched till she passed from sight. Then quickly crept around the inside of the depression, checking at each quarter till he was certain she was gone, sure she didn't have any other companions, goatish or otherwise. The team were looking at him. He put his right fist up and shoved it out from his shoulder; then turned his hands up and waved them back and forth.

The two attachments were staring. He made the OK sign to them, unwilling as yet even to whisper. Recon used sign language in the field, basically American sign but with some additional signals for tactical moves. They'd have to trust him that things were going okay. He checked his watch. Still only 0910.

It was going to be a long day.

THE GOAT lady put them all on edge. Those who had slept now lay glued to the peepholes, ears cocked for more bells. The sleet tapered off into rain again, then at last stopped.

It was even warming up a little, Jake Zeitner thought.

He'd maintained his focus through the march the night

before, wary of his earlier daydreaming. That was the kind of thing that got teams trailed, ambushed, killed. But now he wondered if he should have paid more attention to their tracks. The ground had felt rocky going down into the wadi, so he'd assumed they weren't leaving any. And of course they'd left none in the water. But on the way up here he should have checked their back trail. A patch of damp sand would preserve a footprint. He thought about leaving the hide site, scouting back to make sure. Then thought, No way, not in daytime. They'd just have to hunker down and wait.

Which was the hardest thing to do of all.

He remembered recon school. Foggy cold mornings, on the beach at 0430, runs and group cals carrying inflatable boats over their heads till their arms were dead and the fatigues sawed salt-raw gashes into their skin. Five-mile open-ocean swims with pack and weapon. Then class work in the old concrete-block buildings dug into a sand dune in Virginia Beach, and rehearsing tactics step by step in the scrubby woods overlooking the Chesapeake. The instructors were muscular noncoms with crew cuts, guys who'd fought at Khe Sanh and Hue City. They were marathon runners, SCUBA, Jump, and Ranger qualified, and led every swim and run from the front. They were profane and abusive but he could live with being dropped for push-ups and shouted at, called pussy and limp dick, pogy and asshole bandit. What sobered him was when they quietly asked a man to fall out and wait in the office. That student disappeared; you never saw him again.

Those who survived had gone to Fort A. P. Hill, hundreds of square miles of Rappahannock woods, for weeks in the field, testing and honing their skills. Most of the guys liked that part, but he'd dreaded the dark hours. Waiting on one knee in the dark, no sleeping, no talking, he'd start to imagine monsters coming through the trees at him. Jerk awake with his throat locked on a scream. He just didn't like waiting. Maybe he wasn't really recon material.

No, fuck that. He was twenty-eight now, for Christ's sake. He'd done all right in the Corps, but an E-5 only made nine hundred and twenty-six dollars a month, base pay.

He thought again about the doc. Not about her ass, this time, but the way she'd stitched up the pilot . . . he'd thought about med school once . . . but he was committed with Joel on the store. Firestone was a good company, they could make some real money. Put a wrecker on the road and they could service the interstate from Olean to Hornell. He could run a store. Sometimes he thought he was smarter than the other guys in the platoon. The gunny was sharp, but then you had guys like this Blaisell. Rednecks from down south or out west, yahoos whose idea of intellectual challenge was watching *Twin Peaks* while they were power lifting.

Around noonish a crackle turned his head. F.C. was noshing on a PowerBar. The sight made him hungry. He checked his sector again, then got his ruck open and found the shit-green plastic of an MRE. Pork Patty. There were heater packs in the issue rations, but the team threw them away when they repacked for the field. You could smell hot food hundreds of yards downwind. He ripped it open and squeezed the cold gristly mass into his mouth.

A distant motor stopped his hands. They all lifted their heads. A gas engine, not far off. It sounded like a lawn-mower or a chain saw, high and irregular. Caught Gault looking at him, mouthing, What's that? Giving him the hunched shoulders: I can't see anything.

The buzz persisted, moving till it seemed to come from directly overhead. They lay still. It sounded like an RPV. The little unmanned aircraft were noisy as hell, but so small and so high you couldn't see them. If that was what it was, it was probably theirs. But gradually it too faded back into the sound of the wind.

He looked at his watch. Noon. He reached out and patted the gunny silently on the shoulder, pointed to his watch. Mimed sleeping, pointed at Gault. Who nodded, let himself down onto his ruck, and a moment later was asleep.

Zeitner caught Blaisell's opened eye. He pointed to him and circled the horizon. Blaze made an unhappy mouth, but got up on a knee, picked up his weapon, and took a peephole.

THE AFTERNOON had mostly crept past when the boy found them. The first sign was a clack of stone on stone. Those who were asleep woke without motion or sound; simply opening their eyes as their fingers tightened on weapons. Gault held up his hand for silence, but it was like rebuking the dead.

They listened till it came again: the click-rattle of a pebble, kicked or thrown, landing on rocky ground. And with it the fainter rattles of goats' hooves searching over the bare ground, the occasional baa as they called to one another.

F. C. pointed at his peephole. The sounds came from down along the wadi, the same direction the team had come the night before.

See anything? Gault, signing to him across the hole.

Nichols shook his head. He aligned his rifle carefully, not bringing it to firing position, but lining the barrel up along the bearings he'd marked at dawn. He set his thumb against the safety and checked that the magazine was seated.

A stone hit and bounced a few yards away. It dislodged a little shower of pebbles.

The neigh of the goats, closer. Coming up from the wadi.

Gault pointed to the peepholes and in a moment they were closed. Crouched, the team waited in silence so total their heartbeats thudded in their ears. Head lowered, Maddox imagined she could hear the others' hearts. Her own was whamming away hard enough.

The crunch and rattle of gravel. A cough. Footsteps

crackled, then ceased. Then came again, crossing the knob north of where they crouched.

Lenson's eyes met Blaisell's. The kid was breathing shallowly through his mouth. He gave back a broad grin. Too broad. He had something brown stuck in his front teeth. Dan noticed it with that strange feeling of timelessness, that sense of how important and unique the tiniest thing was, that had always come over him when danger was close.

For a long time then they didn't hear anything. Vertierra had his eyes closed, perhaps to hear better.

A stone struck the sheet, not a large one, but big enough to kick dirt off the bottom of the cloth. They watched it in silence.

Footsteps crunched again. They came over the lip of the knob, stopped, then came on. The air seemed to grow thicker in the pit. The team breathed through open mouths, staring at each other. Then the steps stopped again. For quite some time they couldn't hear anything. No sound at all. As if the whole world had stopped, except for the racketing engines in their chests.

Very slowly, the gunny lifted a corner of the cloth.

The boy was looking right down at him.

GAULT LOOKED up into the kid's face. He was unbearded and black-haired, very thin, with a seamed scar below his nose; perhaps a clumsily repaired harelip. Ten years old? Twelve? It was hard to judge; these people were smaller than Americans, and they looked hungry and careworn. The boy carried a stick like the woman's. He was in dark trousers and a worn jacket. His mouth had dropped open, and his eyes were wide and wondering, fringed with long dark lashes like a girl's. Looking into the muzzle of the silenced MP5, aimed directly at his chest.

Gault felt how cold the metal was as he slipped the safety off. Fighting the sense of horror, all the deeper for the knowledge, embedded it seemed in his very flesh, that he'd done this before. It was every recon marine's nightmare. The kid had to come down. He had to come down into the hole with them. He had to come *now*.

"*Salaam aleikum*," he said to the boy, forcing himself to speak very softly, in case there was somebody else down in the wadi. Detaching his left hand from the forestock, he beckoned him closer. The boy stared back but didn't answer. His parted lips didn't move, nor did he respond to the gesture. Gault noticed a blue rag wound around his throat. Some silver trinket dangled from it.

The sense of doom sank deeper. Holding those dark eyes with his own, he began taking up the slack in the trigger as he gestured again, more urgently now. If the boy came down, the situation was manageable. Duct tape him, stash him away, then when they left, soup him up on enough morphine he'd be out for the rest of the night. If he came down, they wouldn't have to do what he was being forced toward. The team didn't have heavy weapons or close support. Discovered in enemy territory, they'd be wiped out.

The equation was simple. Eight lives to one.

If the only thing that could save his marines' lives was this boy's death, he had no choice.

He knew all this. There was no arguing with it. The only trouble was, he'd already done it.

He'd already shot a child. And he didn't think he could do it again.

His hands were shaking now, the front sight wavering on the boy's chest. He tried again to pull the trigger, and again he failed. The moment drew out, drew out. Behind him he heard the woman mutter, "Don't."

And he couldn't. It might be an operational necessity, but he couldn't do it. Not looking into the dark frightened eyes, so close and wide he could actually make out a tiny image of himself reflected in them; not seeing the dirty small fingers slowly release the stick till it clattered to the ground. He turned his head and hissed to Vertierra, "Grab him, Tony."

But that was a mistake. As soon as their gazes unlocked, the kid flinched as if somebody had goosed him up the ass. He wheeled, stumbling as if his legs had turned to rubber, and pinwheeled into a run. "Get back here!" Gault called, raising his voice; but the kid was sprinting now, full out, waving his arms. Making good time too, zigzagging over the rocks as if he expected a bullet in the back.

A high gibbering scream came back to them. Shit, Gault thought furiously, shit, shit, fuck. We're compromised.

"Okay, everybody, strap it on. We're gonna relocate," he said, reaching for his ruck. They'd have to move out fast. Break contact, then hide up again. The CIA guy, Provanzano, had said this part of Iraq would be empty. Like shit! If you got away from the roads in the States, you hardly saw people. Here they were all over, the peasants or whatever the fuck they were, and their fucking goats scavenging for every withered blade of grass.

Sarsten reached out suddenly and ripped the sheet back. Light flooded in. Gault blinked, grabbing for him, but the SAS man was scrambling out of the hole, boots kicking wet gravel in on them. He was shouting in Arabic. The high thin cries of the boy receded into the gray silence of the wind. Briefly the horizon held two receding figures, one small, one larger. Then they both disappeared over the edge of the knob.

Gault fought the rest of the sheet back and stared with the others where they'd disappeared, wanting to shout, knowing he couldn't. Christ! God! What was Sarsten doing?

"Want me to go after 'em?" said Zeitner, beside him. No point observing noise discipline now. Not with Goat Boy yelling his head off.

"No. We'll head south, then dogleg east and look for cover. Stay together and move fast, and be ready to shoot. Shit! Where the hell's he going?"

Dan was pulling his ruck on, wrapping his elbows in

the unfamiliar straps of the 782 gear. He'd gripped his own weapon as Gault aimed up at the boy. For a moment he'd thought the gunny was going to shoot. Now he was sorry he hadn't. No, he couldn't seriously think that. Could he? A noncombatant. A child . . . He glanced at Vertierra, saw the RTO turning his transmitter on. Their eyes met and Dan understood. He was setting up to call in the extract. What good it would do them in full daylight, he didn't know. Sarsten had taken off after the kid, might even catch him if the boy stumbled. He reproached himself: he should have taken off after him too. Too late now, though.

Then Zeitner was yelling at him and Maddox, cursing them up out of the hole as Blaisell quickly coiled the wire to the claymores, pointing them out into a security perimeter. The team went to their bellies, covered their fire sectors.

When they were all in position, Gault looked around once more, at the bare wet-shining gravel, the empty distance beyond. He listened, extending his senses; lifted his head to scent the wind.

At last he got up and moved out, in a crouch, weapon at his shoulder, toward where Sarsten and the boy had disappeared. At the edge of the knob he dropped to his belly. He motioned: danger front. The team's weapons swung around, aiming at the thud of approaching boots.

It was Sarsten, loping back up from the wadi. Alone. They pointed their weapons to both sides as he approached. Gault went to a knee, waiting as the SAS sergeant jogged up to them.

"We don't have to move," Sarsten said. He was breathing hard. His eyes looked strange, flat, like he was looking through what was right in front of him at something only he could see.

Gault said, "Where'd the kid go, Sergeant?"

"I sorted him out."

"You sorted him out?"

"That's right." Sarsten quirked his mouth upward on

one side; it might have been a sardonic smile. It was hard to tell. The camo paint disguised the features, disguised expressions and identities, leaving only the flat gaze of those empty eyes. They could not be camouflaged or disguised, and looking into Sarsten's, Marc Gault felt suddenly he hadn't understood the man at all, as if he'd spoken to them in some foreign dialect unrelated to any speech he knew.

Lenson reached out, taking a fold of the SAS man's trou. Gault looked and saw it too. Black wetness, grains of gray sand. The SAS bent down and brushed off his knees.

"What did you do?" Gault asked him again.

"What you should have done, Sergeant. I waited for you to. But you didn't."

Maddox said, "He asked you what you did to the boy, Sergeant."

Sarsten smiled, a grim tensing of the lips that did not change the expressionlessness of his eyes. "I persuaded him not to talk."

"What's this dirt on your knees?" Lenson said.

"You bury your trash, don't you?" Sarsten looked back at them coldly. "Look, don't give me this shite. Do you know how I lost my team? One of these fucking shepherds saw us. I captured him. No, no, he said. I won't tell anyone you're here. We all hate Saddam. So I let him go.

"They ambushed us three hours later. Three truckloads of troops. They sorted us out. For fair." He looked down into the hole, at Maddox. "What are you looking at?" he asked her. "It was him or us. You rather it was us? What the hell are you looking at?"

"You," she said.

Gault cleared his throat. "Sergeant." He pointed a few yards off. "The rest of you, back into the site. Rig that sheet again."

"We're not relocating?" Zeitner asked him.

Gault said, voice hard, "Sergeant Sarsten says we don't have to. All right, Sergeant. Follow me."

When they were out of earshot, he squatted, getting them below line of sight if somebody else came over the top of the ridge. Sarsten looked angry. Gault noticed a stain where his knife lay sheathed against his thigh.

Gault told him, "You just fucked up big time, chief."

"Not me, chum. I did a job you didn't have the bottle for. That's all."

"You didn't have to kill him. We had ranger cord and morphine. Bring him back, that's all you had to do."

"And tomorrow morning every jundie's in Iraq out looking for us? What do you think we're out here for, mate? You and your team better switch on. Oh, and by the way. Next time you want an Arab to come over where you are? You go like this." He turned his palm downward and extended the fingers toward the ground, pulled his whole hand back toward him. "Don't do like you did, with your finger. He didn't even know what you wanted."

"You don't make decisions like that on your own. This is a team, not a bunch of independent operators."

"I may be *with* your team, Sarnt, but—"

"Don't bother going there, Sergeant. Your command attached you to me. That puts you under my orders."

Sarsten shrugged, as if to say, So what are you going to do about it? They stared at each other. Finally the Britisher said, "All right, mate, you said what you had to say, and I said what I had to say, and we're still all here together in bandit country. Now what?"

"Now you roger up that you're in line from here on out."

Sarsten hesitated, then nodded, face hard. Gault held his eyes a second more, then got up.

Back at the hide site Maddox looked up at him, then back at Sarsten. The SAS man didn't return her look. He just jumped down into the pit and folded himself against the bank, aligning his M16 along its fire marks again.

Zeitner started to say something. Gault whispered angrily that it was done, too late, to rig the sheet again and shut up.

When they were hidden again something tapped

lightly above their head. Dr. Maddox swallowed, looking up at it. The tapping came again. Again. A worm of water writhed down it. Then the tapping increased, swelled, till the steady roar of the rain isolated them all. Not one of them looked at another. Instead they looked off into the distance, or at the taut dripping cloth close above their faces. And the rain came down again, endless and cold.

11

22 February:
Western Iraq

The sound of the wind filled the night, and the smells of the desert; rain, goat dung, and wet earth, the sharp tense note of faraway smoke. They smelled their wet uniforms and their own body odors and the oily tang of their weapons. They marched through icy darkness, through a lightless river of scent and sound. Only ranger eyes, dots of phosphorescent tape on the back of their gear, saved those without night vision goggles from a collision each time the man ahead stopped. Then came strained seconds of listening, till at last the column would start again with the muffled crunch of boots on sandy gravel, the whisper-zip of a stunted shrub on a trouser leg. The harsh breathing that echoed the wind.

After Sarsten had killed the boy they'd simply waited, there at the hide site. No one speaking. Each occupied with his own thoughts. No one else approached the knob. The afternoon waned with incredible slowness. Then for a lengthy cross section of eternity the desert lit red, the last light dying in a coruscating glow streaked with contrails far to the west. Their eyes had lingered on the gunny, who'd waited motionless, save for an occasional glance at his watch.

At last he'd nodded. And they'd begun sterilizing the area; rolling and stowing the cover sheet, filling in elbow holes and grenade sump, triple-checking for dropped items or wrappings, rubbing out boot prints or any other sign human beings had spent a night here. When he'd looked the ground over, Gault gave Blaisell a compass course with finger numbers, passed the file-ahead signal, and moved them out, all without a word. Checking each man as he passed, expression invisible behind the inhuman insect eyes of the NVGs.

Since then they'd marched in silence. Some could see and some couldn't, but even if they'd wanted to, none of them could speak. So they spoke to themselves, and in the privacy of their hearts whispered what they dared not aloud.

Out at point, first in the slowly moving file that stretched out fifty yards behind him over the desert, Blaze moved step by slow step after the luminescent needle of his hand compass. He carried his weapon shouldered, moving it left to right and back again in slow sweeps synchronized with the arc of his head. Through the green circles of electronic vision coruscating shadows blended and shifted like black smoke.

It took practice and time to view the world at night. The heavy tube of the device, projecting like a downward-displaced unicorn's horn four inches in front of his face, set the muscles of his neck aching. He saw the desert limned in washes of green and black. The distance was hazed. He made out no horizon. Only a few yards ahead did the rocks and gravel emerge into clarity, into definition, swimming toward him as he advanced as if he walked across a sea floor many fathoms down.

He'd been sweating when he started, scared again, but it didn't take long before he was totally concentrated. Now he didn't notice his headache, or anything else, except an occasional flash of pure dread. If they made contact he'd get lit up first. If the ragheads had mines out here he'd step in the shit first. He just hoped it'd be a good-sized charge, not one of the little nut-cutters that popped up to crotch level and blew your balls off. He'd rather just die, quick and clean.

Thinking of dying made him remember the boy. For a moment, realizing what the SAS man had done, he hadn't known what to think. A kid. An unarmed civilian. But suddenly he'd caught on like all at once that this was what they meant when they talked about team loyalty, initiative in the field. It was like code. The goatherd or whatever he was would have called the village in on them. Hell, in another year he'd probably've been carrying a Kalashnikov himself. And understanding that, he'd smiled up at Sarsten, just to show him he knew, one stone killer to another. And Sarsten had narrowed his eyes and given him a cold answering look out of the black-smeared face. Cool as shit. The motherfucker was ice, all right.

He stopped thinking then and froze, one foot off the ground in midstep. Then put it down silently, heel and then toe, and stood without moving as he held his breath, listening with all his being. There. Past the ragged rasp of his breath and the swishing thump of his own heart; past the faint whine of the NVG like a mosquito inside his head. There it was again. Only what was it?

Voices?

He listened, sweating, as they ebbed and went away and came again and went away again. He couldn't make up his mind if it was men talking in the distance or the mutter and whine of the wind. He closed his eyes and turned his head slowly back and forth. Off to the left? He opened his eyes but there was nothing there. Just the wavering shadows, the black of night.

He centered his head where he thought it was and took a slow breath. Keeping his firing hand pointing the weapon, he reached up with his left and toggled the infrared illuminator on.

The world lit up. From murky olive the desert turned the arsenic of a burning flare. Black shadows leapt from the rocks in front of him. But even in its invisible light he saw nothing. No sparkle of return from metal. No shapes of heat source. He swept his head around, scything the beam across the team's front. He got only a confused impression of broken ground dropping away ahead. That one quick sweep, and he released the button and waited tensely for the space of three heartbeats. If anyone was out there with a night vision device, the IR illuminator would look like a searchlight. The wind fell, and rose, and fell again. A fine mist chilled his face.

He heard no more voices.

Inside his head flashed on a tape one of the guys in the LAV platoon had played over and over till they all could hear it even when the player was off. It was an old song by the Cure about killing an Arab. His lips moved soundlessly in the dark, shaping the words. Then he moved forward again.

BEHIND HIM F.C. Nichols waited silently, down on a knee, buried in darkness as a man lies immured in heavy earth. Wishing again, just like he had all the past day, that he had something to tuck in his cheek.

For the last hour he'd followed the ranger eyes on the back of Blaisell's ruck. They bobbed and floated through the Halloween dark, the only thing that gave light in all the world. He had a trick he'd picked up of putting his foot down flat, all at once, rather than heel and then toe. It seemed quieter, on the sand. It seemed to relax his leg muscles too. He got calf cramps on long humps. Then the point had stopped, and he'd stopped too, waiting, peering off into the dark to their left.

F.C. didn't have his goggles on. He'd turned them off. That saved the batteries. Plus he just didn't trust the things. They had their place. But a marine had to be able to do without everything but his rifle. After a while you grew a new sense. You could tell when something was in front of you. He didn't know how it worked, but it worked. You could hear better too. Your smeller got sharp. You could feel differences in the wind, like it was telling you what it had blown over, water or forest or marsh. You became a spider, senses webbing out into the dark and bringing you back more than your mind knew how to know. Feeling, if you were in the woods, the trees all around you; and sensing more sharply ahead, till you could tell if you were about to collide with a bole.

But there weren't any trees out here; and just now, waiting behind the halted scout, he felt the nothing out all around them. The cold wind unimpeded, whispering and then howling in his ears, gave him only the mist and a faraway smell of burning. The flat gravel and sand stretching out and away ahead of their slowly advancing boots.

He frowned. For a moment he'd felt something ahead. He reached out, but it vanished, floating away from the ghostly fingertips he sent after it.

Then the luminous spots danced again, receding, and he heard the crunch of Blaisell's boots. He blinked in the darkness and felt around with his free hand on the ground. Found a small ovoid and rubbed the dirt off it and tucked it into his mouth.

Sucking on the stone, he got up and resumed the march.

BEHIND HIM Gault halted too, looking off to the right. That was his sector. Each man had one. Eyeballs all around. The point man ahead, number two to the left, number three to the right. He didn't need to look ahead; he trusted Blaze for that. The kid had good eyes. Strung kind of tight sometimes, kind of a cheese-dick with his Glock and his smart mouth, but he was a good point. He felt confident about all his men. His mind played with that statement. About all *his* men. About all his *men*?

No, she wasn't the problem, as long as she kept up, kept quiet, and didn't try to pull rank. He only had one worry just now, and it wasn't even the Iraqis. It was Sarsten. The flint-eyed Brit was bad news. He wasn't part of the team, and that was a threat to them all.

The shepherd boy. Granted, he'd been a danger. Still,

Gault thought, we didn't need to kill him. A couple of Syrettes of morphine and some ranger cord, and they'd have been hours on their way by the time he came out of it.

But the kid hadn't cooperated, and he himself had clutched, hesitated. Had fucked up, granted; but Sarsten had taken that as an invitation to take charge. Gault didn't think killing civilians was SAS doctrine. He knew sometimes you had to do things that didn't go in the patrol report. When shit happened, a team leader did what he had to to save his men and accomplish the mission. Men had always done things in wartime they never spoke of afterward. And it was at least half his fault. But what worried him most was that Sarsten hadn't waited for orders. He'd moved out on his own.

A team had room for only one leader. And what had the man's own teammate called him, back at the helicopter?—"the Devil Incarnate." He'd thought it was a joke, a combat nickname. Now he wondered.

Damn it, Blaisell was still holding them up. They had to make distance tonight. More than he'd planned for; the dogleg south and then following the wadi had taken them off a straight line to the meet site.

He slipped the map out again and held it up, focusing the goggles, fighting their clumsy weight and the weird disorientation of monocular vision. The contours of the land, the lines of roads and wadis, blurred and merged. He squinted, trying to figure where they were and how far they had yet to go.

They were coming down out of the higher lands west of the Euphrates. Between them and Baghdad lay three large lakes, or low areas that would become lakes in the rainy season—like now. He saw more from memory than from the map how a network of roads webbed out between the middle lake and the lower. That neck of land was only ten klicks wide. Pipelines, roads, irrigation canals, converged there. The overhead imagery had showed chemical works and an airfield, an open yet presumably intensely patrolled area that men on foot couldn't hope to get through, even at night.

So they wouldn't go through it on foot. One of the tributary roads angled southwest from the neck area, running out into the badlands. It petered out into what the photos showed as a dirt track before finally dying at ruins along a dry wadi bed; then picked up paving again as it curved back toward the lower lake, the Bahr al Milh. That was where he was headed now, to the dirt track along the wadi, west of the lakes. Provanzano had said it was deserted. His imagery guys had gone back over the archives for four weeks and not one shot showed any traffic.

He pondered, wondering again if anyone would show up to meet them. If the contact could be trusted. If Syria could be trusted. If they weren't walking into an ambush. Then he noticed Nichols was up and moving again. He folded the map and stuffed it back, shifted his ruck to a slightly more comfortable position, and got to his feet with a barely suppressed sigh.

WHEN THEY stopped, Vertierra grunted, almost aloud. Then caught himself, and the sound died in his chest. *Silence. Stealth.* He bent and put his hands on his thighs, trying to shift the weight off his back. Behind him the SAS man was a black outline, an occasional clink or grunt or faint clatter of rock. The man did not move silently. Maybe he was tired, but he made a lot of noise. Now he heard the hiss of piss on gravel.

He didn't like the man behind him. Killing the boy . . . a dark-haired, small-boned child who if you didn't look too close might have been a K'iche' . . . it was too much like things he didn't want to remember.

You didn't decide to be a soldier in Guatemala. The military roamed the countryside in big green trucks, stopping every boy who looked like he was over seventeen. If he couldn't produce his *cedula,* his proof of age or military service, they loaded him into the truck then and there. And somehow getting their boots and their uniform and their *automatica* made scared peasant boys into killers of children and women. Like this Sarsten, this man behind him in the dark.

Also the Marine Corps didn't make boots to fit his size feet. He felt the skin rasping away, it felt like a piece of window screening, grinding in where the skin of his heels was blistering away from the flesh. He was sweating too and he had to shit. He hadn't been able to all day at the hide site. Not in front of the woman. He hoped he wasn't getting sick. Not when he had to hump the radio, the extra batteries, along with weapons and ammo and water. The RTO always had more to carry than anyone.

But there wasn't anything he could do about any of these things, so now he stood waiting, bent over, trying to still the trembling in his legs. He figured right here, right in the middle of the file, was the most dangerous place to be. An ambush, they let the point man go by. The tail-end charlie wasn't in the fire zone yet. It was the middle they aimed at, the communicator was the guy who got lit up. He bent over farther, fighting the need to let go in his trousers, praying in a strange mixture of English and Spanish and K'iche'. Not to the High God who had long ago abandoned mankind, but to the Cloud God, he who made the darkness transparent for those who feared him.

SARSTEN FINISHED hosing down the gravel and hoisted and shook and buttoned. He stared out into the darkness, wondering why he couldn't see anything. Then he realized, and turned his goggles off and fumbled out the batteries. He heaved the discards out into the darkness, inserted the new ones, and turned it back on. The twin circles glowed once again.

He was sorry about the shepherd. But he wasn't about to make the same mistake twice. The Americans didn't like it. He remembered how the lot of them looked at him when he came back wiping his knife. Like he was Charles fucking Manson.

So what! What did they think green work was all about! He couldn't even tell who was in charge here. Gault seemed to think he was, but who was the tall serious bloke? Who was the fucking bint, and what was she doing on a combat mission? Something was screwy. If they thought they could swan into Iraq like this they were going to get topped for fair.

He wondered again what exactly they were on about, out here. So far Gault had told him exactly fucking nothing. Okay, need to know, he understood that. The less people knew, the less they could give away if they were captured. The Regiment ran things the same way. But he couldn't help wondering. A hot mission, Gault had said. They were headed east, toward Baghdad. What was in Baghdad the Americans could be interested in, enough to send a team in?

He sat motionless, mouth suddenly coming open in the dark. Christ! There was only one thing. It was crazy, but it made fucking sense.

Somehow the Yanks had figured out where he was, tapped his phone or turned one of his generals to give them the tip. These lads were on their way in for Saddam. An assassination team. Covert as hell. The tall guy was CIA. The woman was some kind of bait. Once you knew that, it made sense. And somehow he'd lucked into it! The glory mission of the whole fucking war!

Somewhere in the back of his head he wondered if he wasn't getting it all wrong, if he wasn't going off himself. But no, he was just tired. Just fucking tuckers. And no fucking wonder.

He peered ahead. They still weren't moving. He grunted and sat down, resting the butt of his rifle on the gravel, and felt in his pocket and clapped two of the little triangular orange tablets into his mouth. Sucking on them, waiting for the lift, the surge, the feeling of super-human alertness and power and confidence it gave him.

Smiling to himself, in the dark.

FOR HOUR after hour Dan had followed the sound of Sarsten's footsteps, trying not to think about anything except putting one boot in front of the other. Trying not to think of what the utter darkness to either side might conceal. Of who might be out here with them, of what might happen.

Or of what *had* happened, back at the hide site.

He'd squatted frozen in the hole, too shocked to move, staring up at Sarsten as he brushed the dirt from his trou and jumped down again into the shallow, stinking trench. He couldn't forget the man's expression, a glittering fixity of eye that had moved from one face to the next, cruel, amused, patronizing. His first thought had been to speak. His second had been the sinking knowledge it was too late. The boy was dead. He'd looked at Gault and seen the same dawning darkness on the team leader's face. Reproach was futile; a waste of breath and a danger to them all.

All he could do was promise himself that when they got back, *if* they got back, he'd charge Sarsten with murder.

The mist sifted down, mingling with his sweat. He pulled his soft hat off, careful to move slowly, silently, and blotted his face with it. The wind and the darkness isolated them, locking each into his own solitary shell. Occasionally, as the patrol made a correction, turning slightly left or right, he missed his step on the uneven rock. Each time this happened he grimaced in the dark. He didn't want to think about turning an ankle out here, or of falling down some unguessable precipice. If the man ahead of him went over a cliff, he'd go blindly after him. He couldn't see the ground he walked on. The sky was black, cut off from the stars by the smoke and overcast. The earth was black, lightless as the sky.

Dan was used to darkness. He knew the blackness of a ship's bridge, the gentle roll of the deck. This wasn't like a night at sea. He couldn't say how, but even in a moonless overcast he'd always felt some form of invisible light rising from the sea. He couldn't say where it came from, or what held it during daylight and radiated it again by night. Or emitted or transmitted it from the cold phosphorescence of drifting organisms a thousand fathoms down, from the dark yet always burning heart of the ocean. Maybe it was imagination, fancy, but he could make his way on deck at night by its intangible luminescence. Could put out a hand and feel steel exactly where he knew it would be, feeling just the way he knew it would feel, cold and slick and gritty with spray-borne salt.

This dark was different, contentless and black as death itself. Only the grating impact of his boots with the desert floor told him a world existed at all. And maybe that too was illusion, maybe he was alone in the infinite formlessness of the void.

Against that nothingness his memory summoned images. The cupping of a white breast. The twining of long white legs, scratchy soft, about his own.

He'd met Blair Titus in Bahrain several years before, during what was for him one of USS *Turner Van Zandt*'s all-too-brief port visits, for her an area tour as defense staffer for Senator Bankey Talmadge. At first he'd been wary of her, wary of love. Disappointed twice, once by divorce and once by death, he'd tried to fight clear. But it hadn't worked. Or maybe neither of them had tried hard enough. They saw each other when they could, camping in the Blue Ridge once, meeting in Philly or Norfolk or Pensacola when she traveled on Armed Services Committee business and the navy shuttled him back and forth about the world. There never seemed to be enough time together.

The price you paid, he'd thought once, for being dedicated to what you did. And once he'd made the sacrifice, not gladly, but with the sense it was appreciated and rewarded. But now when he added it up . . . a medal here, a pat on the back there . . . a letter of reprimand there, and lately the cold feeling when he read a promotion list, went down the Ls to the Ms and back to the Ks, realizing at last he hadn't missed it; his name just wasn't there.

He summoned her again, like summoning a spirit from the darkness. But she didn't seem real out here. More like an actress remembered from a movie, a far-off dream of golden hair and shining body. His mind groped in emptiness, and returned to him.

His daughter, then, smiling aggressively as she stepped into a backhand. But Nan's image too was flat and lifeless, motionless as a photograph. Then he remembered; it *was* a photograph, the one she'd sent him of her Olympic tryouts. She hadn't made the final cuts, but she'd seeded well for her age.

Her life seemed so distant from his own. Life itself, all life, all light, seemed to belong to a world and a time long past. Surely he had always stumbled through this night like a ghost, following other ghosts, speechless and lost in a darkness that would last through eternity; would broaden into the eternal night of a dead universe, expanding slowly into nothingness and silence.

He shivered at the icy caresses of the mist.

BEHIND HIM in the darkness Maddox had recovered some burst of strength, some second wind. Some spurt of endorphins from outrage that blotted out the pain in her feet and the sore spasming in her thighs and calves.

She still didn't believe it. Not one man had objected. They had to have *noticed*. The mud on his uniform. The blood smell when Sarsten slid into the hole. The smirk. She'd moved as far away as she could, and he'd looked at her, once, as he slid in, the contempt and . . . something else in his eyes more than she could meet.

She'd squatted there, paralyzed, going through her options. Scream accusations at him . . . counterproductive. As well as dangerous. Shoot him . . . be realistic. She thought of insisting they go back and dig the boy up, so they could swear they'd seen the body. Maybe take a picture. Gault had a camera. This made more sense. But then she realized Sarsten would have to lead them to the grave.

She'd looked at him again, at the casual way he slumped against his ruck. She could threaten him all she wanted. But then what would happen the next time he was behind her at night? A man who could kill a child without compunction, without orders, without remorse?

So in the end she too had turned her face to the dirt, enraged at herself, at them all. At this insanity men called war.

Now, biting her lips, she hunched her ruck up on her shoulders, cinched the straps tighter, and went on in the dark. She felt dizzy. Her joints felt molten and somehow soft, like hot iron. Her legs shook when she stopped. Her load was too heavy; she realized that now. But she could carry it. She *would* carry it. Determining only one thing: that she'd speak to the gunny about Sarsten as soon as they could talk privately. She wasn't going to let this bastard get away with it.

LAST CAME Zeitner. He'd actually slept a bit during the day, to his surprise. Just now he felt good. Alert. Open to every sound in the night, every flicker in the distance. Through the NVGs it looked like heat lightning, soundless and distant; but something was going down ahead of them. How far ahead he had no idea, whether what he was seeing was antiaircraft fire over Baghdad or bombs or possibly artillery fire farther east.

He too was uncomfortable over what he'd just witnessed. It hadn't seemed necessary. Gunny Gault hadn't told the new man to do that. On the other hand, he hadn't actually seen what went on, and he didn't know what Sarsten had said when the gunny took him aside afterward. Maybe he'd just coldcocked the kid and taped him up and stashed him behind a rock. The dirt, hell, everybody had dirt on their uniform; they'd spent all day in a fucking hole. Maybe he was making stuff up.

It happened, alone in your mind, the way you were alone on patrol. Guys in front of you, but all alone back here. Tail end was the most dangerous position. If they made contact he'd be the last out. He had to emplace the claymore and heave the grenades. The claymore was an iron weight on his chest.

He turned his head and upper body uneasily, aiming his weapon out behind them. Only to find through the goggles the emerald seethe of amplified darkness, and nothing beyond that at all.

THEY MOVED steadily through the hours before midnight. Gault stopped every hour for a five-minute listening halt and breather for the attachments. When they halted, the marines deployed out into their security posture, attention and weapons aimed outward. Lenson and Maddox dropped to their knees, then backward onto their rucks like upended turtles. In the center, covered by the others, Gault, Zeitner, and Sarsten huddled over the map, a poncho over them to shield the disappearing-faint red spot of a combat flashlight.

Five minutes, barely enough time to catch your breath and adjust your gear. Nichols gnawed a PowerBar. Blaisell rubbed his face nervously. Vertierra squatted to finally relieve himself into a Ziploc, sighing with relief.

Then they were on their feet again, humping east once more.

THEY WERE picking their way down a slope covered with small slick flat rocks, shale or slate, when a terrific flash lit the sky to the southeast. A transient pulse of white-hot light; then, twenty or thirty seconds later, a solid detonation each man felt in his gut. They halted in their tracks, waiting for whatever came next. The rumble was like the end of the world. It went on for minutes, only gradually dying away. Blaze stared breathless, thinking, Somebody's getting his ass greased good.

Gault was thinking, That sounded like a fucking nuke. He turned and whispered in the sky-crackling aftermath, "Lenson up."

When Sarsten turned and gave him the word, Dan hustled forward, ruck banging painfully against his kidneys. There had to be a comfortable way to rig the thing, but he hadn't found it yet. A shadow, low to the ground; he stumbled over the patrol leader. A hand grabbed his web gear, pulling him down. A warm breath met his ear.

"Was that a nuclear weapon, Commander?"

He smiled in the dark. Then stopped smiling. Kinnear had given him the proword, after all. Was it possible? How would they know?

Then he remembered the radiac gear. He got his ruck off and went down into it. A rustle, something cold and slick between him and the dark; then the scarlet glow of a combat flashlight. Gault had draped his poncho over them. He set the AN/PDR-43N on the ground and turned it on, knowing he wouldn't get much of a reading, that even if it was a bomb the fission products wouldn't be here for hours even downwind. But the needle didn't move at all. He tried it again, got into the back cover, jiggled the batteries. Nada.

"The gear's down," he whispered to Gault. "But I doubt it was a nuke. An ammo dump, maybe. Do you want me to take this apart? I might be able to fix it, if it's a loose contact."

The gunny just stood up. "Not now. We'll just keep going," he said, and Dan jogged back toward his place.

SHE STARTED feeling faint around two. She'd felt bad for the last few hours. Each time they stopped she'd gone down flat on her back, looking up into the dark, hearing her heart pounding. Her legs throbbed. Then it happened.

The clatter, shockingly loud, brought the column to a halt. Zeitner's head whipped around; he'd been peering behind them, where he'd been seeing things for the last hour. First black curling things, like swollen snakes, at the edge of his vision. Then black ghosts, writhing toward them like like charcoaled, limbless corpses from a George Romero movie. He lifted his weapon, ran a few steps, and fell over something soft.

When he straightened, Sarsten was there too. "She go down?" the SAS murmured.

Zeitner didn't answer. He bent again, felt her shoulder, something softer beneath it; removed his hand quickly. Whispered, "You okay, Major?"

"What's going on?"

"She went down."

Gault knelt, got his ear next to her face. She was breathing, but her skin felt cold. "Major?" he muttered.

She jerked, murmuring something. He sat her up and ran his hands over her shoulders, neck, thighs. No blood, no tangible injury. "You hurt?" he asked her.

"No. I . . . guess I passed out." She tried to struggle up, but he put both hands on her shoulders, keeping her head down.

"We got a problem," Sarsten whispered hoarsely. "They know we're out here."

"I don't think so."

"I'm telling you, Sergeant. I can smell these fuckers by now. They know we're here. Not exactly where, but they're out looking for us."

Gault considered this, considered too that the man confronting him had probably gone sleepless for many days. "Take your security position, Sergeant," he told him.

"Did you hear me? I was out here three days and got ambushed twice. You better start taking this serious, mate."

"I heard you. Take your security position," Gault told him again.

When the SAS faded back into the night, he bent over the doctor again. "You been drinking water? You better drink some more. And give me this." He got her ruck off and swung it over one shoulder. It unbalanced him, but she needed the relief. He got her on her feet then and got them moving again, though not as fast as before; he passed the word up to Blaisell to drop the pace.

BLAZE WAS just as happy to. Not that he couldn't keep it up, though he was getting tired, but he kept hearing things. He didn't like to keep cranking along when he didn't know what was up ahead. So when Nichols grabbed his arm and muttered to slow it down, he just nodded and throttled it back.

An hour went by. They were moving uphill now, up to the lip or edge of a small ridge. He realized Gault was routing them along the high terrain now, along the ridge lines. Not a good idea tactically, but you made better time. Sure a hell of a lot of nothing out here. If there wasn't oil under this part of the world, he'd say leave these badlands to the ragheads. Nobody else would want them, that was for sure.

He came back from his thoughts at a rattle from the dark, and halted, holding up a fist: *Freeze*. He felt the team come taut behind him at the same time his own pulse speeded up. He turned his head from side to side. His ears strained into blackness as his hands tightened on his weapon. He gently touched the selector with his thumb, checking its position.

There: to the left; a clatter of rock.

Another herd of goats? A camel? A dog?

Or men in olive drab and scuttle helmets, a like excitement pounding against the bars of their hearts?

He waited for a long time, peering and listening. He didn't hear the sound again. Didn't see movement. Whatever it was had either moved away or had sensed them too and was waiting them out.

He checked his watch. They couldn't wait forever. He breathed out through a parched mouth, working his shoulders against the straps of his ruck.

Then he motioned Nichols forward, and they moved again, one after the other, into the darkness all around.

BACK NEAR the end of the column, Maureen still felt dizzy, sick at the pit of her stomach.

She'd thought she was in good shape, but rock climbing was different from hiking for miles with weight like an iron burden laid across her shoulders, a hot iron nail hammered into her thighs. But she'd kept on grimly until at last the night turned solid inside her head, and the next thing she knew Gault was bending over her.

Now a foul taste lit her mouth. Her shoulders felt light, as if she was going to rise up and fly, as in a dream. One of them was carrying her pack. No doubt cursing her. The woman. The weak sister. Couldn't carry her load. Couldn't take the pace.

All she could do was keep going. And that was about all she could do, just keep putting one in front of the other. Hydrated, like the gunny said. She had to stay hydrated.

Her canteen was halfway to her lips when she slammed into the man ahead. Something metal clanged like a jeep hitting a brick wall. She dropped the canteen, caught it just in time, screwed the top back. Licked her lips, wondering how they could be wet yet her mouth still so dry. Lenson grunted something and disappeared. She moved quickly after him, afraid of being left behind, but then they collided again. From ahead came muffled shuffling, whispers, a click she couldn't identify.

"Break," the word came back. She turned to pass it on to Zeitner, lowered her pistol, and went on up, joining the circle on the ground, pointing her weapon out again into the surrounding night.

•   •   •

THE NIGHT wore away very slowly, like a wheel grinding black diamond. The terrain was rocky and uneven, and though Gault kept them on the high ground it all tended gradually downhill. This worked with the map, which reassured him, but Blaisell kept stopping. Even when the scout moved, the pace was too slow. They weren't making the distance over time. He'd planned for them to reach the rendezvous well before dawn, and have time to find an ORP and get another hide site dug in. Just in case the contact didn't show, and they had to stand by over daylight. At last he closed Vertierra up, told him he was going forward, and trotted toward the point, ruck slamming against his butt.

Blaze whipped around as he came out of the dark. He muttered, "It's me," and the weapon shadow lowered.

"Gunny?" A murmur so faint he might have imagined it.

He judged the wind gave them enough aural cover. He signaled back for a break and went to a knee. Blaisell joined him. He put his mouth next to the kid's ear and said, "We got to speed this up, Crusty, or we're gonna be still pulling our puds out here at dawn."

"I keep hearing things, Gunny."

"What kind of things? Where?"

"Can't tell. Like I hear voices sometimes. Almost, or like they're real far away."

Gault stood up. Focusing his goggles as sharp as they'd go, he checked their 360. Nothing. But the kid had sharp ears and eyes; that was why he was the scout. They were exposed out here. He was being careful. But maybe it was smarter just to get across this as fast as they could. He ran it all through his head and ducked back down. "It must be the wind. We got to step out here, Blaze. Pick it up."

"Got it," the point man whispered.

He signaled them up and the file moved back into motion. There, the corporal was moving it out now.

Almost too fast. But they had to make some of this time up. He let him go.

And now he was back again in the land of no shadow, submerged again in black so black it quivered in purple and yellow like the afterimages of strobe flashes. Above him the haze cut off the stars. The raw cold air grew a cough in his lungs. He swallowed again and again until it went away.

THEY WERE moving down the side of a wadi, the muddy slanted ground slippery under their boots, when they made contact.

Blaze heard them first, out at point. He didn't see them. He smelled them. Burning tobacco. No shit. It was just registering when he heard someone cough. Someone not in the column. Off to the right, maybe fifty, seventy yards.

He focused the goggles and searched that way.

He heard a faint jingle. He turned his head and clenched his fist in the halt signal; pointed toward the sounds.

Gault heard them too, and saw them: vague warm-green shapes higher along the slope, eighty or a hundred meters distant. He made it as a chance contact. If it was an ambush, they'd be dug in, invisible, the patrol would never see them till it was too late. It was bad enough as it was. The enemy had the high ground. If they had night vision, Soviet or Dutch, the patrol would be clearly visible, infrared-silhouetted against the colder ground.

So far, though, he didn't hear or see anything that indicated they'd been detected. The other patrol was upwind. If they were walking blind, UAT-12 might still be invisible.

"Danger right front. Cover, freeze in place," he whispered, and heard it go down along the line. He dropped too, merging his silhouette with the rocks. His right hand checked the HK, making sure the mag was seated, the selector on safe. He'd checked it sixty times that night, but he still checked it again.

It was probably a night patrol covering the antiaircraft site. Stay low, stay quiet, they'd most likely just go by. Should he set up a hasty ambush? No. His mission wasn't to kill Iraqi dogfaces. It was to stay covert. Avoid compromise, and carry out the reconnaissance.

Unbreathing, unmoving, flat on the ground, they waited. He heard another sound; something like the zip of steel against canvas. Just keep quiet, he told the attachments in his mind. Just let them go on by, whoever they were.

The sounds of men walking on loose rock above them. The clack of stone. The jingle of metal. Another cough.

He lifted his face from the ground and saw their shapes. Couldn't tell how many. Maybe fifty yards away, moving right to left in a diagonal across his original direction of movement. They were going past. They hadn't seen them. He relaxed, letting the tension that had built up in his arms and legs dissipate like a grounded circuit.

Then someone exclaimed, a surprised burst of words. He heard them clearly, but he couldn't splice them together into sense. He heard metal rattle, sling swivels, the click of safeties going off.

Someone called out. A challenge. He hugged the ground, silent and motionless. Even now they might decide it had been nothing, and go on.

Behind him a man laughed, and called a response in Arabic. The voice sounded familiar.

A moment later he realized it was Sarsten.

He was still trying to believe it when a succession of flashes jacked the night open, blinding him with fierce light as the NVGs amplified the muzzle flares. Yelling and shrill cries echoed from the dark.

They were ripped. Compromised. Snarling in anger, not at the Iraqis but at Sarsten, he pulled his weapon to his cheek, aimed at the flashes, and pulled the trigger. A moment of shock on both sides, then automatic fire erupted all over the side of the wadi. The rapid *kak-kak-kak* of AKs fought the muted stuttering of subsonic nine-millimeters. Green tracers flew over their heads, then moved down, arcing and bouncing as they hit rocks, glancing in every direction.

DAN BELLIED himself instinctively into the wet ground as around him the HKs and M16s stuttered and cracked. It took a moment to recall he was supposed to shoot back. He pointed, rather than aimed, and pulled the trigger. Nothing. The selector, damn it . . . it fired then and he pumped rounds into the dark, aiming where he figured chest level should be. Screams and more firing came from their left flank.

"Australian, Australian," the gunny was shouting. "Break contact, six o'clock, two hundred!"

The Australian Peel was a fast reaction to close contact. The first man in line, or closest to the enemy, fired out his magazine and peeled out to the right. In succession, the rest fired out their loads and leapfrogged back, one left, the next right, the next left. Done properly you ended up with a daunted enemy and the squad headed in the opposite direction. Done wrong you ended up with people shot and lost in the dark. Dan heard the command but it didn't register right away; he hadn't been drilled to execute without thought when he was tired and scared. He fired the magazine out and dropped the empty, clattering onto the ground. Groped for it, close to panic. No, forget the fucking empty! He needed another loaded one.

A shadow pounded out of the dark, rushing past. He jerked the weapon up and pulled the trigger. Fortunately it was still unloaded. The bolt slammed shut on an empty chamber.

And as if that foolish and unthinking act had unloaded all his fear, he felt a sudden detachment, a sudden flood of calm. He got to his feet, pulling at his mag pouch. A second shadow flew by, boots pounding earth. He wasn't afraid anymore, but it was hard to think. Hard to remember what he was supposed to be doing. Going with them? Or standing his ground, covering them? "Gault," he screamed. "Maddox!"

But all he heard was the crack of weapons, the steadily growing roar of a firefight in the dark.

BULLETS CRACKED over him. Gault shouted "Australian," gave the rally point, and dropped to a knee to pull off his suppressor. No point in it now, and it dropped the muzzle velocity of an already low-energy slug. Blaisell was firing. The light flared halos in his NVGs. He saw the point breaking right, closer to the enemy, but that was all right, that was the drill. He heard the deeper *boonk . . . boonk* of the 203: Nichols was pumping out grenades, laying forty-millimeter shells like a wall across their front. Flashes and screams, then the last round was in the air and F.C. was up and sprinting all out off to the left.

As soon as his arm-windmilling silhouette was clear, Gault picked out what hostile shapes he could and put rounds on them, sweeping from right to left to give F.C. more time to clear. He couldn't see much, the goggles flared each time he fired, but thought he saw a couple go down.

His magazine ran empty. He surged to his feet and sprinted off to the right with every ounce of adrenaline-boosted speed he could muster as behind him he heard Vertierra start ripping rounds off full auto. The night flickered and glared with fire and behind the lighter weapons he heard the *duh duh duh* of something heavier start up. It was firing tracer, and as each round went over, his goggles flashed like a close bolt of lightning. "Peel off!" he shouted to the attachments as he went by.

The firefight was degenerating into what it became every time he'd been in combat or live fire at night. A welter of impressions, noise, light, and confusion. The only way out was instant action, instant movement, every man knowing exactly what to do and doing it with split-second precision amid flying hot metal. Fire and maneuver, fire and maneuver, until if you were lucky you could disengage.

He ran past a black shape, couldn't tell who; he'd lost count. Then another loomed up, had to be Zeitner because the green ghost-shape had unhooked a square from around his neck and was pulling the little stand-legs out. The ATL held up a gloved hand as Gault pounded by, pulled the time fuze on the claymore, and moved out after him.

The fire slackened, the usual lull after the first ten or fifteen seconds as everyone ran out his first magazine. He scanned the night, looking for the guys who'd already doubled back, and picked one up loping out on the reverse bearing and pounded after him. The cold air was a ripsaw in his throat, but he couldn't stop; if he lost the men ahead, those behind would lose them too.

The chain had to hold. It was all they had. If they were going to get out they had to move together. He thought of the rendezvous and immediately wrote it off. They weren't going to make it, that was all. All he could do was to try to save as much of the team as he could.

A thud and flash behind them as the claymore went off, and a wild burst of shrieks and firing into the dark.

WHEN HE figured it at two hundred meters, F. C. Nichols slowed down. His heart was pounding but he wasn't excited.

Time to punch some targets, that was all.

He picked out a flat section of ground, wound the sling around his left arm, and went down to a three-point stance. He pulled off his goggles and pressed the contact on the side of the night scope. While it spun up he pulled another 5.56 mag out and laid it ready to hand. He turned his head and spat the stone in his mouth out onto the ground. Then laid his cheek to the stock and peered through the sight.

From blackness the hillside leaped toward him, magnified two and a half times into a perfectly visible slope of rock. A trail he'd not made out before led slanting down it. The enemy patrol must have come down it, from the top of the wadi, gradually intersecting their own course. Drawing closer and closer, till they couldn't miss each other. Sweeping the field of view downward, he saw the Iraqi patrol, spread out in open order on their way toward him.

He set in the range and thought for a moment about the misty air. Finally he set in a slight up correction and a couple of clicks of windage. Then quartered the crosshairs on one of the advancing figures and squeezed off. The rifle cracked, recoiled, ejected, and fed. The plume of dust just above his target was clearly visible through the scope when he regained his sight picture. He corrected and the next round dropped his man. He shifted smoothly right, moving legs and body, not just his arms, and breathed in and out and in and half out and squeezed off.

Rounds zipped over his head. They were shooting back, reacting to whoever was putting their men down, but aiming too high. He relaxed, letting the residual tension flow out of his shoulders. He saw them stopping, looking for shelter, looking for the sniper. When they stopped, he shot them. The others went down, taking cover. Now they were all taking cover. The headlong charge was over. Situation under control, thanks to F. C. Nichols.

Then he heard the howl of incoming artillery.

BELATEDLY IT occurred to Dan that he was supposed to fire and move out. Yeah, that was it, this was the one where you peeled out to the side and leapfrogged back.

Which side, he had no idea. He didn't see anyone between him and the flashes, though. If he fired he might hit whoever was left up there. His fumbling hand, numb and senseless as a Novocained jaw, located a fresh mag at last. He jerked the weapon up and somehow got it in. Racked the bolt and thumbed the selector to automatic and let it all go, aiming high just in case someone else was coming toward him he couldn't see.

Then he spun and peeled out, running in the crouch for all he was worth across rocks and sloping slipping scree. God, don't let me break a leg now. Huge tracers arched over him with a zipping noise. Bullets whacked invisibly around him.

Then a dazzling flash of light and a deafening *crack-thud* like a bolt of lightning. He started violently as a rattle sounded across the desert behind him, followed by screams.

He was alone, still sprinting all out but losing his wind fast. No one with him. No, wait, somebody else was wheezing along to his right. As they ran, the gunfire behind them slackened. To occasional pops, then silence. He couldn't breathe anymore. He slowed to an exhausted shamble, scared and embarrassed. The patrol had come unglued. Where were they? For a moment he felt terrified all over again, the panic of a man alone on hostile ground. Then he remembered. Back two hundred yards, and regroup.

SHE'D GONE to her knees at the shout behind them, not understanding the words but knowing it was wrong, whoever was yelling was wrong. The other soldiers would have gone by in the dark. Then the firing started, a terrifying roar. She dropped to her stomach and hugged the ground desperately.

When the lull came, she remembered her pistol. She fumbled for it and got it out and dropped it and scrabbled around for it. She half raised herself and aimed, then hesitated. Wait, wait, weren't they supposed to run? She suddenly realized she was all alone.

Her mouth was open when the earth seemed to heave upward. The darkness split like smashed rubies. She dropped again and tried to crawl down into the ground, tried to burrow into the wet gravel and rocks like a mole.

When it stopped, her ears were ringing. She called out, yelling their names. Gault. Zeitner. Vertierra. No one answered. Her mouth was utterly dry. She got a canteen to it but found it was empty, just a little fluid sloshing in the bottom, like an old coconut. Her finger found a jagged tear in the plastic where something had ripped it open.

A voice, a figure from the dark. She jerked the pistol up. "Who's that?"

"Me. Zeitner."

"Where'd you go? Where'd everybody go?"

"We rebounded back, like Gunny called. Then we couldn't find you. So he sent me back. Let's go, Major, we got to retrograde the fuck out of here."

That sounded good. She was getting up, not yet quite to her feet, when a red light flickered on thirty feet away. She saw the assistant team leader's body, arms flung into the air, a fraction of a second before it hit her. After that last memory—of a shadow suspended in darkness, flying toward her—came nothing.

12

22 February:
Western Iraq

He first regained a sense of self not completely, but only
partially; as perhaps an animal did. A self as yet name-
less, knowing it existed, yet lacking the endless current of
internal speech that is the marrow of the human mind.
Knowing only that it lived, and was in pain. Then sub-
merging again, into the black.

When he surfaced once more, his first thought in the
echo chamber of his mind was What's this in my mouth,
choking me. Then: What is that sound. And: What's
wrong with my back, why can't I move. When he tried to
straighten, the pain became almost too much to bear.

Gradually Dan floated up, not into light or knowledge,
but into torment and a throbbing roar. He could not at first
understand why he was bent into such an impossible
angle. His eyes seemed to be working, but they were covered with a dark cloth, and either there wasn't any light
on the other side of it or what lay over them was too
opaque to sense light through. His tongue explored what
he finally decided was cotton wrapped with rough twine;
a gag, around which he could barely breathe.

Then suddenly, as if he'd blocked it out till then, the
frontier of his self-awareness leaped outward and he
gasped with the agony in his back, his thighs, his wrists.
His whole body felt inflamed, as if he'd been beaten or
kicked while still unconscious. He was lashed into a

chair, but not upright. Instead he was doubled, head forced down even with his ankles. The posture was intensely painful and disorienting. He was also shivering violently, and he realized by the grating of body hair against his cheek that he was naked. The pulsing roar was his laboring heart fighting to push blood through the narrowed arteries of his cramped body. He jerked against the ropes, strained to lift his head. The line became steel wire. There was no give at all, his most frenzied attempt did not even shift the chair. Only the roar became louder, and he found he couldn't get enough air; and the red tide rose quickly up over his panicked mind.

But then it ebbed, and the unconsciousness stepped back. He was sorry to feel it slipping away.

He sat that way for what felt like hours. Now and again he couldn't help struggling. His body made him do it, but he permitted it without hope. Whoever had bound him had done this many times before. For some of that time he prayed. When he did, the pain seemed to recede. Or perhaps he was growing numb, from lack of blood flow or from the unbelievable cold.

But the worst thing was not knowing what had happened to the rest of the team. To Maddox and Gault, Vertierra and Zeitner and Nichols and Blaisell. Sarsten he couldn't care about. He didn't exactly wish him dead, but it would be cosmic justice if one of those bullets flying through the dark had found its mark. But what about the others? Surely the Iraqis hadn't captured them all. The marines were too good, too fast, too smart for that.

Therefore, the mission continued. And if that was true, he was still on the mission too; only his part of it had changed. For if by any word of his the Iraqis suspected their target, they'd double and triple the guards. Move the weapon, if such a thing could be moved.

All he could contribute now was his silence. To keep the existence and goal of Signal Mirror from passing his lips.

He found he wasn't afraid to die. He only feared he wouldn't be strong enough not to.

As the hours passed, his mind circled the same path and only wore it deeper. Till at last it ceased thinking at all, and he hung in darkness, a suffering atom in the midst of a chilling blackness.

Steps, suddenly; the quick opening of a door. The scuffing of heavy boots, and voices in guttural Arabic. He thought, Now they'll untie me, and the idea was so appealing he absolutely did not care what they would do to him after that; only that he'd be able to lift his head, and maybe move his arms.

Instead they lifted him, the chair or rack or whatever he was on as well, and carried it through a doorway (he knew because his shoulder caught on the jamb, and was rammed through with what sounded like a curse) head-first. The second room was as cold as the first, but then came a third and his bearers let him down with grunts and sighs. The legs of whatever supported him grated on some hard rough surface, tile or concrete, as they dragged him around.

Harsh tobacco-smoke. The stink of burning kerosene. It was much warmer here. He heard a cough, a clink of glass. From somewhere the sound of what could be either a radio or a cassette player, a woman singing. He'd always enjoyed Arab music and for a moment the terror stood aside or maybe he stepped outside of it and for several seconds lived in the lilting melody. Words that he did not understand, but a tone of longing and joy deferred that he did. All too well.

A coldness against his skin. Flat and smooth and metal chill. Then it rotated, and he felt the thinness of its edge. It moved idly, almost tenderly along his cheek below his ear. Then rotated again, and with several powerful thrusts sawed through the line holding his head down.

A hand slapped his head upward, and the pain of the suddenly released tension made him cry out into the gag. Then it too was cut, and pulled from his mouth so hard he felt the flesh rip at the side of his lips. He tasted blood.

"Lieutenant Lenson." The voice was that of an older

man, British-accented. He lifted his head, but for a moment couldn't speak. His throat did not seem to be working. Finally he said, "Present."

This seemed to strike several people as comical. He could make out three different laughs, though he sensed more than that in the room. He heard a movement behind him, felt a prod that might be a weapon. But the laughter came from ahead, so he flexed his neck, tilting his head back and working his shoulders, and faced that direction.

"Lenson. And Daniel. Those are Jewish names, aren't they? Are you Jewish, Daniel? Wait a moment—lift it up." Gloved fingers, wool by the feel, bored between his legs and found his penis. Held it up. To silence, and then to renewed laughter, hearty guffaws.

"You can't please a woman with that worm. Are all Americans that tiny?"

He didn't answer. Another voice said, "He does not like women."

"You don't like women, eh, Dan? You give pleasure to men."

More chuckles, but not as many as before. He kept his head up, trying to peer beneath the blindfold. All he could see was a faint bleeding of light.

More seriously now. "What religion are you, Daniel?"

He considered the merits of getting into a religious discussion and decided there were none. To these people, the only safe answer was Christian. "Christian," he said.

"Is your friend Jewish too?"

"Friend?" he said, but the interrogator did not seem inclined to pursue it. Instead there was a mutter of conversation in Arabic or Iraqi, whatever, he thought, they were speaking. Iraqi was a dialect of Arabic. Iraqi, then.

"What are you doing in Iraq, Daniel?"

This too took some thought. And he was not thinking rapidly, or well. So far, though, nothing they'd done to him exceeded the Naval Academy Plebe Indoctrination guidelines, at least as certain firsties had interpreted them when he was at Annapolis. He knew this was different.

There were no rules here, no limits. Still there was a grim reassurance in it, to remember he'd been through trials not unlike this. He cleared his throat and said, "Military operations."

"Let us start with your unit. I believe you will tell us the name of your unit? Will you not?"

This too took some thought, and he hung forward on the ropes to give, he hoped, an impression of weakness and maybe stupidity. Coming across as smart or functional did not seem like the best idea here. His actual assignment was on the staff of the commander, Task Force 151.11 in the Northern Gulf. But this didn't explain why he was in Iraq. Possible answers milled around in his mind. Apparently he thought for too long, because the interrogating voice spoke sharply and he was driven forward by a blow in the back from what felt like a rifle butt. "Your unit!"

"Sorry, I'm . . . not feeling too good. My unit's the First Surveillance and Intelligence Reconnaissance Group."

Some discussion of this; or maybe what was going on was that the first voice was translating, explaining, to someone else taking notes or transcribing the interrogation.

A strange cunning mind within his mind that he recognized but had not heard for a long time, an amoral underdog duplicity that had grown gradually in all his classmates during their first months at Annapolis, that was sly and resourceful and could never be obeyed wholly, for it was concerned only and always with personal advantage, whispered that this was a Good Thing but also a Bad Thing. On the good side, a transcription meant there would be some record that he'd been captured.

On the other hand it meant he was in the hands of professional interrogators.

Another question, pronounced loudly and somewhat pedantically. "Answer more rapidly. What service is this group associated with?"

"The United States Marine Corps."

Another word; another blow, this time much harder, and to the head. His ear caught the steel of the butt and he felt it tear, felt warmth trickle down his neck. He lay forward and tried to breathe, wishing he could see them coming, slip them a little. "Don't begin by lying to me, Lieutenant. You are US Navy. What is the US Navy doing in Iraq?"

"I'm an ANGLICO," he said.

A pause; then a slithering sound, the flip of pages.

"You're an Anglican?"

"No, an ANGLICO—an air and naval gunfire liaison officer. I can call in air strikes, or battleship gunfire."

"You obviously think we're fools. We are far out of range of battleship guns."

"But not of air strikes." He reflected briefly on how much to give them; whether that was enough. He decided to stop there.

But his interrogator didn't want to stop, and through repeated application of the gun butt and also of the odd lit cigarette to his ears and other sensitive areas, Dan gradually invented a mission for UAT-12 he thought might satisfy them. They were a reconnaissance patrol inserted to look for Scud launches. Once they saw one, or located Iraqi forces, they radioed in the location for targeting by aircraft. He let this go bit by bit over what felt like several hours, but knew it was nowhere near that long. The interrogator seemed to have all the time in the world.

Occasionally he would whiff a rich coffee smell, and the harsh tobacco odor was never gone. They were smoking all around him. Finally the interrogator was silent. Dan heard the rapid click of telephone buttons and a long conversation, during which he sat and enjoyed not being burned or hit. In the other room the radio or cassette player came on again, another female vocalist accompanied by what sounded like cowbells.

The rattle of a handset slammed down, and suddenly his head was dragged back. He gasped, but it was only the blindfold coming off. He blinked into the glare, realizing he was directly under a large fluorescent fixture.

The room was pretty much as he'd pictured it, except the walls were painted red to about the height of a man. Above that they were cream. Two large photographs on the wall, one of Saddam in Arab robes and the other of an older Arab he didn't recognize. A table with colorfully enameled demitasse cups. A rusty air conditioner in a painted-over window. Not one but two round kerosene heaters, both throwing a cheerful orange glow out over a floor laid with the square glazed tiles that back in the States would be called Mexican.

Reminding him, in a vivid sudden flash, of his ex-wife's place out in Utah. Seeing it so minutely it was like he was there. A rambling house, with high ceilings and low furniture and expensive-looking modern paintings. Vines on overhead sunshades. A sunlit checkerboard of light and shade on a patio with tiles just like this, and beyond an adobe wall the Rockies floating like tethered balloons. He'd hated the house the moment he stepped in, but now in memory it felt like a faraway vision of Paradise, a lost heaven of safety and comfort and belonging.

Three men sat facing him, all in the drab Iraqi uniform that managed to look at the same time both British and Soviet: green sweaters with shoulder tabs, their trousers tucked into polished Russian-style boots. They could be brothers, all three chunky and mustached. The one on the right had gray in his hair. In front of them on a folding table were objects he recognized. His dog tags—that was where they got the "lieutenant," then; he'd never bothered to change them, just pulled them out of his gray metal academy-issue lockbox and put them on without thinking. The Iraqis were smoking, looking at him. After a moment the oldest spoke, in English. "Cigarette?" The pack was blue. They were smoking Gauloises.

"No, thanks."

"Go ahead. No charge." The others chuckled and for a moment it might have looked almost companionable, four dudes sitting around in a warm room having a smoke and coffee. They must have caught his glance at the tray because one lifted the little teapot inquiringly.

The trouble with this whole scene was that he didn't know what to do. He'd never been to E&E, Escape and Evasion, the school pilots and aircrews told the stories about. Where you learned how to undergo interrogations, what to say, how to escape. The navy didn't consider destroyer officers liable to capture. He'd been trying to remember not just the Code of Conduct, but the GMI training he'd gotten in-theater on surviving a terrorist abduction. They'd been written for skyjackings, but. . . . Whoever wrote them had recommended trying to establish a human relationship with your captors. Accepting small favors was part of that. Establishing a common ground. At last he cleared his throat and said, "Is that Arab coffee? I love Arab coffee."

"Good, good, you love Arab coffee. Give him some," said the older man. For a moment he thought they might free his hands, but instead one of the soldiers held the cup out. He dipped his face and managed to suck about half of it up. It was tepid and sludgy and tasted great, though it stung the inside of his mouth and his lips where the flesh had ripped. He sat back and licked the grounds off his lips.

"I am Major Yaqoub Al-Qadi," said the older man. "Yaquob is the same as your English Jacob. So you can call me Jake."

"Pleased to meet you. Jake."

"It's a pleasure for us too, believe me. We've talked to others of your alliance. An Italian and another American. Pilots."

"Am I being held by the army?"

"By an associated agency," said Al-Qadi.

This sounded ominous, but they gazed on him so benevolently he dared to think the worst might be over. He tried, "Do you think I could have my clothes back?"

"Oh, no, no, we are still interrogating you," said the

major pleasantly. "We find our clients cooperate more quickly if we show them how agreeable things can be when they work with us. We both have the same goal, after all: to keep you alive and well. Things can go well for you if you choose. We can feed you and clothe you, and hold you for return to your home and family when this war is over. Are you a family man, Dan? Are you married?"

Giving them personal information didn't seem like a good idea. He thought of Betts and Nan. No longer his; the way he'd lived his life had somehow made that impossible. But in a sense still his family. His mother, back in Pennsylvania. He hadn't answered her last letter. And Blair; not yet wife, they weren't there and might never get there, but the closest to it he'd come since his marriage blew apart.

He said, "I'm only required to give my name, rank, and serial number."

The Iraqi shook his head. "Not a smart answer, Lieutenant. If we don't get what we need, you'll never see your family again. Which you choose is up to you."

"No, it's up to you. Iraq has obligations to POWs under the Geneva Convention."

"Only toward captured prisoners."

"Well . . . that's me. I'm a captured prisoner of war."

"No," said Al-Qadi. When he gradually stopped smiling, he resembled Stalin. "Not yet. When *we* say you are a POW, then we will turn you over to the army and you will be treated under the convention. But if we decide you are a spy and terrorist, things will go badly. If you do not tell us the truth, you will be sorry you came to Iraq."

"I've told you the truth."

"I am very sorry, but you have not."

Al-Qadi raised his voice, and the man whom till now Dan had not seen behind him went to the door and opened it and called.

Two more men, enlisted, he guessed, dragged a naked mass of blood and meat into the room. Dan stared without recognizing him until Sergeant Zeitner lifted his head. His eyes were swollen closed and blood covered his chest. The sergeant had obviously been beaten much more thoroughly than he had. No one spoke. The stoves gave off a hiss only slightly louder than the assistant team leader's stertorous breathing. A bright red bubble swelled and broke at his nostrils.

"I'm sorry to say Sergeant Zeitner's account of your mission is at variance with yours. Who are we to believe? You or him? Or more likely, neither of you, since you are both concealing what you are really here for?"

Dan stared at Zeitner. His eyes peered out like those of a heavily beaten boxer, blinking slowly and leaking fluid or tears. He couldn't believe Zeitner had told them what UAT-12 was actually out here for. Had he lied too, made up a story? And then of course their fabrications hadn't matched. Good going, Lenson, he told himself accusingly.

He told the major, "His name's Jacob too."

"Well, this Jacob is even more stubborn than I am." The others chuckled. The major lit another cigarette slowly. "Sure you won't have one?"

"No."

"Sergeant?"

Zeitner stared from under swollen lids. He noticed Dan then and blinked, raising his head a little as if to see better. His lips moved but nothing emerged.

"Sergeant?" Dan said. Zeitner didn't respond. He asked Al-Qadi, "Is he wounded? Or did you do that?"

"He was wounded in the battle," said the major. "Actually pretty badly. Our soldiers shoot straight."

"Can't you get him medical attention?"

The major got up and took a turn around the room, fingering his mustache. "Well now. Let us think about that. America has been bombing us for four weeks now. Many, many children hurt and killed. Who do you think should get medical care first? Him, or our children?"

"If you have a medic here, he could look at him. Maybe it wouldn't stop him from helping the children too."

"I'm thinking about it. It might be possible. Tell me something, though. You say you are part of a reconnaissance team. How many men are in this team?"

He was about to answer, figuring that wouldn't tell them much; obviously it was a small unit, recon teams didn't move in force. But instead he caught the warning glance the sergeant gave him. It was just a microsecond of awareness peeping out and then slipping away again, furtive but saying as plainly as any speech: *Don't talk to them.*

Then he understood, and felt shame at his willingness to play. The coffee taste was bitter in his mouth. Zeitner hadn't bothered with games, or guessing what the Iraqis did or didn't know or would or wouldn't believe.

"He hasn't told you a different story," he told the major. "He hasn't told you anything. He hasn't said a word."

"No, he hasn't. But he will now," said Al-Qadi. He spoke to the guard.

Dan didn't see what they did to the man beside him. He'd closed his eyes. He was a fucking coward, that was all. He just couldn't look. But he heard the screams. When they stopped he took a few deep breaths and forced his eyes open again.

"What is your mission, Sergeant?"

Zeitner said, in a hoarse but perfectly clear voice, "All I want is to start a Firestone station."

None of the Iraqis spoke for a few seconds. Dan saw that though the other two officers didn't speak much English, or had not spoken it so far, they looked puzzled, as if they'd understood that. The major said, not taking his gaze off Zeitner, but speaking to Dan: "What is he talking about?"

"I have no idea," Dan said. "He's probably delirious."

"No, I don't think that's it. I think he's laughing at us. He thinks we are stupid!"

"I don't think—"

"You Americans think Iraq is a backward country. You think Saddam is a dictator, that we follow him through fear. But Saddam is our father. We obey him because we love him."

The major launched into what sounded like a rehearsed speech, walking back and forth and talking half the time to the portrait of Saddam. "Before he showed us the way, our country was weak and divided. Coup after coup. Worse than that: we were strangers to our inner selves. Our moral spirit was weakened by the Zionists and their friends the Persians and Kurds. Now it is strong, and therefore our country is strong. We are an advanced country now. There are no more rich and poor, like there were under the king. I remember those days very well. If you were not rich you were dirt under their shoes. Now every child is a child of Saddam. Iraqi citizens are proud to follow such a leader. I myself have fought for him against the Pesh Merga rebels and against the Zionists and the Persian invaders."

Dan thought about answering, but now every word felt like a betrayal of Zeitner's stubborn silence. So he didn't. The major went on for some time, telling them how much Saddam had done in Iraq, how he had won victory against Iran despite America supplying the Ayatollah with weapons and cash. The others sat silently. A pencil was scratching. Dan saw the one on the right was the note taker. Every so often the major paused, waiting for him to disagree, but he didn't. He didn't speak at all.

Finally the major switched back to Arabic, then took his seat again with the others. There was a discussion; then one of the guards left. He came back with a blanket, plain olive drab wool, dirty, with spots of what looked like brown paint. He draped it around Zeitner's shoulders and stood back. Dan felt a shiver run over his own body, his icy flesh craving that blanket. Now that Al-Qadi'd gotten his defense of the Great Saddam off his chest and on the record, maybe he'd get one too.

The guard went over to where the stoves hissed. He came back with a gallon can, an unmarked shiny tin can. He held it up, and the major nodded. The guard unscrewed the cap and poured a stream of fluid around Zeitner's head. It soaked into the blanket, turning the drab wool dark, like a dark collar around his neck.

Dan smelled it from across the room. It was kerosene, or diesel. Whatever they were using in the stoves. He couldn't speak as the man kept pouring. He told himself they wouldn't do it. It was an interrogation trick. Zeitner was moving his head around, blinking, looking down at the blanket as the fuel soaked in. He didn't look as if he understood what was going on. Dan wondered what they'd done to him before they brought him in.

Another enlisted man had come in with fresh coffee while this was going on. He gave the guard with the can a wide berth as he passed, and set the tray in front of the major.

Al-Qadi pulled the sleeves of his sweater down and poured coffee. This time he didn't offer any to Dan. He looked unhappy, as if he didn't want to be part of this, but he didn't look all *that* unhappy. More like someone who had to do a lot of it. He went over to Zeitner and tilted his head back. Looked into his eyes, then let his head drop back down.

"This one doesn't cooperate," he told Dan. "But you will."

He took out the lighter and flipped open the cover. He flicked flame and held it off to the side. Zeitner's gaze followed it. Dan knew from that that he was still there. The flame rose straight and clear, heat shimmering the air.

"Your mission here," the major asked Dan. "Tell me now."

"I told you, we're hunting Scuds—"

The lighter went down to the blanket. The flame played over the wet wool for a moment, then a blue flame curled up. It turned a smoky yellow as the wool wicked fuel up to it. It was only a few inches from Zeitner's face.

"There are no Scuds this close to Baghdad."

"That's what we're here to find out."

"I think you're an assassination team. Sent here to poison our wells. To kill our children."

"No. We're reconnaissance. Marine reconnaissance."

"Yet *you* are navy." Al-Qadi looked down at where the flame had grown, expanding gradually out over the wool as it heated fresh fuel along its edges. It sent a wavering tongue up not far from Zeitner's ear. The marine must have felt the heat, because he rolled his head away; though he couldn't move it far. "Tell me again why you're with them. I just find it interesting."

"I told you, I'm here to call in the air strikes."

"When you find these Scuds."

"That's right. Put the fire out!"

"But the marines must have their own means of calling in air support," the major said thoughtfully. "I believe I have read that in the intelligence about US forces. Yes, I am sure I have. There must be another reason the navy is here. Something to do with the invasion."

Dan said, "What invasion," before he could stop himself. As soon as it was out of his mouth he understood what a mistake it had been. Each word he uttered increased their danger. He should not have spoken at all.

"He's badly wounded," said the officer who was taking notes, speaking English for the first time. His accent was thicker than the major's. "Without medical help he will not live."

"Get him some medical care. Then I'll tell you everything I know."

"No, I think you'll tell us now," said Al-Qadi. He sounded more interested than he had before. "Yes, I think you should tell us more about this invasion. An amphibious landing, is that right? The navy and marines are going to land in Kuwait and drive us out. Of course we are ready. But I wonder just what it is you don't want to tell us. Oh, I can tell there is something you don't want us to know. I have been doing this for many years, you see. You don't have to say a thing. I can tell just by the way you are sitting. I can tell by the way you are holding your head."

Zeitner began to move, jerking against his ropes. The chair rocked. The flames had moved around his head now. They were coming up all around his face. The fuel burned dirty, lifting a dark haze of soot particles and gray smoke. The air in the bunker, or room, or wherever they were, began to darken. The major and the other men watched, looking bored.

Dan thought then, I have to tell them. They mean it; they'll burn him to death.

No one knew they were there. They were totally and completely at their captors' mercy, and Zeitner wasn't going to talk. He, Dan, was the only one who could save them.

Then he understood. To tell them would save Zeitner, and perhaps himself. But it would doom hundreds, maybe thousands, of others. Marines and Coalition allies. Men who'd die if the Iraqis redeployed the Republican Guard from the threatened beaches to the southern border.

This was the hard edge that cut to the heart.

He had to let Jake Zeitner die.

WHEN THE screaming ended, when the charred, blistered face stopped moving, Al-Qadi said something to the guard behind Dan. He heard the slide of metal on leather and a click. Then a shot cracked, deafening in the enclosed space, and he felt wetness and fluid on his naked skin, and smelled the sickeningly sweet scent of brain matter.

When he looked again, Zeitner lay still. The blanket was still burning. Most of the forehead had been blown away by the exiting bullet. He saw the glistening surfaces of brain and blood, the dark cavities of sinus before he looked away, back at the bored men at the table.

The major was talking on the telephone. The conversation was rapid and somehow muted, as if he was making a report to a superior. He listened at the end, said, nodding rapidly, *"Nam, Sayidi,"* and hung up. He seemed to ponder for a moment, and one of the others asked him a question. He replied in a word or two, then looked at Dan.

"I have always found it hard to predict what will make a given man decide to cooperate," he said. "The truly brave will not speak. Like your comrade here. Not for a long time; not for days or weeks. But we know about the American marines, that they have to kill a member of their families before they are accepted into the Marine Corps.

"But most men will submit once they see a friend or wife or child threatened. Occasionally, I would say this of the cowards, one must operate directly on them. I think you are one of the cowards. Otherwise you would have saved your friend. What do you think?"

He sat rigid, still unable to feel or even think through the horror and the disbelief. But dimly he knew anything this man said was a lie. And any reply to him, a mistake. If he'd kept his mouth shut, like Zeitner, they'd have given up eventually and turned them over to the army. Now his fumbling, his fucking cleverness, had killed Jake. And probably himself.

And under that again yet a colder and older part of his mind knew that it was exactly this his interrogators were counting on: that he would act now out of guilt and fear rather than from what he still knew to be his duty. His feelings struggled below the surface of his still numbed mind, like carp tumbling just beneath the surface of a pond too murky yet to see into.

He knew then there was no way they'd release him now. Whatever this was . . . Mukhabarat, secret police, military intelligence . . . he wasn't leaving here alive. So there was no alternative, no way of second-guessing or tricking them. He could tell them what he knew, or he could die as silently as Zeitner had. Those were the only choices left in his life.

He set his teeth and sat looking stonily ahead.

After a moment more the major sighed, and spoke to the guards. The other watchers sat back, gazes gone distant, as if now he was no longer a human being to be reasoned with or threatened or even tormented, but only a thing to be disposed of.

He felt a set of what felt like headphones being slipped around his skull from the back. It fitted tightly and felt wet. He couldn't see what exactly it was. It didn't go over his ears, but pressed against his neck and his temples. The guard lifted a gray wire over his head and handed it to someone out of his view, somewhere behind him.

He felt his courage failing and looked at Zeitner. Whatever they did to him, peace and some form of honor lay on the other side. As long as he didn't talk. He'd spoken all the words he had to say in this life. He thought of biting through his tongue, but decided, Only when I can't stand it anymore. With any luck he could swallow the blood without them noticing, pass out, and die of blood loss. Not much of a hope, but a last despairing tactic.

The first shock was worse than anything he'd expected. He'd touched a cattle fence once as a boy, felt the fiery caress of electricity. This was different, a white hot bar of current that seemed to flow not through his brain but down his back. He arched in the chair and his hands locked, straining against the back of it. A whimpering grunt came through his locked teeth. He couldn't breathe.

He set his jaw and waited, eyes closed, for the next level of pain. It didn't come right away. The major stood by the desk, lighting another Gauloise. He said, "Listen to me. Dan. Are you listening?

"In a little while you will no longer be conscious. Yet you will still be able to speak. What you now think of as your mind will no longer exist. We will be talking to something beneath that. It will tell us what we need to know. That is how this process works. It is much faster than our old procedures. But no one who goes through it is the same afterward.

"Iraqi people are fundamentally kind. We do not like to see suffering, even in animals. Those who administer above me are convinced your presence here has some significance. They want answers and they will not wait. I ask you one last time. One: what your reconnaissance team is here for. Two: everything you know about the seaborne invasion of Kuwait, where it will take place and when, all the forces involved. Otherwise we will have no choice but to proceed." He gave it several seconds, then, when he got no answer, nodded to whoever was behind Dan.

This time there was no pain but only a dazzling whiteness. As if he was immersed, drowning, in a cauldron of incandescent hot metal that for a moment magically did not burn—but only because the enormity of the pain exceeded his brain's ability to sense it. He tried to hold the thought that he couldn't speak. If they found out that the amphibious landing was off, that it'd never happen, they'd move their forces south, away from the coast. The thrust up into Kuwait could fail. It might even lose the war.

But then the pain arrived, so overwhelming he screamed again and again, the sound muffled through jaws welded shut by the current.

When it stopped, he panted for long seconds, feeling warmth beneath him and dripping between his thighs. Smelling his own shit. The pain didn't go away. It had only stepped outside his skull for a moment. He felt it beside him, its hand warm and possessive on his shoulder.

"Where will the Americans attack?" a voice he didn't recognize asked. It sounded friendly. Concerned. And without knowing where or who he was, he told it, "Faylakah Island."

"No—no. I meant the main assault, in Kuwait. Where will the marines land? What will the forces be? How many men?"

And then the memory of self returned, and he knew what he'd said. He swore and cursed, threatened, knowing he was speaking insanity. The voice—he remembered now whose it was—didn't threaten or laugh. It just waited.

In that despairing moment, he knew he'd tell them. They'd burn away his mind, piece by piece, until what was left told them everything. Maybe Dan Lenson would still be sane when it was over. He hoped he wasn't. He couldn't live with that knowledge.

He was opening his mouth, taking a deep breath before he bit down, when strong hands seized him. Jamming, forcing a piece of whittled wood between his teeth. Wedging them just far enough apart so he could speak, but not close his jaws.

"We know what you're thinking," the major said. "We've done this for many years, Dan. We're the experts. Do you understand? The sergeant didn't know. He's only a sergeant. But you're an officer, Dan. You know much more than he does. I think you know what the American plans are.

"You're going to tell us everything now."

HE DIDN'T know till afterward what it meant. His mind wasn't thinking thoughts by then. But his staring eyes registered the sudden blackness in the room. The startled exclamations around him in the dark. Then the clink as a cigarette lighter was flipped open.

Major Al-Qadi's face, lit by the upraised flame.

An appallingly bright flash, a crack so loud he couldn't help crying out. In that brilliance something his eyes could not quite credit. The face of an avuncular Stalin suddenly growing a third nostril. Then another black hole, between two startled eyes.

The flame whipped away toward the floor. The room lit by crack after crack of strobe-swift flame. The flashes, lurid and somehow movementless, illuminated the shapes of men rising from where they sat, trying to draw pistols, reeling back with upthrown hands.

Moving among them, a crouched shadow with goggled head, aiming the spurts of flame. Behind it two others, with the same distorted, inhuman heads, like kachina dolls. He saw without understanding their eyeless eyes, a queer pointed snout that turned from side to side, extended arms tipped with angular darknesses from which the flame leaped, again and again.

Then darkness once more. And in the ringing silence after, moans. The ringing crash as a table overturned, of brass teacups and servingware kicked across a tile floor.

A hand settled on his neck. He flinched away, and heard an insane gibbering burst past the wooden angularity that filled his mouth.

Flashlights, and sight, and with the moving illumination a faint enlightenment within his brain. Figures in desert battle dress, night vision goggles on their faces, and pistols in their hands. From racked memory came an image but not a name; a man in black and denim, big, broad-chested. His hands tilted what was left of Zeitner's head back almost tenderly.

Then he didn't remember anything, and it was all a warm blackness into which he let himself slide.

THEY ALL right?" said Blaisell. He held the Glock in a two-handed shooting stance, guarding the door in case anyone unexpected arrived. Lenson didn't move, and Blaze glanced again, swallowing, at the sagging figure in the other chair. The spatter of blood and white stuff on the floor around it. He looked angrily at the other bodies slumped around the room, across the table, where they'd sat and where they'd died.

Vertierra had taken out the sentry with a knife. Then the gunny had come in from the other side of the building; thumbs up, all clear. They'd searched quickly around the exterior of the building and found the power cable. A snap of cutters, a flash of spark, and the lights in the windows went out. Then to the door. Sarsten, motioning them back, had kicked it open and tossed in the flash-bang. Gault had covered his goggles to avoid flaring them, then followed his weapon through. Vertierra close after, the MP5 ready, and Blaze had the Glock out and went through last. And then another flash-bang and into the room.

They'd followed Sarsten in fast but hardly got to shoot. He couldn't believe what he'd seen. A flare of light, and the SAS soldier had double-tapped the first man, shooting with a smooth unhurried skill that could be seen and still not understood, smooth and rock-accurate. Sarsten fired and moved till not a man was left standing and the magazine had clattered away empty and another one snickered in. And then he, Blaze, saw the guard coming from behind the guys strapped down in the chairs, starting to bring up the AK, ready to fire even though to him it must have been still pitch dark in the room, and he put the sights on him and squeezed the trigger until the guard reeled back and hit the wall and fell. Pictures under glass shattered down from it. All in the green weird light of amplified infrared.

He looked at Sarsten again with awe. He'd never seen anyone handle a pistol like that.

Gault came over and looked at Lenson. "Cut him loose. Get some clothes on him. His ruck's in the front room."

"What about Jake?"

"I'll look at him. You take care of Lenson. Get moving, we can't stay long."

They found stove fuel, several gallons, and poured it over desk and couch and the bodies. When all the tins were empty, they backed out. Vertierra threw in a white phosphorous grenade. As they humped away, Gault and Sarsten carrying Lenson and he and Tex-Mex what remained of Jake Zeitner, the building suddenly lit the night for a hundred yards around. The glare increased as the roof exploded, then gradually waned. It popped and crackled as ammunition cooked off.

They collected the doc, who'd stood security outside,

and went about four hundred meters south, away from any possibility of being backlighted, and knelt with their E-tools. They wrapped Zeitner in his poncho liner and got enough dirt and rocks piled on top of him to keep the dogs off. They divided up his food and ammunition and drank what was left in his canteens. Not talking, just sitting on the rock pile. They rested there for five minutes, while Gault took a GPS reading on the grave site. Then they walked back to the vehicle Vertierra had found parked a little way from the building, and shoved off.

For a long time Blaze kept looking back at the fire flickering on the horizon, like a Viking pyre. Then it died down and he couldn't even pick out the spot on the black desert, receding already into the distance, where it had been.

13

0500 23 February: Western Iraq

Gault kept low in the vehicle, his goggled head thrust forward. It was still dark, though barely, but since they were on a road, of sorts, eyes might be on them in the waning night. At the rate the light was coming, a good set of night glasses might give them away.

They were descending a trail of some sort, just grooves worn down into the dirt. From time to time pumping stations or farms slid past. Only a few were lit. Gault figured the bombing had knocked out the Iraqi power grid. The glow was probably gasoline lanterns. There'd be militia there, sleeping in the dark with weapons beside them. He glanced left and caught the shapeless blur of the driver. Vertierra. Tony, Gault, and F.C. were in the front seat. The others were wedged tight in the back, lying down in each others' laps so their heads didn't show.

It was a Soviet-made command car, the same kind the Syrians used. The suspension telegraphed every bump and pothole straight up his spinal column. The RTO had found it parked behind the building prior to their going in after Zeitner and Lenson. He'd gotten to it first and held up the keys in triumph. When they got in after burying Jake, Gault had studied the map for a few seconds, then pointed northeast. "That way. And for Christ's sake keep us in low gear." Tony had started it, clutched, and managed to kill the engine. He did it again while they hissed insults at him, called him Low Rider, told him to let them drive, but he finally got it moving. Gault told them to have their weapons under cover but ready. If they came to a roadblock or a patrol they'd have to react fast.

Now, passing through a village, every window dark, every occupant asleep except for a barking dog, he wondered if going vehicular had been smart. Generally you stayed clear of roads in hostile territory. But it was the only way they'd make the linkup in time. With the firefight, and the major's problems on the march, and now Lenson to carry, they couldn't hump wadis anymore. It was this or abort. And he wasn't about to abort. Not after the price they'd paid.

He felt angry and guilty. Angry at Sarsten's insane taunt, the shout that had started the firefight. Guilty that he'd gotten to the intel post too late to save Jake. He missed the New Yorker's understated competence already. Son of a bitch, and the bitterest part was Zeitner had already pulled the pin on the Corps. If not for Saddam he'd have been out, managing that tire store upstate with Daro. He'd met Daro. Not the kind of woman he cared for, but Jake had. Fuck! Now he was a corpse in a poncho, getting cold under a pile of rocks.

Clinging to the windshield, looking ahead for the first indication of roadblock or minefield, he forced himself to go over the linkup procedure once again.

IN THE back, huddled on the right side, Dan wasn't thinking clearly. He couldn't be where he was. With the team again, in the backseat of a car? Yet this was Major Maddox beside him. He could feel the silky prickle of her hair, which had come unpinned and was lying across his shoulder. Part of it curled against his chin. He felt the hard metal of his weapon too, lying across his lap. He dug his fingers into it till he felt the nails bending back. He wanted to bring it up and pull the trigger, kill someone, but when he tried, Maddox pressed the barrel back down. Then laid her glove along his cheek, a caress that startled him, that made his confused rage lower its head and close its eyes.

Someone was talking to him, but he couldn't listen. The words didn't make sense.

He blinked into the grinding dark. He could drag back Al-Qadi's face. The smell of burning wool. Then, just for a strobe flash, Zeitner's exposed brain, the red gristle that had a moment before been a human face.

He turned his head and vomited again, but all that came up was bile and acid. It burned his lips and he ground his sleeve against them, relishing the ability to move, relishing the ability to choose his pain even if he couldn't control his mind. It careened out of control, frenziedly replaying what it had seen and suffered. The deafening crack of a pistol by his ear. Zeitner's head flying apart.

The silver-laced whiteness when the current was turned on.

Beyond that, he didn't remember. Not remembering didn't bother him. He wished he could forget it all. But he couldn't; he was only blocking part of it, and the thought of why his mind might be doing that terrified him. He'd screwed everything up, everything. Thought he was so smart, stringing the interrogators on. His mouth had cost the sergeant his life. Had he told them about the landing? *What* had he told them? He got only an image for an answer: a black telephone being lowered slowly back into its cradle.

What did that mean? Had Al-Qadi phoned it in, that single essential element of information—that the massive assault force off Kuwait was *only a diversion*—before Blaisell and Sarsten and the rest had burst in?

He lowered his head between his hands and groaned. And again he felt her hand on his neck. So terrifyingly inadequate against the horror bubbling in his skull, yet still comforting despite its impotence, maybe because it was so unequal to what the universe confronted them with; a single human contact he braced like a shoring timber against the darkness outside.

SHE WORRIED about Lenson. His skin was icy. They'd gotten his clothes back on, but that didn't mean he wasn't hypothermic. Shock hypothermia, exacerbated by torture. He responded to touch, but didn't answer when she asked how he felt. He might retreat into catatonia. Some trauma survivors never spoke again.

She didn't kid herself. She'd be happy to turn back. Let somebody else deal with Saddam and Al-Syori. Burying Zeitner had taken all the fun away. And there'd been damn little to start with.

She couldn't help thinking that if he hadn't come back for her during the shelling, he'd probably still be alive.

Then she remembered what might happen if they failed, and rubbed her face hard, trying to balance thousands of Israeli lives against her own. Back at 'Ar'ar it had seemed clear. Out here, she wasn't sure it made a convincing trade-off.

She reached up to adjust the goggles. Zeitner's goggles, passed on now to her. They were heavy and awkward, but she couldn't believe the view. Being able to see in the dark was godlike. She could see every turn in the road, and the green-outlines-on-black-shadow of darkened buildings going by. They were going generally downhill, though the road was so bumpy and had so many turns it was hard to tell. The engine seemed very loud, and the gears ground when Sergeant Vertierra shifted. The heater worked, though. She felt its dragon breath even back here in the rear.

The warmth, initially welcome, made her legs come to life, and that was bad. Pain lanced up her ankles. She needed rest, elevation, ice. But all she could manage was a handful of the fat white ibuprofens. So when she'd seen the jeep in the light of the flames, heard the engine start up, it was sweet. She looked at her watch, remembering the linkup was supposed to be at dawn; and already the night was wearing thin, a threadbare old black dress.

She stripped off her glove and put her hand on Lenson's neck. He felt warmer. The heater would help. She got a pulse, weak but regular. She called his name, shook him, but he still didn't respond.

She glanced at her watch, couldn't find it, cocked the goggles around till she could. "PB time," she told them all, and felt in her breast pocket for the card. Plastic snapped as they thumbed pills out, swallowed them dry or with the tilt of a canteen. She popped hers, then snapped off another and pushed it between Lenson's lips. Studied him for a few seconds, then shifted around in her seat and got out her gas kit. The diazepam autoinjector was provided as an anticonvulsant, but it would serve as a tranquilizer too. Diazepam was the generic name for Valium, after all. She pulled out the injector and twisted off the cap. The spring would drive the needle through the uniform cloth, so she didn't need to roll up his sleeve.

She was positioning it against his arm when Gault turned in his seat. "What are you doing?" he said. He didn't sound happy.

"Giving him a sedative."

"Put it away."

"I'm sorry, are you the doctor here?" It came out sharper than she intended.

"Listen up, Major." Gault glanced front, then at her again. "You don't give anybody in this team anything until I approve it. Understand me? I want him able to walk and carry a weapon."

"He's suffered major psychological trauma."

"Not as much as Jake Zeitner did." Gault stared her down, and despite herself she dropped her eyes, wondering if he blamed her. "If he can walk and return fire, leave him alone. Hear me? Put it away. Now."

Pressing her lips together, she kept her head down. And after a moment, she felt him turn his attention back to the road.

WHEN THE light grew, they saw the lake. It sprawled below them, a great sheet of gray-brown water reflecting the even more colorless sky. A motionless mist hung over it, a pearly curtain hiding whatever lay on the far shore. The land sloped down to it. Power pylons stood like giants with upstretched arms. There was a highway down there too, and along it some sort of construction, though at this distance they couldn't tell yet what kind. Gault kept checking his watch.

"We're running out of time," Nichols said from the backseat. Gault nodded without turning his head.

"Where the fuck are we?" Sarsten said. He'd slept up to now; just fallen asleep in the back as soon as he'd hit the seat. Now he sat up, looking at the water. He sounded up again, almost hectic, and Gault wondered if he'd taken another of the orange tablets he'd seen him swallowing before. They had to be stimulants, Benzedrine or Dexedrine, something like it.

"This is where we split up, Sergeant," Gault told him. "You can help cover the meet-up, then we'll go on in from there."

"Meaning what, mate? You're ditching me?"

That's exactly what I'm doing, you fucking lunatic asshole, he wanted to shout into his face. But made himself say instead, "No, just that you've done your mission. No point taking on ours too."

"I told you that back at the fucking LZ."

Gault couldn't disagree with that at all. It had been his mistake, taking him. So he tried to keep his tone reasonable. "You're right. You're right; I should have just let you extract with the rest of your team. But look, Sergeant. I'm glad we had you along back there. But we wouldn't have had the contact at all if you hadn't decided you were going to show off your Arabic."

"Show off my . . . oh, get fooking serious, mate. They knew we were there. That's what they were yelling. I was telling them not to shoot, we were friends. Some jundie was just too fucking heavy on the trigger."

"Forget it. We're going into urban reconnaissance mode now. We're trained for it. You're not. You've got your own backup extract routine, right? Now you've got a vehicle to get you there."

"Fucking shite," said Sarsten, but he didn't say anything more because just then two trucks turned out of a side road ahead.

Gault faced front, focusing the goggles on them. Two heavy trucks, canvas tops, the kind that carried troops. They were accelerating, moving at thirty or even forty, way faster than he'd drive on these shitty roads. Vertierra let up on the gas, tossing them forward as the jeep slowed. Gault told him, "Keep your speed up, Tony. Watch which way they turn. If they go down toward the lake, fall in behind."

But they didn't. As their track intersected the one the team was on, the trucks braked in a spray of mud and water. Then they turned uphill, toward them, one after the other. As they got closer he saw they were Soviet-made, like the jeep.

"Get your hats off," said Sarsten, behind them. "And get the fucking cammie paint off your face."

Gault whipped his cover off, pulled off Vertierra's, scrubbed at his face with his sleeve. Most of the paint was gone anyway with the rain and wear of the long night. He glanced back to see Lenson staring obliviously off to the right, to see Maddox and Blaisell and Nichols come up from rubbing their faces. With their stubble, they might look like Iraqis, at least through a window going by at high speed. The men, at least. "Drop your head forward. Like you're asleep," he told Maddox. To Vertierra he said, "Step on the fucking gas, get us up to fifty."

"Man, I'm at seventy now. This speedometer's hosed."

"It's in kilometers," Lenson said, startling them all. After a moment Gault said, "Back with us, Commander? That's good. He's right, RTO. So get us up to a hundred. Or whatever, just fuckin' go!"

The lead truck was almost on them. Gault made out the driver and another man in the cab. Both in the drab Iraqi battle dress. Vertierra raised a lazy wave, hanging his arm out the window. Then the truck was towering over them, abreast, then past, the next coming up, a blast of wind, a splash and clatter of road grit against metal and glass. The second driver looked down as they passed. Gault saw dark eyes fix on his own through the dirty windshield, but they didn't widen, he didn't look surprised or point.

They rounded a bend in the road and he saw the rendezvous point. It had been briefed to them as an abandoned restaurant on a one-lane road five klicks south of the lake. The light was coming now, and he could see for miles in every direction except across the lake, where the rose-tinted mist cut off his sight line north. The land was under cultivation, it was open. The only building actually on this road was a mile east of them. He guessed it was a couple of miles south of the lakefront. There was the marsh behind it, like on the map. He got the map out of his thigh pocket and checked it again, tried to eye-shoot a bearing on the lake and the marsh. It looked about right.

He told Vertierra, "Downshift and head out cross-country, about forty degrees to your right."

The only problem was the RTO didn't bother to slow down first. They went off the track at speed, hit the embankment, and sailed through the air for twenty feet before the wheels whammed down again with a jolt that bottomed out the springs and whipcracked their heads forward. Blaisell started yelling and Sarsten told him coldly to shut up.

Vertierra wrestled with the wheel, cursing in whatever

language he spoke when he wasn't speaking English, and
they came out of a near-rollover back down onto four
wheels. They were bouncing downhill on a gravelly long
slope dotted with bushes and crossed with shallow
ditches and, here and there, white-painted iron pipes jutting up out of the soil. The ground looked like it had been
plowed long ago, then abandoned. Gault yelled at
Vertierra to slow down before he rolled them, killed them
all, and the RTO yelled back he couldn't do everything at
once. Each time they hit a ditch the shocks bottomed with
a tremendous jolt and dust boiled up from the floormats.
Then they hit a rise. The back seemed to dip down and
the wheels spun, and the jeep stopped moving forward
and slid backward instead. They yelled at him to gun it,
but the wheels just spun and they searched the dash without finding anything that looked like a four-wheel-drive
shiftover.

Finally Gault said, "Forget it; Sarsten can back it out.
We can dog it the rest of the way. That hollow in the field.
Dismount and let's go."

TONY SPILLED out with the rest, and tossed the keys to
Gault. Who caught them in midair, and handed them to
Sarsten. The Britisher seemed about to speak, then didn't.
He put the keys in his pocket. The others turned and ran
for the shallow fold of land the gunny had pointed out.

It seemed like a long way across the open field. As he
leaped one of the ditches, the ruck slamming against his
back, canteens jumping around, Tony wondered why the
gunny wasn't filtering them across, making it covert.
Then he knew. They were late. If they missed this linkup,
they'd have come all this way and lost Zeitner for nothing.

The hollow was deeper than it looked from up-slope,
with scraggly dry-looking bushes screening the edge.
When they were all down, panting from the sprint, Gault
gave him the 'put out security' signal. Tony stared at

him, then remembered he was assistant team leader, now that Jake was gone.

He passed the order, and the team went to their positions in silence. He searched his own sector over the sights of his weapon, observing how they bobbed with his breathing, looking for movement, any sign they'd been seen. Not that troops dismounting from a vehicle was probably that rare a sight here.

Okay, he had to start thinking like the ATL. He took out his compass and glanced from it to the terrain around him. He was facing the lake. To his right ran the road and on the road was the building. The only movement was ducks above the lake and an occasional vehicle on the distant highway.

He rolled over on his left side and took out the little binoculars Zeitner had carried. The building didn't look too different from West Texas: a hut or shack with a rusted tin roof, a chicken run or goat pen wired up behind it. Brush and small trees, green despite the cold; denser, lusher growth than uphill because it was close to the water. Tires leaned against what might be either adobe or some kind of pink-painted concrete. He focused finer and saw faded red spray paint on the wall. Arabic writing, but below that were block Roman letters. They read RESS TARANT.

The team lay motionless, casing their sectors for fifteen minutes before he felt someone's hand on his boot. He tucked the glasses back inside his blouse and low-crawled back to where the gunny and Nichols waited, at the bottom of a ditch, screened by the bushes.

Gault said that they were here, but he didn't see anyone waiting. Their contact might be late. Or maybe he'd already been and left. Regardless, he was going to go down to the restaurant and see what happened. "I'll do a leader's recon. If everything looks kosher, I'll pat the top of my head and you come on in. Got that? What's the signal?"

"Pat your head; means come on in."

The gunny nodded. "We'll do linkup the way we rehearsed it. Me down front, the lance corporal giving me flank cover. The rest of the team in reserve back here with you. If there's hostile contact, rally point's back where we left Jake. Tony, what's your withdrawal route going to be?"

He hadn't expected the question. He tried to concentrate, and sketched a route on the ground with his finger.

When he was done, Gault nodded again, then went over hand signals during the contact. If he scratched the back of his neck while he was talking to the guy, that meant for Nichols to shoot him. Scratching his ass meant everything was cool. The sniper repeated it.

The bushes at the top of the hollow moved, and he whipped his sights around to cover them. He stared when Sarsten came over the crest, staying on his belly, and slid down in a little shower of dirt and rocks to join them.

"I'm b-a-a-ck," he drawled, grinning. With his dark, arched eyebrows he did look a little like Jack Nicholson.

"What's the matter?" Nichols said. "Jeep won't start?"

"I didn't try it. Let me get this straight. If I heard what I thought I heard, up there? You're joining up with an Iraqi?"

"He's a resistance member," Gault said, sounding angry. Vertierra studied his face. The gunny was pissed, but he was holding it back. Why?

"Ballocks! There's no resistance left in Iraq. Saddam killed them off years ago, and terrified everybody else. They're just sucking you white-eyes in."

The gunny's face hardened. "We have to take the risk, Sergeant. But you don't. You've got a vehicle, if you want it. Go ahead and execute your extract."

"Oh, I don't know," Sarsten said. He unhooked a canteen, unscrewed the cap, and took a pull. "I sort of thought we were getting to be squaddies."

Tony was behind the SAS man. He lifted his weapon slightly; caught Gault's eye. The gunny hesitated, then shook his head just an infinitesimal fraction. He said, "I

appreciate the offer, but we're trained for urban reconnaissance. You can carry out your extract plan."

Sarsten smiled, but didn't move to leave. He had
pulled his ruck around and was feeling in it.

Maddox slid a few feet down from the top. "You need
a direct order?" she said harshly. "The gunnery sergeant
detached you. That means you leave now."

Sarsten shook his head. He found what he was looking
for in his pack, shook something out, slapped it into his
mouth. He followed the tablets with another gulp of water
and capped his canteen.

"You wankers need me," he said. "I saved your mate
here. I speak Arabic. If things go to shite and you have to
go clandestine, I can save your stones."

Tony glanced at the gunny, tense for the signal to take
him. The SAS was big, he was hard, but if all four of
them piled on they could cable-tie him, no sweat. But
Gault didn't give a sign. He just lay there. Finally he
said, "So far you've acted like a loose cannon, Sergeant.
Will I have compliance now?"

No, Tony thought. No way! He frowned, trying to get
the message across, but Gault wouldn't look at him.

"Absolutely," the Englishman said.

"That doesn't mean just to me. You take orders from
Sergeant Vertierra too. From *any* member of the team.
You execute what you're told to do, when you're told to
do it, and not a lick more. You don't act on your own and
you don't speak unless spoken to."

"Just tell me what to do, Bwana," said Sarsten. Shrug-
ging, turning his palms out like a rebuked child. Smiling.

"Give me your med kit," Gault said.

Sarsten watched as the gunny buttoned the stimulant
tablets into his own breast pocket. For a moment he
seemed about to speak, but didn't.

"Take security facing south," Gault said, and without a
word back, the SAS rolled over out of the group and to
the edge of the depression, propping his rifle at the ready
and squinting into the growing light.

·   ·   ·

WHEN THEY broke up, F.C. edged up to the crest and
looked out over the field. Nothing moved but the birds
over the lake. Some kind of black duck. He checked the
rifle again and crouched, not wanting to do this, but
knowing he had to. Then pistoned his legs and shot suddenly up out over the edge and doglegged out to the
right.

He took it in a rush, bent low, trotting zigzag from one
bush to the next, then dropping to scan around before the
next burst. He made his way across the field, taking
advantage of every stunted bush, down into the marsh.

When he reached it the land dropped, went dark, went
soft. His boots sucked in clingy mud, and the smell of the
marsh came up around him. It was a familiar smell. It
smelled like Carolina pluff mud. The grass was tall,
whispering and brown around him. A rustle ran among
the roots, and he brought his weapon up and froze till it
scurried away. Low to the ground like that he figured it
for something like a water rat or a nutria. If they had
nutria in Iraq. Rats, he was pretty sure, were everywhere.

He was still feeling dark about Jake, and having the
Brit back aboard didn't help. For a couple minutes there
he'd thought he was gone. Then he'd come back. F.C.
grinned tightly to himself, remembering how ready Tony
had been to take the asshole from behind. He couldn't see
what other choice the gunny had, though. Not if the guy
wouldn't leave. You couldn't tie him up and leave him for
the Iraqis. Not after seeing what they'd done to Zeitner
and the navy guy, Lenson. The only other choice was to
kill him.

It was a temptation, that was for sure.

Fifty yards in, he came to an irrigation canal about four
feet wide. It was shored up with pieces of plywood, which
had gone rotten and were falling in. The water was murky
gray and stank of chemicals. It was six inches deep, ooz-
ing slowly toward the lake. He followed it, working his

way gradually closer to the road, till he came to a culvert where he could see across a waste of brown dead grass to the restaurant, or used-tire place, or whatever it was.

He decided that was as close as he was going to get without breaking cover and started setting up for the shot from a belly hide. He got his grease kit out and rubbed it between his hands and smeared on more camo paint, nice and thick. Garnished his bush cover with some of the brown grass. Then raised his head very slowly, breaking silhouette off to the side of the culvert.

According to the mil-markings on his reticle, the building was two hundred meters away. He watched the wind on the tasseled tops of the marsh grass and dialed in a correction. Then shouldered the rifle and put his crosshairs on the building again.

It jumped close through the scope, and he saw now it was abandoned, windows broken, the tires propped in front rotten, with strips of tread falling off. It looked like the kind of store along the back roads at home that sold recaps to colored and poor whites. He ran the scope carefully along under the eaves, over the roof, looking for loopholes or loose tin or pried-off boards. An attic was a favorite sniper position. He checked a pile of sand off to the left but saw no sign of anyone.

He sank back and lowered the rifle slowly and looked to his left. Gault was lying behind a bush watching him. F. C. gave him a thumbs-up and glued his face back to the scope. It bobbed with his breathing and he slowed it down, felt his heartbeat slow, felt everything slow and collapse down into the magic circle through which he looked. His finger left the guard and touched the trigger very lightly, then let up. His thumb found the safety and, as Gault's head bobbed into the field of view, very slowly eased it off.

GAULT WENT out in the other direction from the hide site. You never went straight in at an objective. A sniper could backtrack you and target the rest of your team. He felt time ebbing away like blood. He went along north through the brush at a high crawl, then dropped into a cut where he could walk bent over. Over the top, low crawl now, then a rush to the cover of another fold of land. Two hundred meters out, he boxed right, then right again and came in from the northwest.

He was still on edge from the face-off with Sarsten. He'd almost given Vertierra the nod to coldcock him. Only one thing stopped him. No, two. The first was that with Zeitner gone he was a man short. Sarsten was a shooter and a damn good one. They might need that. But he also remembered the old saying: Whoever lies first gets believed. If Sarsten got back first, they'd have to refute his version of the events on the knob. The SAS man was smart enough, cunning enough, that if his version got out first that would become the official record. The fact that they'd be accusing an ally, not an American, of a war crime, would make it even harder.

That could end up looking very bad for Team Twelve. No, on the whole, he preferred the guy inside the tent pissing out, rather than outside the tent pissing in. Especially if he lived up to his word and toned down from here on out. Taking away his speed might help.

He stopped fifty yards from the abandoned building, lying in the underbrush, listening and waiting. He took the time to open out his senses, smelling the dank of the marsh and the distant lake. The oily, shitty odor that lingered everywhere. The closer-in smells of smoke, maybe from the city that couldn't be far off now, that had to be on the far side of that misty lake. The rustle of wind in the grass, rising now from the dead calm of dawn, and the distant diesel snorting of a truck up on the highway. Even under the overcast, the light was growing fast. He felt naked under it. He was used to moving in the dark now, and he felt the morning radiance like a tumor must feel the radiation that is trying to kill it.

He shook this thought off and glanced to his right. He had to look close, exactly where he'd told him to be, to see Nichols. The sniper inclined his head slowly. Gault nodded back and looked behind him. The others were well concealed too. If he bit into a shit sandwich, they'd be able to get out.

Satisfied, he returned sight and attention to the building. It waited in the wind and the growing light. A black bird fluttered down and disappeared in the wire behind it. He waited, but it didn't fly out again.

The diesel snorting came again, louder, and he pulled back into the brush.

It was the same truck he'd heard heading along the lake. Coming toward them, it was a Toyota eight-wheeler with a noncommittal grille. It had been blue once but now was streaked with rust. The bumper was crushed. Behind the cab was a big cylindrical tank. It looked like a gasoline tanker. It snorted blue smoke, pulling itself up the slight grade, and passed the pink building, going about fifteen miles an hour. He saw the driver's head poke out, craning around.

The truck downshifted, snorted, downshifted, and rumbled slowly to a halt, there in the middle of the deserted road, among the deserted-looking fields. It stood there for a time, chuffing smoke, then backed around slowly and pulled off onto the berm, facing in the direction it had come from, about thirty yards from the building.

Not *at* the building, like it was supposed to be. Where the meet point was. Just *near* it. Meaning it might be their contact, or it might not.

The driver cranked the window down, reached out, and opened the door from outside. Gault heard the hinges screeching fifty yards away. The guy climbed down, put his hands to his back, and stretched, looking up and down the road. Gault watched him intently. Glancing toward Nichols, he saw the sniper gathered into his scope, tracking the Iraqi as he moved around the truck, checking the tires. Then he was out of sight, behind it.

Nichols could still see him, though. Through the powerful optics the driver looked close enough to hit with a rock. He was young and heavily mustached, in black pants and shoes with high plastic heels and a light blue jacket. Behind the truck he pulled out his cock and stood pissing down into the marsh. He stood there for some time looking around. Then he zipped up and adjusted his balls and went heavily back to the truck and hauled himself up into the cab.

The tail of a green rag came out the window and started flapping around as the driver scrubbed at his windshield with it.

When the guy had come back around the truck playing with his balls Gault had just about concluded he was nothing more than a passerby. Till the rag came out.

That was the signal, a green cloth. This was their boy. He felt his heart speed up. He took a few breaths, making himself chill out as he glassed the road again. He didn't see anyone else coming.

It was always tense when you met a contact for the first time. Usually the other guy was armed, and just as nervous about you. Not a good situation no matter how you looked at it. No sudden motions. No jokes. Jokes could be taken the wrong way by a man who feared for his life. Real slow, real calm. He had to remember not to scratch the back of his neck without meaning it. Same with scratching his ass, of course.

He ducked down in the brush and pulled off his ruck. Checked his weapon again and laid it on top of his pack. Took off his war belt too, and his hat, so he didn't look so much like a soldier from a distance. He pulled out his phrase book and reviewed the opening dialogue he'd penciled inside the cover. Just to make sure.

When he looked at the truck again, the guy was still sitting there, the engine was still running, but he'd put the rag away.

Gault took a deep breath, hoisted himself to his feet, and started jogging toward him.

THE GUY watched him through the windshield as he came up. He didn't move, just watched. Dark mustache, like all the other Iraqi men they'd seen. Saddam's fashion influence. Gault lifted a hand as he approached, but got no response. He jogged up to the cab and stopped a couple yards off. The guy looked down. Up close he looked about twenty to twenty-five, with a heavy growth of dark brown beard under the mustache. Longer hair than on the soldiers, and tinted glasses like Daniel Ortega. Gault said, in his very best Arabic, "*Sabaah al-khair, sidi.*"

The man's mouth went tight, as if he'd said some kind of curse. He didn't answer in Arabic, though. He just said, "Uh."

Gault cleared his throat. "I understand we're to meet here. I'm Gunnery Sergeant Gault, US Marine Corps."

"You call me Ted." He didn't move his head, but his eyes were searching the low bushes, the slope down which Gault had come.

"I was told to meet someone called Samir."

"No Samir. He alone?"

"No. I have others with me." Including one who's got his crosshairs on your ass right now, he thought of adding; but didn't. It would not be what you'd call building trust. He might be in somebody's sights himself. He looked at the roof of the building. Up close he could see gaps in the tin, but not what was behind them. Nor could he see into the broken windows. He wished they'd gotten here earlier. He wondered about the Samir/Ted thing. The word he'd got was that the Syrian asset was named Samir. The name might change passed from hand to hand, but it didn't seem likely it would change that much. On the other hand, the identification signal had been right.

"Are he ready go Baghdad?"

He looked steadily up. "Ted"—it obviously wasn't his

name, but in the guy's situation, basically a traitor leading enemy nationals to their target, Gault wouldn't have given his real name either—had a boil on his cheek he fingered from time to time. His eyes were shifty behind the glasses and his face looked wet. I'd be sweating too, Gault thought. In fact, I am. Maybe his name *was* Samir, he just didn't want them to know it in case they got captured.

He didn't like standing out here in the open, in the growing daylight. He threw a glance over his shoulder, toward the lake. No traffic yet, but anyone could turn off the highway and drive up this way. To see a white-eye in camouflage battle dress talking to a guy in a water truck. He said, "How about if I get up in the cab with you?"

"What?"

"Into the truck." He pointed, and the Iraqi hesitated, then nodded.

Gault trotted around the back, staying alert, inspecting it as he went. A brace of spigots came off a manifold, hanging over the rear bumper. A water truck, it looked like; how they got drinking water to the outlying villages. The passenger-side door banged open with a tinny creak, then slammed behind him with a boom.

The first thing he noticed was the folding-stock AK laid across the seat between them. All Gault had was his .45, cocked and locked and pushed down into his belt with the battle dress jacket pulled down over it. Sitting this high, he could see all the way down to the lake now. The front seat was worn plastic with the springs showing in places. The interior smelled of harsh tobacco, sweat, piss, diesel exhaust and cheap cologne. It felt hot after the freezing air in the open. The Iraqi was lighting a cigarette. He glanced doubtfully at Gault, then held the pack out. He took one and bent forward for a light. The appearance of trust, at least.

"We go Baghdad, yes?" the Iraqi said.

"*Na'am*. Yes. That's what we're here for."

"You fight Saddam, yes?"

"That's right. And you?"

"Saddam enemy of my people." He pronounced it *beoble*. "Of all Iraqi people. Soon now all fight him. Then he fall."

The guy's English wasn't flawless, but aside from his all-purpose pronouns and his habit of replacing every *p* with a *b* he was understandable. Gault smiled encouragingly. "That's right. Saddam will fall. Then Iraqi people build democracy, right?"

"Not *your* democracy," the Iraqi said. He stared straight at Gault, about as hostile as he could be. "*Islam* democracy."

Well, *o*-kay, Gault thought. He swallowed and looked out the window, started a reassuring wave, then realized it might look like a motion toward his neck. He'd screwed up. Up here in the cab no one could see him scratch his ass. Next time . . . to hell with next time; he had to worry about now. He noticed the assault rifle on the seat had the safety off. He sucked in harsh raw smoke, barely stopped a cough. "They say you know where *hijurat ababeel* is."

"No. I don't know where he—where he *is*."

Gault went quiet inside. He said carefully, "We were told you worked on it."

"Work on it? Sure. I work on it. Up until last year. But I don't know to little bit where he is. He never let me there. Brecautions. Security. But I get you close enough you find. Get your man in truck."

He looked around the cab. The smoke was starting to get to him, and his stomach was pumping out gallons of acid. "I have too many guys."

"Not here. The back. In *back*." He gestured emphatically over his shoulder.

"In back?" Gault twisted, thinking he must have missed something, but the only thing behind them, up close against the little oval window in the rear of the cab, was the peeling painted metal of the tank. Then he understood, and said, "You mean, inside the tank? What, it's empty?"

Ted nodded. He pulled the backrest forward and put his hand down behind it, down into a gap that disappeared when he pushed it back again. "They climb in from top. Put guns behind seat. Get in water tank."

"Okay, but we'll keep our weapons with us."

"No. No guns inside tank. Make noise. Guns up here." He patted the seat again. "Give back when we get to shop."

"Shop? What kind of shop?"

"Guns up here. No guns in tank." The Iraqi looked down the road. "*Bi sir'a!* Get man in now, fast. No argue."

Gault rubbed his hands together, not liking this. Separated from their weapons, they were helpless. If this was a trap . . . not only would the mission be compromised, they'd all be prisoners. On the other hand, this lad was their only lead to the objective, the only way to carry the mission forward. It was a command decision and he stalled for a moment, unwilling to accept it. Instead he said, "We can't give you our weapons."

Ted didn't even bother to answer him. He just gunned the accelerator and put the truck in first. "All right, okay," Gault told him quickly, feeling the irrevocability, feeling the wrongness but seeing no other choice. "Okay. I'm going to lean past you and call them in."

THEY CAME in slowly, then at the double time when he pumped his fist in the hurry-up signal. They were so painfully exposed in the daylight. He kept looking toward the highway, then at the overcast. If the Iraqis had any aircraft up. . . .

They panted up, and from anonymous running targets, rucks jouncing on their backs, became individuals again, became his troops. They huddled on the building side of the truck, and he said down to Vertierra, "Sergeant, hand up the shoulder weapons."

"Say again, Gunny?"

He saw the doubt in their faces. He repeated the order and added, "We're going in the water tank. That's the only way he'll take us. Hand them up and go up the ladder there, there's a hatch on top."

"No fucking way I'm giving up my rifle," said Sarsten.

"Fine with me, Sergeant. See you back in Saudi."

The SAS hesitated, then handed it up, cursing. Gault checked the safety, then placed it carefully behind the seat. Vertierra's followed, then Lenson's. Maddox was looking up; she touched her side, raised her eyebrows; the pistol? He shook his head silently.

"Is all?" the driver said. Gault said yeah, they were climbing in now. The tank behind them boomed as someone struck the metal.

"They must stay quiet."

"I'll keep them that way."

"You in tank too."

He hesitated on his way down from the cab. The Iraqi was looking at him with a strange expression. Maybe he'd called this wrong. All the son of a bitch had to do now was drive them to the local Republican Guard barracks. On the other hand, they still had grenades and sidearms. Ted hadn't disarmed them completely.

"You're driving us to *hijurat ababeel*?" he asked him.

For answer he got another revving of the engine, another clash of gears. The dark eyebrows, the dark eyes turned on him for a fraction of a second. Then another press of the throttle.

"Get into tank," Ted said.

Gault swung down, got his boots on the rickety rusting ladder, and boosted himself up over the curve of the water tank. He felt naked. A marine didn't turn his rifle over. This all felt wrong. Very wrong.

But it was the only choice he could see.

14

0800 23 February:
Western Iraq

Blaze dropped into the tank, quick-drawing his Glock as
he let go of the hatch rim. He had it pointed by the time
his boots splashed into a foot of water.

He stared blindly at nothing. At the dark. It smelled
musty, choking, like stale water underground.

Like a cave. And with that thought, the smell unlocked
a door.

That summer the river went down, and somebody had
discovered the hole. The kids had dared each other to go
in. He and another boy had been the only ones brave
enough. Inside, past the narrow entrance they'd had to
wriggle through, had been a pool of water. It smelled like
lime and wet and rottenness, as if animals had hidden
here to die and decay. They'd crawled through it, the cold
mud dragging at them in the dark, and then lain there, the
rock close above their heads. And little by little the light
from behind showed them a narrow passage, inward,
totally dark, a passage to a cold hell. Looking at it he'd
understood suddenly that whoever went in there would
never come out. They'd dared each other in whispers, but
in the end neither had had the guts to go on.

He pushed through the memory as through cobwebs
and sloshed forward a step and looked around again.
Behind him someone else dropped and landed softly.
Light came in through the circle in the overhead, but not

much, and it was instantly sucked up, absorbed, obliterated by the dark. He felt a premonitory childish horror, a creeping of the skin just like he'd felt years ago in the cave, twelve years old and looking at his own death.

A thud, a splash, a grunt. Vertierra said close to his ear, "Make a hole. Move aft, marine."

He laughed disbelievingly, as much from being scared as anything else. " 'Aft'? Where the fuck is *aft*? We're in a fucking milk truck, dipshit."

Vertierra put his little dark big-nosed face close in the dim. "You don't say 'dipshit' to me, man. You address me like a fucking marine, Corporal, that clear?"

He started to react, had his hand up to punch the fucker, when Parris Island cut in just in time. He wanted to say, fuck you, Mex boy, you're ATL material like I'm President George Fucking Bush. But instead said, "Aye, aye, Sergeant," and melted back into the darkness, walking crouched over with his hands out until his head caught some kind of internal stiffener and he reeled back with a groan.

WHAT THE fuck is that?" Sarsten muttered beside him. Gault turned his head, still unable to see. After the morning light, the inside of the tank was like night again.

"Blaze. He hit his head."

"Everybody get down. He's going to start up."

"Hey—No! No!"

Maddox's near-scream rang in their ears, bent and focused by the curving metal around them. Gault flung his arm up instinctively at the hollow bang just above them, then realized both what it was and why she'd screamed. What the hollow grating was, then the sound of heavy boots above them pacing back toward the ladder.

Ted had just slammed the hatch above them. It was battened down, sealed tight, maybe locked for all they knew. Yeah, the grating sound was probably a dogging bar. He stared into the dark, starting to sweat again, then groped for his combat flash. By its sudden light, welcome but not all that bright, they looked around the interior.

It wasn't shiny stainless, what you'd expect, but rusty, corroded iron. A discolored pool down the center was dirty water bottomed with sticky mud. It was slippery as hell under their boots. Vertical stiffeners, or maybe baffles to keep the load from sloshing from side to side, came down from the overhead to welded-in bar stock along the floor. It all looked like it had been slapped together in some back-alley garage. Four holes low to the after bulkhead led, he figured, to the manifold and spigots he'd seen on the back. In the flash, he saw something else unsettling: six sets of startled eyes, all looking up at the sealed hatch. It had been the only way out. Which meant that till somebody decided to let them out, they were staying here.

"Everybody okay?" he said, not too loud. "Major, put the pistol away. You too, Blaze."

"We're fucking locked down here, Gunny. You trust that raghead? What'd he say, anyway?"

"He's taking us into the city, Corporal. Just like in the plan. So cool the fuck out, all right?"

The world lurched and began moving. A grinding roar came from below, a hollow rumble from all around them accompanied by the pop and clink of gravel kicked up from the wheels. The remaining water flooded aft, piling up near the manifold. Gault squatted again, but a jolt put him on his ass in the mud.

A moan. He sent the beam forward again, searching. Maddox's eyes were blasted wide, and sweat gleamed on her face.

"Problem, Doctor?"

"Nothing . . . well, technically, something . . . I have these anxiety attacks. In closed-in spaces."

"Can you secure the pistol, Doc?"

She seemed to realize she was still holding the Beretta. She flinched, and checked the safety and holstered it. So far, okay. He duckwalked over to her. "What is it? Claustrophobia?"

"Maybe." She shook her head, and he heard her breathing, rapid and shallow, felt the warmth of it on his face. "It doesn't feel real good."

Wonderful, he thought. If they had to go sewer-crawling. . . . The tank interior was dark, swaying and rumbling as they gathered speed, but there was enough headroom to stand up. He'd had troops fall out from claustrophobia before, the first time they put on their chem gear. Usually you could talk them through it, or get their attention on something else. He tried for a comforting tone. "It's just getting used to it. Take some deep breaths. Think about the sky." He looked past her to Lenson. "How's he doing? Commander, how are you doing?"

The navy officer blinked. "Better. I think."

"Talk to me. Still a little shook, huh?"

"I watched them shoot Zeitner. Burn him alive. Then shoot him."

"I know. I saw what they left of him. How about you, Commander? Want to talk about it?"

"No," Lenson said. He rubbed a hand across his mouth, looked down at it as if expecting to see something there. "Not now."

Gault sat back again and checked his watch. From the map, it would be ninety, ninety-five kilometers into Baghdad. The truck had been pointed north, and he hadn't felt a turn yet. So they should be on this heading for a little while before they got to hard surface.

Ten minutes after they started, the truck heaved upward suddenly, booming and rattling. The rattle of pebbles against iron fell away. He held his breath, waiting for the turn, and there it was; a lean to the right, dragging his upper body toward the far side of the tank. The motion gentled, and the engine roared again, geared up, and from the smoothness now he figured they were on the hardball. He felt for his compass, then let his hand drop; no point to it, they were enclosed in a cocoon of iron. Same for the GPS. No radio signal could penetrate to them here. Then he caught Nichols's light, probing into a corner.

"Gunny. Over here. Got a hole."

F.C. had found a weak spot in a weld with his KA-BAR. He leaned back and Gault applied his eye.

To see countryside going by. He was looking out the right side, out to the south, if they were traveling east. He couldn't get a fix on the sun through the overcast, though, and there were no shadows. But he couldn't see the lake. If they were going west, he'd be looking right out over it. So they were headed east, as promised.

On the other hand, if Ted boy was driving them to Mukhabarat Central, they'd be heading into Baghdad anyway.

"I make us going east," Nichols drawled beside him.

"How you figure?"

"The wind. I saw smoke coming off one of those farms. Somebody burning something."

"I concur, based on not seeing the lake. The wind, that's pretty sharp, Lance Corporal."

"No problem, Gunny. I had to mike it out, setting up for the shot."

Sarsten moved up, wriggling over Maddox and Lenson to get up to them. The truck was still gathering speed, the gears changing every once in a while, the tires whining underneath them. He wanted to see out too, and Gault edged back, letting him press his eye to the hole. They were tumbled close together, lying on each other, when Maddox said, sounding strangled, "I really don't think we're going to have enough air in here for long."

BLAZE HAD his back against the bulkhead, knees up and hands locked around them. He was still pissed about getting his ass chewed by the ATL. Hah, yeah, big fucking deal. Old Tex-Mex acting like he's fucking God, when all he is is the fucking RTO. Everybody knew the dumbest guy got to mule pack the radio. A ray of light shot across the dark as someone shifted, and he saw the others clustered in a knot, saw for the fraction of a second an upside-down picture on the other side of the tank; an upside-down road, upside-down buildings going by. He blinked, but it was gone, leaving him doubting he'd seen it. Weird. He got his M&M and nut gorp out and chased a handful with a drink from his canteen.

Another flash of light, and in front of it someone moving toward him. Walking like the Incredible Hulk, arms down. It lurched as the truck jostled. He heard a whine and drone, a whoosh on the far side of the iron. Then the shape sank down beside him and he smelled the other guy; they could all smell each other now.

Sarsten said, "What a fucking wank-up. You lads always run your missions in milk trucks?"

He laughed, had to; the guy just had such a deadpan delivery. "I don't know. I'm low man on this one."

"First time we got to talk. I'm Vic Sarsten."

"Uh—hi, Sergeant."

"We don't use ranks in the SAS. Not on ops. Just call me Vic, or Vickers. You're Nichols?"

"No. Denny Blaisell. I'm the scout."

They shook hands and started to talk, kind of easy. Sarsten had such a dry sense of humor that the first couple of times he said something outrageous Blaze wasn't sure if he heard him right. Then he started to laugh.

GAULT WAS looking out the peep, the truck was slowing, when he saw an Iraqi trooper by the side of the road, mouth O'd in a yell to someone out of the field of view; then another soldier; then a litter of wire and shattered concrete with uniformed men standing around it. He pulled back and groped along through the mud, then jammed his glove over the hole. All they needed was to have somebody spot an eyeball looking out of the side of a truck. He told Nichols to find a piece of rust-scale and hold it over the hole; they were coming up to a roadblock.

The brakes came on, screeching and complaining, brake shoes rubbing metal. He put his flash on his face and mimed *silence* to the others. They waited, unmoving, barely breathing. Gault suddenly remembered that German sub movie, what was it, yeah, *Das Boot*. All the guys sweating it out while the destroyer rumbled overhead. Waiting for the depth charges to go off.

A sudden blow against the metal next to his ear made him start back and nearly drop the light. A few seconds, then another blow, farther down the tank. Someone was walking down the truck, hammering on it. They waited, motionless in the dark, barely breathing.

Then he heard boots at ear level, moving up. Someone was climbing the ladder. He reached out and his hand found a shoulder. He pulled it toward him and murmured into Maddox's ear, "Cover the hatch. If it opens, start shooting."

He heard safeties click off in the dark, and pulled out his own .45. And waited grimly, holding it.

The boots were off the ladder now. Footsteps paced over their heads. He stared where the hatch was. Whoever opened it would get two or three pistol rounds in the face. After that they'd have to take out the checkpoint with grenades. Then retrieve their weapons from the cab, if they were still there, and try to scatter and escape individually.

He didn't expect very good odds in the daylight. But he couldn't think of anything else to do.

A hollow thud as a boot contacted the hatch coaming. But then, instead of the grating noise as it undogged, the steps went on, to the back of the truck. Then forward again, faster now, and a series of thuds as someone went down the ladder and jumped off onto the roadway. A distant shout, then the renewed roar of diesels.

When they got moving again, groaning back into

motion, only not as fast as before, the pavement was rougher. They jolted over what sounded like steel plates, then went through a series of hairpin turns. The truck body lurched over, as if they were negotiating the side of a hill. Then they speeded up for a time, followed by another tortuous passage. When the ride turned rough for the third time, Gault couldn't stand it any longer. He motioned the lance corporal aside and applied his eye to the hole again.

They were passing what looked at first glance like a junkyard on fire. Then he saw it had been a neighborhood, buildings, shopfronts. It had been battered apart by a gigantic hammer. Rows of bodies lay by the roadside, crudely wrapped in bloodstained cloth. Around them others lifted arms and faces, wailing to the sky. Women in shapeless black clothing wandered here and there. One was close enough for him to see her face. It looked stunned and dead. As she bent he saw her arm was gone from the elbow down. The stump was covered by brightly colored cloth, what looked like part of a child's pajamas. Wavering veils of gray smoke blew over the scene, giving it the sense of dream, of nightmare.

NICHOLS HAD a cleaning patch in his cheek. It seemed to help calm things down to have something to chew on, even if it was just a square of cotton. He missed having his rifle in his arms, but he didn't worry about it. You just had to take it as it came.

A flash of light drew his eye. For a moment he saw Gault's face, sharp, intent, outlined by daylight. Then it eclipsed the source, and he couldn't see it anymore. He sat back again, trying to relax into the curved iron.

Slowly, over the sound of the engine and the thunder of the wheels, he made out a voice. It was Sarsten's. He was talking a few feet away, in the dark, a steady flow of syllabic sound that only now and then penetrated to reach his ear and his understanding.

Then the other voice, Blaisell's, said with dawning understanding, "Fuck, you're putting me on, man. Aren't you?" and the other voice chuckled and said, "Hey, I had you going there though," and after a second Blaisell chuckled too.

Riding in the darkness, Nichols listened, eyes squinted. But no more words came his way.

MADDOX WAS breathing shallowly when the truck's brakes gave a long, shivering moan. A weird creepy sound, like the complaint of a ghost. It shuddered to a halt, the iron beneath and around them angled upward. The engine ticked over, and with her ear to the metal she heard shouting in Iraqi. No one moved inside the hollow shell of darkness. She dragged breath after breath down into the hollow fear inside her, into the panic that fluttered her heart.

It wasn't actually a surprise. She'd felt it before, as she zipped her space suit closed and slammed the air lock shut behind her, entering Level Four. It had struck her in aircraft. Sometimes even when she was riding in a car, and someone else was driving.

She was thinking this when the motor accelerated and the truck began moving again, upward, then downward, then slowing, easing its bulk and its weight slowly forward with a series of squeaks and shudders, jerking forward so that her head nodded. Then the engine died, popping and rumbling to a halt, and around her shadows rose in silence, and she rose too, facing the hatch, wanting to claw at the metal with her fingernails. She didn't care if the whole Iraqi Army was on the other side. She wanted out, out, *out*.

The boots dragged themselves up, over the curved rim of their dark sky, then paused above them. A hollow cough came through the iron. Then the scrape of metal slowly moving against rough metal.

She was fast, but she was still second or third below

the circle of light that blinked open above them. The man-figures bent, then one rose suddenly toward the light. He went up quietly and quickly through the opening. The men below regrouped, and a second sucked upward. Then she felt hands grip her legs and arms. They half pushed, half threw her up through the hatch, and she caught the lip with her arms and dragged her legs up and out of the iron ring.

Outside. She breathed in fresh air, or at least fresher, cool with a hint of dust so that she sneezed suddenly, before she could remember she was supposed to stifle it. She swallowed quickly, guiltily, but no one said anything. Ducking her head to avoid a web of truss work and beams, dusty and neglected-looking, only a few feet above. A roof or ceiling of some sort. She crept forward on gloves and knees over the curving tank and then reoriented herself and fitted her boots to rungs leading over it and down.

She stood on black concrete, rough and unevenly planed, as if it had been poured too quickly to level properly. Above the truck hung fluorescent tubes, whole, but lightless. The only illumination came from the truck's headlights, which were still on though the clatter of the worn-out engine had stopped. They lit everything in stark shadows, a confused jumble of large objects half revealed and half in shadow. She smelled diesel exhaust and burnt rubber and hot metal, like the smell when something goes wrong with your car and you keep driving because it's dark and you can't stop but you know something's going very seriously wrong.

Gault dropped to the concrete, holding his pistol. His camo trou were muddy and dripping. He didn't look at her, just immediately headed for the cab. Nichols was already there, pulling weapons out from behind the seat and passing them down. When the gunny had his, he checked it quickly, breaking it down to look inside. Checking it hadn't been tampered with, she guessed. He looked up and saw her watching him, slapped the weapon back together, and jogged back. Without words, he directed the men out around the truck with a pointed finger.

Then she and Sarsten and Gault were alone with the Iraqi, who was staring at her. Gault was looking in his little phrase book, while Sarsten spoke rapidly in Arabic. The Iraqi replied, a few short words, but his eyes stayed on her. Then he reached out suddenly, and pulled off her bush hat. She grabbed for it but he held it away, staring at her hair.

GAULT HADN'T expected this. He cursed himself, knowing he should have anticipated it. But he hadn't, and now the Iraqi was yelling a mile a minute, shaking the major's hat like it was a cobra he was trying to kill. He was talking too fast to catch a word, except maybe for *hurmah*—woman. Sarsten was standing back now. Only occasionally did he interject a word. Gault looked off into the garage, or warehouse, or wherever they were, and realized time was passing, they weren't moving, and that someone might overhear. So he put his hand out, over Ted's mouth. The Iraqi threw his hand off. Gault said angrily, "Tell him to shut up, will you?"

"Isma'! Tkalam be sout wati," Sarsten told the guy.

"You bring woman—this is *haram. Mush taiyyib!* Forbidden. You are fools."

"She's a doctor."

"Doktoor?" He stared at her, and Maddox, bless her, coolly took out a medical pack and held it up. The red cross on it silenced the Iraqi. He rubbed the boil on the side of his face, breathing hard. Shaking his head.

Sarsten spoke then, smiling. He patted Maddox as if she were a pet, not noticing, or pretending not to see, the look she gave him. He said several sentences with the words woman and good in them. Then he smiled. And after a moment Ted smiled too, only in a puzzled, still angry way.

"You really are fools," he said again, and Gault noticed the guy's English was getting better the more he spoke it.

He didn't like this place. He felt exposed, though he couldn't tell exactly why. It was an open-bay building, poured-in-place concrete or maybe the prefab type of tilt-up walls. The ceiling was light-duty: corrugated steel, held up by the truss work. He kept looking toward a line of light. Now that his eyes were adapting he saw it was a gap along the bottom sill of the sort of rolling door you saw on warehouses. It looked like a garage, except he didn't see any fuel pumps or tools. Maybe a service area, where trucks pulled in for unloading or maintenance. He didn't want that door to roll up all of a sudden. Too many unwelcome surprises could be on the other side. He pulled his city map out and squatted on the concrete. Clicked his light on. "Where are we?" he asked the Iraqi, pointing at the map.

Ted looked at Maddox, then at Sarsten. He still looked angry, but finally he squatted. Gault handed him a pencil, and he studied the map a moment, then made a firm mark and looked up. Gault bent close, wiping sweat off his face.

The mark, not a cross but a dot, was almost perfectly centered in the city map. Just south of one of the eastward-swooping bends of the river. Above a white strip representing the Baghdad/Muthenna Airfield. On one of a scatter of the black squares and rectangles that meant buildings. Streets and rail sidings threaded them. Ted had placed his dot just north of the airfield, in a built-up area the map called Al Fajr.

He glanced up as Vertierra went to a knee beside him. The RTO put his face close and muttered, "I found a window. Back of the building. Looks like we're in a truck park. A bombed building back of us."

"Any other doors?"

"One, in back. I've got Nichols posted there."

"Okay. Maintain the perimeter. Keep out of sight from outside," Gault asked Ted. "Okay, my friend. My *good* friend."

He patted the Iraqi's shoulder, then, remembering how the Arabs liked to touch each other, reached around him and gave him a shoulder-hug. "Thank you so much for helping us. *Shukrahn*. Bringing us into town in your truck. Very, very smart! They tell me you know the way from here on. Make me happy and tell me that's true."

Ted nodded. He pointed straight down. And grinned.

Gault stood and looked at the floor again. It was still concrete, still as roughly finished. Where it met the wall a considerable amount of dirt and the kind of debris smokers left behind, butts and crumpled packs and burnt-out matches, had been push-broomed into a little shoal. "Under here?" he said.

Sarsten began to speak, and Gault wheeled on him at once. "I'll ask the questions."

"Just trying to help."

"If I need it I'll ask. Right now I want you on security by that entrance." He pointed to the light.

The SAS raised his eyebrows, started to speak. Then smiled.

He got up and jogged away toward the entrance, cradling his rifle. Gault turned back to Ted. "You're telling me it's right underneath us?"

"*La*. Not *beneath*, not *here*. But that is how you get to it." He pointed down again.

"Where does it lead?"

"That way." He pointed. "Where you want to go."

Gault was frowning over this statement when he remembered the Finnish map, the guided tour to the sewers of Baghdad. He got it out too and laid it next to the city map. He took out his compass and oriented them both, then exchanged it for the GPS. He waited till it picked up the satellites. Ted watched silently. When the latitude and longitude came up, Gault plotted it. It came out on top of the penciled dot, and he nodded, impressed. They were right where the Iraqi said they were: north of the airport, south of the river.

Ted had observed this without saying a word, looking at the maps, then at the device. Now he pointed to one of the dotted lines on the Finnish map. "This one. Here. Down to the river—through Al 'Atifiyah."

Gault transferred the position to the Finnish map, as closely as he could—it didn't have lat/long markings, just the call-outs for elevation and the river and some of the principal streets—and sat back on his heels. He felt uneasy again, and again he couldn't say why.

"Where exactly are the missiles?" he asked Ted.

"Mee-sles?" The word didn't register, he could see that.

"Flying Stones. *Hijurat ababeel*. You said you worked on it."

"Work on it? No. I didn't say that."

"You didn't?" Gault looked at him; hadn't he said he did, back in the truck? *"Mutta'assif*. I'm sorry. I thought you did. Well, you said you knew where it was, right? Where is it?"

For answer the Iraqi extended his hand. Gault watched it travel across the map, his breath withheld. The moving finger reached east. It reached across the river. It came down on the tongue of land created as the Tigris writhed from south to east, in the center of the city, creating a bulge of land that under his flashlight showed a cluster of black squares north of a bridge. The bridge was called the Jisr 17th Tammit. "Jisr," he knew, meant bridge. But the cluster of buildings was labeled in English.

"The Medical City," said Ted, picking absently at his boil. He grinned, showing teeth that made Gault look away. "Big hospital. For important peoples. Saddam Hussein, he goes to there."

Gault examined a cluster of buildings overprinted in red adjacent to it. Red meant government buildings, on the CIA map. The key number was forty-five. He expected them to be some sort of health department buildings, or maybe housing for medical staff. But when he turned the map over and read the entry under forty-five, he saw they were the Defense Ministry and the Headquarters of the Iraqi Army.

"Son of a bitch," he muttered. "Get the commander over here."

Then he remembered: he hadn't seen Lenson get out of the tanker.

He looked up, but Maddox was already climbing the ladder again. Her boots grated on iron. The sound made shivers run down his back; he hadn't enjoyed being entombed in there either. He heard her calling, muffled by the metal.

He studied the map as the naval officer emerged, then let himself down step by step to the concrete.

"Commander. You okay?"

Lenson rubbed his face slowly. He still looked dazed, but he seemed to be trying to focus as Gault explained. When he got to the Medical City bit, he blinked. "It's a hospital?"

"This Medical City, it's a hospital, right?" Gault asked Ted. "Like a national hospital?" The Iraqi nodded. "And that's where Flying Stones is?"

"That is what they say."

A flame flared inches from his face. Gault looked at him. The man looked back levelly, unconcerned, sucking another of his cigarettes, and flicked the burnt match against the wall to lie smoking with the others. Making his voice calm, he said, "That's what *they* say. What do you mean? Haven't *you* been there?"

"*La, la.* No. I told you. I have not been to it."

"How can you take us there if you haven't been there?"

Ted raised his eyebrows. "I? Oh, no, no. I not take you there. No. You go. *You. I* not take you."

"Oh, yes, you will."

"No. No. I will not go."

Gault raised his voice wearily. "Sergeant Sarsten? A little translation help, please. We seem to have a serious misunderstanding here."

• • •

WHEN THEY had it straightened out, or as straightened as it was going to get, he felt the sinking feeling again. "Ted" insisted he'd never been told to take them directly to the site. Nor did he know exactly where it was. He'd heard it was beneath the Medical City. He didn't know exactly where beneath it, but he'd been told it was close to the river. No, he wouldn't say who'd told him. No, he couldn't go and get his boss, the one who passed information out of the country to Damascus. He'd left the city when the bombing started. In fact, Ted wouldn't admit he was working for the Syrians, only that he was doing Allah's work helping the enemies of Saddam, the enemy of Allah. They *were* the enemies of Saddam, were they not? They were Americans. Their wonderful radio there would tell them where to go. They had no further need of him, surely. Together they whipsawed him for nearly fifteen minutes, but in the end concluded either he knew nothing more, or he wasn't going to give it up without more forceful persuasion.

Sarsten got up from his heels and motioned him aside. A few feet distant he said, "Shall I take the piss out of him, then?"

Gault looked back at the guy. He was smoking again, squatting and looking pleased with himself. He kept stealing glances at Maddox, who was sitting on the running board of the truck with Lenson. He wondered if it was worth some field interrogation. Wiring his hands behind him, a few slaps to loosen his mouth. He decided it was too soon for that, and told the SAS no. This guy was the closest thing they had to an ally. Converting him into another hostile wasn't going to help. "Maybe if he keeps this up," he told Sarsten.

"Just give me the word, Gunny. We'll make him sing."

He strolled back and Ted stood. "So, you will go now?" he said, grinning and spitting out a shred of tobacco. The cigarette smelled rank, like some old cigar.

"Go down underground. Find Saddam's secret. Win the war." He grinned wider, looking sideways at Maddox.

"Like shit," Gault muttered under his breath. "You're going with us," he said aloud.

Ted just smiled and shook his head.

He was considering strangling the fucker, stinking breath and all, when the tremor hit. A jolt against the soles of their boots, a sway and humming in the truss work overhead. Seconds later the sound arrived. He listened to the thuds of distant bombs, eyes on the Iraqi—who didn't react at all, as if he heard it every day. He probably did; he'd had four weeks to get used to it.

Gault wiped sweat off his face again. Like every mission, planning it was different from doing it. Time was passing. He had to do something. He got up and began quartering the garage, running his flash over the concrete. Aside from the surface roughness, it was unmarked. No sign of joints or accesses. Monolithic. He couldn't tell if it was part of a larger slab, if the garage they were in was part of a larger building. If there were adjoining buildings, shouldn't there be doors to them? "Reinforced?" he asked the Iraqi, pointing at the floor, but got only a blank look. Sarsten and Maddox watched him. Lenson stared at the wall.

He went on his knees to the map, checked the GPS again. The tremor came again, closer. He glanced at the overhead and saw Maddox looking up too. They were too close to the airport, and way too close to the railyard. Whether the explosions they heard were bombs or Tomahawks, freight-handling facilities attracted ordnance. He didn't want to be here when the US Air Force decided it was time to catch up on their quota of truck parks.

Finally he went around to the back of the truck. Vertierra was down on one knee, weapon cradled, watching the gate door. The gray light silvered his sweating face. He looked muddy and exhausted. "Get Nichols on deck to rig for breaching," Gault told him.

* * *

F.C. WAS still chewing on the cleaning patch. It was getting soggy-ragged, but it kept his jaw busy. Kneeling on the cold concrete, its whorls and ridges pressing into his knees through the battle dress, he checked that the rifle was on safe, then laid it carefully aside. He shrugged his ruck off and swung it around to face him. He pulled the charges out and set them on the concrete, then laid his demo card beside them.

The smell of the explosive brought back Quantico in the summer. The heat. The mosquitoes. The woods, green and dripping with summer rain.

The Corps taught breaching in the classroom first. Scarred wooden tables and plastic chairs whose feet left rust rings on the linoleum tile. C-4, TNT, tetrytol, ammonium nitrate, military dynamite. How to calculate charges to cut steel I-beams, rectangular sections, concrete T-beams, timber. How to crater roads and destroy a bridge abutment. Saddle charges, diamond charges, platter charges, a counter-force charge, where you blew through a standing column from both sides at once. Some math, not a lot; basic arithmetic, simple tables; procedures a man could remember under stress, at night, under fire.

After the classroom you went to the dummy explosives. Kindergarten clay that you shaped with your hands, kneaded into plasticity and molded to shape. Bright candy yellow, grass green, sky blue. The primary colors of a child's world. They practiced setting up out at Combat Town. How to blow a door, a brick wall four feet thick, how to cut through sheet steel or demolish a stick-built house. Then at last the real thing, waxy stiff blocks of gray explosive. Their first live charge was a quarter-pound of C-4 on a concrete block. It made a neat, perfectly cut hole.

The problem was, at school you always knew what you were blowing through. Here, it was anybody's guess. He struck the concrete with the heel of his hand, but of course got nothing back. At least two feet thick, and judging by the fact trucks parked here, most likely steel reinforced.

He checked the demo card. An untamped charge on reinforced concrete between one and three feet thick required fourteen pounds of TNT. He didn't carry TNT. He had twenty pounds of C-16, Detasheet, in five-pound blocks, and eight detonators. The blocks were skinned with olive drab plastic. He peeled a couple and pressed them together, making a single square from the two dense-feeling rectangles, and leaned his weight on them to mash them into the whorls and indentations of the concrete. Considered adding another, then looked at the flimsy roof overhead and decided not to.

"We need to move the truck," he told Gault. "I want the engine block over the point of detonation."

"You sure about that?"

"I want something to absorb the back blast. We don't want the roof taking off."

A tremor; a wait; a distant thud. Lenson got up and walked toward them.

"Tomahawks," he said.

"Is that what it is, Commander?" said Gault. Nichols watched his pale eyes examine the naval officer's face.

Lenson looked pale but better than he had that morning. F.C. remembered getting him out of the blockhouse. He hadn't been able to walk then. He decided he wasn't going to let the fucking Iraqis capture him. Not while he still had a weapon, even if it was just his KA-BAR.

Lenson nodded. Said something about hearing them before, the sound was the same. Gault nodded, and after a moment Lenson went back to sit beside Maddox again.

To F.C. the gunny said, "Well, whatever it is, maybe it'll cover us setting this off. I'll get him to move the truck. You're all ready to go?"

"Just got to stick the detonator in."

"Before or after?"

"Get the truck over it first. Then I'll crawl under and set it."

The only trouble was Ted Man didn't want to move the truck. He said it was his. And after a while F.C. started to think maybe it wasn't such a hot idea after all. What if they just blew the wheels off? They didn't have jacks, or time, to pry a goddamn truck out of the way. Finally he went over to where the gunny and the Iraqi were arguing and said he'd changed his mind. Gault gave him a pissed-off look. Instead they moved the truck farther away. This Ted readily agreed to. He jockeyed it back and forth while the diesel fumes filled the garage.

When he finally turned the engine off again, F.C. dropped to his knees over the charge. Oil had dripped from the truck where it had parked, making a black pool that reminded him of blood. He had the cap ready and pressed it down into the explosive. Then looked to the TL.

Gault nodded, and he twisted and pulled the fuze igniter. Grabbed his rifle and jumped to his feet, and ran after the gunny for the back of the garage.

In an adjoining room they flattened themselves along the wall, just in case the roof came down. Through a window he saw empty rails, a lowering sky, the distant sky-pricking needle of a minaret.

The charge went off with a clap that left their ears ringing. The walls shook. Pieces of insulation and straw—the remains of birds' nests, he saw—fell from the roof. A clang and clatter of metal resounded from the bay area.

When they went back in, the air milled with smoke. It smelled like a firing range. He fanned the haze away and looked down. The charge had blasted a hemispherical absence in the concrete. At the bottom was a two-foot circle of tan gravel. The end of a rebar came out of one side of the cut, then took a sharp angle downward. He looked around the garage. Ted was running his hands over gouges in the side of the cab. There were holes in the overhead, too, through which they could see the sky.

"E-tools," Gault said, looking into the hole. "And hurry up. We don't have much time."

·   ·   ·

THERE WAS room for one man at a time to work in the hole. They went in headfirst and worked hanging upside down, legs hooked over the edge, pitching the dirt up and out onto the concrete floor. Each man dug furiously for ten minutes, then backed out to give the next one a turn. Ted came over with a sledge from his truck and they used that to hammer off more concrete around the lip of the penetration. The work went fairly fast until the dirt began caving in on them. They dug it out around the perimeter of the hole, under the concrete, and kept going down.

In an hour they were six feet down, the "on" digger inside the hole, his head under the level of the foundation. Gault, squatting beside it, didn't like the way he was starting to feel. Each time he jumped in he worked furiously in the dusty air, coughing, twisting awkwardly to throw spadefuls of the loose soil into the bucket they'd lowered to get the tailings out of the pit. The sand shifted under his boots, caving in as he went down. At each plunge of the blade, he expected the ring of concrete, but it didn't come. The spades grated and sparked through a layer of weathered, burnt brick, and he wondered what ancient catastrophe or war had left it there. They said Baghdad was older than Rome. He dug till his shoulders ached and his throat was coated with the dry fine dust, then dropped the tool and wriggled out as Blaisell thrust his boots through the hole. Ted sat chain-smoking, grimly eyeing his truck. Maddox took her turn, though she didn't last long, and after a while Lenson got up and insisted on digging too.

Gault didn't mind underground work. They'd done some during the UAT workup, trying to refine tactics and weaponry for fighting in built-up areas. Building on stuff they'd read about Stalingrad and Hue City and the tunnels at Cu Chi. A city engineer had taken them into the drains of downtown San Antonio, and they'd war-gamed against a police squad. What worried him was how little time they had. G day was tomorrow. He kept the men digging as fast as they could, rotating them in and out. But so far he didn't see anything like what he wanted. The ground looked undisturbed. He checked the map again, remembering what the army engineer had said about what got built probably not matching what was on the plan. If they didn't find this thing pretty fucking soon, he'd have to come up with some other way to get to the objective.

At last he jumped to his feet, grabbed another tool, and slid feetfirst in beside Sarsten. The SAS grunted angrily at being crowded, but Gault attacked the side of the deepening hole, digging not downward, but off to the north.

Six feet on, the steel blade cut chips out of a terracotta surface. For a moment he thought it was an old wall, buried here. Then he recognized it. The old square pipes he remembered seeing in pits along the road when he was a kid. Sarsten wriggled over beside him. Working side by side, they uncovered three feet of it.

"That what you wanted?" the SAS asked him.

He shook his head. The Finnish map showed a major new line here, built in the eighties. This was smaller, something that might serve to drain a block, and it had been here a long time. He called for the sledge, and when F.C. handed it down, tapped it on the pipe, swung back, and whanged it dead center.

It busted apart, and a putrid smell of cold water and ancient shit welled out where they crouched. He reached in and through and felt the far side of it, slick and wet. He fitted the broken pieces roughly back into place and hastily covered it back up with dirt. And was turning away when he thought, Okay, this isn't it; but where does it go? Sooner or later, it's got to drain into something.

Half an hour later, digging along it as it headed east, they struck the top of the new line. The old terra-cotta was crudely cemented into its roof. The new drain was about eight feet down, of fresh gray concrete. He yelled to Nichols, who slapped a pound of Detasheet on it and scrambled out. The bang, muffled by the earth, was barely noticeable.

They dropped through the smoking hole, one after the other, into the hollow echoing darkness of the Baghdad sewers.

15

1200 23 February: Western Baghdad

Maureen looked past her dangling boots into the black hole the others had vanished into. Her hands were numb. She felt dizzy. She knew she was hyperventilating, but knowing it didn't help. Gunny Gault was hurrying them in, using those laser-beam eyes like cattle prods. Listening to the Iraqi protest, watching him scrabble against the concrete as the men below him pulled on his legs, hadn't helped a bit. A clammy sweat broke under her arms, all over her body. She didn't want to go in there. She didn't want to. She took a deep breath and let it out. Another.

She let go, and slid down and in until her boots splashed. She crouched there, terrified, looking up at the tiny perforation of light far above.

Like the others, she carried her weapon—in her case, just the Beretta, in its nylon holster belted to her LBE— and the load-bearing belt itself. They'd stripped what they'd need out of their rucks when they weren't digging. Vertierra told them to eat, stick some PowerBars or gorp in their pockets, and drink as much water as they could hold. Take flashlights, NVGs, spare batteries, ammo, grenades, E-tools, chemical protective gear, and their weapons. She and Lenson were to take whatever gear they'd require at the objective. Sarsten had climbed up onto the water truck and they'd handed up the stripped rucks one by one. They'd remain behind, hidden from prying eyes even if someone came into the garage. If they found the hole, the shattered concrete, they'd know *something* had been going on. But it would most likely be taken for a dud bomb, fallen through the overhead and burying itself, and given a wide berth.

A light ahead, an echoing voice. She slowly became aware of the smell. A humid, musty, old-detergent reek, mixed with a dead earthiness that made her think of pathology labs deep in ancient basements, the kind with stone slabs and cold water. And the smell of human shit, of course. She looked ahead, to where beams danced down a long lightless lumen. Then up again, her eyes unwilling to leave what little brightness dwelt above, what little fresh air touched her sweating face.

"Come on," muttered Lenson. He touched her arm. "Let's go. We got to move out."

Nichols's face appeared above her, then his footgear. They slid down toward her, kicking dirt into her face. Like being buried, she thought. She turned her head, with a physical effort that was like stepping through some invisible wall, and took a step into the dark. Then another. Her shaking fingers found her flashlight and switched it on. The light trembled as it bounced out ahead.

The drain was oval-shaped, a little lower than she was tall, so that she had to walk bent forward at the waist, and about six feet wide. The bottom was covered with a foot or two of viscous-looking sewage. It was flowing on ahead of her, eddying around her boots. It ran fairly fast; the current tugged at her ankles. It was icy cold. She could see her breath puffing out white in the beam of her light. Beneath the surface the concrete bottom was slick, coated with some sort of algal slime. Ahead came a splash and a muffled curse as someone went down. Her boots slipped too, and she flung out her arms instinctively. Her gloves scraped rough concrete and found no handhold, but she caught her balance. And a good thing, too, she thought, looking at the all-too-natural things that floated past her.

The air was breathable, though, and she sucked more of it in, trying to disregard the smell. A steady splash and rattle came from ahead, from the others, and the rasping echo of her own breathing. Too fast again, too ragged. She took another deep breath, trying to slow it down, and rubbed the back of her glove over her face and waded after them, sliding her feet along in the muck rather than lifting them from the bottom.

Lenson turned as she came up to him. He pointed his light at the overhead, and she saw something sticking down from the roof. A roughly sawn, jagged edge. Water was pissing down from it. She nodded and ducked under it, weaving her head out of the way. Already she was losing the smells, or her olfactory sense was burning out. Her boot toe felt a joint between the pipe sections and she saw, running her light up the side, that each section was about twenty feet long. She couldn't image how they'd gotten this thing down here, underneath buildings and so forth. Unless they'd built the buildings—poured the foundation of the garage, for example—after they'd laid this pipe.

A blue-gray radiance ahead . . . reaching it, she straightened for a moment and found herself at the bottom of a shaft that came down from shadowy recesses above. Like looking up in a cathedral. Far away at the very top, light shone through two small holes, rimmed the outline of a circle. She felt a little better, realizing there were other ways of escape. They couldn't use them, she knew that—couldn't climb out in the middle of a street, or whatever lay above—but it was nice to know they were there.

GAULT WADED along, bent over till his neck brushed the roof. He'd expected low, and he'd expected shit; the engineer had said the storm drains were sewers too here, like they used to be in the States years ago. What he liked was the steady flow of air on his face. Airflow meant he didn't have to worry about gas buildup, methane and the other nasties you could run into underground. They had masks, but you still needed oxygen.

He'd expected turds, but it actually wasn't as bad as he'd expected. He guessed it was because the air war had knocked out the power supply. No electricity, no pumps; and in a flat land like Iraq, no water pressure. No water pressure, no flush toilets, and no flushing, no shit. Or at least, less of it. The rain that had fallen over the last few days had washed this narrow passage as clean probably as it had been since it was installed. Judging by the slime underfoot, and the brown discoloration along the sides, most of the time it was three feet deep in crap.

He was counting steps, but now his attention moved from *eighty-nine, ninety* and what his boots were splashing through to where they were headed. He had them back in column order, with Blaze at point. He could hear Ted muttering to himself behind him. After the Iraqi, Vertierra, looking shrunken without the bulky radio gear he'd toted all the way from the LZ; Sarsten; Lenson; Maddox; and then Nichols taking the rear. Eight people, strung out along a long narrow hollowness here beneath the ground.

He wondered what was above them, what they were burrowing beneath, and recalled the map, the visual image he'd impressed on his mind like taking a photograph. Between the airfield and the Tigris lay a mosque and a bus garage, then a scattering of the green crosses that meant orchard. That was strange, an orchard in the heart of the city. Then would come the river. Just about a straight kilometer . . . maybe he should have put Tony as tail end. There were pros and cons both ways. He checked his compass again. The needle was meandering first one way, then the other. A lot of metal around them. Probably, in the concrete itself. But so far it ran straight as a stretched cord. Be nice if it took them all the way to the river. Once he got there, he'd have to think of something else. They couldn't swim the river in daylight. He'd just have to recon in and see.

The dark ahead was utter dark, utter cold, and he heard things moving up ahead. He didn't like it down here, but there were worse places to be. Ten or fifteen feet straight up above them, for instance. In the streets of a capital under siege from the air.

Another jolt, the kind they'd felt in the garage, rocked the drain around them. He halted, startled, then forced himself into motion again. Down here it felt closer, stronger, a whipcrack that shook scabs of dried crap down into the beams of their lights. If a bomb collapsed the drain, they'd be buried. He felt sweat break on his forehead at the same time he was freezing.

The wind blew in his face. He went on until he counted a hundred and fifty paces, three hundred meters, then called softly to the point man and went down on one knee. The sloshing behind him slowed. Then came faint splashes as one after the other they took knees too. He turned his head and whispered, "Step count?"

Vertierra tilted his head forward. He breathed into his ear, "A little short of three hundred meters."

Behind him Ted said loudly, "I go back now, please."

Gault turned instantly and reached. Grabbed the front of the Iraqi's shirt before he could evade. He shook him, hard, and hissed, "Keep quiet! They can hear us under here."

"I don't think—"

But the protest cut off with a wheeze, and Gault saw Sarsten had taken over. With a knee in the back and a hand over his mouth, the Iraqi's eyes shone terrified in the light of his flashlight. Gault blinked it twice and the SAS's hand removed itself. "Keep quiet," he mouthed to the Iraqi again. The guy had to shut up. They had no idea how close a basement or another tunnel might be above them. There were also such things as geophones.

The asset didn't say anything else, just looked scared

and pissed, which was okay by Gault, as long as he kept
the noise down. He directed the beam farther back;
glimpsed Lenson's and Maddox's faces like mud-
smeared moons. Nichols he couldn't see, but as tail end
he'd be lagging back, turning and listening behind them
to make sure of their six.

Vertierra, a hoarse whisper behind him: "We've got to
keep a serious eye on this knucklehead."

"If he keeps making noise, I'll fucking kill him,"
Gault muttered back. Then he glanced at his watch, and
got up again off his knee. Checked the safety on his
weapon. And a moment more they were all moving forward again, filling the narrow tube with the rapid *slosh,
slosh* of eight people walking into the darkness.

UP IN front, Blaze waded steadily ahead. He felt Gault
like a pressure behind him, pushing him along. He moved
without light, navigating by feel and by the faint back-
gleams of the flashlights behind him. He had his NVGs
on, and in their tiny whine the green and black patterns
shifted and fell into recurrent patterns that over and over
again showed him the same thing: the tube, too low to
stand erect in, continually narrowing ahead; the black
dots of roaches, scurrying away as they sensed light,
motion, sound, threat; the slowly roiling surface of the
sewage, with bits of paper, sticks, turds, and once the
limp soggy body of a dead kitten all hurrying on past and
ahead of him as if eager to reach some fated destination.
The twin burdens of the night vision goggles, poking out
ahead of his face, and the awkward bent posture sent an
ache corkscrewing into his back. He fingered his weapon,
starting every time the scratching, scuttling sound came
from ahead. Rats? Crabs? As long as it was going the
other way, who cared?

He didn't like this, but it was probably the safest way
of getting across town. As long as nobody figured out
they were down here. Covert in the culvert, he thought,

and grinned. Have to tell Vic that one. He hadn't seen any graffiti, anything to show anybody ever came down here. It'd be a bad place to get ambushed, though. You wouldn't even need to send troops down. Just seal off both ends, pour in some gas, and drop in a match. He shivered. Christ!

His goggles picked out the black side oval of an intersection ahead. He signaled back to hold up, and heard the splashing stop as the team halted. Weapon to his shoulder, he rocked slowly from side to side as he went forward, placing his boots on alternate sides of the centerline. The slow swish of water echoed out ahead of him. It came steadily nearer, eerily, as if it were flowing along a moving tunnel toward him, and he himself was standing still. He leaned out to the right and toggled his infrared, tried to shine it in, but couldn't see much.

Corner drill. Just like Combat Town. He angled out, hugging the wall, keeping the muzzle of the suppressed MP5 as close to the axis of the new tunnel as he could. But when he came abreast it was empty, just another sewer, slanting in and slightly down, filled with darkness and the rush of more water, a lot more. This one wasn't oval prefab, like the one they were in, but more like a big corrugated-steel pipe, the bottom half reinforced with concrete.

Past it, the joined streams were faster and much deeper. Another flash of his IR illuminator showed him white water over rocks and tree branches and what looked like an overturned shopping cart. The flood surged out, creamed halfway up the side of their drain, then turned and hurtled downward.

Blaze shivered, imagining what it must be like down here during a storm. There'd be fucking tons of water tearing along, loaded with debris. He wished he'd taken a closer look at the sky when they were back in the garage, looking out at the minarets. How much warning would they have, if it started to rain again?

He lifted his head, peering under the green seethe of

the screens, and looked ahead, into darkness. Only darkness, and when he bent forward again, the moving shadows of the cockroaches—black in the luminescent green—fleeing endlessly away down the dark tunnel ahead.

Come on, he motioned, and the splashes behind him resumed.

F.C. SPAT his cleaning patch into the sewage. Then grabbed for it, splashing in the murky stuff he waded through. Too late. The current whirled it away, toward the others, and passed out of sight down the tunnel. He didn't think a chewed-up wad of gauze was going to give them away. But it wasn't recon style. He wiped a sleeve over his mouth, wishing for about the millionth time that he had just a thumbnail of Copie to tuck under his lip.

It wasn't an easy way to move, crouched over, bent forward but looking back. He'd tried to walk backward, but slipped twice, going down on his ass in the slimy shit-water. He'd kept his weapon and his face out of it, but still. Forget that maneuver. Now he just crab-shuffled along, keeping his head turned back as much of the time as he could. He kept his light off, figuring anybody behind them would be using lights and he'd rather see them first than the other way around. This whole drain-crawling thing was new, and he was almost enjoying himself. It'd be a good story to tell when they got back.

Too bad Jake wasn't going home. He had a sudden image of the way the ATL's head had looked, the sweetish-coppery odor of blood and brain fluid. The oil stink of kerosene as he'd poured the stove fuel out, shaking it gurgling over the bodies. The way the flame caught and grew and merged into a yellow roar that filled the room with heat and light.

A painful blow to the back of his head knocked his NVGs askew. He crouched under the projection that came down from the roof. A bent metal bar, jagged, and he touched the back of his head to feel his own blood, as slick-slippery on his fingers as Zeitner's had been.

TWENTY MINUTES on, they came to the chute. It was at another intersection, this one with a dead-ended drain leading off to the right, a body-small oval-shaped feeder leading off to the left, and the remains of what looked like a bedstead, complete with springs, caught and hanging on a rusty projection of corrugated steel where they met. Blaisell had halted when he reached it, looking down. Gault aimed his flashlight where the corporal pointed, motioning to the rest of the file to hold up.

The sewer dropped into darkness, and his light found no bottom. The water, which had become deeper and more turbulent with each feeder, poured out over it in a dark curve. A hollow continuous roar filled their ears, and spray and mist filled their mouths and glistened in icy beads on their skin. Gault blinked into the black, trying to piece together a map from the shadows, trying to come up with something better than grabbing his balls and jumping in. Once one of them went down this thing, they'd be committed. He couldn't see any way of coming back up, not this steep, not with that much water going down. He glanced back and saw their faces studying him, weary and drawn, the men's cheeks dark with stubble and the camo paint that after days in the field caked solid in the creases and lines of their weathered skin, Maddox's exactly the same except for the lack of beard.

Okay, he wasn't too proud to ask for help. "Any ideas?" he asked Vertierra. The RTO just shook his head, looking down the throat of the monster.

They were all three standing there looking down when somebody ducked under his arm. It was Dr. Maddox. "Oh, a chute," she said. She pointed her light down it, then above and around. "How do you guys descend these?"

"I'm thinking about that very topic."

"I do some rock climbing. I'd just rappel down."

He looked at her. "What would you use for gear?"

"Gear's nice, but you don't have to have it."

"What about the line?"

"I'd leave it here, and use it on the way back."

"Okay, that sounds good. Want to give it a try?"

She looked surprised. "Me? You want me to go first?"

"You sound like you know what you're doing. Sure."
Blaisell, who was curled up in the little side feeder, made
a face behind her. Just for that, Gault told him, "Corporal,
you anchor the Major. Anything happens to her, your ass
is history, copy?"

"Right, Gunny." He rolled out of his niche, grinning.

SHE FELT like a kid who's just been dared to do something. Fine, she *wanted* to do something. Sitting still in
the dark, feeling closed in, was almost more than she
could take. As long as she could distract herself, it was
standable. Whenever she let herself think about where
she actually was, she started sweating again.

So that now when Gault uncoiled the line from around
his waist and handed it over she held it to her flashlight,
seeing what she had. Green woven strapping, about five-
eighths or a little more, not rope but better, covered with
nylon sheath; a bit stretchy but more than strong enough.
She bent over and clambered back up the sewer and
wrenched at the bedstead till she got a piece of iron free.
About three feet long, and pretty sturdy. She waded back
and braced it in one of the side feeders and tested it with
a tug. The pull set it. All right. She clove-hitched the
strapping to it and let the current drag her back through
the team. They pressed against the walls to let her pass,
and she came to where the concrete ended and tightened
up, legs sticking out over the edge while she looked
things over. The water funneled past her with a roar,
cresting up over her back and shoulders and spraying an
icy shower over her head.

"Maybe one of us should do this," Nichols said, glancing at Gault. "Not the doc."

Gault looked at her, but she didn't bother to respond. She was wrapping the line around her body. She kept it high, under her right armpit, around her back; up under her left armpit and across her chest, then across her back once more. Rock climbing, she'd have done it different. Just attach her figure eight to her harness, jump over the edge, and rap on down. Here she didn't have a harness or a figure eight, or the right boots, or the rest of her climbing rack, but the instructor at Seneca Rocks had shown them how to body rappel, and she thought she could do it. Unless the rope slipped, or the makeshift anchor pulled out.

She pushed that from her mind and edged around on the perch, fighting the pressure of the water, and asked them to shine their lights down after her. She turned hers off and buttoned it into her shirt. She found the end of the line and put two knots in it—one to warn her the end was coming up, the other a couple of yards from the end itself. If she got to those and there wasn't any bottom, she was going to have to climb back up, or more realistically, they were going to have to haul her back up. She gave them the idea: one yank, everything's okay; two yanks, come on down; three yanks, pull me back up.

Then she turned quickly, before she had a chance to get scared, braced her boots, and started down.

The first step or two her head was clear, but then she was suddenly underwater and the sheer force of falling tons almost knocked her off her feet. She tucked her chin against the roar and buffet, fighting to stay upright. She couldn't stay here, that was for sure. She let go a little with her right hand and the strapping slid around her and she walked on down. After four or five bounces her head came out of the sewage and she snatched a breath, though a mouthful of the sewer flow came with it. She could practically taste the pathogens going down. For sure fecal *Escherichia coli*, the pseudomonas family, the vibrios, the Aerobacters, salmonella . . . beaucoup protozoans and helminths, echinococcus, cryptosporidium, giardia. . . . If there was tidal backflow from the river, bilharziasis was a possibility too. Well, she had the Cipro. She made a mental note to give everybody a good heavy dose.

All this time she'd been bouncing down, or rather, getting slammed around by the water while her head was being bashed into the top of the pipe. She missed her climbing helmet. There wasn't much air room. The lights from above glared in her eyes, but they gave her a little visibility. Enough to see where, a few feet below her boots, the air space ended altogether.

She hung there on the line, looking down at it and feeling more and more like she just couldn't do this.

The curving fall plunged down and outward till it hit the opposite side of the drain, what was the ceiling a few yards above, what was here the slanted wall at her back. Leaving no air bubble between them, and giving no guarantee one existed beyond. She'd never been in a drain before, or a sewer, or whatever this place was. She didn't think a four-by-six oval would neck down that radically. A blood vessel wouldn't, but she had to admit she didn't know what kind of rules applied here, or if, whatever they were, they'd been followed.

She clung there, staring at it, smashed and buffeted by the icy water. Sometimes it submerged her, and she gasped and coughed. When you were in doubt on a rock face you could hang. Take your time, recover, think it through. She couldn't hang here. She was losing feeling in her hands. Plus, the team was waiting on her.

Thinking of them, she finally took a deep breath, then another—oxygenating her bloodstream—and kicked off and let go everything but the line.

The current grabbed her instantly and snatched her off her feet. She shot downward boots first, into blackness. The strap whipped through her gloves with frightening speed. She felt the first knot and almost instantly afterward the second. She only just got a glove on the tag end. She gripped desperately hard, flailing with her legs, kicking to find footing before she lost her grip and was swept away.

Then she had it, the hard slick concrete against the soles of her boots. She got her other glove on the strap, pulled upright, and stood sideways, leaning against the pressure. Her upward-straining lips found nothing but the cold foul rushing fluid that submerged the rest of her body. She struggled desperately to tiptoe, heart hammering, out of air and at the end of her strength. If she didn't let go, she'd drown here. If she did let go, she'd never be able to make it back against the current.

Without warning, her face broke free into darkness and cold spray-laden air.

She panted for several minutes, recovering her breath and letting the shakes work themselves out of her arms.

She went several yards down the larger drain before she found a place to anchor the line. Here the drain made a sharp left, not a planned one, she thought, judging by the ragged edges where the cut section had been set off. In the glow of her combat flashlight, pale cones hung down from the joint. She touched one with a gloved finger. It was a stalactite, but not hard; soft and friable, damp, detaching at her touch to drop into the stream that foamed and tugged around her chest. She found a knob of concrete and tied the rope off with a half hitch, then tugged hard twice. An answering tug came back.

Several minutes later Blaisell emerged into the air space, weapon slung over his back, coughing and sputtering. He wiped his face, blinking at her. Finally he muttered, "I'll take point," and headed down the sewer.

The gunny came next. He looked carefully around, then bent and found the line again and gave it two more tugs.

They came through one after the other, with Ted silent and angry-looking, scared-looking. She smiled at him, but he turned his eyes from her and spat.

Lenson came up not even breathing hard, as did

Sarsten. The SAS gave her a smile as he moved past, and a hug around the waist that almost pulled her off her feet. "Good leadership, Major."

"Thanks." She didn't care for the hug, but maybe it was a guy thing. A teammate kind of thing, like in football. They hugged each other after a touchdown, didn't they?

Vertierra emerged looking shaken. He stood, then slipped and went down and came up again with the same shocked expression unaltered. The water was so high and he was so short he had to crane his head back to breathe. She pressed his arm, asked if he was all right. He nodded silently, face turned away, and went on.

Nichols came last. When he got his footing, he panted for a moment, recovering, then shook himself like a dog till spray flew off his short hair. "Who took this line through?" he said. When she said she had, he said, "Good work."

She was shivering hard and her head hurt, actually the adrenaline was ebbing and everything was starting to hurt, but his remark lit a warm little pilot flame of pleasure. She said "Thanks," making it offhand, and bent under the surface to check the line one last time. She wanted to make sure it'd be there when they came back. It seemed solid, and she turned, glad *that* was over, and began once more wading downstream.

Not too long after that, she saw the tiny distant shimmer of gray daylight, very small, and very bright.

THE TIGRIS was broad and looked calm at first because it was so big, but when Gault looked closer it was roiling and muddy, full of power and debris. Upstream, a bridge lay crumpled, waves cresting over it as if over rocks in rapids. Black smoke rose in the distance above the far bank, and again, closer in, to their right. The sky was gray but it wasn't raining.

He was glad of that. If it had been, not one of them would have gotten through that sewer alive. He looked at the river again, estimating it at two fifty or three hundred meters across, an amazing thing in a land he'd thought of, before he got here, as parched desert. Then rolled slowly back from the steel-pipe screen that barred their exit, moving back into what, to any observer, would be the shadowy recesses of the sewer outfall. He checked his watch again. Twilight in three hours.

The rest of the team was sitting half in, half out of the flood, backs curled into the curve of the sewer and boots braced against the bottom. They held their weapons against their chests, or tucked them behind their heads to keep them out of the water. Ted's face was gray. His beard stubble looked shockingly dark against it. He'd lost his Daniel Ortega sunglasses in the chute, and he blinked into the dirty light, shivering like a wet kitten. Nobody said anything, so Gault didn't either. He got his camo kit out of his wet gear and smeared fresh green over his face and the backs of his hands. Vertierra was doing the same. When they were cammied up again, he let the current take them back to the grating. They lay there limply, like floating masses of wet garbage shoaled up against the bars, and he looked out again, slitted cold gaze examining everything that lay before them in the failing light of late afternoon.

Their eyes were only millimeters above the level of the river. It swept steadily past, cold and brown and filled with eddies and turbulence. He couldn't see above them on the embankment, on this side. The collapsed bridge lay about seven hundred meters upstream. Downstream, the river made a bend to the left and passed out of sight. For a moment he thought he heard voices; then decided it was just the roar of the river, the endless rushing clamor that was really all they could hear.

Beside him Vertierra shifted uneasily. Gault floated motionless, accepting the discomfort and cold, and lifted his eyes.

The river foamed along the far bank. Shallower there, then, probably submerged rocks. A concrete embankment rose above it fifteen or twenty feet. At the top of the embankment stood tiny figures that after a moment he recognized as fishermen. Above them were palm trees, then buildings. They were set back from the river's edge. Sizable, modernistic concrete structures of six or eight stories. Others rose behind them. They all seemed the same age and style. A brick chimney towered beyond the buildings, tapering against the gray sky like a pointless minaret. Even farther upstream, farther north, the gray stacks of a power plant rose. No smoke came from them.

Other buildings, downstream, showed the ragged outlines and rising smoke of bomb damage. But the area across the river seemed undamaged, at least that he could see.

He thought he heard voices again, accompanied this time by a metallic clacking. A rapid mechanical rattling, like pawls jumping against gear teeth. It sounded familiar, though he couldn't remember where he'd heard it before. He couldn't tell where it was coming from either. Their angle of vision wasn't that great, looking out from inside the outflow. Maybe behind, above him? He moved right up to the grate, thrusting his face between the thick galvanized bars to see out. A few more meters of the bank came into view. It was concrete, sloped downward. Here and there a metallic glitter. He stared at them for a few minutes but couldn't tell what they were.

Other side, then . . . with some grunting and splashing he and the RTO changed sides. On the downstream view, not much different. He looked at every inch of what he could see. That was how you noticed things, not trusting the first glance. Taking a close look at everything, letting it all sink in. They had to move, couldn't stop here, but moving before you knew where you were going was the way people spotted you.

That was how he noticed the manhole cover. It was hard to see from where he was. He was looking at it from the side, not from the top. But he was pretty sure it was a manhole cover. He pulled back and lifted the damp map above the water with his wet gloves. A thin blue line stretched across the river. Not one of the sewers. Not a drain either. Just a line, unmarked by call-outs or legends. But nothing showed above the surface.

He returned his attention to the river. It was foaming past faster than any body of water he'd ever crossed. Swimming it would be very dangerous. Even roped together, they'd be swept downstream. If another dropped bridge waited around the corner, they'd be in among it, maybe pinned against it, before they could reach the far bank. Even if by some miracle they did get across in one piece, they'd be way downstream of where they needed to go. Still, it was a possibility. He wouldn't rule it out yet.

He checked his watch. The trouble was, it would be almost four more hours till full dark. They couldn't swim across in the light. Not with the fishermen watching. And the invasion of Kuwait was going to start at 0400 tomorrow.

The only movement was the river. That and a car, creeping along on the far bank until it passed out of sight. A road, then, between riverbank and buildings. For a moment he wondered if maybe they *could* swim it in daylight, take a chance they wouldn't be spotted.

Something came drifting down the river, something dark. Part of it lifted above the surface, upraised, like an imploring hand. As it came abreast of him, swept steadily along, Gault saw it was a fallen tree. The imploring hand was a limb, broken short to a stump.

He was wondering if they could use something like that to float across, when a *crackcrackcrack* pealed out and white cones leaped up around the tree. He felt Vertierra flinch, reacting to the sound of gunfire from just above their heads.

The voices again; a pause, then the ratcheting noise resumed. He still didn't know what it was, but whoever was up there had rifles. AKs, by the sound. Therefore, most likely, troops. Men bored enough to fire at passing logs. Therefore, some sort of garrison.

Then he realized what the glints were, scattered here
and there along the slope, and with that the ratcheting
sound too made sense.

They were below an antiaircraft battery, sited here,
where the river gave a wide field of fire. He'd heard that
sound aboard ship, during floats in the Med. A memory:
hot days, the smells of paint and stack gas and food and
diesel fuel. Topside lines of marines exercising on deck,
and the ship's company working on the AA guns. The
mechanical noise was either maintenance or drill. Or
maybe whatever machine loaded the cartridges into belts.
The metallic glints were empty cartridges, lying where
the guns' mechanisms had ejected them.

He lay there, going over their possible routes across,
and at last concluded there were only two. He didn't want
to swim that river unless he had to. He didn't want to wait
until dark either.

But maybe there was another way.

DAN LAY with his arms wrapped around himself. Gray
stinking water slid endlessly down over him, and it was
cold. Along with the others, he'd tried to climb out of it,
edging up the sides or trying niches and corners to hoist
himself a few inches higher, but there was no place to rest
here in the outflow that wasn't underwater. So at last he
gave up and sat braced against the current, eyelids droop-
ing shut. Not really thinking at all, and not wanting to.

Then someone was shaking him awake. Vertierra,
hands cupped to confine his murmur. "Gunny wants you
down front."

When he neared the circle of light, the doctor was
already there. She held pills out. He swallowed them obe-
diently as Gault told them both to be completely silent,
there were troops right above them. He told them to float
slowly up to the grate, to take their time and look things
over. Then come back and they'd talk.

Dan looked out over the river. The city seemed ominously silent and strangely empty. He saw a few figures moving about on a shattered bridge, and once in a while a car moving along the far bank. That was all, except for the everlasting rush of the river, carrying along debris and foam in whirling eddies.

When they rejoined the gunny, Gault pulled their heads close in to his. He murmured, "That's the objective. Those buildings right across from us. It's a hospital complex. The buildings to the right are the Ministry of Defence."

"I know," Dan said.

Gault frowned. "You do?"

He had to force himself to speak. Above all else he wanted to sit quietly and do nothing, not even breathe. But behind the apathy he was beginning to remember what they were here for, beginning to argue himself back into participation in the mission. Not for himself. For Zeitner. Maybe even, in a strange way, and his thoughts grew confused again at this point, for the shepherd boy. And a hot spark of anger ignited, like a charged wire being pulled apart, at Saddam and Bush and Major, all the politicians whose greed and incompetence had so mismanaged things that now other men had to kill and maim each other to settle the matter. At humankind, all too eager to follow their gods and leaders into war. And maybe most of all, at Whoever had intended and continued such a fucked and evil world. He swallowed the cloying taste of shit that even the air tasted of now and coughed into his armpit and said, "I was doing targeting, remember? We hit the Defence Ministry the first day of the air war."

"You know where we are?"

"Basically. Don't you have us on the map there?"

Gault unfolded it and they went over it again. Maddox said, "Ted said it was at the hospital complex?"

"Correct."

"Well, that might make sense," Dan said, studying the map in the light of Gault's flash. "What's the last thir we'd target? A major medical facility. Where's he going to keep his ultimate deterrent? Right in the capital. Right next to the MOD. It could be."

"If it's really there," the doc put in.

Dan nodded unwillingly. The same thought he'd carried all this way with him: that Flying Stones, Hijurat Ababeel, Project 985, whatever, might all be just the Iraqi equivalent of Area 51 or the Face on Mars or the boy who needed pull tabs for a kidney operation, an urban legend that in the end would dissolve into mist.

Maddox went on, "And if we can find it. I count twelve buildings on this map. How do we know which one it's in? And how do we get into it, if we find it?"

"He's no help?" Dan glanced at the shivering Iraqi.

"No. Says he doesn't know."

"You believe him?"

The gunny said quietly that that was hard to say; his story had changed over the course of the day. First he'd said he'd worked on the weapon; later he'd denied it, said he knew nothing about it. First he'd said he knew where it was, then he'd backed off that too. Maddox looked at Dan. "We'll talk to him," she said. "See what we can get. Do we have time, Gunny Sergeant?"

Gault checked his watch. "We can't move till dark. Not with them up above us. He's all yours."

So now they were squatting up-sewer with Ted. Maddox had plumped herself down next to him. Dan squished down on the other side. The Iraqi looked uncomfortable, but there was nowhere to go. After their descent of the chute, and without his glasses, he looked less truculent. He was also shivering hard, just like both of them. And the doctor was saying, disbelief and scorn plain in her voice, "You're telling me you worked on it, but you don't know what it is."

"I didn't make it. I work in shop where they make it. The part that causes death."

"The part that . . . you mean the warhead?"

"That is it. Not the . . . mee-sle. The warhead."

Dan caught Maddox's eye, gave her an encouraging nod. *Go on.* "So it's definitely a missile," she told Ted. "Well, that's helpful. But not much. What's in the warhead?"

"I don't know."

"I mean, just in general. Chemicals? Biologicals? Some sort of radioactive weapon?"

Ted mumbled, "The boss said it was a ray of light."

They looked at each other across him. "Excuse me?" Maddox said to him. "What exactly did he say?"

"He said it . . . *was* ray of light out of Saddam's forehead, like Tammuz, that it would conquer the Zionists and Americans. Saddam thinks he is Nebuchadnezzar. He will bring the Jews into a new captivity."

Dan wondered what to make out of this. None of the briefings had mentioned any kind of laser or beam weapon, and he was pretty sure anything like that was beyond the Iraqi capability. Tammuz, though, was interesting; it was another name for the long-range upgraded Scud. On the other hand, he dimly remembered something about Tammuz being the son of Ishtar—no, he wasn't sure of that—anyway, some early Babylonian god.

"Tammuz, the missile? Or Tammuz, the god?"

Ted shrugged. "That all *jahilia*," he said. He didn't bother to explain what "jahilia" was, but it didn't sound like he meant it as praise.

"So, you worked on the warhead," Maddox said. "Tell us about it. What was your job?"

"Drive machine," he said, pushing with his hands, then extending them and lifting.

"Forklift?" Dan said encouragingly.

"*Aywa!* Forkleeft."

Dan tried for heartiness, anything other than the exhaustion and guilt that was hardening around his heart like a leaden shell. "Okay! Now we're getting someplace. The forklift man. You move the warheads around. Good. Tell me about them. What are they like?"

"Concrete. It's concrete, hollow." Ted swallowed,

looked around the drain. Then reached up, and sketched a diagram with his finger on the muck that coated the arching overhead. "Hollow, yes? With tube through middle. Holes in the tube. Hole at the nose. Nose plug, make it out of . . . plastic, like glass."

Dan looked at it, groping through his exhaustion for what the guy was talking about. The challenge with any ballistic warhead was to bring it through the high-speed, high-temperature atmospheric reentry. Concrete could be a way to do it. Heavy, but it'd protect whatever was inside from the heat. The plug was strange, though. "Plastic, like glass." Fiberglas? But Fiberglas would burn through, wouldn't it?

"Where exactly did you work?"

"I work in Karbala. But I live in Baghdad, in Al Quds. And one day man say to me, you know, that where this going, not far from Al Quds. And I say, where? And he tell me here." He pointed toward the far bank. "Four of them, I remember now. He say, number four."

Maddox said, "You're telling us you don't know what the payload was?"

Ted said he didn't know, a liquid, he thought. When they asked him what kind of liquid, he just shrugged again. All he seemed to know was that whatever it was, the man had told him it was in Medical City.

Dan stared at him in the tunnel dim. So that if this turkey was telling the truth, the only actual link was a chance remark that might as far as any of them knew simply be rumor. But that somebody had reported to the Syrians as a fact, and they'd handed on through who knew how many hands and ears till it reached US Defense Intelligence. Growing its own layers of legend and accretion at each passage from hand to hand, language to language, like a grain of sand around which more and more layers of shit wrapped themselves. Making an unemployed forklift driver an "insider," a "mole," an "engineer."

"Why exactly are you helping us, Ted?" he said, making his voice as friendly as he could muster, lying waist-deep in runoff and wanting to throttle the guy.

"I want kill Saddam."

"You're a friend of Syria, do I understand that right?"

"I don't care for Syria, or for America, or the Jews. I follow Ali. Anyone who kills Saddam, I help them." He glared at Maddox. "But woman soldier, this *haram*. Not according to their nature, or Allah's will."

Dan was thinking how a lot of American servicemen agreed with him when Maddox jerked her head up-tunnel. He fought his way against the current after her. A few feet was enough for the rushing water to mask their voices. She said, "I'm sorry, this is horseshit. He's obviously a hopeless bullshitter. But it was all there was, so our intel people believed what the Syrians told them. There's nothing here. We've lost one man getting here. If we try to cross that river, those troops out there will either shoot us or we'll all drown."

"You think so? I think we could make it after dark. Find something that floats and hang on to it."

"That's not exactly the point." She glanced toward the leaden disk that was the exit, the malformed humps between them and the light that were the others. "Look, we're just the attachments, you and me. The gunny's the team leader. But once we get to the objective, we're in charge. Right? Well, we're at the objective, and I'm asking if you've seen enough."

"What are you suggesting? You want us to turn around and go home?" He rubbed his face. The cold separateness, the numbness was ebbing. Now he could feel; but what he felt was ineradicable guilt and desperate fear. He didn't want to be captured again. He wouldn't be able to stop babbling. He'd do anything to avoid the Electric Walk-man again. If there was anything they didn't know, he'd tell them. He'd make it up. Sign things. He wasn't proud feeling this, but it was the truth. Maybe that was why he was looking forward to the river. He could let go, just let go, and he wouldn't have to feel anything ever again.

Looking at him, Maddox said, "You know, you're still in shock."

"Not anymore."

"You think you're okay, but there are aftereffects. You're going to carry them for a long time. Maybe for the rest of your life."

He cleared his throat and put his hands over his eyes. White hot lightning spiked through his vision, and he uncovered them quickly. "I'm all right. Look. We're *not* at the objective. Not yet. We've got to at least try and find it. If we can go back and honestly say we looked and there's nothing there, it's scuttlebutt, a rumor, that frees the CINC to act. Otherwise he's got to keep in the back of his mind that Saddam's got some kind of hole card, some last-ditch terror weapon that if the Allies push him too far, he'll use."

Maddox said angrily, "How many lives is that worth? You heard this bozo. He's fucking clueless. A concrete warhead? Come on."

Dan said, "The Manhattan Project probably had a lot of clueless gofers too. Guys who only saw their little piece of the tail fin or the left hand frammous nut to the number three packing gland or whatever. That's how security compartmentation works. It doesn't mean this thing doesn't exist. And a concrete warhead sort of makes sense. With a nose plug, and a central tunnel." He rubbed his face again, trying to convince himself more than her. "So the plug burns through, then air pressure blows whatever's inside out the back in a plume. Dispersal, see? Whatever's inside gets air-mixed and scattered, instead of plowing into the ground and getting buried. Actually it'd be pretty clever, wouldn't depend on a lot of circuitry, stuff we can fry or jam."

"So you think it could be real?"

He shrugged. It was hard arguing with her, because he wanted to go back too. He *desperately* wanted to go back. He didn't want to cross this stormy river. Those ominously silent buildings gave him the same feeling he'd had as a kid, following the reluctant Frodo toward Mordor to destroy the mysterious Ring that the Dark Lord, Sauron, needed to complete his power. But they just couldn't stop three hundred meters short of what they'd come so far to find. It was perfectly clear to him that in the cold equations of intelligence, all their lives would be well spent finding out exactly what lay over there. If there was nothing, *nada, rien, nichevo,* that would be precisely as important as if it was actually some hellish weapon, some horror of chemistry or biology or physics twisted to the purpose of mass death.

Faced with that need to know, his own terror and all their lives were not enough to balance against it.

"Whatever I think, we've got to go," he told her. "If you don't feel it's necessary, stay here. I might not know exactly what I'm looking at, but if it's there, I can target it. And that's really all they need."

He was turning away when she gripped his arm. She brought her face so close he could smell her breath, like ripe apples amid the putrid breath of the sewer. She said, "If the rest of you are going, I am too."

"Gee, this is just like arguing with my ex-wife. You just said there's nothing there."

"That's what I think. But if I'm wrong, I need to see it. If it's something Fayzah Al-Syori's managed to petridish, we have to find out exactly what it is."

"But there's still probably nothing there?"

"That's my call, yeah," she said.

"All right," Dan said. "So let's go see the gunny. Now that we agree."

GAULT WATCHED them as they came up. Vertierra was up at the grate bars. The *scrape, scrape* of his wire saw underwater was just audible. He wondered what they'd decided. He guessed they'd go for it. There was really no other choice.

"Well?" he said.

"He doesn't give you much to go on," Lenson said. "But it sounds like there might be something there. Or there might not. The only way to find out is to go in and look."

He looked to Maddox. She nodded darkly, and Gault said after a moment, feeling the irrevocability and doom of the words, "All right then. The sergeant says he'll be through this grille pretty soon. I'll go out first. Just sit tight till I get back."

HALF AN hour later Gault decided it was time. Vertierra had edged back by then, carrying the sawed-through length of grate bar. He told him to put it in a side drain, and to smear the cut edges with mud so they didn't gleam. He pulled off his load-bearing vest and bush hat and gave them to Blaisell. He left his MP5 and his NVGs behind too. Held his .45 a moment, then handed it over as well. Reluctantly, but knowing that if the AA troops saw him, a pistol wasn't going to help. The only thing he could do then was lead them away from the others. He wouldn't come back, but they might be able to keep on.

Feeling strangely light, he ducked and slid between the smooth cold bars, out into the river sliding by. It tugged at him, but he lingered there, anchored by one hand. Looking upward, over the outflow.

He couldn't see the gun, but he could hear the men. He heard music too; it sounded like a cassette recorder, with a man singing, the caterwauling, falsetto Arabic that sounded strange at first to Western ears, but that after months in Saudi did not strike his ear now as exotic or foreign. It was just music, with the same mixture of sadness and longing and joy he heard in Merle Haggard or Tanya Tucker or Tammy Wynette. Then he saw a flicker, and pushed himself out and started drifting downstream, watching firelight reflected off some sort of overhead cover. A tent flap or a piece of metal; they'd screened it from the air. But that was good news. For men staring into a fire, the dark would be hard to penetrate.

And the dusk was gaining fast. Light was fading from the sky. Maybe, he thought again, he should wait for full night. One faint light, he couldn't tell from what, glowed out across the river. Aside from that the city was blacked out. He thought again, with a chill, how empty it seemed. But he knew it was only a seeming. There were probably more troops per square meter in the capital than anywhere else between here and Kuwait. Saddam took his security seriously.

While this went through his mind, the current was trucking him downstream. The farther out he got, the faster he could feel it taking him. The Tigris was anything but clean, but after the stone crap-stink of the sewer it felt wonderfully refreshing, flowing around and under his filthy battle dress. When he guessed he'd gone twenty yards, he began swimming slowly, keeping his arms underwater, back toward the bank he'd just left.

A few seconds later his knees brushed concrete. He low-crawled a few feet up on the slanted concrete. It was slick and stinking, as well it should be, he thought, downstream of a sewer discharge. He lay there for some minutes, looking and listening, till he was sure no one, no sentry or picket, or just some stray soldier come down to take a leak, watched from the bank above.

He low-crawled very slowly up the slope; waited; and then began his slow wriggling traverse. The wind brought the music to him clearly again. A woman was singing now. He remembered Baghdad Betty. He hadn't caught the program where she warned her audience how Bart Simpson was raping their women at home, but guys had told him about it. He smiled faintly in the dark.

Eventually he found the manhole, by ramming it with his head. It was raised a little above the sloping level of the bank. He rested by it for a time, listening to the music and the night, then lifted an arm and worked his fingers

around the edge. He found a thumbhole and tried it. No
good. He tried prying it up with his knife. The blade
snapped off. He shoved the useless hilt carefully back in
a pocket and tried prying with his fingers some more. He
must have loosened it, because this time it lifted, just a
bit, and then his muddy wet swollen fingers slipped and it
fell back with a clang.

He waited, tense with dread, but the music must have
covered the sound. No one came to investigate. But
sooner or later, they would. He couldn't lie out in the
open forever. A flare, a curious sentry with a flashlight, a
fisherman; sooner or later compromise was inevitable.

He rolled up and over it like a predatory starfish
mounting an oyster, braced himself over the lid, levered it
up, set it aside. Swung his legs in, and carefully and quietly and quickly lowered himself with his arms until he
felt iron rungs beneath his searching toes.

The trunk was very narrow and completely dark. That
was okay. He didn't need a lot of space, and he didn't
need any light at all. He went down and down till his
boots splashed. More water. He looked up, at a circle of
black outlined by greater blackness. Only someone peering straight down would see his light. He turned it on,
masking all but the faintest bleed of scarlet with his
cupped hand.

OKAY, but what about the lads on the gun?" Sarsten
smiled slowly. "Want me to make some more martyrs?"

Gault said no. They were here to recon, not fight.
Killing men on guard would only lead to a search. They
would follow the way he'd gone already: into the water,
downstream, then a short crawl to the manhole. Nichols
and Blaisell would overwatch as they moved down the
embankment. Everything they didn't need, canteens, web
gear, everything except the chemical gear and their
weapons, would stay here, cached in the side drains.
They'd cross, recon for no more than two hours, then

return to the garage and squirt transmit their report from there.

Sarsten's voice murmured as he explained it to Ted. The Iraqi protested, voice going high. The SAS murmured again, and he subsided, though Gault saw his eyes shining in the dark. *"Ma-arif asbah,"* he said.

"What's the trouble?"

"This fucking *manyouk* says he can't swim." The sound of a slap.

"Goddamn it, Sarsten, knock off hitting him."

"He's making too much noise. The major says he doesn't know anything. Why are we taking him with us, anyway?"

"Because I said so. Tell him to float on his back and you'll tow him. All right, follow me," he said, and slid out between the bars.

He reached the manhole first and lay beside it in the dark until they all joined him. He could hear Ted gasping and whimpering, then another smack of flesh on flesh. Well, maybe it would motivate the guy. He raised his head slightly and saw the dancing firelight.

A plane droned somewhere far off, and he tensed. Then a firework rose slowly and detonated above the city.

Shouts, yells, the sudden explosion of an engine starting. He heard the clanking sound again as the plane drew closer. Gault grabbed the body closest to him and pushed it toward the manhole. Two figures held back, swaying together. They writhed for a few seconds, then one went limp.

Arcs of fire rose, crisscrossing, and the hammer and stutter of automatic guns swelled and grew into a discordant cacophony. He couldn't hear the aircraft anymore, only the guns. Then a renewed clanking, a shout of command, and a ball of flame lit the whole embankment, catching him as he levered himself over and dropped into the trunk. The blast clapped his ears, making them sing, and smoke and paper fragments blew past. His groping boots found the topmost rung, kicking something soft, and he grabbed the cover and dragged it over his head. It fell into place with a clang as the battery settled into steady firing, *pa-pam, pa-pam*.

The trunk was about thirty inches wide. Just enough for him to slide and wriggle downward past others clinging to the rungs. Then someone clicked his flashlight on and he was face to face with Ted. The Iraqi was hanging by his arms, thrust through the steel ladder rungs. By his motionless, open eyes and protruding tongue, he was quite plainly dead.

Below him Sarsten murmured, "He was trying to yell for help. The first chance he had, he'd have given us away."

Gault looked into the dead eyes. They stared back without expression. "You son of a bitch. We needed this guy."

"Like hell we did. He didn't know a thing."

"I told you to leave those decisions to me."

"There wouldn't have been any decisions if he'd gotten to shout at that AA crew. And you said, if he kept making noise, to slot him."

"I didn't say that."

"You absolutely *did* say that, mate. And my squaddy here heard you. Didn't you, Denny lad?"

Blaisell said, "Uh, yeah. I guess. Right, Gunny. Didn't you?"

Gault was too furious to speak. He climbed over the others, slid past them as they clung to the rungs. His stomach was knotting on itself. Not just at Sarsten's homicidal disobedience. His repeated insubordination, his refusal to leave the team. But now he was pulling Blaisell into his orbit, like some murderous dark star. And added to all that, like multiplying his anger by his dread, was what he had to do now. And he had to do it first. No one else would unless he led the way.

He got to the bottom and clicked his flash on and swung it around.

The trunk, thirty feet beneath the surface. It ended in an inch or two of water on the floor, a thick bundle of cables, and, leading off to the side, a black circular opening only an inch or two wider than a big man's shoulders.

Shining his light down it the first time, he'd seen the interior recede, curving into the darkness. The cables took a wide bend in and then followed it, laced tight against the curving overhead with cable straps.

It was a cable run, some sort of utility conduit. The steel interior of the pipe, that was what it was, a steel pipe just wide enough to let a worker wriggle in for repairs, shone with moisture. The cables were rubber-coated in shades of black and dull brown. Some were thick as his wrist. Others, newer-looking, were pencil-thin. They looked like communications, maybe some power; he didn't know and didn't care. All he needed to know was that they emerged on the other side of the river, and that there was no block or barrier along the way.

Unfortunately, the only way to find that out was to crawl it.

Quickly, because his thighs were already trembling, his balls shrunken by cold and fear till they burrowed into his crotch, he bent and shoved himself headfirst into the tunnel. His weapon caught crosswise across the entrance and he reoriented it, pulled it in, laid it on his chest as he stretched out on his back. The curved steel was cold and hard under him. Water dripped off one of the cables onto his face.

The dread congealed inside his gut, sucking warmth out of him. His arms were shaking. He'd never been this afraid.

Then he remembered, and with remembering came a sardonic humor. Why should Sid Gault be afraid to die? He'd killed his son. He'd destroyed his wife's life, and his own. What reason did he have to live?

Smiling grimly, bracing his boots, he shoved himself backward into the darkness.

.   .   .

NEXT BEHIND him, Blaisell watched the gunny's legs disappear with open-mouthed disbelief. The guy couldn't be serious. There wasn't enough room in there to sit up. But he'd just lain down on his back and braced his boots against the bottom and shoved himself in. He was either cold as ice or crazy as shit. He bent down and shone his light in after him. "What the hell's this?" he called.

"This is how we get across the river. You coming?" said Gault hollowly. Not very loud, or maybe the confinement of the pipe muffled his voice. He added, "Marine?"

That jibe at the end pissed him off. He grunted, "Yeah, fuck, does a fat lady fart?" and contorted himself around and slid in.

But once he was in it the tube was even tighter than he'd thought. Lying on his back, he could lift his head up and practically kiss the cables above his face. This must be how they got their comms across the river, he thought.

He braced his boots and shoved himself a couple of feet in. He had a bad thought then, and wondered if it had occurred to the gunny. What if there wasn't any way out at the other end? They couldn't turn around. They'd have to squirm back boots first. That could take a long time. Seven of them, strung out like ants going through a straw. If somebody passed out or went apeshit, there was no way back.

A hollow grunt came back. The gunny, pushing himself along. Cloth scraped. Metal banged. Blaze heard a harsh confined roar of breathing. He heard the river rushing past on the other side of the steel, above him.

He braced his boots and pushed himself another couple of feet into the tunnel. Working himself along with his elbows too, but mainly pushing with his feet. Staring at the overhead, black cables stencilled with numbers and letters. His breath sawed at his throat. Time to hang tough, cowboy. Recon marines didn't lose it. Only three hundred meters. He could do three hundred meters, pushing along on his back. Then they'd be out of here.

He took a breath, braced his boots, and pushed himself another foot downward, into the cold.

VERTIERRA WATCHED the boots disappear with a dull stare. He felt himself shivering. They had to cross the river. He'd waited for it with dull apprehension. Why hadn't Gunny just swam it? It looked dangerous, but at least you could breathe. He'd hated the sewer, especially the chute; the moments when the plunging water filled his mouth, when he couldn't breathe.

He shuddered. He also hadn't liked seeing Sarsten twist the Iraqi's head, suddenly, from behind.

The guy was loop the loop. Certifiable. *Demente.* First the little boy. Then everybody at the Mukhabarat post. Sure, they were the enemy. But he'd seen the guy's face while he was doing it. Sarsten had been enjoying himself. And now, their contact, their only link to the resistance. He wasn't going to let this crazy asshole behind him.

"You're next," Sarsten said, behind him.

He flinched. "No, you."

"You sure?"

"Sure, sure. You go ahead."

The SAS's shoulders were so wide it looked for a minute as though he wasn't going to fit. He hunched them up and crawled in. On his belly, rather than on his back the way Blaze had. Tony wondered which way the gunny had gone in. He'd been above, he hadn't seen. They were working their way down the ladder one by one as those below crawled into the pipe.

The doctor was hanging back above him. He looked up to see that her face was white. She said, "Where did everybody go?"

"In there." He pointed.

"My God, what . . . they went in there? Where does it go?"

"I don't know," he said. It was the truth. "I guess the gunny figures under the river, to the other side."

"Under the river. . . . Oh my God. I can't do this."

"Sure you can," he said, though he was afraid himself. But somehow seeing a woman's fear made it easier for him to be brave. Or at least to act brave, because he didn't feel it at all. He bent down and looked in again. At least he was small. He'd have more room in there than the big crazy Brit. He tucked his light into his shirt, clutched his weapon to his chest, and crawled in.

HIS BOOTS kicked in the water, against the concrete, and then were out of sight. Maureen stood looking down where they'd been, at the faint flashes of light that reflected back out, arced as if reflected off a curved mirror. Her fist dug into her mouth.

"You okay?" Lenson said, above her. She barely heard.

"I can't do this," she said again.

She knew without any doubt it was true. This was the end. The sewer had been bad enough. She'd barely been able to hang on inside the trunk, which was so narrow one person could only slide past another by pressing himself lover-close into her. That was what Sarsten had done, after whatever had happened as he got in; she hadn't seen it. But he'd pressed against her as he climbed down, and she didn't think it had been an accident because she'd felt his erection, hard, poking into her belly.

Not that it mattered. They'd have to leave her here. She just couldn't lie down and shove herself headfirst into a pipe under a river. Just could not. She heard a strange high sound, and put her fist to her teeth again. It had been the start of a sob, the whimper of a terrified child.

And maybe it was that, the sob, that made her suddenly realize *she had no choice*. She couldn't stay here, not when the rest were going on. If they didn't come back, she'd be in the middle of the city, alone. She'd never get out. All around them, at the top of the trunk, soldiers. She could imagine what the Iraqis would do to a woman, one in the most forbidden dress of all: an enemy uniform. Gang rape would be only the beginning.

But this terror felt like death. She could tell herself it was psychological, only a phobic attack, but that didn't help. There was more terror in the idea of being trapped in the pipe than there was in the idea of being at the mercy of the Iraqis above her.

Above her Lenson said, "It's only a couple hundred yards. Then we'll be out."

"I can't. I can't."

"How about if we go next? F. C. and I? Then you'll be last. There won't be anybody behind you. If things get too tight in there, you can work your way back out first. How's that sound?" He looked up and whispered, "That all right with you, Corporal?" She didn't hear the answer but it must have been yes, because Lenson looked down again. "That'd be better, wouldn't it?"

"Maybe a little," she whispered through dry lips, though she still had no intention of doing it. And pressed herself back, into the cables and wires, as Lenson clambered quickly down and swung himself in.

DAN FOUND himself on his back, looking over his head toward a very small pair of boots—Vertierra's boots—that were scraping and pushing into the dark. The pipe *was* very narrow. It had machined-looking rings in it, probably where it had been polished prior to shipping. The marks were just above his eyes as he too began shoving himself along, trying not to think about where he was and how close he was hemmed in. His breath rasped shallowly and he slowed it.

It was like scuba diving. The same constriction, the same sense of confining space. He wasn't wearing a mask, but the closeness of the pipe was like the inside of a mask. He tried to think of the river water above him, leaving out the half inch, or however thick the pipe was, of steel. Gather his legs up, till his knees hit the cables. Place his heels, then straighten his legs. Each time he did this he gained six inches, inchworming along head downward. If he could have bent his legs all the way he could have gotten more thrust, but there wasn't room.

The cables traveled slowly past his upward-staring eyes. They looked like telephone cables, or data cables of some sort. One of them was new, pencil-thin; he figured it for fiber-optic, cored with a strand of glass you could push megabytes of computer data through. He shoved and straightened and shoved again. Some yards in, he realized he should have been counting each shove, instead of thinking about the cables. Then he'd have some idea how far there was yet to go. However, he didn't mind this too much. He could do this. It was better than sitting in a chair, looking at Major Yaqoub Al-Qadi.

Yeah. It was a lot better than that.

Behind him, he heard a ripping sound, and a low mutter of "Shee-it."

F.C. PULLED again with mild annoyance at where his mag pouch had hung up on the cable holder, a metal bracket that fixed the cables to a curved metal rib that ran around the top of the pipe every meter and a half. They had sharp edges that somebody had bent back in order to wire in a new cable, and each one tried to snag you. He got free and shoved himself a few feet farther in, rested, shoved. His Colt was a weight on his chest. He felt water under his back, seeping up to wash cold around his neck. This was a bummer. He could think of lots of things he'd enjoy doing more. The upside was that whatever you earned in a combat zone was totally tax free. So on top of hostile fire pay and jump pay, which almost everybody in the recon community qualified for, it was like another twenty percent raise. Not bad! But what would really light his stogie right now would be just enough Skoal

Wintergreen to stuff a mosquito's ass. His mouth started to water. He gathered up his legs and shoved again, not too fast, not too slow, just keeping up with Lenson.

TWENTY YARDS ahead, folding himself along like an inverted inchworm, Gault was thinking about the water.

He'd first noticed it a few yards back, as a coldness at the small of his ass. Then it licked the back of his neck. As he moved steadily on, it kept rising, slowly lapping up toward his ears when he relaxed his neck between thrusts, laying his skull back against the curved hard bottom of the tube.

He wasn't sure, but figuring a foot each time he pushed, he was about a hundred meters in by now. A third of the way across. Thinking of it as a third done helped. Or had, until he started wondering where the water was coming from. He didn't think it was from the river. He hadn't seen any leaks or drips, or rather, just an occasional drip of what seemed to be condensation. The steel interior wasn't new. The metal was rusty here and there where it had been gouged by workers adding cables, or perhaps splicing in new. But it looked in good shape, or he wouldn't have started this thing.

He figured it was leakage from the access trunks. They were concrete, and there had to be a gap where the steel and concrete met. It wasn't much of a leak. But it didn't have to be much. Just a little bit. As long as the power was on, and the pump was working, pumping whatever accumulated out of the bottom of the U, it would be all right.

Only now the pumps weren't working. Probably not since the air war had started, knocking out the city's power. Four weeks, a trickle of water running in, sliding downhill. Slowly pooling, here at the bottom of the tube. Or maybe just the condensation would be enough, given all that time.

He pushed again, and the water rolled ahead of him and then rolled back, rising to cover his ears. He lifted his head out of it, trying to shine his light ahead as he craned his skull back to look ahead. The beam reflected away, off water, off the interior of the pipe, till it was swallowed by a blackness he couldn't see the end of.

The question was: did it, at any point, fill the tube completely?

If it did, how far did that zone of total fill extend? Far enough for him to push through underwater? And not just him, for all of them to get through? He was particularly worried about the doc. She had problems with confined spaces. Being in here on his back, underwater, was bad enough for him. If she freaked, she'd drown.

He shouted back down the tube, knowing it was a risk, but those behind couldn't hear otherwise: "Corporal, you there?"

"Yea, Gunny."

"Everything okay back there?"

"Yea, Gunny."

"I'm running into some water up here. Hold up while I investigate."

"Roger that, Gunny."

Gault pushed himself forward, keeping track of each thrust. If he could get to 150 yards and still have an air space, they could probably make it. But he could feel the pipe slanting down faster now. That was bad news. The sharper the slope, the more chance water would fill the lowest bend. And it was rising fast now, up to his cheeks, over his mouth when he laid his head back down to rest. So instead he had to keep his head lifted, craning up, to keep his lips and nose where they could suck the dank, still air.

He came to a sudden halt, blouse snagged by one of the cable holders or straps or whatever they were that stuck down from time to time. While he was freeing himself the water sloshed, getting in his eyes, and he inhaled some through his nose and choked, coughed. Faintly he heard Blaisell yelling after him, asking if he was okay. He yelled back Yeah, to hold everybody where they were.

At what he figured at 140 yards in, he had no more than an inch of air space left at the top of the pipe. He was almost sitting up, or as close to it as he could come, jackknifed halfway through a sit-up with his rump hard against the bottom and his face jammed up into the cable-work. He took a breath and held it and squeezed himself slowly around, aiming flashlight and eyes down the pipe.

Just ahead, he saw where water met steel. He floated, face submerged, as he thought about it. Figuring three hundred meters across the river, which was only a guess, it could be more, it could be less, he had another ten yards past that meeting point to the centerline of the river. Past that the pipe ought to start angling up again. The water had to be the same height on the far side, right?

He figured that at most, he'd have to go twenty yards underwater before he came up in the air pocket on the other side. He thought he could make that. He was breathing hard already, but he should be able to make it twenty yards.

On the other hand, what if he figured wrong? What if it kept going down instead of heading back up again? Or if he ran into some kind of anti-intrusion barrier?

It might be that the smart thing to do was turn back. It would be harder going back than coming in. They'd be pulling themselves uphill with their arms, instead of pushing downhill with their legs. It'd be slow. But they could do it, and nobody would drown.

But then they'd still be on the wrong side of the river. And thinking of the Tigris again, the way it foamed and roared in flood, and the darkness, and the lights at the AA battery, he figured they had maybe an even chance of getting across without losing somebody.

While if he screwed up here, or guessed wrong, the only one who wouldn't make it through the water plug would be him.

He rolled slowly over to his back again, bringing his nose back up into the narrow tapering slice of air at the top, and floated there sucking at it as his hands moved around his uniform. He got the hank of ranger cord and started backing out. It was as slow as he'd feared, humping yourself uphill backward. But he finally saw the glow of Blaisell's flash ahead, making luminous circles in the pipe as the light reflected down toward him.

Talking toward his feet, he explained the plan. The corporal would take the hank of cord as Gault spun it out behind. Blaisell would lash it around his upper body, and hand the rest of the hank on to the man behind him. The seven-strand nylon was good for a breaking strain of 550 pounds. That should be sufficient not only for tug-signaling, but to help pull anyone through who was having trouble. The faster they got through, the less chance of problems.

"I'll be real fucking glad when we're out of here, Gunny." Blaisell's mutter echoed down the pipe.

"If it don't suck, it ain't duty, Blaze. How's the others doing?"

"I don't know. I can only talk to Sarsten. He wants to know, quote, 'what the fooking holdup is.'"

"Pass the word back I've got solid water up here, but I don't think it's more than ten or fifteen yards through. I'll go first. Same as when the doc went through the chute. One tug, okay; two tugs, come on; three tugs, I'm in trouble. Don't follow me if I get in trouble. If you can't pull me back out, cut the line and pass the word for everybody to creepy-crawl back out. Then it's the staff sergeant's turn at team leader."

Blaisell said he had it. Gault rested for a few seconds, staring at the overhead. He wanted to say a prayer, but he couldn't think of any. Finally he just thought, Please don't let this thing be flooded more than twenty yards. That seemed to be about the extent of his needs on earth just now.

He braced his heels and started inching downward again. The water rose, cold and dark, over his shoulders, up to his neck. He turned his flashlight off and stuffed it inside his blouse so he could use both hands. The water rose over his ears, and he heard through it distant clunks and thuds, transmitted through the steel, as the others got moving. His breath gasped in the narrow confines. The water splashed and rose, to his forehead, above his head. He positioned his lips just above the water, in the narrow gap that remained between the cold rubber-smelling cables. Checking his watch, the tritium-glowing numerals distinct in the dark, he took three deep breaths, sucking each all the way into his lungs, and held the last one.

He rolled slowly, belly down, and began pulling himself rapidly along the conduit, into the dark.

THIRTY YARDS behind him, Maddox lay shuddering, eyes open, staring at the steel and listening to the hollow indecipherable roar coming down the tube. Voices, but she couldn't make out what they were saying.

What the fuck were they doing up there? Being in here was bad enough, without at least the illusion of movement.

She couldn't believe she'd followed these fools into this. Crawling under a river through a thirty-inch pipe. Unable to raise her arms or sit up. She tried to stay calm, but inside her skull her mind was screaming. She bit her lips to keep from sobbing, and couldn't feel her teeth. She was hyperventilating. Getting dizzy. She tried to control her breathing, telling herself she could still get out. Nothing lay between her and the surface but her pride. But the terror seemed to turn and bite its own tail, and spiral faster and faster until her mouth was dry and she was gasping for breath again.

Her hand moved over her body, into her BDU pocket. She felt the lumpy hardness of the autoinjector kit. Ten milligrams of Valium would take her through this. Just jam it into her thigh and she could relax. And that knowledge, that there was something she could do, helped her not do it.

The roaring slowly died away, and she heard the river

once more. It whispered to her from the far side of the steel. She felt the cold through the metal. It seemed to want her. She shivered again. Why the *fuck* weren't they moving?

Then she heard Nichols, explaining something about ranger cord. She took a deep breath and tried to listen, tried to understand what he was telling her. Something about water. Something about tying herself on the line.

When she understood, she closed her eyes.

MOUTH SEALED tight, Gault pulled himself as rapidly as he could through complete and utter blackness. The water was icy cold around him. He felt his muscles shudder, cramping up. He was losing heat fast. But he had to keep going. Too late to go back. Worming backward, like when he went back to talk to Blaze, your boots caught on the stringers, your elbows rammed into the cable clamps. The human body wasn't designed to be rammed backward through a thirty-inch pipe. He'd never make it back to the air space.

The only way now was forward, and he pushed himself grimly on, locking his toes on the cables and pushing, head down, sometimes ramming his face into unseeable projections. His hands were down by his crotch. He couldn't put them above his head, and he needed them to keep paying out the cord. If it got caught on something, they were all in shit city. Images flew through his head as he started to lose it. Started to run out of breath.

That *had* to be twenty yards by now. But when he came up and opened his eyes they were still underwater. His straining lips found nothing but cold liquid.

He ducked his head again and pushed along. His heart began to hammer. This was too far. The attachments wouldn't be able to make this. Well, maybe the commander, he'd said he was a diver, but the doc wasn't going to. No way. Tony had trouble in the water too; he never mentioned it, but Gault had seen his face back in the sewer when they came to the deep places.

No, no, no . . . this was just too far. His lungs started to ache. He ignored them, levering himself farther into the dark. Too far. Knowing it was over, he was dead. There just wasn't any air space. He'd rolled the dice and crapped out. . . . He was out of air, he couldn't hold his breath any longer . . . his fingers tingled madly, his legs started to thrash and kick, he was done. This was it.

Cory, he thought. *Cory. It's Dad.* His dead son's face alive again before his sealed eyes. Flashes of bloody light painting the dark like distant artillery by night. He turned his body awkwardly, shoving with numb spasming hands against the cold painted steel, and pushed his mouth with despairing force up against the overhead.

He sucked air from an echoing space about four inches high, enough to push his whole face into. Which meant he could have come up a little earlier. He couldn't tell how far he'd gone. It felt like more than twenty yards. Anyway he should only be about a hundred to a hundred and fifty yards from the far shore now. He gasped down the air with a moaning sound that echoed in the rippling darkness. Brought his watch up at last when his heart slowed down to something like normal, and was astonished to learn from its luminous hands he'd been underwater for forty-five seconds. That didn't sound like too much. The doc should be able to make that.

He pushed himself a few meters farther on, noting that the water dropped steadily. Soon he'd be out of it entirely and crawling through dry pipe again. Judging that was far enough, he braced his feet, wrapped the cord around his hands, and gave it two hearty pulls.

WHEN THEY passed the word back to him, Tony Vertierra was already gasping for breath. It was as if those who had gone ahead had breathed the life out of the dark air. Taken all the oxygen, leaving only a cold staleness that he sucked at again and again but that did not satisfy the emptiness inside his lungs, and the terrible fear in his heart.

He lay on his back, holding his head up from the icy water, and felt the line go tight against his back. For a moment he braced himself, eyes closed in the dark. He didn't want to put his head under. He couldn't put his head under. Not here.

Because it seemed like he'd been here before. Though he knew that was impossible. He'd never been deep under the Tigris, cramped so tight he couldn't raise his hands more than a foot in front of his face.

The line tightened again, insistent, calling with the peremptory insistence of duty. *Hijo de la gran puta*, he thought. The terror suddenly seemed too big to fit inside his chest, and he gasped and gasped at the air that was not good air and then, with a refusing paroxysm, pulled his head backward and under and began pushing blindly and spasmodically along through the submerged lumen of the tube.

Then, all at once, Tony Vertierra remembered. What up to now somehow had gotten lost, or had been too much to remember. That he had not known, or not known what to do with. Although it was all down there, deep down under the wavering black water.

Black, nothing but black in front of his open, staring eyes.

IT HAD begun not with the helicopters, but with shots. The Sunday market, the market square. His family were potters, and as a small boy he had sat with his mother on the market blanket as she sold the goods they baked, the bowls and tall squarish pots for storing cornmeal. It was the hungry time, before the corn was harvested, and they sold their pots not for money, but for dried corn. It was still on the cob, and his mother and his aunts soaked it in lime and water and made their own *maza* for the tortillas.

But that day, instead, the shooting began, and his mother had grabbed for his hand and they ran. Leaving the pots, their stall, everything but her few remaining coins, which she pushed hurriedly into her zipper purse and dropped down the front of her *huipil*. They had to reach the ravine. It was where the villagers had always hidden when there was trouble.

But then shooting came from there too. The village was surrounded. Smoke roared up from the fields. The corn was burning. The people stopped then. They saw the soldiers coming up the street from Petán. Petán was the next village. Then A Tun saw a man with them. The man was wearing a black hood. You could not see his face. As he walked, he pointed at this man, at that woman. The soldiers shot them immediately and they whirled around and fell down, just as in the game the children played.

The man in the hood saw them, and pointed in their direction.

His mother had lifted him then and dropped him into the well. Held him for a long moment, her thin hard hands gripping his so tightly as she whispered, *Match'aw taj, dih.*

Don't speak, dear.

And he had clung to her, too frightened even to look down; but she'd looked up, and let go, pushed his clawing hands away. And suddenly he was falling, out of her arms, down into the wet and narrow darkness. Where he'd struggled to keep his head above the water for hours, unable to hold to the slick stones for long, not knowing, then, how to swim. Surrounded by the dark and the smell of the water, the smell of death. While from above, faint, as if from another world down to the World Under that his grandfather had told him stories of, came the shouts and screams and the crackle of shooting.

And he had not made a sound. Till so much later it was dark above him, someone had let down a bucket.

He had never seen her again.

He remembered all this now, what despite all his

remembering he had not remembered for so long. And the slick interior of a steel conduit became the cold rough stone of a well, and he himself became again a terrified child. So that when he felt something sharp pressing into his side he first tried to push it away, to slide past. But it hung fast to him, and he struggled with it, there in the cold, in the darkness. Till at last there was no more breath, not in all the world. Till he saw her face again in the circle of sky, looking down, calling down to him with the gentle voice he remembered so well.

He smiled in the darkness, remembering. At last.

16

Medical City Complex, Baghdad

They climbed out half an hour later, clambering slowly out into a trunk that looked like a copy of the one through which they'd entered. It was narrow and vertical and dark. Folding himself around the pipe exit, standing upright on shaky knees, Dan closed his eyes in exhausted relief. He'd been in combat, he'd had to abandon ship, but just now he didn't think either experience had been as terrifying as just crawling through that pipe.

"Give me a hand with his legs," hissed Sarsten. Dan flinched, and bent to help pull Vertierra's unresisting body out into the trunk.

He'd glided through the water trap pretty easily, though his heart had been going about a mile a minute. Diving was different than going headfirst and without any air supply into the darkness. But knowing there was a way through, having it passed back mouth to mouth that Gault was okay on the other side, made it possible to trust the team and go.

But the RTO hadn't made it. Sarsten had pulled him through by main force after the flailing had stopped, clearing the way for Dan. He didn't know what had gone wrong. The only evidence of struggle was a rip in the sergeant's trousers.

Looking into Tony's narrow dark visage, unknown to him five days before, now more familiar than his own battered swollen face would probably be, he felt suddenly like smashing things. How could human beings keep thinking war was a solution? As long as one man could become a god, then other men would die. As long as the Saddam Husseins and Hitlers, the Stalins and Maos and Pol Pots, could demand sacrifice, the sacrifice would continue. As Jake had died, and now Tony. As they all might, and thousands more with them in the Mother of All Battles that was about to start.

He looked on the slack, lifeless cheeks, and knew that in seconds or minutes or hours, he could be dead as well.

But wasn't that always true, every day you opened your eyes?

And what did that tell you about life?

He wrapped his arms around the sergeant's wet body and boosted him up, with Sarsten and the others pulling from above, until the limp burden rose. Then Dan turned and bent again and gave Nichols a hand up.

AT THE top Gault crouched in a narrow underground space that was concrete on three sides and on the top, and earth on the fourth side, looking down at Vertierra. The gaunt Indian features looked relaxed, free at last. For a moment he envied him. He looked at Sarsten, then put his mouth to the other's ear. "Okay, what happened?"

"I don't know. I felt him jerking, on the line. I was pulling, it was taut, but I slacked off when I felt that. Figured he might be snagged and need slack to back up. Then after a couple of seconds I pulled again. I felt him come, but when he got to me he wasn't breathing. I couldn't get to him to do mouth-to-mouth."

Gault nodded, then jerked his gaze away. He couldn't fixate. They were on the objective. He had to improvise, adapt, and overcome. Find this thing, or confirm it didn't exist, and get the word back.

He looked around, taking deep breaths to regain control. The only way out seemed to be a black gap that opened at the top of the earthen wall, a foot-wide aperture with darkness on the far side. He started stripping his weapon, shaking the water out.

Nichols clambered up out of the trunk, then stopped, gaping down at Vertierra. He looked questioningly at Gault, who shook his head somberly.

When the doc came up and saw Vertierra, she immediately went to her knees and started clearing the sergeant's airway. Gault put his mouth close to her ear, conscious of the darkness around them as if it had ears. Murmured, "He drowned. Sarsten pulled him on through."

She nodded, still holding the RTO's wrist, intent on his face. Then gently replaced Vertierra's wrist on his chest.

All this time Gault had been reassembling his MP5. He finished and worked the bolt, stripping a round into the chamber. He checked the safety, then stood for a quick look down the tunnel. His flash only illuminated the first few feet, shining over a lip of earth to show pipes and cables stretching away. He felt a breath of warm air welling up from it. It felt good on his chilled skin.

"Listen up," he whispered. "We're tactical from here on in." He told Nichols, "You and me, we'll do a quick recon. The rest of you, strip your weapons out and wring out your uniforms. Total quiet! Make sure you get all the water out of the suppressors and the barrels. We'll be right back."

A moment later he and the corporal were on their way, up and over, kicking back the dirt with elbows and knees, weapons cradled ready in their arms.

F.C. FOLLOWED the gunny, wondering what they were getting themselves into now. He hadn't minded the pipe that much. Tight quarters, but it was restful and a couple of times he'd nodded off, waiting there for Lenson to get moving ahead of him. The doc took it hard, though. She tried to keep it down but he'd heard her

sobbing behind him. So he'd talked to her, tried to get
her attention off where they were. Asked her where she
was from, where she learned to rappel so good, stuff
like that. Just to get her mind off it.

Then they'd started moving again, and Lenson had
passed the word back they'd have to hold their breath for
a while. That was okay with him. He had no trouble with
it. But Tony did, it looked like. It had rattled him some
seeing him lying there all slack and wet. But not a whole
lot. Maybe he should be more shaken up about it. He and
Tony had been in the platoon together for three years
now. But hell, he was totally exhausted, asleep on his
fucking feet. Zoned. At the stage where you just kept
walking, even if your buddy wasn't next to you anymore.

But you couldn't go into a tactical situation like that.
So he tried to talk himself back into the mindset. Be the
hunter, not the victim. Keep your situational awareness.
Take rounds and return fire. It was getting harder to snap
back into it though. It was also dark ahead, a void opening on the far side of the lip. He didn't like the look of
that at all.

The gunny gave him a halt signal, and he held up.
Gault squeezed through a narrow gap, following some
cables, and disappeared. The scrape and clack of falling
rock and sliding earth came from the other side, and then
silence.

After some minutes, a low mutter: "Come on
through."

When F.C. scrambled over the lip, the ground fell
away. He slid downward a few feet on loose dusty-clay-
smelling earth and stones and came to rest on a hard
floor. Crouched there in the darkness, he reached inside
his blouse for his goggles. They were wet, of course, but
the AN/PVS-7s were waterproof as long as you didn't
submerge them so far the pressure breached the seals.
Three feet, was what he'd heard. He turned them on and
the corridor ahead rose into existence out of the black,
but so dim, with so little ambient light for the goggles to

magnify, that ahead of him Gault was reaching up to flick on his IR illuminator.

Then all at once it was flooded with the invisible light, and he swiveled his head, going to a tactical stance, weapon to his shoulder, finger off the trigger, knees bent. Looking along the barrel, so all he had to do was drop his head and his eye would find the sights.

They were in a bunkerlike corridor six feet wide and eight feet high, so long he couldn't see the end. Pipes and wires ran along the overhead and both walls. They ranged from an inch or two, like water pipes, to one huge insulated mother three feet across. The air was still and dry and loaded with a penetrating heat that made sweat break on his forehead. The walls were concrete. The floor felt gritty under his boots. There were fluorescent blocks overhead every few yards, but they were dark.

He caught Gault's signal and slid back to cover him. Two-man team. Shuffling forward, more like a slide than a run. Head steady, lead with the weapon. Easing his boots down carefully, trying to keep it quiet even though the grit crunched like sand. The corridor seemed to be deserted, but there might be people not far away. Microphones were a possibility too.

Door, Gault signaled. F. C. saw it to their right, a two-leaf that looked like it opened out. It was ajar.

They moved into the drill, a little rusty, but both knowing how it ought to go from weeks at Combat Town. He remembered the concrete block buildings, like a little abandoned village, and the room-clearing drills. The hours in full gear, sweating, fighting your way up stairwells and across roofs while you sucked the choking haze of the navy smoke floats the staff used to cut down their vision. Drilling till it went smooth as a machine. Gault went to one knee and edged in, and F. C. thought, Right corner, and shifted his weapon to his left shoulder. Gault flicked the door open with his suppressor and went in, low, head and weapon searching to the left, and F. C. went in after him aiming to his strong side around the jamb.

His barrel pointed at stacks of old air conditioners and broken toilets. They stood piled against the walls, nearly to the ceiling: old Fedders and White window units, broken grilles hanging off them. And old commodes, cracked, broken, discolored. Then he saw in the emerald light of the IR that the floor was covered with snakes.

He sucked in his breath, finger twitching toward the trigger, before he saw they were just power cords, uncoiling over the floor from the busted air conditioners. The room smelled like old cement and rat piss. Gault's infrared beam glared around, throwing weird writhing shadows that seemed about to jump out at them. Then it glared back toward him, making his screen fluoresce and waver, and the gunny jerked his head backward toward the door.

Five meters down the corridor, the whir of electric motors behind another door. They double-teamed it, high-low, and found themselves covering a pump room. Gault put his mouth next to F. C.'s ear. "So why aren't the lights on?"

He thought, Because it's dark out, and they don't want to get bombed if there's a light leak. "Blackout?" he murmured.

"Maybe. Let's get the rest of the team up."

They trotted back to the lip, boots squishing as the water drained down into them off their battle dress, and the gunny low-crawled up the bank. F. C. turned to cover the corridor behind them. It still made him uneasy. They hadn't gone that far down it. It had to lead somewhere. At some point, they were going to run into somebody. Who would it be, and who'd shoot first?

Then he told himself, There's not going to be any shooting. Nobody knows we're here. We'll check it out, confirm there's nothing here, and head back. Make that squirt transmission—they were all trained to operate the radio; the RTO was better at it but they could work it without him—and head back for the extract.

Down on one knee, he held the darkness prisoner before the sights of his M16.

WITH GAULT and Nichols gone ahead, Dan had occupied himself tearing his weapon down as directed. He looked doubtfully at the rounds in his magazine. They were supposed to be sealed, waterproof. He sure hoped so.

When the gunny reappeared, he motioned them brusquely to their feet. "Turn those lights off," he told them. "We're going in tactical. There's a steam tunnel on the far side."

"What's a steam tunnel?" Maddox asked him.

"A utility tunnel. Takes steam from a central boiler to the other buildings in the hospital complex. Looks like they've got other stuff running through it too. Power, phone lines, water, maybe natural gas. Okay?"

"Right, I just wondered—"

"I figure if there's anything here, it'll either open off this corridor, or there'll be a side-route way to get to it. We'll go in quick and quiet, in the dark. IR, no visible light. I want the attachments to stay back here, with their safeties on and their mouths shut. Sarsten, you hang with them. If we find anything, I'll be back. Commander, come with me a minute."

They nodded, and he pulled his legs up and over and disappeared.

Dan scrambled up after him and down about fifty yards of low-ceilinged, dirt-sided crawlway. He noticed that the new cable, the one he'd figured for fiber-optic, ran off to his right. Then it disappeared, zagging away into the dark. He felt his way after the others. Then he sensed open space, though of course he couldn't see a thing.

Gault's voice, next to his ear. "Commander."

"Yeah."

"Here's the plan. Give us one hour. If we're not back

by then, take charge and retrograde. If you hear firing, assume command and pull out. Make sure they can't follow trail back to the river crossing. Understand what I'm saying?"

"I think so."

"Let's hear it."

"Give you one hour, then get back across the river. Erase our tracks behind us. Same if I hear firing."

He felt the hand clamp his shoulder, then let go. Heard the three marines sliding down the far side, into some dark space filled with echoes.

He wished he'd said good luck. Checking his watch, to start the hour's wait, he saw it was nearly midnight. They didn't have much time. If they found anything, they were going to have to clear the area, fast, and call in the strike. Before 0400. And, he hoped, be out of the city by then too.

BLAZE FELL in behind F.C., turning his goggles on and trying to swallow his fear. Seeing Vertierra die was a shaker. That was two, fucking *two* guys down. He'd never been on a patrol where they'd taken casualties.

On the other hand, he'd never been in a war before. This is it, boy, he told himself. On the fucking objective. Fucking Baghdad, Iraq. You better fucking forget about scoring and start thinking about saving your ass. He touched the Glock for luck, put his MP to his shoulder, and concentrated on backing up the others.

They went down the corridor fairly fast, not running, but moving in the shuffle, head down to the weapon, weapons pointing everywhere they looked. It reminded him of a passageway on a ship, cramped and crowded with pipes. Heat like when he'd gone down to the engine room once, on a float, on the *Okinawa*. Down there the sailors worked in T-shirts or bare chests, skin shining with sweat, and after a couple of minutes you were ready to go back to troop berthing. Sweat was running down his face now, but he kept his head down and his eyes front. Doors along the way. Gault checked each one, F.C. covering him, Blaze covering the corridor while they were inside. Then they popped back out, swept the passage, and moved to the next.

After fifty meters the corridor took a forty-five to the right. A hundred meters after that, still meeting no one, they reached an intersection. They'd heard machinery noise for a while. Now it was louder. The pipes were getting louder too, as if they were getting close to wherever the steam was coming from. The gunny went to his belly for the intersection, scoped it out from the corner, then waved them up. He pointed Blaisell to the right.

He edged cautiously around, then sprinted across to the far wall and went to cover behind one of the pipes. He could feel the heat coming off it, radiating off it like a Hummer that's been out in the Saudi sun all day. He reflected grimly that it wasn't much good as cover. If a bullet hit it instead of him, the steam would fucking boil him like a lobster. He adjusted the goggles and peered ahead, down another corridor, wider than the one they'd just come out of. The hum of machinery grew louder.

He dragged his sleeve across his forehead, wishing he could stop sweating.

GAULT CROUCHED, looking to left and right. After a bend the corridor split. One branch led off to the right. The other led to the left, where it branched again some thirty meters down. All were dark except for a faint shine at the far end of the leftmost corridor. Very faint, just tickling the image intensifier. The right-hand corridor was wider, and the machinery sound was coming from that direction. Toward the light, or toward the sound? He decided for the sound, mainly because he figured that way led east, downriver, toward where the map had located the Defence Ministry. A subterranean facility, if there was any, would probably lie in that direction. He caught Blaze

and F.C.'s faces, cyclopean eyes turned back to his, and
signaled them out to the right.

Now, moving on, he caught light ahead here as well.
The air grew humid, and he heard the hiss of a steam
leak. His goggles picked the hot steam up as a luminescent mist, glowing in the long wavelengths of infrared.
He moved toward it, was briefly surrounded by a drifting,
sparkling light; then it was past.

Beyond lay more doors, hasped and locked. He hesitated, then waved the team on. What he sought would not
be guarded with a padlock but by armed men. The light
grew closer.

Finally he made out a single low-wattage bulb glowing
by a stairwell. Beneath it was a switch panel. Maybe that
was the arrangement: the corridor lights down here
stayed out until someone needed them. He bent and
touched the concrete at the foot of the stairs. It was
smooth, free of the old grit he'd felt crunching under his
boots. So people used it; it was an active trail.

He was looking up the stair, wondering where it led,
when down the corridor the fluorescents suddenly came
on. Far enough away they didn't blank his goggles, but he
turned them off and pushed them down anyway, flatten-
ing back into the stairwell. More lights came on, reaching
along the passage toward them.

Someone was coming, walking rapidly and decisively
toward them. As the figure advanced, light moved ahead
of it. He heard the click of footsteps.

He motioned the others back into the stairwell, and
moved them up a flight. The light moved toward them.
Looking down, he saw legs go by. A woman's legs, in a
tan pants suit and high heels, striding along at a brisk,
confident pace. The roof of the stairwell cut off his view
of the upper part of her body. Her steps clicked away into
the echoes. Shortly after that the lights went off again.

He looked at his watch. Nearly midnight. He called
Blaze and F.C. in. In terse sentences he told them to
patrol out to the end of the corridor and report back. They

nodded and moved out. Gault took the center of the third corridor and started to jog, the MP5 at port arms, the world bouncing and rocking in a green and black glow.

MAUREEN LAY in darkness for an interminable time, feeling heat on her face and the cold of the bare earth under her. Hearing nothing but the black thud and rush of her own blood. They waited in silence, and as time stretched on, the earth-cold crept inside her damp clothes until her limbs went stiff and numb. And her mind began spinning thoughts, images, and then fantasies, until she was halfway dreaming. But even in dream the terror still followed. Wherever she went she felt its inchoate, enveloping horror. Something stalked her, and she would not see its face until it was too late.

She fumbled out her flash and illuminated her watch face. Then flinched back as it was pushed into the dirt. "What the hell—"

"Anybody tell you to shine that in my eyes? Keep it the fuck off."

"Look, Sergeant—"

"Shut up," Sarsten whispered, and his voice sounded so eager to kill her, or somebody, that she didn't say anything else at all.

At last she heard the slide and grate of footsteps, and stiffened. Pulled the Beretta out and aimed into the darkness. Beside her she heard Lenson and Sarsten bring their weapons up too. The sounds came closer.

"It's us," Nichols muttered. She breathed out and holstered the pistol.

"Anything tasty?" Sarsten said in a low voice.

"Just these utility tunnels. We went through them. Not a thing."

"You sure?"

"There's nothing here," Gault said, and his voice had the ring of iron in the blackness. As if to underscore it, a white light flashed on.

She blinked in its glare, letting air out again, feeling taut muscles untense, loosen down to the tips of her toes. So it was all rumor, all part of the fog and loose talk of war. Or maybe something that had some root in reality, but it wasn't here. It wasn't here.

They could go home.

She was looking at her watch again, figuring how long it would take them to get back to the truck, when Lenson said, "There's one more place we ought to look, Gunnery Sergeant."

DAN HAD thought about this during the hour they'd lain in the dark. He'd been aware of something nagging him, but hadn't been able to grab it. But then, at last, he had.

The thin little cable, the new-looking one. He'd noticed it back in the first trunk. Noticed it again during the dead time in the conduit, waiting for the boots ahead of him to start moving again. Even reached out and tweaked it. A plastic-skinned, insubstantial bit of wire. Only it wasn't wire; its flexibility under his questioning fingers told him that. It was glass fiber.

Glass meant high-data-rate, broad band-width digital communications. He'd seen it used to link missile transporters with command vans. They were starting to install it in the States for commercial phone lines. So he hadn't thought twice about it. But later, lying in the dark, he'd suddenly asked himself, What's it doing *here*?

And where had it gone, after crossing the Tigris?

So that after a while, puzzling it over in his tired mind, he'd turned around, an awkward crab in the dark, and crawled back toward the river. Till Sarsten had hissed, "Where in bloody hell d'ye think you're going?"

"Checking out one of these cables, Sergeant."

"You just sit tight. The way you were told."

Dan hadn't bothered to answer, just kept crawling. For a moment he expected the Britisher to come after him, but he hadn't. And feeling his way through the dark back to the trunk he'd located the cable again, followed it, on his belly in the damp dirt with one hand sliding along it, till he found where it turned right. And followed that, till the earth fell away and a deeper darkness opened ahead. Into which he'd peered; gotten his flashlight out; then paused, finger on the switch. And at last put it away again, and crawled back to where the others waited.

"Someplace else, huh? Where's that?" Gault said now.

Dan said, "Follow me."

WHEN HE pushed his boots through the hole, Gault smelled something funny. A chemical smell. The air was colder here, much colder. As cold as the winter earth.

He had to kick at the dirt, knock dried hard clods of it away. Whoever had run the cable—maybe not that long ago; the commander said this was new technology stuff—had simply dug a hole and pushed it through. The original opening hadn't been large enough for a human body. But on the other side the thin flexible glass snake joined a twisting bundle of larger wires, cable-tied together and running off into the dark.

All this he saw with his fingertips, not by eyes and light. He kicked a few more times, twisting and corkscrewing himself through the dirt. Then his boots hit solidity, and he pushed once more and dropped through, a fetus become infant, expelled from the Iraqi earth's icy womb.

He landed with a clatter of iron, and crouched, grimacing as echoes reverberated from the dark. Reached up to turn his NVGs on. Then something hard slammed him in the head, and he reached up to grab his weapon, pushed through behind him. He rubbed his sleeve over it, cleaning off the loose soil. Then stepped off the pile of loose metal as the goggles whined, powering up, and bleached the darkness into green-tinted black. But still not into sight, till he pressed the button and the IR beam shone out.

He was in a low, roughly cast concrete channel through the earth. It looked like a watercourse, curved at the bottom, almost like the sewer had been. The cables ran along its floor in thick bundles that looked relaxed and heavy. The floor slanted downward. He couldn't see where it ended.

But he heard something. Distant, muffled, not all that clear. It might be an animal. It might be the sound of a man in pain. Or even the squeal of unoiled machinery. It came from down the tunnel, from the darkness where his beam didn't reach.

He crouched into a tactical stance and followed his weapon. The trough under his feet flattened and leveled. The sound grew louder, but no clearer. He ducked under an overhang, placing his boots carefully. Making no noise at all. He was in complete darkness, able to see nothing but random speckles in the screens unless he let go of his weapon to press the illuminator.

At last he reached the source of the noise. He pressed the illuminator and examined it carefully, covering it with his weapon. Then retreated, step by step, still noiselessly, until he reached the upper entrance again. Where Nichols waited. His put his mouth to the corporal's ear and whispered, "Send down the doc. And tell her to wear her NVGs."

SHE FUMBLED awkwardly with the goggles. They were heavy and kept sliding down her face. But she could see again, a relief after so long in darkness.

But now she saw in two dimensions, not three, by an eerie wash of bright green light. It came from where Gunny Gault was down on one knee. The team leader's head was a blaze of light, throwing utterly black shadows away down the tunnel.

She looked again at the man in the blankets.

He lay comma-curled against the concrete, occupying a folded blanket on the floor of the tunnel. Another blanket had been laid over him, but he'd kicked it off. He spoke rapidly, in a slurred, high-pitched mumble; then convulsed in a spasm of coughing that lasted for several seconds. After which he lay for a time quiet, save for a panting breath; then the murmuring started again. His eyes were open but didn't seem to see her.

Of course they didn't, she reminded herself. To him, without the sorcerer's vision, the darkness was complete. She looked down the tunnel again but saw only the moving shadows of her team members, slipping past her.

Two other blanket-wrapped bundles, a few yards down the tunnel, would be motionless forever. She'd checked them already and confirmed that this soldier was the only one still alive.

She knelt, fumbled with the focus knob on the goggles until she had as sharp a picture as she'd get. She took a pair of latex gloves from her pocket and slipped them on, feeling the dirt and crud gritty against the smooth rubber skin. Then turned back the blanket. He must have felt it, but he didn't respond. That was consistent with the weak steady murmur.

He was youngish—early twenties, she guessed—with several days' stubble and the omnipresent mustache. Dark bits of gravel or dirt stuck to his cheeks and forehead. His cheeks were hollow and his prominent lips were blistered. Dark, sweat-damp hair, longer than a US soldier would sport, stuck to his forehead. A dark fluid had trickled from his nose across his cheek and down into the blanket. He coughed again, face turned upward, and she sat back on her heels, thinking.

She laid her palm on his face, then to the side of his neck, feeling for a pulse. It was weak and rapid. He felt hot, yet he was shivering. She noticed the gravel on his skin again and tried to brush it away. It felt strange, soft, and clung to his face. She brushed at it again, puzzled, before she realized it wasn't small stones, or dirt, sticking to the damp of his sweating flesh, as she'd thought.

Her hand stopped and she blinked rapidly. A chill

caterpillared up her shoulder blades and over her neck. She removed her hand slowly, holding it away from her, holding her breath.

Coughing; elevated temperature; delirium. Flat, soft, dark skin lesions. Extensive petechiae. Mucosal hemorrhage.

"Stand back from us," she said aloud. "Move away. Down the tunnel."

"Keep your voice down!"

She said in a fierce whisper, "All right. But get away! And don't go near those bodies either."

She heard mutters, then the scuffle as the remainder of the team moved past. She stayed on her knees, taking shallow, slow breaths, keeping her face turned away.

She waited till the others had passed, till they were shuffles receding down the tunnel. Then, with a quick motion, pulled the blanket down to the soldier's feet. He still had his boots on, she noted. She unbuttoned his uniform, trousers and shirt, and pushed them apart to reveal his trunk. Nothing. Or only a few of the dark, slightly raised specks.

She wondered what color they'd be in visible light.

His hands. She lifted one lightly, feeling the fever through her gloves. Then she unbuttoned his cuff and slipped one of his sleeves up to reveal the forearm. It was as heavily dotted as his face. The small, soft, flat-looking bumps ran from the backs of the hands up the forearms, disappearing into the sleeves. All the bumps looked more or less the same.

The trunk less affected than face and arms. Centripetal distribution. Synchronous development. Then death . . . if she could judge by the bodies down the corridor. She thought of doing a scraping of one of the lesions. But she didn't have a kit for a Tzanck prep. In a lab, she could do immunofluorescence. But she wasn't in a lab. She was in a tunnel deep in Iraq.

She'd always been taught that no diagnostic sign was absolutely pathognomonic in and of itself. There was no definitive diagnosis till you got the lab work. But she didn't think this was varicella.

In fact, there was really only one thing it could be. She'd never seen it. She'd only read about it. The last natural case of variola major had been reported in 1977.

She looked at her hands. The man had been coughing, maybe for hours before they got here. Coughing in the confined space, the still air of the tunnel. By the looks of things, the others had died here, going through exactly the same process.

She'd never seen a case of hemorrhagic smallpox. But this looked like the clinical descriptions.

She looked at the soldier for a moment more, wondering who had put him and the others down here, who had abandoned them to die. Then she wondered how many more had been infected, and where they were now. She thought of her kit. Would morphine do him any good? She doubted it. She buttoned his clothing again and smoothed the blanket over him. He shuddered, and his legs thrashed briefly. Then he subsided again into that feverish simulacrum of sleep.

She stripped off her gloves, peeling them carefully off inside out, so that at no point did her bare fingers touch the outer surface, and dropped them on the blanket with him. Her skin itched and crawled. Shuddering with the knowledge that any precaution she took now was probably too late. She'd leaned close over him, breathed air he'd just exhaled. She looked at him for a moment more, wondering who had done this to him. She was very much afraid she knew, though.

She got up slowly. Skirted the two blanket-covered corpses, giving them only a glance as she passed. Then headed down the tunnel after the rest of the team.

17

0100 24 February: Medical City Complex, Baghdad

Light outlined the rectangle of a thin steel door set into roughly poured concrete. Gault had pressed his shoulder against it, bending it outward ever so slightly. Now, lying on his belly, blinking into what seemed like blinding light, he peered with one eye through the crack.

The room beyond was concrete-walled and concrete-ceilinged, capped by a barrel vault some twenty feet up. Caged industrial lamps burned saffron. The floor was concrete too, flat and gray and covered with dust and pieces of pipe and piles of rough lumber. Large pieces of machinery in turquoise blue, chrome yellow, the bright colors of playground equipment, were spaced across the floor. Puddles of liquid gleamed darkly here and there. He could hear motors running, the hiss of air or steam, and a rhythmic thumping that reminded him of those creatures who lived underground in the movie *The Time Machine*. He couldn't remember what they were called.

He watched for some time, but saw no one and heard no sign of activity, no voices, no footsteps, no clang of tools. So that at last he felt around the edge of the door, apparently an access to the comm tunnel down which they'd come. His fingers encountered a crude latch and turned it slowly, till it slipped off its catch and the door began to swing outward. He caught it and eased it back, put the latch on again, testing it, making sure it wouldn't pop open unexpectedly.

He pulled a Ziploc out of his battle dress and took a booklet of papers out of it. He tore one of the flimsy sheets of M8 chemical agent detector paper off and rubbed it carefully around the edge of the door. He waited, then examined it. Its pinkish hue didn't change. He looked at the door again.

Suddenly he remembered what those creatures were called. Morlocks, that was it. Blue hairy monsters that came up at night to kidnap and eat people who lived on the surface.

He grabbed a handful of dirt and tossed it back down the tunnel.

Nichols leaned in as Gault, hands cupped around his ear, explained in a whisper what he was going to do. A leader's recon. Nichols was not to cover him. Nor come after him, if he didn't return. He would wait for half an hour, then rig the door with a claymore and withdraw. Squirt the report from the garage and get the fuck out of Dodge.

The corporal nodded. He didn't have any questions, and Gault started rigging his MOPP gear.

MOPP meant mission-oriented protective posture. The gear included the field gas mask and gloves, the coveralls and injectors every soldier in the Gulf carried now to protect himself against gas, nerve agents, mustard, whatever Saddam had managed to buy or make to kill human beings as quickly and efficiently as bug spray. He already had the oversuit on. The charcoal lining was wet, but he couldn't stop to wonder if that made it less effective. It was all he had. He checked the closure flap on the front and Velcroed the cuffs tight around his boots. He set the hood ready to pull up and then took out his mask.

A quick check, filter cartridge tight, webbing tight, and he placed it against his face and peeled the rubber "spider" back over his skull till it snapped tight, snugging

the facepiece against cheeks and forehead and jaw as he
pulled on the straps. Feeling the familiar sense of suffo-
cation, the nose-prickling smell like the inside of a new
tire. He put his palm over the filter and breathed in. The
mask sucked tight, molding to his face.

Peering out through the lenses, working more by feel
than by sight, he pulled the hood over his head and
snugged it around the mask with the drawstring.

Gloves next. He peeled his sleeves back and drew on
the white cotton undergloves, a memory-echo of dress
white gloves with the full dress uniform, polished rifles,
gold buttons. Then over them black butyl rubber over-
gloves, heavy and thick. Held his hands out to Nichols,
who tugged the suit sleeves down and Velcroed the cuffs
blood-tight around the wrists.

Moving clumsily now, feeling nothing through the
cloth and rubber, Gault tore another sheet of the paper off
and stuck it to the sleeve patch, and put the rest of the
booklet into its little pocket. He put three skin decon kits
into one cargo pocket and his atropine injector kits into
the other. On top of that he jammed the thirty-five-
millimeter camera, ready to hand. Nichols peered into his
mask. Gault blinked at him, sucking air through the filter.
It was hot inside the mask and hard to breathe, but if any
of those puddles out there were nerve or blister agents, he
preferred working for his oxygen to the alternative.

Lights meant people, and if anyone saw him he'd have
to take them out fast and quiet. He started to blow through
the suppressor on his MP5, then remembered the mask.
He handed his weapon to Nichols instead. The corporal
cleared it and handed it back. Gault pulled back the bolt
with his clumsy rubber flipper for a visual check. Made
sure he had a cartridge in the chamber, and worked the
safety off and back on again. Got the spare mags and put
them in the pocket with the atropine and 2-PAM chloride.

He nodded to Nichols. The corporal kneaded his
shoulder and moved back to let him pass. Gault squatted,
turned the latch, and bent quickly to squeeze out through

the access. He heard the faint clang and the grate of the latch, and stood alone in the light.

TEN MINUTES later he was flattened against the west wall, looking down at two oblate shapes swathed in cheerful blue plastic.

He had alternately observed and rushed across the vaulted space, zigging from stacks of tanked gas to a diesel generator set to a row of large stainless-steel boxes that as he neared he realized were refrigerators; at least they hummed like Frigidaires, and the doors sealed with rubber gaskets. He had carefully avoided stepping in the pools of liquid here and there on the floor. Now he was against the far wall from where he'd entered. He was careful to keep his body out of sight and only break the line of the equipment down low, near the floor.

At the far end of the hall, men were moving. Some were in the olive Iraqi uniform. Others wore green rubber suits. All wore the Soviet-issue gas mask; he couldn't recall the model designation but he recognized it from briefings. Those who were armed carried their Kalashnikovs slung. He watched them for perhaps five minutes. A lot of activity, but not much noise. Maybe because of the masks. An officer pointed. Then the growl of a vehicle engine, and the back corner of a truck moved into view, taillights glowing and mud flaps swinging as it braked, paused, then moved forward out of his field of view once more.

When he'd seen enough for the moment, he moved back toward the palleted shapes. He examined them for a time, then went back to the wall and observed again. The truck did not reappear.

The faint click of a camera shutter bounced off the walls, off the curving ceiling. Followed by the sound of film being advanced, and then another shutter click.

At last he decided it was time to go. He trotted to the fridges. Crouched there, he tried the door handles. Each

and every one was locked. He blinked behind the mask
lenses, feeling sweat drip and burn into his eyes. He
concentrated on breathing in and out, slow and easy. If
the hostiles at the far end of the bunker thought they
needed to wear masks, he sure as hell wanted his sealed
tight.

Checking the far end of the vault again, he felt for the
book of detector paper. Clumsily tore off a flimsy page,
bent, and pressed it to a stain on the concrete. Rubbed the
dye-impregnated paper back and forth, scrubbing it in,
then picked it up and counted to twenty, watching the far
end of the vault, before holding it close to his eyes with
his rubber-coated fingers.

DAN WATCHED tensely as the door cracked open. He and
the others covered it with their weapons.

It was Gault. Nichols swung it wide and the gunny
toothpasted himself awkwardly through, like a grown-up
playing hide-and-seek, bent over, trying not to tear his
suit. Nichols latched the door behind him, and the team
leader pushed his hood back and tore his mask off. He
breathed hard through a reddened, sweat-covered face.
The corporal gave him an interrogative thumbs up. He
grinned, short and sharp, and pointed up the tunnel.
Nichols reared back, giving him room to squirm by. The
gunny pointed at him, then forked two fingers to his eyes;
pointed to the door. The corporal nodded, and Gault
turned to head back where the others waited. Dan saw the
mask in his hand and the detection paper stuck to his
overgarment.

"Come on back with the others, Commander," Gault
whispered. "You and the doc both need to hear this."

Maddox and Blaisell were sitting side by side. She
looked pale. Sarsten was an arm's length up-tunnel, rifle
across his knees. He looked very interested, almost avid.
Dan went to a knee, and together they all stared at the

team leader as he took a knee too, breathing still ragged, and briefed them on what he'd observed.

"It's a work space; looks like where they load the warheads. There are two empty ones on pallets on the west side of the room. That's where the refrigerators are too."

"You're sure they're refrigerators?" Maddox asked him.

"That's affirmative. Big stainless industrial-type freezers. I tried 'em, but they're locked. It's obviously a handling area. Tanks, for liquid. Hoses and pumps. A lot of leakage on the deck, but there's no reaction from the chemical detector paper. There's a rack with green suits on it."

"What kind of suits?"

"Like chemical protective suits. Rubber, or plastic."

Maddox asked him, "With hoods? Do they have hoods attached to the suits?"

"Correct. Beyond is another room. The whole thing looks like one long hall, all with the arched roof. Partitions in between, but I can see troops moving around farther down. Some are in battle dress and gas masks. Others have the full-body dress-out. Looks like Soviet-bloc chemical suits."

"This has to be it, then," Dan said. "It's in the right place. It's underground. We just have to decide what the most likely active agent is, confirm our location, then call in our strike. Agreed?"

He looked rapidly around, gathering their glances to his, taking command. It felt like time, felt like far past time, and he felt suddenly anxious to do what had to be done and get the hell out. "Gunny Gault, that consistent with your understanding of this mission?"

Gault hesitated a moment, then said, "Yes, sir." He nodded down-tunnel. "I'd like to ascertain exactly what they've got down there, but it may not be worth the risk. If they see one of us, realize they've been compromised, they can evacuate and relocate."

"I agree, it's not worth the risk. We'll get a GPS fix. Then we can start back." Dan pointed at the detector paper. "You said you tested what was on the floor. What else did you test?"

"The access door; any patch of liquid I saw, any stain on the deck."

"Did you test the refrigerators?"

"They were locked. I tested the deck just in front of them. In case anything had leaked or spilled. Again, nothing."

"You waited for it to develop?"

"Twenty seconds. No reaction."

He started to fish out the used papers, but Dan waved him off. "You know your job. Tell me about these warheads you saw."

"They're on pallets, covered with blue shipping wrap. I tore the wrap off one. It's about two meters high, maybe a meter in diameter. They shipped them base up with two-by-four braces holding them vertical."

"What's the material? Metal?"

"A metal skin on the outside, just sheet aluminum, looks like. On the inside, concrete, just like Ted said."

Dan nodded. They'd doubted the Iraqi, but he'd told the truth as far as he knew it. "Anything inside?"

"No. They're hollow, with a cast steel base that looks like it screws in. The bases are on the same pallet, but not installed."

"Did you get pictures?"

Gault nodded, patting one of his pockets. Dan said, "Good. All right then. We've established that whatever it is, it's a liquid. Both from what Ted said and from examining one of the casings designed to take it. That crosses off two of the possibilities the DIA and CIA gave us: radioactive waste and a crude nuclear bomb. It leaves chemicals and bugs.

"You checked the environment and came up with no response on the chemicals. That plus the refrigerating equipment tells me it's a bug." He looked at Maddox.

"Doc? You agree? There's no reason to refrigerate a chemical weapon."

SHE SHIFTED uneasily, wondering if she should tell them. Was it necessary? Was it smart? Then she thought, I've probably been infected. They've been exposed; but being exposed and being infected were not the same. The more often they were exposed, of course, the higher the probability of infection. But if they knew, they could take precautions against another exposure. It might save some of them. So she took a breath and said, "I agree. And I'm pretty sure I know what the infectious agent is."

They looked at her, waiting. She took another breath and said, "I expected either anthrax or botulinum toxin. But based on the casualties back in the access tunnel, it's neither."

"Okay, what is it?" said Gault.

"I can't be certain without lab tests. Basing a diagnosis on symptomology's more of an art than a science. But I'm pretty sure we're looking at smallpox."

She could tell from their faces they weren't sure how to take that. "I thought that was, like, extinct," Blaisell said.

"That's right."

Gault said, "I know it's bad shit. But not as deadly as anthrax, right?"

"I'm afraid this is worse than anthrax," she said.

Sarsten whispered a laugh. "Worse? How could it be *worse?* They both kill you, right?"

She concentrated, trying to get it across in words they'd understand. "The difference is that variola—that's smallpox—is naturally infectious by aerosol.

"See, the anthrax in a warhead or a bomb is artificially aerosolized. That's what we mean by 'weaponizing.' It's hard to do, to get the spores milled down and coated so they can float and be inhaled. The weaponized material will infect the people who breathe those specific spores. But those people, in turn, *won't* pass it on to others.

"Smallpox is different. It aerosols naturally. So instead of a limited infected population, what you have is an epidemic."

She could see they didn't like that. God knows, she didn't like telling them.

"It couldn't be anthrax?" Lenson asked her. "You're sure?"

"No. It's inconsistent with the clinical manifestation I saw back in that tunnel. It could be camel pox, or some other member of the family. There are twenty or thirty different vertebrate poxviruses. But I doubt it. Most of those either don't affect humans or they manifest as a mild illness. That man's dying. The two others with him are dead. I'm not an expert on virus weapons. But I know smallpox had several clinical variants, due to differences in both strain virulence and host response. What he has looks like something they used to call hemorrhagic smallpox."

She thought, but didn't add, that the hemorrhagic variant was both the rarest, the deadliest, and the most rapidly progressing. And she did not want to follow down that chain of reasoning, because it meant the virus had been engineered; deliberately increased in virulence, artificially selected to enhance lethality and leap easily from host to host.

And worst of all, it meant that someone had to have used human beings in that engineering. Helpless victims, sacrificed to breed the deadliest possible version of an already horrendous disease.

Lenson broke into her thoughts again. "The troops we stumbled over in the tunnel. How'd they get it?"

"I don't know. There could have been an accident loading the warheads. Or when it was shipped in here. Who knows? Anyway the material leaked somehow. They were infected. And I'd bet they're not the only ones."

Gault said slowly, "You said it can spread from person to person."

He'd understood, then. She nodded. "That's right,

Gunny. Variola major's extremely infectious."

Blaisell leaned forward. His voice was suddenly angry, as if she'd just cheated him at poker. "What're you saying? You saying we got it now?"

"Not necessarily. But we've just been exposed."

"We got shots. Back at 'Ar'ar.'"

"For anthrax and botulism. I'm afraid they won't do us any good with this."

"Can you give us antibiotics?" Gault said. "Out of your kit?"

"I'm sorry. Antibiotics don't kill viruses."

Lenson said, "So now what happens?"

"You mean, to us? The first sign will be a fever. Then comes rigor, vomiting, headache, followed by the characteristic pox pustules. Followed by systemic toxicity, and either slow recovery or death." She paused. "It's a nightmare virus. A cough can pass it. Your bedding's infected. Your clothes are infected. Just breathing in the same room, that's a reliable mode of transmission. Meaning, once it starts, we can't stop it or isolate it. All we can do is immunize around the edges and wait till it burns itself out."

"Casualties?" Lenson asked softly.

"Released over a city?" she asked him. "A plume, on the wind? Classic variola kills forty percent of an unvaccinated population. The hemorrhagic variant's going to be higher. Much higher. I'd say, in the hundreds of thousands. Maybe in the millions."

"And you're saying we'll get it?"

"That's right," she said somberly. "Not all of us, probably. But there's no way to tell how many, or who."

She took another deep breath, admitting the truth to herself as much as to them.

"But it's not just us, now. Because we can pass it on, even if we don't show the symptoms yet. Before we're even sick.

"Right now we may be walking biological weapons. Loaded with the most deadly disease that has ever existed on earth."

18

0200 24 February

They sat, backs propped against the walls, a few meters up the corridor. In the dim near-dark, each held his weapon across his lap, or upright, propped between dirty, toe-scraped boots. All but Nichols. Gault had left F.C. down-tunnel as an OP, to watch for roving guards, arrivals, deliveries, activity, anything they hadn't seen so far.

Dan dragged a hand down his face, feeling the buildup of dirt and sweat and camo paint like a viscous paste. He had enough beard to qualify as one of the Faithful. He couldn't believe how tired he felt. How unutterably, bone-wearily exhausted. He'd gone without sleep before. As a staff officer in the Med, as an exec escorting tankers during Operation Earnest Will, as a captain-in-all-but-name in the China Sea. It had been hard then, fighting the motion of a ship in a seaway, sometimes in storms; resisting the nervous exhaustion of day after night on watch, not to mention other anxieties. . . . But added to sleep-lessness and fear this time was the sheer physical wear of marching under heavy rucks, crawling up and down through subterranean drains and ways. Hours of hard work and moments of terror, adrenaline surge followed by the burned-out emptiness of an exhausted body and a mind driven to the edge of sanity. The marines looked worn too, but it didn't seem to slow them down. They were hardened to it. He and Maddox weren't. Each time he stopped moving now he had to fight the droop of his head, the slackening of his bruised sinews and exhausted muscles. He wanted sleep.

No. It had gone beyond that. The darkness in his heart had advanced, like a gangrenous infection that gained a little each day.

Sometimes he wanted to die.

But they'd reached their objective at last, and he wasn't a useless caboose anymore, following the troopies and trying his best to act like one. Now he had to be the engine. Had to make decisions, and make them stick, and those decisions had to be right.

He muttered hoarsely, "All right. First of all, we've got to figure out exactly where we are. Gunny. Can you get a reading off the GPS?"

Gault stirred. "I'll try. We're pretty far underground here."

"How far? Anybody keep track?"

They contributed different guesses; the average seemed to be about forty feet. That sounded about right, and Dan got out his pad to compose the message. The shorter, the better. The less time it took to transmit, the harder it would be for the Iraqi Army's direction-finding stations to triangulate them. Something like FLYING STONES LOCATED GRID SQUARE such and such, BUNKER SYSTEM FORTY FEET BELOW SURFACE, CONTENTS BIOWEAPONS SMALLPOX. He regarded it and then scribbled over it. Tried PROJECT 985 CONFIRMED BIOWEAPON SUSPECT ACTIVE AGENT SMALLPOX. BUNKER SYSTEM GRID SQUARE CONSISTS CONCRETE BUNKER SYSTEM. . . . He cursed and scribbled that one out too, blinking, fighting exhaustion and the overwhelming desire to sleep.

A Tomahawk strike took time to design. The targeting facility had to program the flight path, actually tell the missile not just where to go, but how to get there, what radar-navigation marks to check and when and where it would pick them up. During the last seconds of flight, an electro-optical terminal-guidance system took over. It compared the expected image from the target area with the actual infrared image it observed. If you had clear weather and a high-contrast target, you could actually tell the missile which window of a building to fly into.

But even after the mission was in the can, it took more time to transmit to the launching platform—in this case, the destroyers and subs in the Red Sea and Persian Gulf. When he'd started with the program, in the early eighties, someone had to physically transport the tapes to the launching platform. Now they could download targeting data by satellite, but it still wasn't an instantaneous process.

He checked his watch, feeling the passing seconds like quicksand sucking at his legs. Because if Saddam's threat was real, the suited and masked troops Gault had seen were carrying out their launch preparations now.

Could he streamline the targeting process? He'd plotted missions to downtown Baghdad at the start of the air war. He remembered one used the river as a nav marker. Maybe they could use that profile, that already-plotted course. Tomahawks came in so low and fast he didn't think the AA battery would be a problem. The direction of flight would be in from the river. That would be good; the missile, flying only a hundred feet off the deck, would avoid the buildings behind them. But what if there were buildings in front . . . That depended . . . he was so fucking tired, his mind wouldn't work . . . first he had to make sure exactly where they were.

"I can't get GPS here," Gault said, looking up from the set.

"Damn it. Okay, give me the map."

The team leader flattened it on the powdery concrete. Blaisell positioned his flash, leaning to shield them. They worked from the toppled bridge and where the map showed the cable crossing. When they had it argued to an agreement, Dan shook his head slowly. Then looked up at Gault.

"What's 'Building 61'?"

Gault flipped the map over. Ran his finger down the numbered list. "Al Mustashfa Al Humhuri. A 'child welfare hospital,' it says here."

"*Mustashfá* means hospital," Sarsten put in.

"Thanks," Dan said. He pushed what that meant aside for the moment. "Okay, a UTS grid coordinate? I want it down to ten meters."

Gault read it out and he wrote it down. "Okay, that's where we are; one end of the complex. You said it extends southward, right? How far?"

"I couldn't see the end. At least a hundred meters."

"You saw trucks. Right?"

"I saw what looked the rear end, yeah. Mud flaps and lights."

Sarsten asked him, "Color?"

"Military green."

The SAS said, "The Scuds will be on those trucks. They're TELs, transporter-erector-launchers. What we were trying to find out in the desert. Huge things, six big wheels, dual cabs. Carry the missile in the bed between."

Gault said, "I didn't see anything that looked like a missile. Warheads, but no missiles. They could be in silos."

Dan said, "Silos are possible, but I don't think likely. This whole installation strikes me as something they ginned up on short notice. This area was probably underground parking, or maybe an ambulance station. No, the sergeant here's probably right: they're on transporters. So there's got to be some way to get them up to ground level. Most likely, a ramp. With me so far?"

The gunny said, "Everything you say makes sense, Commander. But we haven't actually seen it."

"We don't have to *see* it to know it's got to be there. You ID'd the goddamn warheads. That's enough." He looked at the map again, noted the road between the hospital and the river; remembered palm trees bending in the dusk, a car moving along above the river. "Actually it's a great location. They don't need to go far. Just enough to clear the buildings. They erect and launch and scoot back down here for a reload. Let's call the tunnel a hundred meters long. That'll give the targeters notice that it's an elongated rather than a point target."

"You don't think if they hit one end of this thing, it would wipe out the rest?"

"Tomahawk doesn't have that big a warhead."

"Can it go through forty feet of dirt?" Sarsten said.

Dan rubbed his face again, thinking about it. He didn't like the SAS man's tone, but he had a point. Saddam had located his last-ditch deterrent deep beneath a children's hospital. It was totally consistent with the way the guy had operated to date. Using Western hostages as human shields. Putting beaten-up, captured pilots on TV. Siting his surface-to-air missile batteries in residential neighborhoods.

He was getting a bad feeling. An effective Tomahawk strike would be difficult. Maybe impossible.

Tomahawk was an air-breathing missile, like a miniature aircraft. It didn't dead-drop like a bomb, it flew in at an angle. You could select an up-and-over approach, but that only steepened the angle, didn't make it straight down. The warhead had been developed for use against ships. It would go through the armor of a Kynda-class cruiser, it would penetrate several feet of concrete, but it wouldn't burrow down through dirt. It was really at its best against aboveground buildings, aircraft shelters and so forth.

Tasked with eliminating Saddam's underground command bunkers, the air force had hastily pasted together a penetrating bomb. It might punch through forty feet of soil and however much concrete was in that arched overhead. But bunker busters had to fall vertically, gathering the kinetic energy to penetrate. He couldn't see Schwarzkopf signing off on dropping one through a children's hospital. Not after the uproar over the Amiriya shelter attack.

He saw Sarsten's sardonic glare, and dropped his eyes. Still trying to goad his reluctant brain into something resembling coherent thought.

"You can't bomb it," Maddox said in a low voice. He started.

"What?"

"You're coming to the same conclusion I came to. If you bomb this facility, you'll spread the virus all over the city. I saw the map. There are residential neighborhoods all around us."

"So what?" said Sarsten. "Give Saddam a taste of his own medicine."

She told him contemptuously, "I'm not talking about him. I guarantee you, whatever this is, *he's* been immunized against it. We're talking about innocent people. Kids."

"*Raghead* kids," said Blaisell.

"That's enough, marine," Gault said sharply.

A stir down the tunnel, a movement in the shadows. Weapons whipped around. It was Nichols. He murmured, "Troops. Coming this way."

"Side tunnel," said Gault, and they moved quickly off into the shadows. They waited there for several minutes, but nothing happened. No one came.

Dan was conscious of the minutes passing, time bleeding away. He took the penciled scrap of his message out again and reread it. He was sweating again. He was remembering what Admiral Kinnear had offered him.

Desert Moonlight.

A two-hundred-kiloton W-80 nuclear weapon, on call.

He held the scrap of paper, trying to steady down, trying to think it through. Kinnear wouldn't have given him a nuke on call unless he thought it might be needed. Unless he thought Dan might face a situation like this. But was it even sane, to think about using a nuclear weapon in downtown Baghdad?

Then he thought, Was it sane to think about unleashing

the deadliest disease in human history? And not just on
Israel—what Dr. Maddox said made it clear the thing
would spread far beyond whatever its original target was.

So that no, Saddam Hussein was not sane, not in the
Western meaning of the word. Deterrence theory had
always presupposed a rational actor. Saddam acted by a
different code. One that could wipe out a nation as cold-
bloodedly as he killed his own associates. One that could
use sick children, like the ones in the hospital above them
now, as human shields.

A nuke would trump Saddam's ace. It might even ster-
ilize the horror he'd loaded into the warheads a few
meters away. But a nuclear detonation, even below-
ground, would cause enormous collateral damage in the
middle of a city. Would vaporize the hospital and everyone in it.

They'd be playing Saddam's game. And precisely at
his moral level.

It's not your decision, he told himself desperately. The
paper trembled in his hands. *Kinnear told you that. It's a
recommendation, not a release. They'll make the decision. Not you.*

But he knew that whatever his mind told him, the
responsibility was his. If he'd learned anything from his
career, the disasters and setbacks and sometimes the
equivocal shadowy half victories, he'd learned that.
Orders from above didn't exculpate a man. Policy didn't
exculpate a man. Passing the buck didn't exculpate a
man. Like an infection, responsibility stayed with you
even as you handed it on.

The responsibility was his.

GAULT DIDN'T like what he was seeing. The commander
had looked bad since they'd rescued him. Now his hands
were shaking. The gunny stood and said in a low voice,
"Sir? Let's you and me and the doctor go talk this out."

He raised his eyebrows at Maddox. And after a moment she stood too, and they went around the corner a few steps. He reached out with both hands to their shoulders and pulled their heads in to his. Murmured, standing there, "We need a decision, sir. Right now."

"What's your call, Gunny?"

"Haul ass, ASAP. Before somebody decides to come back and check on their casualties, the guys in the tunnel here. Or brings in the next one. Get back across the river and do our transmission. Let Higher know what we found."

Maddox said, "It's not that simple, Gunny. The commander's problem is that we can't just leave and report this."

Gault looked at her. She looked exhausted, eyes hollow, hair matted with dirt and dried mud. "Why not?"

"Because it does no good if we do. They can't bomb it."

He stared at her. "Sure they can. Or he can call in a missile strike."

"No, he can't. I told you how serious this is. Smallpox doesn't exist in nature anymore. Human beings were the only reservoir. A thousand years ago, we had natural resistance, those who didn't die from it. Contracted from low-level infections, exposure to the less virulent strains. A hundred years ago, we used to inoculate. But now we're vulnerable. We're *all* vulnerable. We can't take the risk of spreading a plume of the pathogens across the city. Because the disease won't stay here."

Gault watched the commander. Lenson didn't seem to agree with her, but he didn't say he disagreed either. After a moment he started talking about how it might not be possible to destroy it anyway, plume or no; since the facility was buried, and beneath a hospital, he wasn't sure either a Tomahawk or an air strike could wipe it out.

Gault thought about that, and it seemed they were both avoiding the obvious. "So we do what, Major? Just leave them here? Then Saddam fires them as soon as the ground attack starts. You get the same germs, only over Tel Aviv instead of Baghdad. *That's* your only choice."

"But I don't think he will," Maddox said. "It wouldn't make sense. Not if this is his ultimate deterrent. If he uses it, he loses it; there's nothing more to threaten us with. No, he won't launch. He can't."

"I wish I could believe that," Lenson said. "That'd make everything real simple. But I don't think this guy works that way. He made the threat. He has the capability. He knows if we invade, we won't stop till his regime is history. I'd say the odds are good he'll follow through. Anyway, that's not our decision, whether to bomb it or not."

Gault looked from one to the other. He didn't care what they decided, but it would be nice to have some leadership. He looked at his watch. Five more minutes. If they didn't make up their fucking minds by then, he was pulling out.

"It isn't our decision?" Maddox was saying.

"No. That's not our bailiwick, Doc."

Gault folded his arms. He said softly, "I agree with the commander, Major. Our mission's not to guess what Saddam's going to do. It's to locate and report what he's got. The commander's eyes and ears. That's what a recon team is. And that's all it is."

She lowered her head, looking angry and frightened and very, very tired. "You're saying—what? That there's nothing we can actually do?"

"Like what? We're not armed for a raid, and there aren't enough of us. We're a recon team, Doc. Not a strike force."

"We've got weapons. Guns. Grenades."

"And there are only six of us. I saw a couple dozen armed troops strolling around out there. Probably more back wherever they bunk and hang out. And a reaction team on call too, I guarantee that. Light armor. Maybe even tanks." He gave it a pause, waited. But neither of them said anything.

• • •

SHE WATCHED the gunny's expression, watched the iron come back into it. His arms were folded and his lips were grim. "I'm not saying to kill them," she said, but she heard the uncertainty in her voice and was ashamed.

"Then what *are* you saying?" Lenson asked her.

She hesitated, not sure how to answer. She didn't want to die. She didn't want any of the team to die. But given what Gault described—refrigerators and warheads and filling equipment—and the dead and dying men in the tunnel behind them, Al-Syori had done her duty for her master. She'd given Saddam a more terrifying weapon than anyone had imagined. He'd already fired Scuds. He'd used chemical weapons on his own people. Once the ground war started, he'd be doomed. There was no way out for him. Maybe the commander was right. Why shouldn't he pull the world down with him as he fell?

He'd use it. Of course he would.

But now Lenson was saying they couldn't do anything. The gunny was saying that they should just leave.

Wedged in the dilemma, she groped for a solution. "We can't just go back. Just let him do this. If we can't bomb it, then what? Isn't there *any* way to stop this?"

DAN LOOKED at her face close to his. He had the uncomfortable feeling they were all converging. Closing in from different angles on the same ugly necessity.

He said to Gault, "I'm starting to think she's right, Gunny. Granted, going overt isn't in our mission statement. But sometimes the mission changes."

"I know that," Gault said. "Sir."

"This may be one of those times," said Dan, holding his gaze.

Gault looked at him squarely. The marine's eyes were blue and cold, staring out from a network of fatigue lines and congealed camo paint. "You ever sent men to die before, sir?"

"Yes," Dan said. He blinked away the images of a sinking, burning ship, the cries of drowning men he couldn't stop to rescue. "Too many."

"I've seen dead marines too." Gault looked away. "If it takes the team to accomplish the mission, it takes the team. I'm just pointing out that if we go overt, probabilities are we won't make it out of here."

"What about your men?" Maddox asked him.

"They're marines," Gault told her. "They'll do what has to be done."

Dan said, "And you'll back me up on that decision?"

Gault hesitated, just for a moment, then his expression turned hard again, unyielding and emotionless. "You're in charge on the objective, sir. That's how it was briefed."

"Wait a minute," Maddox said. "Let's not go that way yet. Commander, you're our missile expert here. Any way we can fuck them up without taking them all on in a frontal assault?"

Dan had thought about cutting the cable, but then realized that Scuds didn't need the data more sophisticated missiles required. They were ballistic birds, rock-simple, not much harder to aim than an artillery piece. Shoot them up at the right angle and they'd come down in the right place. Point and shoot, like a cheap camera. Fly and die. Their launch points were probably presurveyed; a few spots of paint on the road topside would do that.

"Power?" Maddox suggested. "Do they need power to launch?"

"Yeah, but they'd get that from the transporters."

"Anything else? Fuel?"

Dan lifted his head as he realized a shadow stood near them. It was Sarsten. "What is it, Sergeant?"

The SAS stood just far enough away that they couldn't see his face. "Just wondered how long it was going to take you wankers to figure this out. You there yet?"

"Where?" Maddox said, and her voice was suspicious.

"I can't believe it," Sarsten said. He stroked his

weapon like a cradled cat. "I knew it was something special, but I never thought this. At first I thought you were up to topping Saddam. A wet mission, like the Sovs say. Then I thought you were just tossers, crawling through the sewers on the say-so of that Teddy boy. I never figured you to come up with the prize."

"We're making a decision," Dan told him.

"Making a decision? That shouldn't take long. I get to put in my tuppence worth? You can't bomb it. Collapse this tunnel, the hospital'll come down into it. The poncing paper-tearers back in London and Washington will never check off on bombing a hospital anyway. No, we've got to do this lot ourselves."

"With what?" Gault said.

"Why, with whatever we got, mate. Whatever we have or can scrape up."

Maddox said then, "There's something else we have to do."

"What's that?" Dan said.

"Get a sample. Whatever this is, we've got to bring some back."

"That could be tough," Gault said. "This isn't going to be like in a lab, Doc."

"Do you absolutely have to?" Dan asked her.

"Yes. I absolutely do," she told him. "To document what they have. Without a sample, we're just guessing. With one, we might be able to stop this, or at least confine it to a geographic area if it goes epidemic." She hesitated, looking up at them. "Look, that's my job. You get me in there, I'll get what I need. But I can't emphasize enough how important it is that we come back with specimens. With proof."

They stood together in silence, in the dim light and the close limestone smell of the tunnel. Each confronting what he didn't want to confront. Then the gunny said slowly, "Well, there's one thing we can do they can't."

"What's that?" Dan said.

Gault said, "We're the Morlocks. We can see in the dark."

19

0300 24 February

Gault waited on a knee, watching them dress out. He didn't usually pay much attention to the way he felt. But after thirteen years in this business, you knew when you were taking too many risks. Going against superior force in an unfamiliar environment without drill was asking to have your butt whipped. The only thing on their side would be surprise. In the dark and the confusion . . . No man could predict how an action would turn out. You just did the best you could, and relied on your team, relied on firepower. Relied on Luck or God or whoever you believed took care of you in battle.

He slotted the bolt and checked the chamber one more time. For himself, he didn't feel much interest. He'd been dead inside for a long time now. If the end of life meant the end of remembering, he was ready. More than.

Nichols got up and stood against the wall. Gault dropped his mask, pulled his hood up, and went forward. They checked each other, the Velcro and drawstrings that were supposed to seal out gas or germs. F.C. looked good, so Gault sent him forward along the line.

When he came to the doc, he stopped. She wasn't in the issue MOPP gear. Instead, gleaming white coveralls covered her from toe to neck. Her hood was of the same material; white booties covered her feet. She was carefully winding silver duct tape around where her booties tucked into trouser legs. She'd already taped where white rubber gloves met her sleeves. She wore a hood and what looked like a soft-sided cooler bag with a shoulder strap over her shoulder. Her pistol belt was buckled over the suit.

He said, "You absolutely sure you need to do this?"

"It's why I came, Gunny."

"We can't get the stuff for you?"

"It's got to be done right. To avoid contamination, false results. And I don't have time to train you."

He looked at her for a second more, weighing the assured tone of her voice, noting the smooth, tight over-lappings of the tape, not a wrinkle, not a crease. Then moved on.

Blaisell's stubbled face disappeared under the mask as he pulled it down. Gault waited as he pulled the straps tight, watched the sides of the rubber facepiece pull in as the corporal checked the seal. He blinked through the goggles at Gault.

"Okay in there, Crusty?"

The buzzing voice through the diaphragm. "Does a fat lady fart, Gunny?" And he realized Blaze was giving him that silly grin.

"We'll go in tactical all the way. Take the fight to them. Stay with me."

Sarsten next. The SAS ran his gaze down him, inspecting him as he knew he was being inspected. They nodded curtly to each other and Gault slid past.

And the Navy. He reached out to pull on Lenson's mask; it was seated firmly. The commander checked the bolt on his weapon, pointing it down-tunnel. Gault caught his eye and held it, looking for fear, and found none. They nodded and he turned, giving the follow-me signal.

Single file, they moved out after him.

MAUREEN FELT around her wrists, checking the tape where it sealed the gloves to her sleeves. She'd used a double glove procedure. You put one pair on under the cuff of the disposable coverall, then cut a thumbhole into the cuff of the coverall and shoved the thumb through. Then you put the second glove on over the cuff. This kept the inner glove on, but let you change the outer one. She'd figured this one out after she sweated through the tape while she was working with a culture of *Burkholderia mallei*. No one in Level Four depended on just one set of gloves. They tore too easily, on a corner of an equipment cabinet, the edge of a slide. You changed the outer ones whenever you thought they might have been contaminated. And took everything slowly . . . and . . . carefully.

She looked ahead, to where the others shuffled along. In Building 1425 they had shower rooms and ultraviolet baths next to the hot areas, so you could transition from dirty work clothes back to field clothes without contamination. Here, they'd use the tunnel as the transition zone from dirty to gray to clean, and just leave what was contaminated behind.

If they got out.

Gault, in the lead, gave them the hold-up sign. She shuffled to a stop. Waiting there, she reviewed what she was going to do. The Smart Tickets, the sampling swabs, the sample vials. Her mouth was parched and her breath came in short gasps. But it was too late to reach for a canteen. She was sealed in, impermeable plastic and rubber protecting the fragile skin bag of enzymes and plasma that was a human being. Before she unsealed she'd either be dead, or this whole thing would be over.

She swallowed again, took a deep breath through the *clack-hiss* of her respirator, and stood waiting.

BLAZE WAS geared up, ready to strap it on and go. The gunny had given them the frag order. He and Gault were the first fire team, with the diesel generator set as their first objective and the Iraqi security force as their second. Nichols, Lenson, Sarsten, and the doc were the second

fire team. They'd divide into two subteams when they
reached the transporters; Nichols and Lenson in the dis-
abling team and Sarsten covering the doc while she did
whatever she had to do up at the front end.

A hasty plan, but a plan. And judging by what the
gunny said, there'd be no shortage of ragheads to light
up. He checked his HK, then patted where he'd stuck the
loaded Glock and then his fighting knife. Fear and excitement streamed through his brain, too fast and fluid to jell
into words.

Ahead of him Gault bent low, peering through the
door. Then rose and flipped the latch off and pushed it
open, bending and squirming through. Blaze went
through after him, but his web gear caught on the door's
edge and hung him up for a second before he jerked free.
Jesus Crumb, he thought.

By then Gault was ten strides ahead, moving in the
gliding tactical shuffle across an open space under bright
lights. Blaze squinted, pulling the MP5 up to his shoulder. He snapped the selector to single shots and loped
after him, twisting as he cleared the door to sweep their
right flank with the muzzle. His breath was fogging his
mask. But the flexible urethane was clear enough that he
could see there wasn't anyone there. A lot of gear,
though. Equipment enclosures, big boxes, forklifts. Like
the shipping dock of some manufacturing company.
Nobody in sight. The lights glaring out high above. He
looked ahead again to see Gault breaking left, looking
left, and he moved to follow, sweeping gaze and arc of
fire out to the right. The shuffle and scuff of their boots
on concrete muffled by the hood, his breath closed in and
harsh in his ears.

Gault reached the generator switchboard and cornered
around it weak-side. Checked the space beyond; then
lowered his weapon and unbuttoned a panel door. He sur-
veyed it quickly, mask lenses bent close. Then reached in
with a gloved hand.

The clatter of the diesel suddenly rose in pitch, going

faster and faster. Gault swiveled around and pointed to
Blaisell, then to it, as the lights began to die.

Blaze pulled his NVGs down and turned them on as
the lamps above them went from yellow to dim red to
dark. When he climbed up on the little fold-out operator's
platform, the screens showed him the diesel board. He
didn't know the language on the labels, it looked like
Dutch or German, but he'd run a dozer one summer in
Montana and he pulled what looked like a choke and that
must have been the stop cable because that did it; the
engine tapered off and died. He backed off and put a
burst through the control panel to make sure it stayed that
way. The suppressor went *poppoppoppoppop,* punching
neat holes through the steel. He was lining up to give it
another burst when Gault grabbed his shoulder from
behind, spun him around, and pointed into the darkness.

F.C. LED the second party. Once in the open he headed
them off to the right, toward where Gault said he'd seen
refrigerators and, beyond them, trucks. They were about
fifty meters in when the lights flickered and went out. He
pulled the NVGs down with one hand and cut them on,
and the world went green and black. Mostly black,
though, except for the blurs of heat sources ahead, the
ghostly circles above of the dark but still-hot lamps; so he
turned the IR illuminator on. There, now he could see.

He wasn't sure he totally rogered up to this plan. They
were supposed to disable the missiles, but not catastrophi-
cally. Turn them into Iraqi government surplus, but not
blow them all over hell. So he'd made up the last of his
Detasheet into one-pound charges. He and the commander
would set them, then fall back to cover the doc while she
took her samples. He had doubts about it even while Gault
had explained it—like, what were all the Rackies going to
be doing meanwhile?—but he'd kept them to himself. Had
to keep a positive attitude, that was all.

Big steel boxes, square-edged, smooth metal surfaces

giving him a ghostly IR reflection of himself. A big-eyed bug-man carrying a black rifle. From the ghostly blur of heat behind them he figured these were the refrigerators. Leave them to the right and go on . . . a partition beyond, an open archway to another space. He looked back to make sure his team was still there.

They were. And there were Gault and Blaze, coming in from the left to rejoin. More faceless monsters in rumpled MOPP gear, masks jutting snoutlike, NVGs sticking out above that. Gliding along, weapons to their shoulders, covering each hidey-corner as they passed it.

Gault pointed at him and then ahead. He moved out in that direction, and suddenly there they were.

Three Iraqis, unarmed but masked. He took them out on burst fire, the unsuppressed clatter of high-velocity 5.56 rounds suddenly filling the arched tunnel beyond as the troops halted, started to run, jerked as the bullets hit, then fell. F.C. kept on going over them, pointing his weapon at each man's head as he passed. One moved and he shot him again.

Keep going, keep going, men shouting ahead now, moving on. Into a larger area beyond that echoed, flicker-shadowed with running shapes amid huge lightless wheeled bulks. He kept the rifle to his shoulder and flicked the selector to semiauto, moving the scope from one figure to the next. At each crack, hot bright gas flared out from the comp ports like a sudden star. Then the first ripping snaps of return fire, light blasting the darkness apart. He wheeled and pounded down the aisle between two of what he could see clearly now were missile transporters, wheels higher than his head, and on them the dimly visible cylinders they had come so far to find.

DAN DIDN'T have his goggles on, but once the firing started he didn't need them. The gun flashes showed huge objects around them, looming nearly to the arched overhead. He saw the outline of a massive tire and knew instantly what they were. He'd deployed with air force transporter-erector-launchers when he was with the cruise missile office. These were the Soviet version, bigger and beefier, great eight-wheeled beasts with hulking slab sides, up which he stared as from the bottom of a cliff. Ahead of him Nichols fired, the unsilenced 5.56 shockingly loud. Dan pulled his own weapon to his shoulder and went after him, down in the semicrouch like they'd drilled, aiming wherever he looked.

Suddenly headlights came on beside him. They pointed forward, illuminating the vehicle ahead. Above his head a door swung open, an interior light came on. A soldier looked down at him from an operator's cab, silhouetted.

Dan had already swung to look up. His bullets slammed the driver back into the cab and bounced off the inside of the windshield. When he stopped firing, a leg hung out of the still-open door, swinging, boot dangling toe-down in an awful attitude of casual relaxation.

He didn't feel anything yet, just the numbness that came with killing. He stepped up on an access ladder to look inside, to see if there was anyone else in the cab, but there wasn't.

The backwash of the headlights gave him sight now. When he looked for Nichols, the lance corporal was far ahead, halfway down the length of the next vehicle. Dan dropped back to the concrete and ran after him, down the aisle formed by the trucks, till the floor slanted up beneath his boots. Nichols had stopped there and was peering around the nose of the lead transporter. Dan stopped too, looking up a ramp to a blank, corrugated-looking wall that gleamed like dull steel.

The way out. The way up. The direction the transporters were facing. So all they had to do was start their engines and drive up, through what must be power doors up there, and swing around onto the riverfront promenade. Stop at presurveyed marks, erect, and fire. Shoot and scoot, just like they were doing in the western desert.

A rattle of fire bounced down from the curved overhead, focused as by a parabolic reflector to a painful loudness right at his ear. The sound was deafening, the headlights were shining directly at him, he heard shouting and the thud of running boots. One truck back he saw Sarsten and the doc climbing up onto the bed of one of the transporters. One truck in front, one behind it. Two side by side, the empty aisle between them. Two by two. Four trucks in all. "Ted" had told the truth. Not that it had done him any good.

A hand on his shoulder, a porcine snout at his ear. The buzzing of the voice emitter diaphragm. "Ready to blow 'em, Commander?"

Dan nodded, looking up at the curved cylinder of the missile far above. He slung his weapon, grabbed a hand-hold, and pulled himself aboard.

PINNED DOWN, Gault thought. He bobbed up and fired, then dropped and duckwalked along under cover of the palleted freight as bullets zipped over him and whacked into the boxes. But he couldn't see, and he could yell inside the mask as loud as he wanted and his fire team couldn't hear him.

With a sudden convulsive movement he tore it off and stuffed it into a side pocket of the clumsy coat. He'd rather breathe germs than catch a bullet. He grabbed the suppressor and twisted it off too, feeling its heat through the thick rubber glove. He bobbed up, picked out a muzzle flash, and fired. A man reeled out of cover and fell, his AK clattering to the concrete and discharging, the bullet cracking above their heads. A fine rain of concrete fragments, dust drifting down like heavy smoke.

No lights overhead, but the gun flashes and flashlights and headlights, a confusion of sudden light and utter dark, made the goggles useless too; they dangled at his neck, still turned on.

He and Blaisell had taken out the five or six troops that'd come charging out of some area to the left, just

charging out without any idea what they were doing. He
and the corporal had mowed them down on full auto,
holding the jerking HKs level with the ground and just
hosing them along, brass pinging and tinkling away. Then
slapped in fresh magazines and moved forward, past what
looked like a stairwell, dark and empty; laying fire into
where the troops had come from, some sort of quarter-
deck or personnel area to the left of where the trucks
were parked. Glass windows back there; he could hear
the rounds smashing through them. Between him and
them, pallets of cardboard boxes, food or some sort of
consumables. Whatever it was, it soaked up fire just fine,
giving a solid thud as each projectile hit.

That was good. What wasn't so good was how rapidly
that fire had started coming back, and in such volume.
None of them heavies, sounded like they were all AK-
types, but five to seven weapons were hosing it out and
for the first time he worried about his own ammo. Then
he remembered the dead men behind him, their weapons
lying not far from flung-out arms. Kalashnikovs were
crudely finished compared to an HK or an M16, but they
never jammed and they'd kill a man just as dead.

He wasn't nervous anymore. Every atom of his mind
was locked into putting down the men opposite. In Combat Town they taught you to move toward the threat. Take
the fight to the enemy, keep him under stress and off balance. But that only worked when you outnumbered him,
or were at least equal. Advancing into this would just end
up getting them chopped, and not only that, leaving the
second team, with the attachments, uncovered.

He popped up to fire again, putting rounds into where
the fire was coming from, then dropped again. Looked
anxiously toward the transporters. Only two were visible
from this angle, parked nose to ass, close under the curve
of the ceiling. He'd heard one burst from over there and
then no more. Well, maybe that was good. He and
Blaisell drawing fire, keeping the Iraqis bottled up while
the doc and the commander did their work.

This was the objective. Everything they'd done and suffered up to now had been to put them here. Jake and Tony had died for it. All he had to do now was keep everybody alive for five more minutes, till the attachments did what they had to do, then cover them as they fell back. He had to keep the security force fixed, at least keep their heads down.

It might work. It just might. Getting out would be tough, but maybe they could do that too.

He popped his head up and fired, and saw a dark object sail out of the darkness where the guns flashed. It hit concrete and bounced. He ducked as it exploded, then stood again, firing; but seeing as he did—too late to stop it—scuttle helmets moving out toward his left, moving to flank him. He yelled that to Blaisell, and saw a grenade fly out of his position. But it fell wide, missing the Iraqis, and then he couldn't see them anymore.

He fired the mag out and moved, trying to work his way back now. If they got flanked and cut off, they'd be dead in short order. But he had to keep their attention away from the transporters. He glanced that way again, but still couldn't see the doc or the commander.

Then he told himself that was good; they were doing what they had to do over there and keeping out of sight. And tried to make himself believe it. He fired till he ran dry again, dropped the mag and slapped in another and fired again. Wondering all the time where the Iraqis to his left had gone.

HIGH ON the blind side of the transporter, standing close against the rounded length it carried on its bed, Maddox heard the firing swell to a steady roar. Gault was over there, and Blaisell. She didn't know how long they could hold the Iraqis off. She had to hurry.

But she didn't know what to do, how to get at what she had to have. She ran her hand over the smooth surface, feeling its cold hardness, its smoothness. Then a discontinuity. She traced it round the curve away from her. The missile-warhead join? She flicked her combat flash on and ran it over the side, looking for a way in. Some access, some way to fill it, perhaps. But she didn't see any. Just that smooth metal skin.

Then she shifted her boots, and heard in a lull in the firing an unmistakable sound; the squish of liquid. She looked down and realized she didn't have a problem after all. Or at least, a different one than she'd had a moment before.

For a frozen second of horror she couldn't think, couldn't move, just looked down at her boots. Her problem wasn't going to be getting to whatever was inside this thing. Because she was standing in it.

A deafening explosion, so close and confined it made her ears buzz. She shook herself out of it. The Smart Tickets were the first thing she had to do. She pulled them hurriedly from her kit.

Smart Tickets were immunochromatographic assays, rather like the pregnancy strips sold over the counter in pharmacies. A basic antigen-antibody reaction with a chromogen attached to the antibody. Samples could be collected as either a liquid suspension or on a swab, then placed in contact with a test strip. If it contained the target antigen, its reaction with the antibody-chromogen complex produced a color signal visible to the naked eye.

She split out a leaf of it, bent, and pressed it into the pool. She could feel its coldness through the double layer of gloves. The coldness of liquid death, if she wanted to get melodramatic. Perspiration ran under her respirator. She absolutely could not touch her face with anything around here. Pools of it on the truck. Leaking warheads. No wonder they had casualties. Not only didn't the Iraqis mind killing Israeli civilians, they didn't seem to care that much even about their handling crews.

"Hold this," she snapped, handing the flashlight over. Sarsten had been looking over the missile, his back to her, aiming his weapon toward the racket of the firefight. At her order he frowned down. "What?"

"Hold this, I said. I have to have light."

The strip was still orange. No color change at all. So whatever this stuff was, it wasn't anthrax. She went quickly through the others, bowing to dab each in the puddle, counting the seconds, then examining it under the flash. Negative for botulinum toxin . . . negative for *Clostridium perfringens* . . . the mycotoxins (both trichopycenes and aflatoxins) test was negative too.

She looked closely at the fluid again, wondering if it could be fuel, or water. Or even urine, if one of the guards got caught short, although up here would be a funny place to go. No, it was definitely coming from the warhead. Then she saw the runnel, a faint shine of fresh liquid, where it had come out of a filling port. And understood why she hadn't noticed it before. The fill port was beneath the missile. Meaning that they'd filled the warhead separately, then hoisted it up here and bolted it on.

She didn't have a test strip for smallpox. Fort Detrick didn't make one. It had been soberly considered, and at last judged unthinkable, that any human being would unchain that demon again. That anyone would unleash again a scourge that had destroyed millions of human beings down the centuries, toppled empires, depopulated whole continents, a plague that killed and killed without reason or remorse.

But as a doctor, she knew death didn't come in millions. It came one individual at a time. A child, a mother, a young man, and with each death a universe of heartbreak and loss. What madman would open the door for it to return to a world that had fought free of it?

But obviously someone had. Had gone to the trouble of manufacturing it, designing a special dispensing warhead . . . she didn't want to think about how they'd tested it. She thought again of the bodies back in the tunnel, of the young Iraqi, dying as she stood over him.

Sarsten was still holding the light. He said impatiently, words buzzing through the mask: "You done, then?"

"No," she said, trying to snap out of the horror. Looking again at what she stood in. God help her, there was enough on her boots to kill thousands.

Hands shaking, she reached back into her kit.

THIRTY METERS away, Dan was at the rear of another missile. He and Nichols together. The sniper had set his rifle aside. They both had flashlights out, searching around a shroud or base ring that circled the nozzle. One of Nichols's premade charges lay like a hunk of window putty against the rocket casing. To which Nichols pointed, now, not saying anything, a cock of his masked head asking the question as plainly as words could. More plainly, given the clamor of gunfire that was steadily rising now under the curved ceiling close above them.

"No," Dan said, but the word was caught and smothered by the mouth cup, held close and absorbed by rubber and activated charcoal and sweating flesh. He shook his head instead; tried to steady down and think.

Scuds were liquid-fueled missiles, with storable propellants. But the outer shell of a rocket was the merest skin, and the fuselage little more than a tin can full of flammable fuel. A pound of C-16 wouldn't just breach the casing, it would scatter burning fuel the length and width of this cavern. Four pounds of Detasheet, on four airframes, would turn this subterranean parking garage into a very respectable approximation of Hell.

But if he understood what Maddox had been trying to tell them, they couldn't do that, attractive though the prospect might be in the short run. Catastrophic destruction would send a plume of pathogen up those stairwells and out that ramp door along with the fire and smoke.

He had to disable the missiles, not destroy them. And at that thought, the faintest possible smile curved his lips. For just once the military had actually sent the best man for the job. Who better than an ex-missile engineer to disable a missile?

Shots clattered overhead and he flinched. For some reason he'd assumed the Iraqis wouldn't fire toward the transporters. But too many rounds were in the air now, in too close a space. He heard yelling, an officer or noncom urging his men to the attack. Gault and Blaisell couldn't hold them for much longer. They were outnumbered. The Iraqis had unlimited ammunition. Once they realized how small the opposing team was, a rush would finish the firefight.

Sweat trickled into his eyes and he couldn't fling it off. He blinked rapidly and brought his face close to the collar. Disable but not destroy. A tricky distinction. Maybe one you really couldn't make.

Then Nichols pushed the light in a little farther, working it past the ring, and he saw a swelling curve, the lip of a smooth circle of metal. And smiled again, beneath the mask.

A FEW meters ahead of them, Maureen dumped the cooler bag down on a dry part of the transporter bed and dived into it looking for swabs. Her sample kit had rayon swabs and several small plastic sample vials, fifteen- and fifty-milliliter conical tubes, all carefully sealed in Ziploc bags to keep them clean and dry. Unfortunately, her flashlight showed brownish water sliding around in the corners of most of them. Sterile water would have been no problem, but murky, runoff-laden Tigris River water sounded like the ultimate contaminant. Finally she found the swabs and one clean fifty-milliliter tube. She fished them out very carefully, making sure she didn't touch the outside of the bag with her right glove. She'd gotten some of the leakage on her right hand while she was sampling with the tickets.

She was trying to think straight, but it was getting harder. She felt as if carbon dioxide was building up in

the hood. She tried to breathe slowly, and the dizziness
backed off a little. An outer enclosure . . . she got out
another Ziploc and held it out to Sarsten. The SAS just
looked at it. *"Take it,"* she hissed.

"And do what? Give you a sperm sample?"

She ignored that. "Hold it open for me. Don't touch
anything; just hold it so I can drop things in."

He hesitated. For a moment she was afraid he'd argue.
She'd had enough of this macho clown. The next step
was pulling her gun on him. But finally he tucked the
flashlight under his arm and laid his weapon aside and
knelt down.

Blowing out, trying to think past her fear and rage, she
got one of the swabs out and squatted down on her boot
heels. Holding it by the very corner, in her right glove,
she dipped it into the leakage; rolled it into a curl; then
eased the cap off the tube with her left thumb. Brought
the swab close, and dropped it in.

And missed. The dampened swab hit her knee and
clung there. She flicked it off instantly, but saw the dark
stain it left, felt the coolness against her skin through the
plastic material of the suit. Shit, shit, shit. Now her outer
suit was contaminated. If she was wrong and this was a
nerve agent. . . . She wasn't sure she'd be able to tell if
she *did* get a dose of organophosphates, she was shaking
so hard. She searched desperately around her feet for the
swab. It was gone. Sarsten cleared his throat, irritating
her anew. She plucked out another from the cooler bag.
Her last clean one.

In any normal sampling, she'd return the samples,
tubes or swabs, to a team member who'd stayed back in
the "clean area." That person would hold open a second
bag for the contaminated team member to drop his sample bag into. That way they could transport the sample
safely, in their bare hands if they liked, since the outer
bag was clean.

By now she had another sample taken up, and by dint
of holding her breath, had managed to get it into the tube.

She capped it and sealed the bag tightly over it, using her left, clean hand.

Normally, now she'd have a dunk tank, containing 1:10 bleach, set up to rinse the first bag in before placing it into the second bag. Household bleach was the decon solution of choice. She'd never been in a part of the world where they couldn't find it. Even in Zaire, where she'd gone two years ago to help look for Ebola, they could buy Javelle, the French version of Clorox.

Here she didn't have any decontaminant but the dandruff shampoo, and that wouldn't do much against smallpox. But on the slim remaining chance that they were still dealing with anthrax, and for the mechanical cleaning action, she squirted it out over the bag and her gloves and rubbed it up thoroughly, scrubbing in between her fingers and around the seal of the Ziploc.

"Major, you better pull your finger out," Sarsten told her. "We're going to have one lot of thoroughly excited jundies crawling up our arse very soon."

"I'm ready, here it comes. Don't let it touch till it's fully inside."

The SAS pulled the lips of his bag open and she dropped hers in. Watched as he sealed it, then made him double it over and put it into yet a third bag. That would have to do. She took it out of his hands and pulled her softsider open and dropped it in, careful not to touch the exterior fabric with her glove.

"That's it?" he said.

"That's it."

At just that moment someone began firing at them from the darkness above, from the direction they'd come from, back toward the refrigerators. Sarsten gave a muffled grunt and fell back against the cab. She stared into the darkness, reaching for her Beretta. But he was already aiming past her. His gun went off practically in her ear. Four rapid detonations, and the Iraqis spun and fell, rifles clattering away.

"You hit?"

"Caught a packet. Not a bad one," he told her, but she heard the shock in his voice. She couldn't see a wound, but the way he hunched forward told her it was the upper body. "You take the next lot," he told her.

"Forget it. You're the shooter here." She straightened and felt her legs cramp, so bad she nearly fell; caught out, by reflex, at a metal jut; felt the sharpness of it, but too late, felt her glove tear, deep, then her skin, a tear right down into flesh. It didn't hurt yet, but when she held it up she saw the stain of blood welling up through the sliced latex. In her right glove. In her *contaminated* right glove.

"Fantastic," she said aloud.

"What?"

"Nothing." She climbed down the access rungs and reached up to help him. Sarsten nearly fell into her arms, staggered as his feet hit concrete, but managed to stay upright. She saw him blinking through the mask lenses. More firing from the far side, the boom of another grenade, so close, fragments whined past like wasps. The eerie buzz of men shouting in gas masks.

She took a step and then, looking at the bodies on the concrete, stopped dead. Put the flashlight on one of them, on the blouse, the pants suit, and moved it up to the masked face.

"Fayzah?" she said.

DAN JOGGED forward along the right side of the trans-porters, next to the curving wall, to the truck closest to the exit. He didn't feel tired anymore, or scared. He didn't know how long it would last, but right then he felt like he could leap tall buildings at a single bound. He had his weapon in his right hand, cradled ready to fire pistol-fashion, and the two lumps of C-16 Nichols had given him in his left.

When he got to the lead truck he hesitated, looking at the ladder. His left arm didn't reach above his head very well, hadn't since a fiery night in the Irish Sea years before. Okay, that was the one cradling the explosive; but what to do with his weapon? Finally he stretched up on tiptoe and set it atop a fenderlike protrusion above the rear wheel. Then pulled himself up, holding the C-16 close to his chest.

On top of the carrier frame, close against the missile's drab-colored metal, he slid along its length to vestigial-looking fins. Behind them a protective shroud covered its base. He pulled at it and at last discovered it hinged upward, probably for maintenance access. He fumbled at it for another few seconds and discovered the toggle hinge that held it open.

All *right*. He bent over and thrust his arm deep into the base ring. When he felt the lip of the engine nozzle, a bell-shaped machining that directed the exhaust jet, he plunged his other arm in with the kneaded ball of explosive. He pushed it up against the smooth curved metal of the chamber's lip. Then took the detonator Nichols had given him and reached in again and pushed its tube into the yielding clay of the explosive.

Deep breath, deep breath, making sure he was ready. Then he twisted and pulled and let go. He pulled his arm back and bent to retrieve his weapon. Then went quickly forward along the missile, holding on to a steel erector-arm that cradled it as a brace cradles a weak leg. When he could go no farther, he ducked and tucked, making himself as small as possible, crouching to use the missile body itself as cover.

The charge went off with an earsplitting crack. When he looked back, sparks were still falling and the air was thick with black smoke. Twisted metal jutted up. That engine wouldn't be going to Israel. Or anywhere else. But just to make sure, he backed off and fired a full magazine of nine-millimeter slugs into the area he figured for the guidance section. Some missed, going low, but that was enough. He only had two magazines left.

He jumped down to the floor. Staggered at a flash of pain in his knee, then went to a crouch and swept the area, weapon to his shoulder.

Another flat crack and burst of sparks from behind told him Nichols was working on the far side. Bullets sang over them, ricocheting off the vaulting. The Iraqis were getting over whatever qualms they might have had about firing on the transporters. That wasn't good. Soon they'd come over in person.

One more missile and he'd be done. He reached it, panting inside the mask, and pulled himself up. Fitted the second handful of explosive and to his astonishment managed to do it all a second time. This time he aimed more carefully, stitching all his bullets into the guidance compartment. A workmanlike job. The second hunk of explosive was slightly larger than the first, and when it went off, a sizable chunk of the nozzle took off and slammed into the overhead.

Nichols, running past, M16 to his shoulder. A tinny voice: "Australian Peel." This time Dan remembered: firing and pulling back by turns. He slapped in his last full magazine and sprayed the transporters, then corrected and sent his last few rounds into the dark alleys between them.

MAUREEN LOOKED down at the woman who lay at her feet, covering her with the drawn nine-millimeter. The others were in the Iraqi drab uniforms, but she wasn't. She was in civilian clothing, tan pants and a flowered blouse. She saw one bare foot, and a shoe lying a little distance away. A woman's shoe, a spiky-heeled, expensive-looking one: Manolo Blahnik or Prada. And with a quick motion she bent and saw the dark hair spilling out behind the straps of the respirator mask, looked into dark eyes that blinked up into hers.

"Fayzah?" she said again, uncertain.

Al-Syori didn't answer, and Maureen wondered if she recognized her. Or if she was in shock. Or if it really wasn't her; it was hard to tell through the mask. She squatted and pulled the woman's blouse aside, looking for the wound. It was her shoulder; the slug must have knocked her down, dazed her. The woman looked like Fayzah, a few years older, that was all, with strands of gray now in the long glossy black hair she remembered. "I'm Maureen Maddox," she said. "We studied together. At Ohio State. *Staphylococcus aureus*? The twenty-three-to-twenty-nine kilodalton proteins?"

"Maureen," the woman said. Her voice was weak, but even through the mask Maddox recognized it. "What . . . what are you doing here?"

"Stopping you." She glanced back at the missiles, then back down. "So it's true, it was you. It's variola. Small-pox. Isn't it?"

Al-Syori didn't answer. Just stared back up at her, eyes huge and disbelieving. Maureen slid her hand under her shoulder. "How could you do it? You're a doc-tor, for God's sake. How could you do something like this?"

"You know nothing about it." Al-Syori struggled to sit up. She was surprisingly strong, and pushed Maureen's helping arm aside. She pulled her blouse open with her uninjured arm, tearing the buttons off to peer down at the entry wound. She wore a lacy brassiere beneath it; expen-sive, like the shoes, Maureen thought. There was blood now, and the bruise was growing dark, the flesh purpling and going puffy around it. Then she looked up again, and her eyes were suddenly full of fear. "Get out of here, Maureen."

"I intend to. Believe me."

"But first, do me a favor. Will you? Please?"

"What?"

"Shoot me."

Maddox said stupidly, "What?"

Al-Syori spoke quickly. "I see you have a pistol. I said, *shoot me*. Do you think I wanted to do this? You must know better. But when *he* has your family, you do what he wants." She pointed between her eyes. "Right there. If you kill me, he can't punish my family. And I won't have to do this anymore."

Maureen stood slowly, looking down at her. The pistol drooped in her hand. She said, "I'm not—I'm not going to shoot you."

"Then go. Go! There are hundreds more soldiers on the way. Run! Get out of here!"

Al-Syori was sitting up now, face contorted with pain. Impelled by her tone, Maddox turned. She ran a few steps, looking for the others.

Then stopped.

Stopped, remembering what she'd forgotten, and faced the woman she recognized again. It was important, what she'd forgotten. Without "Doctor Death," Saddam wouldn't have a biological weapons program. Fayzah had been the driving force behind actually producing this deadliness, and directing it against human beings. Not just against troops. Against innocents, children, old people, noncombatants. Smallpox wasn't a weapon. It was a plague from Hell.

If anything a human being did could be called diabolical, this was.

She turned, to see her classmate picking herself slowly off the concrete. Fayzah looked up at her. Just for a moment, Maureen saw the triumph in her eyes. Before it was replaced by realization.

The Beretta bucked in her hand. The shot thundered in her ears.

She lowered the pistol, shaking. Appalled at what she'd done. The physician. The guardian of life. She felt like her cortex was splitting, shaking apart within her skull in a cerebral earthquake.

A laugh behind her. A chuckle, muffled by plastic and rubber.

She wheeled, to find Sarsten watching. He was slumped against one of the huge wheels of the transporters. She saw his eyes crinkle through the eyepieces.

"See?" he said. "Don't honk at me, mate. I'm not the only murderer out here."

She whipped the pistol up again, fingers tightening, and aimed at his chest. The front sight trembled in the flickering light, the growing roar of sound.

GAULT HADN'T fallen back, they'd pushed him back. It was that or be flanked, and the way the cover was distributed here, to be flanked was to die. He'd not heard fire from Blaisell for a time, and was getting set for a rush in his direction when he heard the crack of a Glock.

At last he made out a yell from over by the trucks. It was Nichols. Fire team two, mission complete, pulling back. Gault yelled, "Fall back. Fall back," then hosed his last magazine into the booth area. He followed it with his last grenade and hauled ass, running doubled over as he zagged among the pallets.

Behind him the fire built to a roar, bullets hissing past and smashing into machinery and boxes, into the walls. A flare popped up, hit the overhead, and flew down, bouncing and throwing thick, soft-looking sparks and billows of white smoke from the floor.

Sarsten, Lenson, F.C. and the Doc were laying down a base of fire from behind the refrigerators as Gault pounded up. He scooped up an AK from the floor, got a mag pouch too, heavy with rounds. Stood pressed up against the back of the big steel box, sucking air and fumbling with the heavy curved magazine. Then poked around the fridge weak-side and put a burst on an Iraqi who showed himself. The bullets kicked up concrete dust all around the soldier, but he scrambled back to cover without being hit.

"The missiles?" he said.

Dan said, "Out of action."

Maddox, in a flat voice that buzzed through her speaking diaphragm, said, "You should have kept your mask on, Gunny."

"I know," he said. "Too late now."

She remembered what Al-Syori had said. "There's a reaction team on its way. A big one."

"I think they're already here." Gault ducked his head out and fired another burst. He pulled back and panted, wishing he had some water.

Blaisell slid in. His face was bloody under the mask. His hood was pulled back so you could see where it was coming from, a scalp gash under his high-and-tight. He had his Glock in one hand, and did a speed reload without looking at it.

"You hit?" Gault asked Sarsten. The SAS nodded. Then he fired again. He had an AK too. He was firing single shots, picking his targets, resting the stock on a box and steadying it with his wounded arm.

F. C. was using the grenade launcher attached to his rifle, lobbing the golfball-sized projectiles. When they exploded, screams burst out. Then his bandolier was empty. He lowered his rifle, looking down at it sadly. "Gimme a round," he said. Gault worked his action till a cartridge spun out. Nichols caught it, pushed the takedown pin down on his M16, and pivoted the receiver up. He pulled the bolt out and pushed it down into his cargo pocket. He swung, holding it by the barrel, and pinwheeled the useless weapon off into the darkness.

Bullets hit the stainless steel shielding them with dull puncturing thuds. Gault could hear the rounds smashing things inside. He yelled above the clamor, "Fighting withdrawal to the tunnel. F.C., take your attachments and withdraw toward the river. Set the claymore behind you. The rest of us will fight rear guard and withdraw east, into the hospital service area. That'll draw them away from you. Forget about transmitting. Just get to the truck and get the hell out while it's still dark."

"Leaving you guys?" Dan asked him. "There's got to be another way to do it."

"There isn't, sir," Gault told him. He was searching his chemical oversuit; he found the camera and held it out. "Look, we don't have time to fucking debate. You made the decision to go overt. This is how it plays out. Getting you and the doc back is the mission now. *Go*, F.C.! Don't worry about us. We'll make it."

Dan took the camera, then hesitated, looking into Gault's eyes. He wanted to say how he wished it could be different; that he respected the man beside him more than he'd ever respected anyone before. But the gunny turned coolly away, firing again around the freezer. He motioned angrily to Sarsten, and pointed left.

"You heard the gunny. Let's get moving, sir," Nichols said. "No shit, we don't have time to hang around. If they rush us, we're fucked."

A series of ponderous explosions, close together, and the freezer shook. "Heavy MG," Sarsten yelled. "On the right, elevated."

Dan looked off to the left, searching for Blaisell. He couldn't see the corporal. But his eyes locked, just for a second, on Sarsten's. The SAS's chem suit was soaked with blood. He too had pulled his mask off. Under it his skin was smeared with camo paint and burnt powder. But he was still aiming and firing, though his whole upper body jerked each time the butt slammed back into his shoulder. Dan leaned down and yelled, "We're pulling out."

"Suit yourself, mate."

"That means you too. Let's go."

"Not me, mate. I'm on my chinstrap here." He fired again and the action of the Kalashnikov locked back. He struggled with it, his other arm nearly useless to brace it, and dropped the empty magazine with a clatter of steel. He put his thumb and forefinger together and jiggled his wrist. Pointed a finger at Dan and winked. "Take care, wanker," he said. Then pushed a fresh magazine home and aimed again.

Dan looked at Gault. "Take good care of yourself, Gunny."

Gault nodded, not looking at him. The last thing Dan heard him say was, "It don't matter, sir. Give that little girl of yours a kiss for me. *All right!* Skirmish line, out to the left, on my command, *go!*"

THE AFTERIMAGE

17 March: Maximum Biocontainment Patient Care Suite, US Army Medical Research Institute of Infectious Diseases, Fort Detrick, Maryland

When the heavy steel door of the air lock finally sucked open, the pressure change patting his face and clicking in his ears, Dan saw for the first time what they'd dreamed of for weeks: the green-painted cinder-block corridor, the gray smooth tile floor. The rumble of wheels on concrete: a tired-looking man in blue coveralls, pushing a cart stacked high with cages. They were empty, but he caught the stink of animal excrement.

He stood irresolute, almost afraid for a moment to step out. To face what lay beyond and after and next.

The Slammer had been their world for two weeks. After the extraction, their helo had flown directly from Iraq to King Khalid airfield in Saudi. His memories of this period were confused. The water truck wouldn't start when they returned. So Nichols had hot-wired a taxi and they'd driven till the tank was empty, hid over during daylight, then walked through the next night to reach the extract point.

By then they'd been dead on their feet, exhausted and hallucinating. Maybe he'd hallucinated the spooky figures in orange suits and green hoods. Imagined being helped into a sealed litter, tented with thick, clear plastic. The plastic zipping closed behind him. Then the long flight, gloved hands of the aeromedical isolation team reaching in to minister to his bodily needs. Looking through the sheeting at the blurs of the other passengers' faces, sealed away too, racked alongside him like so many Typhoid Marys.

Since then they'd been here. Playing cards and watching CNN in a cramped four-bed isolation unit deep in the bowels of the Institute of Infectious Diseases. Four hospital beds, but six patients in the bare smooth-walled room: Dr. Maddox, Corporal Nichols, and Dan himself, plus the aircrew from the helo, pilot, copilot, and gunner. So it was even more cramped with the folding cots set up. The Space Suits had to maneuver around them and the air hoses snagged and they were always cursing and pulling at them. Space Suits: that was what they called the nurses and doctors who came packaged in big blue inflated suits, gloved and hooded and supplied with air from outside. But then after that first annoyance they'd stop pulling suddenly and look toward their patients, fear in their eyes behind the clear plastic face shields. And the patients would smile grimly back. Knowing.

Dan had asked for paper on the second day, and started writing. He had a lot he wanted to get down. Just in case he didn't make it through this. The first thing to complete was his after-action report. He wanted to make sure whoever needed to know these things knew everything they'd done, everything they'd observed. And how well everyone on the team had done. Whatever happened, they deserved that.

Maddox went down first. When she did, they moved her into the room adjoining, where they kept the stretcher transit isolators, the negative-pressure coffins they'd flown them back in.

By then they'd had all the shots, the inoculations, the experimental antivirals. Dan didn't bother keeping track. Just sat, feeling estranged from everything, waiting for it to start. Waiting to get sick, then actually being sick, sicker than hell. From the drugs; the side effects felt like intestinal flu, complete with vomiting and agonizing shits.

They knew it was smallpox by then. The cultures from the sample the doc had brought back confirmed her call. But there wasn't any antidote or antitoxin for variola major, let alone the virulent and mortal variant Dr. Al-Syori had weaponized. So all the army could do was vaccinate them, pump them tick-tight with antivirals, and wait.

So they waited; watching the news images flicker across the screen; tanks plunging forward, skies full of helicopters, berms exploding, hundreds of prisoners walking toward the cameras with their hands in the air. A road of abandoned burning vehicles. The Kuwaiti flag going up side by side with the Stars and Stripes. The fiery plumes of burning wells stretching off to the flat horizon. And at last, a tent in the desert, men in olive drab and mustaches sitting down opposite the Allies.

And he'd watched and listened, taut with apprehension and guilt; but not once had there been any indication the Iraqis had wheeled, reoriented their forces, to face south. So either he hadn't talked, there in the bunker, or the word had gotten to the Iraqi command structure too late to do them any good.

All that time they waited to see who'd be next. But no one else came down with it. Only the doc. They listened to the Space Suits in the next room, and watched through a window as they worked around Maddox's bed. Watched till the end, all the way to the body bag, and when it was gone, the disinfecting cookers on the floor generating a formaldehyde cloud so thick that nothing lived on the far side of the glass but a writhing whiteness of utter sterility, utter lifelessness.

He'd watched that deadly mist, mind blank. Remembering a fog rising from a silvery lake in Iraq, and the delicate rose as the first morning light touched it.

THE PHONE call came in several days after the cease-fire. He picked it up, and for a moment didn't recognize the voice. Then he did. "Corporal Blaisell," he said.

"Hey, sir, it's Blaze. Tricky tracking you down, but they finally gave me your number. You're where—some army hospital?"

"That's right. I'm glad you called." Dan thought about asking if Blaisell had gotten sick, then realized if he had, he'd probably be dead. So instead he said, "How are you? *Where* are you?"

"I'm still in Saudi. They flew me back to a field hospital after the ragheads let me go. They're going to operate again, then fly me back home."

"They took you prisoner?"

"Right, I get the POW medal now. Along with the Purple Heart, how about that? Bad news, though. They killed the gunny and Sarsten. When we finally ran out of ammo. I took a couple of rounds, but they operated and I pulled through. Somebody scored my Glock while I was out, though. Some son-of-a-bitching Iraqi's walking around with it now. Who made it from your end of the team?"

"F.C.'s here. They had us quarantined. It was smallpox, all right. The doc was the only one who came down with it, though."

"How is she? She pull through?"

"No. She didn't make it."

A brief silence, then "Too bad. She had balls. Well, I'm glad you made it okay, sir. You're a good man."

"You are too, Blaze. By the way, I'm doing some medal write-ups. For everybody. I think you deserve something, and this has mostly been an Army war. . . . I figure if we can make a case for some of our guys, the Navy Department might want to play catch-up."

"You don't need to do that, sir."

"It'd help your career. If you're staying in."

"I got nothing better to do, sir. Not like Jake." A pause, and they both listened to the faint crackle and drone of whatever connections lay between them. "Well . . . is F.C. there, you said?"

He'd handed the phone off and gone back to the television. And that was the only thing he'd heard from the outside, other than the TV news. Nobody from CINC-CENT or NAVCENT had ever called. He had no orders; it was as if the Signal Mirror team had been forgotten in the heady aftermath of victory. He'd talked to his mom on the phone, and to Blair once, but that was all.

So he was feeling both lonely and disoriented as the door whooshed open, and he watched the empty cages rumbling by, wondering what had happened to the monkeys. And at last he stepped through, into the hallway, and saw her waiting. For a moment he couldn't believe it.

"Blair?" he said, astonished.

Blair Titus hesitated; glanced at the doctors with her. They smiled and she ran the few steps between them and hugged him. He felt her cool cheek against his. She was wearing a blue wool suit, a power-look outfit, with an open neckline and a little American flag pin on her lapel. Her hair was shorter than he remembered it, but it looked good on her. "You look terrific," he told her.

"Thanks. I just drove up from Washington. They told me you were getting out this afternoon. God, the Beltway traffic; I just made it." She looked at him searchingly, holding him out at arm's length. "But you're okay?"

"I'm okay."

"Really? Your face—" He felt her finger trace the line of his ear, where the sutures had just come out.

"Really. It looked a lot worse two weeks ago."

"They told me about the major. The one who died."

Dan said, "She was a good soldier."

"I'm so sorry. I'm just glad the casualty lists were so light." She tried to smile, as if she thought he didn't want to talk about it. "Anyway, I'm glad you made it. Let's go to lunch. There's a nice place called Tauraso's out in Frederick. You've probably had enough army food for a while."

"It'd be nice just to see the sky again."

She started to turn away, then turned back and held him again. Tight, this time. Into his ear she murmured, "We spend too much time apart."

"That's true."

"But maybe we can make it work. Other people do."

"Make it work?" He blinked, still not feeling he was with the program. The aftereffect of all the drugs, or maybe the sudden pressure change from inside to outside, made his head feel like it was stuffed with used rags.

She said, her mouth still so close against his ear he could feel her breath, like a recon marine passing a message on patrol, "You asked me once, and I said no. Well. At lunch. Today. Ask me again."

Dan looked at her, not sure anymore what he wanted to do. She seemed so self-assured, so confident, so separate, so . . . powerful. He'd always thought two people had to need each other, to make a life together. Was it worth trying again, after he'd screwed up one marriage?

He no more had the answer to that question than he understood what had happened in Iraq. The decisions and terror and violence. What others had done, and what he'd done himself.

But you couldn't wait till you had the right answers. Some things would become clearer with time. Others, he'd change his mind about as the years went by. And some, he'd never fathom. No one knew or could see ahead. That was why human beings needed something beyond themselves. To make sense of the world. Or to reassure themselves the world *did* make sense, no matter how often it didn't.

Sometimes you just had to take it on faith. So that now

he said, surrendering to the future, "All right. I'll ask you again."

She held out her hand, and he took it, and they walked down the hall, toward doors that opened to distant blue mountains.

16 May: Baghdad

The Tigris flowed quietly at last under an empty blue spring sky, green and somehow thick-looking, as if composed of a liquid more viscous than water. The group moved slowly along a tree-lined boulevard. Some wore coveralls and carried respirator masks, sample kits, and detector equipment; others were in drab uniforms, shoulder boards, and black berets. One Iraqi carried a camcorder, filming every step they took, but none were armed. They reached the entrance, a wide ramp sloping down from the river. The hospital rose above it, story after story, untouched. An Iraqi in a white coat hurried toward them, carrying a clipboard.

Steel doors rumbled up as they trudged down the ramp. The interior was dark, and a faint smell of diesel fuel welled up from it.

Colonel Anders Paulik, US Marine Corps, was the leader of the inspection team. He stopped to consult a GPS receiver and a map, confirming their exact location. The others waited patiently. He looked back at the river, then down at the doors again. Finally he pulled his half-face respirator from its belt pouch and seated it over mouth and nose. He tested it, pulled the straps tighter, then led the way forward.

The huge interior was empty. Vaulted ceilings caged lightless fixtures. The flashlights made pale beams that probed uncertainly about in the gloom. "Can't we get some light down here?" Paulik asked, voice muffled by the mask.

His escort, an Iraqi general, had not bothered with breathing protection. He said loftily, as if such matters were beneath his notice: "Sorry, no. Lights don't work."

Paulik did not respond. He moved forward, following the pale searching of his beam. Sending it down the long open vaulting, smelling even through the mask of fuel and mold and another smell, a faint, bitter chemical after-taste. Water dripped from the ceiling. His boots splashed through it. Behind him the technicians fanned out, intent on instruments and sampling kits.

Paulik kept walking, hearing the Iraqis close behind him. Along with the general was the man in the white coat, who had been introduced as the director of the medical center. The colonel pushed his light beam into what looked like an abandoned control booth. The concrete was starred with bullet marks. Glass lay in shattered sheets across the offices within. A chair lay where it had been knocked over. Nothing else remained save the concrete floor, dusty and bare, showing still-faint outlines where heavy objects had rested, black tire marks where vehicles had passed.

"What was this area?" he asked the escort. The general turned and spoke in Arabic to the man in the white coat.

They faced him again. "It was storage space," the general said. "For the hospital. Now it is unused."

"What happened here? What were these bullet spalls from?"

"Those are not bullet marks," said the doctor, in English, though he had spoken to the general in Arabic. "Those are where forklifts ran into the concrete."

"This was a storage site for biological weapons," Paulik said. Both men shook their heads, but said nothing.

"You owe me the truth. Your president agreed to a full accounting and destruction of all nuclear, chemical, and biological weapons."

The general looked upward, to the ceiling, or to Heaven. "No, never. As I have told you so many times. We never manufactured such weapons. This was never a storage site for such things. Nor did we have the type of weapons you allege."

Paulik held his gaze for a long moment. "You're so full of shit," he said.

The general didn't answer. Paulik stared him down, then called to the technicians: "Take samples here. And here. And over there, next to the wall. That's where the refrigerators were."

The Iraqis watched, saying nothing. When he looked back at them again, they were smiling.

TOMAHAWK
DAVID POYER

Once Lieutenant Dan Lenson had a ship and a family. Now he is on his own, deep within Washington's military industrial complex. His task: shepherd a controversial weapon through the Navy's testing process to deployment. But powerful forces are lined up against the Tomahawk missile—and against Lenson. And for Dan Lenson, separating his enemies from his friends is the beginning of the most dangerous war of all…

"There can be no better writer of modern sea adventure around today."
—Clive Cussler

"This demanding, excellent novel is probably the best so far in a major contemporary seafaring saga."
—*Booklist*

"An imaginative, thought-provoking premise rich in possibilities."
—*USA Today*

T 1/01

READ ALL OF THE SPELLBINDING NOVELS BY
DAVID POYER

"Poyer knows what he is writing about when it comes to anything on, above, or below the water." —*The New York Times Book Review*

"The best military suspense writing to come along in years!"
—Stephen Coonts, author of *Cuba* and *Fortunes of War*

THE MED
A powerful and fast-moving tale of the Navy-Marine Corps team in action, on a dangerous mission in the volatile Eastern Mediterranean. An explosive start to David Poyer's compelling series featuring Naval officer Dan Lenson.

THE GULF
When a U.S. destroyer is attacked, commanding officer Benjamin Shaker vows revenge—and it's up to Dan Lenson to prevent Shaker from releasing a deadly nuclear warhead...

THE CIRCLE
Junior officer Dan Lenson heads into the dark waters of the Arctic Circle with the *Ryan*, an aging WWII destroyer. But as he and his crew struggle on the choppy ocean, they discover a more dangerous foe within the creaking ship...

THE PASSAGE
Officer Dan Lenson must man the USS *Barrett*, the Navy's most sophisticated destroyer containing a powerful top-secret computer, through the treacherous Windward Passage between the U.S. and Cuba. But when the system develops a sinister virus and a sailor takes his own life, Lenson will undergo the most dangerous mission of his career...

**AVAILABLE WHEREVER BOOKS ARE SOLD
FROM ST. MARTIN'S PAPERBACKS**

POY 6/99